S0-BFM-423

"YOU DESERVE A GOOD, HARD SPANKING."

Jessie pulled back on her arm but couldn't loosen the iron grip James had over her wrist. "No!" she protested. "You can't be serious!" She jerked hard on her arm and began swinging with her other fist to fight him off.

He only grinned at her attempts. "You should try picking on someone your own size," he told her.

"You horse's ass," she shouted. "I'll get even with you for this if it's the last thing I ever do!" Just then, a spark of fear flew through her and she grabbed him around the neck to keep from falling.

James was unprepared for the feeling of her arm around his neck and her breasts flush with his chest. He felt as though his heart had suddenly dropped to his toes, then rushed back upward, sending blood pounding through his body. He stopped moving and released her wrist, wrapping his other arm around her waist, supporting her there.

It was at that moment she felt the change and became aware of the heat emanating from his body into hers. She suddenly felt the strong muscles of his chest pressed against her breasts, felt the rippled surface of his stomach flush against her abdomen. With a surprised intake of air, she raised her eyes to meet his gaze.

"Jessie?" he rasped. Lowering his head, he saw the look of surprise in Jessie's eyes just before he claimed her lips in a devouring kiss. . . .

CRITICS CHEER THE WESTERN ROMANCES FROM

FAYE ADAMS

LADY OF THE GUN

"Fast and exciting with an . . . enchanting mix of characters, Adams has created an adventure to remember. The plot is loaded with danger, passion, and tense gun fighting at high noon. You won't be able to put this thriller down."
—Laurel Gainer, *Affaire de Coeur*

"*Lady of the Gun* is a gripping tale of revenge and honor, obsession and passion. Faye Adams entertains readers with her sensitive, determined heroine and the strong hero at her side."
—Maria C. Ferrer, *Romantic Times*

"A sharp plot . . . stirring romance. . . . Superb. . . . I've yet to read a better western romance!"
—Gloria Miller, *The Literary Times*

ROSEBUD

"For anyone who loves a western romance, *Rosebud* is the definite book to read. The novel is original, humorous and has a special charm about it that will please anyone who reads it."

—Harriet Klausner, *Affaire de Coeur*

"*Rosebud* is sure to please western romance fans."
—Frances L. Trainor, *Romantic Times*

THE GOODNIGHT LOVING TRAIL

"Ms. Adams packs comedy and tragedy into a bang-up romance peopled with all the diverse characters making up the cattle drive, a bunch we soon know well. And, as in real life, we never learn just what happens to a couple of them. Maybe they'll appear in a sequel? We can hope."

—*Rendezvous*

"Faye Adams' adroit touch of sexual tension makes this an accomplished western romance that is highly entertaining."
—Gary Benninger, *Romantic Times*

Books by Faye Adams

Under a Texas Moon
Lady of the Gun
The Goodnight Loving Trail
Rosebud

Published by POCKET BOOKS

For orders other than by individual consumers, Pocket Books grants a discount on the purchase of **10 or more** copies of single titles for special markets or premium use. For further details, please write to the Vice-President of Special Markets, Pocket Books, 1633 Broadway, New York, NY 10019-6785, 8th Floor.

For information on how individual consumers can place orders, please write to Mail Order Department, Simon & Schuster Inc., 200 Old Tappan Road, Old Tappan, NJ 07675.

FAYE ADAMS

UNDER A TEXAS MOON

POCKET BOOKS
New York London Toronto Sydney Tokyo Singapore

The sale of this book without its cover is unauthorized. If you purchased this book without a cover, you should be aware that it was reported to the publisher as "unsold and destroyed." Neither the author nor the publisher has received payment for the sale of this "stripped book."

This book is a work of fiction. Names, characters, places and incidents are products of the author's imagination or are used fictitiously. Any resemblance to actual events or locales or persons, living or dead, is entirely coincidental.

An *Original* Publication of POCKET BOOKS

POCKET BOOKS, a division of Simon & Schuster Inc.
1230 Avenue of the Americas, New York, NY 10020

Copyright © 1996 by Faye Swoboda

All rights reserved, including the right to reproduce this book or portions thereof in any form whatsoever. For information address Pocket Books, 1230 Avenue of the Americas, New York, NY 10020

ISBN: 0-671-52727-4

First Pocket Books printing December 1996

10 9 8 7 6 5 4 3 2 1

POCKET and colophon are registered trademarks of Simon & Schuster Inc.

Cover art by Darryl Zudeck

Printed in the U.S.A.

*This book is dedicated
to my sister, and partner in crime,
Kaye. Thank you for all the dreams,
schemes, adventures, and scathingly
brilliant ideas!*

lashes shadow her cheeks in the way she'd seen her friends do. "I won't trouble you further, Jamie. I'll go on

UNDER A TEXAS MOON

❊ Prologue ❊

1880

Jessie grasped the banister finials in anger, her fingers stiff, her knuckles white from the force of her grip. How could they think of sending her away? How could they dare? Clenching her jaw so tightly her teeth felt as though they might crack, she leaned forward on the stairs slightly, straining to hear more of her parents' conversation.

"I just don't like the idea of sending her so far away," Rachel said quietly, staring out the dining room window, knowing how Jessie was going to take the news.

Sin looked at his wife and could sense the tension in her stance. "It's what's best for Jessie, Rachel. She's gotten too wild. She won't even listen to you anymore. And she can barely read or write. She needs an education." He glanced down at his hands, folded before him on the table, then added softly, "You know I'm right."

Rachel turned to face her husband, a look of defeat on her lovely face. "You might be right, but it doesn't make it any easier. Charleston is so far from here. She'll be so alone."

"She won't be alone. She'll be with my aunt Lizzie, and there will be lots of girls in the school. She'll make friends."

Rachel gave him a derisive stare. "In case you've forgotten, Jessie doesn't exactly make friends easily. She's not like other girls her age."

Sin pushed himself away from the table and stood to face his wife. "Which is why we're doing this. It's for her own good. If we do nothing she'll end up being a cowhand and nothing more. She's fourteen, and I don't think she can even add two and two."

"You're exaggerating," Rachel argued.

"Maybe, but not by much. When was the last time you know for sure she attended school?"

Rachel lowered her eyes. "The teacher told me it was over two weeks ago," she said, her voice barely above a whisper.

"And then the sheriff brought her home for sneaking into the Rosebud. She's lucky we happen to own that saloon. If she'd snuck into the Wagonwheel, there'd have been hell to pay. Can you even imagine what the proprietor would have done if he'd found her in there?" Sin asked, an incredulous tone to his voice. He then took a step closer to Rachel and put his arm across her shoulders. "We've been over this a hundred times in the last month. The girls' school is the best solution. Aunt Lizzie is looking forward to having her." He put one finger under his wife's chin and tilted her head up. Looking into the emerald green eyes he loved so much, eyes that were mirrored exactly in his daughter Jessie's face, he tried to smile. "It's for the best," he assured.

Rachel felt her heart rate increase slightly as she looked into her husband's eyes. Even after years of marriage he had this effect on her. "I suppose you're right. When do we tell her?" she asked.

"The sooner the better. School starts in a month and a

half, and we'll need all that time to get her used to the idea."

The dining room doors burst open with such force that one of them crashed into the wall behind it, the knob breaking a hole in the wallpaper that decorated the room. Rachel and Sin both jumped at the intrusion.

"I won't go! And you can't make me!" shouted Jessie, her hands clenched into defiant fists at her sides.

Sin studied his daughter for a moment before he spoke. She was so small, so delicate in appearance, especially now, standing in her cotton nightgown, her black hair a wild mass of curls around her head. It was hard to believe that this tiny creature could ride and shoot better than most men, could outswear the toughest cowboy, and had recently decided she didn't need to attend school and had begun sneaking into saloons. Sighing, he pictured the lady she could become, would become, if he had anything to do with it. "Your mother and I have decided you're to attend the Charleston School for Girls," he said in his sternest voice.

"I won't go!" Jessie shouted again.

"You will go," Sin argued, his voice getting louder.

"You'll have to tie me up to get me there, and I'll run away the first chance I get," Jessie fought back.

Rachel leveled her gaze on her daughter, meeting her glare in kind. "You will attend the school, Jessie," she said quietly, but firmly.

Jessie's heart lurched with sadness that her mother wasn't on her side in this. It was her mother she most wanted to be like. Her mother rode horses and shot guns. It was her mother who'd first said cuss words in front of her, and now Rachel wanted to send her to a school for girls. "I don't want to be like those drippy, sissy girls in town. I want to be like you," she argued.

Rachel's intake of air was audible. Jessie's wild ways, her rebellion, her defiance, was an attempt to emulate her! This, like no argument Sin had put forward, convinced her that sending Jessie to Charleston was the right thing. Reaching out to her daughter, she motioned for her to come closer. Then taking her hand, she guided her to sit on the window seat with her.

"I don't want to go, Mother," Jessie said before her mother could speak.

Rachel looked down at her small daughter. "I love you, Jessie," she began, "and I want what's best for you. So does your father. This decision, to send you to Charleston, has been a difficult one for us to make." She glanced up at Sin, standing near the table, watching and listening. "But we feel it's the right thing for you. You need an education. You need to learn how to be more ladylike."

"But you're not ladylike," Jessie said through clenched teeth.

"Because no one ever taught me different, Jessie. My life was hard, though I'm not saying I'd change any of it. I loved my life. But I want a better life for you. I want you to have all the opportunities, all the chances I never had. You can't take advantage of everything that's out in the world if you don't have an education. And you certainly won't be very successful in life if you're continually offending people by your words and actions. That's why we're sending you to Charleston to school," Rachel explained softly.

Jessie listened to her mother's words. She heard the hopeful tone in her voice and saw the expectant look in her father's eyes when she glanced up at him. It didn't matter. They wanted to send her away. They wanted her to become something she wasn't. And she'd be damned if she was going to make it easy on them. "No!" she burst out. "I won't go to Charleston. It isn't home. I'll never live anywhere but here on the Triple X. I'm going to live forever in Texas!"

❧ 1 ❧

1884
Charleston

Jessie pushed open the kitchen door with a quick shove and practically bounced into the room, followed closely by her best friend, Mary Blakely. She glanced around at the servants busily getting ready for the party that evening and saw her mother sitting at the table, a pitcher of cold lemonade in front of her collecting moisture in the warm afternoon air. "Mother, it was a wonderful ride," she said breathlessly, her cheeks reddened, and stray black curls caressing her face. "Mary nearly had a heart attack when I chose to ride Tornado," she laughed.

"I did not," denied Mary as she pulled the hat pin from her derby and tugged it from her head, releasing several long, light brown strands with the action. "I just don't see why you have to ride the craziest horse on the place.

Jessie laughed again. "He's not crazy. He just likes to run. Isn't that right, Mother?"

Rachel smiled at her daughter, then took a small sip of the lemonade she'd come to the kitchen to get. Jessie had grown into an incredibly beautiful woman in the past four years, and despite a very rocky beginning, she'd not only gotten used to her life in Charleston, but excelled in school and mastered the art of being a lady. Even now, with her face flushed from her ride and her hair a bit disheveled, she looked the epitome of grace and elegance. Only when she was truly vexed about something would the old, wilder Jessie emerge. "Tornado does like to run," Rachel agreed with her daughter.

"See, Mary. I told you so," Jessie said, then giggled when her friend made a face at her. Pulling off her riding gloves and hat, she glanced around the enormous kitchen of her parents' new home at the numerous servants working diligently on the food for the party. "Where's Father?" she asked, dropping the hat and gloves on the table.

"With the horses, of course. I'm surprised you didn't see him," answered Rachel.

"That barn is so big I could have walked right past him," observed Jessie. Unbuttoning the top three buttons of her linen riding habit, she crossed the kitchen and pulled two glasses from the cupboard. Spying a giant fruit salad one of the cooks was preparing, she leaned forward and sniffed. "Heavenly," she murmured, and was rewarded with a bite of pineapple.

Smiling broadly, she returned to where her mother sat at the table and filled the glasses with lemonade from the pitcher. Handing one to her friend, she sat down. "Why did Father insist on everything being so large?" she asked.

Rachel looked around the kitchen of her new home. She and Sin had begun spending more and more time in Charleston as their Thoroughbred horse breeding business became increasingly successful. In the last two years they'd made only one trip back to the Triple X, their ranch in Texas, and finally, about ten months before, decided they should stop pretending they were ever going back to live there permanently. Construction on the new house had begun immediately. "Your father wanted it this way," she answered, smiling.

Jessie grinned and sipped her lemonade. She was glad

her parents lived in Charleston now. "Has my dress arrived yet?" she asked, her thoughts once again straying to the party.

"Yes, about an hour ago. I'm sorry I forgot to tell you right away," answered Rachel.

Jessie squealed with delight, a sound echoed by Mary, and the two girls jumped to their feet. "Where is it?" Jessie asked.

"In your room," replied Rachel.

"I can't wait to see how it finally turned out," squeaked Mary, grasping Jessie's arm in excitement. "Let's go."

Jessie leaned forward and gave her mother a quick hug. "Do you mind if we—"

"Go look at your dress," Rachel told her, and winked. Watching the two girls leave the room, she was filled with a warm glow of happiness. The decision to educate Jessie in Charleston had been the right one, after all.

"I'm so glad my mother decided to use candles to light the room," said Jessie as she let her eyes sweep the ballroom several hours later.

"Mmmm," agreed Mary. "Everything is so beautiful." Then, as the grandfather clock began to strike eleven, "I can't believe the night's almost over."

Jessie nodded. Glancing down at the white satin gown that reflected the candlelight, she once again marveled at the way the seamstress had turned yards and yards of flat fabric into the beautiful creation that hugged her body and revealed curves that caused her father to raise his eyebrows in concern. She smiled warmly. The evening had been perfect, the food delicious, the music wonderful, the guests gracious. "Let's sneak outside to the patio for a few minutes. My feet are killing me," she told her friend, wincing to emphasize her pain.

Mary giggled. "I'd love to, but it looks like your feet won't get to rest just yet. Frederick Chasen is winding his way through the crowd to claim you for another dance."

"No," Jessie groaned. "Frederick is really very nice,

but I need to sit this one out." She grabbed her friend by the wrist. "Run for it," she whispered.

Mary's eyes opened wide. "You can't be serious. He's almost here."

"Come on, Mary," Jessie urged.

"We can't. He's looking right at us. He'd know we were running away from him. It would hurt his feelings," Mary argued.

Jessie made sure no one was looking then stuck just the tip of her tongue out at her friend. "If I didn't know better, I'd think you had a crush on Frederick," she teased.

"As if it would do me any good if I did," answered Mary quietly, then adding, "Frederick sees no one but you whenever you're around. For that matter, being invisible next to you is becoming my most common pastime," she teased.

"Pooh," responded Jessie. Just then, Frederick touched her on the shoulder. Putting on her most dazzling smile, she turned toward him. "Yes, Frederick?"

"May I . . . I believe I have the honor of the next dance," he stumbled over his words.

Jessie brought her dance card up to inspect the list inside it. "I'm sorry, Frederick. William Sennet has the next dance."

Frederick smiled broadly at that. "He did, but I made an arrangement with him. Now the dance belongs to me," he announced proudly.

"An arrangement?" Jessie asked.

"I agreed to clean his father's barn for him."

Jessie heard Mary's surprised giggle and had to bite the inside of her lower lip to keep from laughing herself. "Well then, I suppose I can't refuse you," she managed to answer graciously a few seconds later. Frederick led her to the dance floor.

Turning in Frederick's arms, Jessie was able to allow her thoughts to wander. Frederick never spoke while they were dancing, only stared down at her with large, puppy-dog eyes. She'd found it very disconcerting the first few times she'd danced with him, but now she actually enjoyed the quiet and allowed her thoughts to run freely as he spun her in time to the music. The sound of his voice this time surprised her. "What's that, Frederick?"

"I said, you're the most beautiful woman here, Jessie. You're the most beautiful woman I've ever seen," he blurted.

Jessie blinked rapidly several times at his outburst. "Why, thank you," she answered.

"I mean it, Jessie. I've been wanting to tell you for so long, but I never had the courage. You're the most beautiful woman in the world," he gushed.

Jessie's first instinct was to tell him he was repeating himself, but it was obvious he was sincere and quite smitten with her. She felt him pull her slightly closer to him, his hand at her back tightening its grip. Looking up at his thin, handsome face, she wondered what she should do. "Thank you again, Frederick," she said. "I'm flattered."

"I don't want you to be flattered, Jessie. I want you to allow me to court you, with your parents' permission, of course."

Jessie stared hard at the face she already knew quite well. Frederick Chasen had been her friend for several years. He was soft-spoken, educated, and came from a good family. He was quite nice looking, with light brown eyes, sandy blond hair, and a tall, thin frame. She supposed he was quite attractive, but she'd never felt anything more than friendship for him. His outburst tonight was going to change all that. Could she feel something for him other than friendship, she wondered? Perhaps, she heard her mind answer. "I . . . suppose," she responded.

Frederick stopped dancing abruptly, causing Jessie to stumble a bit. "Frederick?" she said.

"Pardon me, Jessie." He took her hand and kissed it softly once. "You've made me so happy. I'll go speak to your father at once." He turned on his heel and began looking for Sin and Rachel in the large crowd.

Moments later, Jessie was standing alone in the middle of the dance floor. Shrugging, she walked to the side where Mary waited.

"What was that all about?" Mary questioned urgently.

"Frederick asked to court me. When I said yes, he took off like a coyote after a jackrabbit looking for my father," she answered, her eyes scanning the room for her parents.

Mary giggled. "I love the way you talk sometimes," she said.

Jessie looked back at her friend and grinned. "I sometimes forget myself." She scanned the room again. "I wonder if I've done the right thing."

Mary touched her friend on the arm, questioning with her action.

"I'm not in love with Frederick. I just didn't know what to say when he asked to court me. He is pleasant to be around. And he is a friend," Jessie explained.

"Pleasant? You describe him as pleasant?" Mary commented. "Maybe you should have turned him down. I mean, if you're really not in love with him."

Jessie's emerald green eyes lowered slightly, her search of the room ended. She then lifted her gaze to meet her friend's. "I've never been in love with anyone," she confessed.

"Never?" Mary asked incredulously. The girls at school had talked endlessly about their love lives. Each girl trying to outdo the other with stories about hand-holding and stolen kisses. Each professed undying love for several different young men before their time at school was complete. Even Mary herself had enjoyed several light dalliances with gentlemen she'd met through the years. One of the gentlemen in question had even touched her breast, through her clothes of course, but she had definitely won the respect of the other girls and the reputation for being quite worldly. Now, in retrospect, she realized Jessie had never really joined in those particular conversations. Instead, she'd listened intently to the other girls' stories, then acted very mysterious when asked about her own love life. "You mean, never?" Mary asked again with emphasis.

Jessie glanced downward in embarrassment.

"But you're gorgeous!" Mary exclaimed.

"That hasn't always been the case," Jessie responded, remembering, with some horror, the hellion she'd been when her parents had forced to her leave Texas.

"But someone . . . I mean . . . There had to be one time." Mary stammered.

Jessie let her thoughts stray back in time. "Well, I suppose there was one young man, but I was just a kid."

"Tell," insisted Mary.

"I was only twelve," said Jessie, remembering. "I'd run away to join my sister's cattle drive to Montana."

"And you met someone?" Mary urged.

"My sister's brother-in-law. He was the younger brother of the man who owned the cattle that collided with my sister's herd. The man, Luke, and my sister, Tish, eventually got married, but when I met Jamie I sort of, I don't know."

"Did he make you tingle?" Mary whispered, leaning forward conspiratorially.

"No, of course not. I was just a kid. I just had a crush on him." She stopped and smiled. "I even told my sister I was going to marry him some day."

Mary narrowed her eyes. "So, what happened to him?"

Jessie sighed. "He's the manager of my family's ranch, the Triple X, in Texas."

"And?"

Jessie shrugged. "And nothing. I haven't seen him since the cattle drive. He's probably fat and bald by now."

Mary dropped her shoulders in disgust. "I swear, Jessie. You're positively depressing."

Jessie giggled at her friend's expression. "You're just sorry I didn't have some wild and juicy tale to tell you."

"Well, yes, but I'll bet you're sorry, too," Mary answered.

A short time later, Jessie saw her parents approaching her. She knew what they wanted to tell her, and she could see by their happy expressions that they approved of Frederick.

"Hello, Mary," Sin acknowledged first. "Jessie, we have something to discuss with you," began Sin as he neared his daughter.

"Perhaps I should leave you alone," suggested Mary.

"No, that's not necessary." Sin grinned at Rachel for a moment. "I'm sure Jessie would just run to tell you what we've said anyway," he teased.

"What do you want to tell me?" inquired Jessie, returning the conversation to its purpose.

"Frederick has just asked permission to court you," said Sin, a flash of pride in his eyes.

"And you said yes, of course," Jessie commented, smiling softly.

Sin nodded. "We think Frederick is a fine young man." He then looked toward Rachel again. "I'm a little surprised he didn't ask for her hand in marriage," he commented.

Jessie raised one delicately arched brow slightly. "I'd be surprised if he had," she said.

"It's going to happen soon I think," said Sin. "Which is the reason your mother and I thought we'd share some good news with you tonight."

Jessie looked at both her parents curiously. Mary listened intently just a step away.

"We've sold the Triple X and sent half the money to Tish and put the other half in your account, Jessie. The money is yours to do with as you wish, and with the way things look with Frederick, I'm assuming it will be used as part of your dowry. Of course, Frederick is only the first in what I'm sure will become a long . . ."

Jessie stood stock still as her father's words hit her. They'd sold the Triple X? They'd sold the Triple X! She didn't hear much of what he'd said after that. Something about a dowry. It didn't matter. How could they have sold the Triple X? Her heart began to beat wildly in her chest. Blood pounded in her ears. She began to feel both hot and cold at the same time and a sound like rushing wind filled her ears.

She could see her father's mouth moving as he continued speaking. She could see her mother's face, beautiful as she agreed with her husband. But she couldn't hear. And she was beginning to have a hard time breathing. How could they have sold the Triple X? Why would they do such a thing? And why did it matter so much to her? "You can't be serious," she whispered.

Rachel looked at her daughter and noticed how pale she'd become. "Sin?" she stopped his speech. "Jessie, are you all right?"

Jessie continued staring at them. "You didn't really?" she murmured.

"Jessie, what's wrong?" asked Mary.

"Tell me you didn't really sell the Triple X," Jessie said, her voice louder, but raspy.

Sin frowned in concern. "Yes, Jessie, we did. We discussed it and decided it was—"

"Whom did you discuss it with, certainly not with me!" Jessie interrupted, her voice carrying past her parents to several people standing nearby.

Rachel heard the surprised whispers behind them. "Perhaps we should discuss this in some other room?"

"Why discuss it now? You didn't feel the need to discuss it with me when it mattered." Jessie's voice continued to rise. "How could you do this?" she demanded.

Sin's surprise at her response to their news was fast being replaced by anger at her lack of decorum. "Jessie, we will not have a scene here," he said quietly, sternly.

"Jessie, maybe we could go into the hall?" suggested Mary.

Jessie swung to face her friend. "You don't understand what they've done!" she nearly shouted, drawing attention from the rest of the guests in the room. She could see Frederick's shocked expression as he walked closer to them. It didn't matter. Suddenly nothing mattered except that her parents had sold the Triple X.

"Excuse us for a few minutes, folks," Sin turned and addressed the crowd. "Just a little family matter. I'm sure you all know how it is sometimes," he said jovially. Smiles and nods passed through the room. He then turned and once again faced his daughter. "We will take this into the parlor." Taking Jessie's arm in a firm grasp, he led her from the room.

Jessie was surprised to feel the strength in her father's fingers. His anger was evident as he guided her toward the parlor, but she didn't care. She was angry herself, more angry than she could ever remember being except when her parents sent her from the Triple X in the first place. All those years ago they'd sent her away for being unruly, uncontrollable. She'd vowed to go back, to live on the Triple X forever. Somehow during the years she'd forgotten that promise to herself. And now it was too late. They'd sold the place, and all her old feelings had surfaced at once. She was filled with powerful feelings of anger, regret, guilt. She'd let herself down. She'd become exactly what she'd promised herself she'd never be. Glancing down at the white satin dress she wore, she now felt ridiculous. She'd dressed up and put herself on display. This was not who she was, but what could she do about it? Especially now that the Triple X was gone.

"What's gotten into you?" asked Rachel as soon as the door closed behind them.

Jessie turned to face her mother, emerald eyes sparking with barely controlled rage. "You sold the ranch without even telling me, without even asking me what I thought about it. How could you do that?"

"We didn't think we had to discuss our business decisions with our daughter," replied Sin.

"This was more than a business decision. The Triple X is my home," she stopped herself for the space of a second, "was my home," she emphasized to her father.

"We never knew you'd feel this way, Jessie," said

14

Rachel. "I can't remember the last time you even mentioned the Triple X, let alone talked of returning to it."

Jessie faced her mother again. "I know. And I'll feel that guilt for a long time. But what about you? What about your loyalty to family, to Grandpa? He and Grandma are buried on the Triple X. You once fought Father so hard for ownership of the ranch that he almost left forever. If he had, I'd never have been born. And now you just sell out? What happened to you, Mother?" she accused.

Rachel leveled her gaze on her daughter. "What you say about my fighting your father is true. But that was a different time and different circumstances. The Triple X was all I had then. I thought it was all I'd ever have. I was wrong. Life has been good to me since I met your father. And I've learned through the years that it doesn't matter where we live. As long as I'm with him, I'm happy. And as far as my loyalty to family goes, the ranch is still in the family. I'd never sell to an outsider. We've sold the ranch to Jamie Bonner."

"Jamie? The manager? He wanted it?" Jessie asked in surprise.

"Jamie's been asking to buy the place for years," answered Sin.

Jessie lowered her eyes in defeat. Tears began to sting her lids. "It's really gone," she said quietly. She turned and crossed the room, sitting on a small settee.

Rachel watched her daughter with concern. Touching her husband on the arm, they crossed to stand in front of Jessie's small, dejected frame. "It'll be all right, Jessie. You were just surprised by the news. You'll get used to the idea," Rachel said softly.

The heat of rebellion burned in Jessie's chest. Lifting her moist eyes to her parents, she spoke, "I'll never get used to it. Write to Jamie. Tell him you've changed your minds," she said vehemently.

Rachel and Sin exchanged glances. "We haven't," they said practically in unison. "Besides," added Sin, "Jamie wouldn't back out of the sale even if he could. He's wanted the Triple X from day one."

Jessie's mind raced to remember Jamie Bonner. Her memories had faded with time, faded and become rose colored. His face was a handsome blur, soft brown eyes grinning at her, a tall, thin, boyish body riding away from her. She could remember his laughter and that he had a quick but amenable temper. But none of these memories helped her now. "What if I talked to him?" she finally asked.

"Writing to him won't change his mind, Jessie. He's worked the ranch for a long time. He's earned the right to be the owner," Sin answered.

"I didn't say I wanted to write to him. I said, what if I talked to him," Jessie responded.

"Face to face?" asked Rachel.

"Yes. What if I went to the Triple X and asked him to sell?"

"I forbid it." Sin's voice was stern.

Rachel looked startled at her husband.

"You forbid—" Jessie began.

"You are not going to the Triple X and you are not going to try to convince Jamie to sell the ranch back to us. Your mother and I made a decision. We're sticking by that decision."

"But—"

"But nothing," Sin interrupted. Then, kneeling in front of Jessie, he softened his tone a bit. "I'm sorry this was such an unpleasant surprise for you, but the sale stands."

Jessie raised her eyes, lowering her lids slightly, and leveled her jaw as she looked at her father. She didn't respond, but sat there staring at him.

Sin was startled by how strongly Jessie resembled her mother at that moment. The same defiant expression he'd seen so often on Rachel's face through the years he now saw on his daughter's. "Do you understand me, Jessie?"

"I understand how you feel," she answered.

"Are you saying—"

"I said, I understand how you feel. Now, if you'll excuse me, I have guests to attend to," she said stiffly, standing.

Sin raised himself up and looked down on her.

Jessie walked past her parents and headed for the door before anything more could be said. She didn't want them pinning her down to any promises she'd regret later. She had a plan. She knew they'd be angry, but, to use their own words, they'd get used to it.

The notes were written: one to her parents, one to Mary. They stood side by side, propped up against her pillow. Her mother would find them in the morning, but not too early, as they'd expect her to sleep late the morning after the party.

Sticking her head out her bedroom window, Jessie surveyed the ground below. The trellis was beneath the window. She'd only have to reach for it a little. Pulling her head back in, she picked up her valise and tossed it out the window, saying a little prayer that the sound of its landing wouldn't waken anyone. Taking a deep breath and letting it out slowly, she swung one leg out the window. For a moment she couldn't find a foothold and her leg waggled precariously back and forth as she hung onto the window sill. Gritting her teeth, she kept feeling with her foot until she finally, gratefully, felt the top of the trellis. Sighing, she swung her other leg outside and began the climb downward. Her fashionable, high-heeled boots weren't made for midnight escapes down spindly structures, but she managed to keep a tight grip and was soon standing on the ground. Picking up her valise, she twisted one way and then the next, looking to make sure no one was out and about at this late hour who could alert the household of her escape. Satisfied she was alone, she grinned, a mischievous upturn of the corners of her mouth, and headed across the lawn and toward the street. If things continued to go well she'd be on a train and heading for Texas before morning.

"Jesus Christ!" cursed James Bonner as he held the telegram tightly in his gloved fist. "This is all I need," he said disgustedly.

"What is it, James? Bad news?" asked Sam, the telegraph operator.

James leaned his head back slightly, trying to gain some control of his temper, and sighed. "No, not bad, Sam. Just damned inconvenient." He shoved the crumpled telegram into his pants pocket and started to leave the office.

"Anything I can do?" offered Sam, pushing his glasses up to rest higher on the bridge of his thin nose.

James stopped at the door and turned back to the old man. "Not unless you want to come out to my place and help baby-sit three children," he responded.

"Three? I thought your brother's children were twins."

"They are, but now Jessie Braddock is headed this way." He shook his head in frustration.

"Sorry," offered Sam, remembering the wild little girl that had torn up the prairie on horseback.

James sighed again and pushed his way out through the screen door of the office. He stood on the sidewalk for a moment, not relishing the idea of retrieving his nephews from the general store where he'd left them to pick out candy while he tended to business. Why he ever agreed to let his brother Luke's twin five-year-olds stay with him for the summer while Luke and his wife Tish went to England in search of new breeding stock, he'd never know. But how could he have known five-year-old boys could be so much trouble? And now Jessie Braddock, hell on horseback, was on her way as well.

Stepping off the sidewalk, he thought about the telegram in his pocket and clenched his jaw, remembering Sin's warning about Jessie's reason for this visit. "It'll be a cold day in hell before I give up the Triple X, Jessie," he mouthed. Just then he heard a shrieking cry coming from the general store. "Oh no, they're at it again!" he fumed, and began racing toward the store.

"You've ruined the whole barrel!" screeched Mrs. Medley, the storekeeper's wife, as James ran through the doors. "Do you know how much a whole barrel of pickles costs? Well, do you!" she demanded, glaring down at the two identical troublemakers.

"What have they done now?" asked James as he stomped closer to the two boys.

Mrs. Medley changed the aim of her angry stare to James. "They've ruined a whole barrel of pickles is what they've done," she announced. "A whole barrel," she added more loudly for emphasis.

James glared down at the angelic faces that stared back up at him. "What did you do?" he demanded.

Both boys shrugged. "I didn't do it," they answered in unison.

James gritted his teeth and sighed through his nose. This answer, their standard answer to any question regarding guilt, frustrated him almost beyond endurance. Neither one would ever own up to his shenanigans, and it didn't feel right punishing both of them when one was probably innocent. Most of the time he'd end up yelling at them until he was hoarse, then letting them off the hook, unable to determine who the culprit was in any given situation.

Looking at the barrel of pickles, then at Mrs. Medley, he ventured, "Are you sure the barrel is ruined? What did they do to it?"

"Look!" she nearly shouted.

James glanced at the barrel again and still didn't see anything so terribly wrong. "Did they spill something in it?" he asked.

Mrs. Medley rolled her eyes impatiently. "Look more closely. When you do, I think you'll notice that several pickles have grown legs!" Her voice rose several decibels as she spoke.

James blinked several times when he heard her strange explanation, then as he leaned over the barrel to inspect further, he realized why she was so upset. Floating dead in the brine at the top of the pickle barrel were the bodies of two enormous frogs. Staring at them for a moment, he was speechless. Then turning to face his nephews, he glowered at them. "Why?" was the one word he could trust himself to say.

" 'Coz they match," the two voices answered together.

James looked back at the dead frogs. Their color and texture did, indeed, match the pickles perfectly.

"The frogs didn't know they'd die in there, Uncle James," Jeremy offered.

"They though they'd like it in there," added Jamie, James's namesake.

"Do frogs start out as pickles?" asked Jeremy.

"Or are pickles just frogs with their legs cut off?" asked Jamie.

James hung his head in defeat and tried not to laugh as he wondered how much the barrel of pickles was going to cost him.

❊ 2 ❊

Jessie stuck her head out the window of the stage as it came to an abrupt halt, dust flying, harness chains jingling, and leather and wood creaking. She let her eyes search the main street of Mesa City. It had been a long, arduous, filthy trip, but she'd finally made it. And during the trip, as each hard mile passed under her, she became more and more certain she was doing the right thing. "I'm nearly home," she whispered as she saw familiar buildings and faces.

"What's that, Miss?" asked the elderly gentleman who'd shared the stage with her for the last two hundred miles.

Jessie brought her gaze back around to look at him. "Nothing really, Mr. Anderson. It just feels so good to be back in Mesa City," she answered politely.

He nodded in acknowledgment of her statement and smiled, wiping a trickle of perspiration from his temple. "It's been quite a few years since I last visited my daughter and grandchildren here. I don't remember it being quite this warm before," he commented.

Jessie, too, felt the heat, wishing she could loosen her corset and wipe the perspiration that ran between her breasts in itchy little trails. "It does seem quite warm for spring, doesn't it?"

21

"Everybody out!" shouted the stage driver as though he spoke to a crowd instead of just two passengers. Throwing open the door, he secured it with a leather strap, then began yelling to the stationmaster to give him a hand with the luggage.

Jessie sighed. The stage driver had been surly and abrupt the entire trip, making their various stops less than pleasant. He'd scolded her for taking too long getting back to the stage when she'd had a hard time finding the convenience at one particularly rustic place he'd chosen to rest the horses. Closing her eyes for just a second, she thought, it doesn't matter now. I'm nearly home.

Minutes later, she was standing on the wooden sidewalk outside the stage office, her valise at her feet. Glancing around her, she took in the changes the small town had gone through during her absence. The Shady Place restaurant was still there, though the sign proclaiming they served the best coffee in town had faded with time. The general store looked the same, as did the telegraph office and several other small businesses she remembered. She noticed that the Wagonwheel Saloon had undergone a name change, the big red letters on the marquee now read, The Cattlemen's Club. She pursed her lips a bit as she noticed the scantily clad women sitting on the window ledges on the second floor, advertising their wares. "Club, indeed," she mused.

Bringing her attention back to matters at hand, she picked up her valise and began walking in the direction of the livery. She couldn't wait to get to the Triple X.

James scanned the horizon and removed his hat, wiping the sweat from his brow with the back of his gloved hand. He placed the hat snugly back in place, tugging the brim low over his eyes. "Damn," he murmured at the cloudless sky. He'd been looking for some sign of rain, hoping to see the beginnings of a spring storm brewing, certain he'd sensed a change in the air.

Looking back over his shoulder, he squinted in the

direction of the house. He was several miles away. It would be inconvenient to go back now, but suddenly he wondered what his nephews were doing. Had they gotten into more mischief? Is that what was bothering him? He was filled with a sense of foreboding. Shaking his head, he turned his mount toward home.

Jessie could see the ranch from some distance away and her eyes began to feel the stinging threat of tears. Blinking rapidly to stop them, she slapped the buggy reins against the rump of the worn-out horse the livery man had given her, trying to get a little more speed out of the sorry animal. "Hurry, boy," she urged, but the animal kept up the steady, slow pace he'd started the second they'd left town. "Why did I get stuck with you now that I'm so close," she complained to the plodding animal.

Scanning the buildings, she searched out the house first. It looked pretty much the same as when she'd left, though an addition of some kind had been built on near the back of the house. The barn and other outbuildings looked freshly painted, the corrals sturdy. Several horses stood at the ready in the corrals and a small herd of cattle filled another fenced-off area. She couldn't see any hands around the place, but realized the men would probably be out working the range this time of day.

Slapping the reins more firmly against the horse's rump, she tried again to hurry him up, but was only disappointed when the animal acted as though nothing had happened. Sighing, she whispered, "I guess I'll get there when I get there."

As she neared the buildings, her head was swamped with memories of her childhood, memories she'd all but pushed completely from her mind. Most of her memories revolved around her love of horses and the hours she'd spent in the saddle, riding hell-bent for leather, her hair flying behind her like a banshee's, across the open range of the Triple X. Without even realizing she was doing it, she guided the horse and buggy toward the barn and pulled them to a stop in front of the open double doors of the large building.

Climbing down from the small conveyance, she moved toward the doors, the cool, dark interior of the barn beckoning to her. Stepping inside, she stopped and waited for her eyes to become accustomed to the dim light, then moved farther in, the smells of manure and oats and molasses filling her nostrils. She remembered the hours she'd spent working in this barn. The work had been hard, but she'd loved it. She'd learned how to shoe horses here. She'd seen births and deaths here. She'd helped with both. She'd had a real sense of what life was about here. She wondered how she'd allowed herself to forget all this.

The sound of horses in the stalls pulled her along. She smiled as she neared one stall and saw a new foal standing beneath its mother. "Hey, little one. How are you?" she whispered, suddenly envious of the people who'd seen this little life brought into the world. The foal turned toward her. "My name's Jessie." Tugging one soft gray leather glove from her hand, she reached into the stall to pat the tiny nose of the baby animal. "You're sure a pretty thing," she continued to whisper.

A sound deeper in the interior of the barn caught her attention. When she turned she saw a big grey and white striped cat scurry into the tack room. "And who might you be?" she said to the cat, smiling. There had always been several cats around the place when she was growing up. Cats were necessary to keep the field mice from setting up housekeeping inside the barn, but she'd always made pets of the tough felines and wanted to meet this descendant of her former friends. Scratching the under-jaw of the foal for just a second longer, she said, "I'll see you later," then turned to follow the cat.

Walking quietly to the doorway that led into the tack room, she stopped to search with her eyes. She didn't want to frighten the cat away. As she scanned the room her eyes fell on something that took her breath for a second. High on a shelf was her old saddle, the initials

J.B. barely visible under a thick coat of dust. The small saddle, unused for so long, saddened her, causing her to close her eyes in memory. She'd spent every spare moment of her life in this saddle on the back of her horse. There was nothing like the feeling of freedom she'd get from letting the animal have its head and then just hanging on with her knees. She'd spread her arms out wide and let her head hang back, her hair slapping wildly in the wind behind her. Now, standing still, her eyes closed, she tilted her head slightly back. She could almost feel the wind in her face and hear the thunder of the horse's hooves beneath her. She could feel the tears behind her lids long before they began to fall.

James stood silently in the doorway of the barn studying the young woman silhouetted by the light coming in through the tack room window. Her eyes were closed and she seemed to be lost in some reverie. Emotions warred within him as he took in every detail of her appearance. He knew it had to be Jessie. Her arrival was the source of the premonition that had brought him back to the house. But this couldn't be Jessie, not the Jessie he remembered. His dark brown eyes narrowed as he remembered the wild child she'd been, all long black curls, green eyes, and smart mouth. Stepping into the dark quiet of the barn, he decided to interrupt her thoughts. He needed to see if this small, delicate creature was, in fact, Jessie Braddock, and if it was, he needed to spell out straightaway that she wasn't going to convince him to give up the Triple X now that it was his.

Certain she'd turn when she heard him approaching, he became suspicious when she remained with her eyes closed, her back turned a little toward him as he neared. He wondered at her tactics. The Jessie he remembered wouldn't have ridden to the Triple X in a buggy and she wouldn't have been standing peacefully daydreaming in the barn. She'd have come in on horseback, shouting to the heavens her claim on the ranch and causing more than a few blushes by her expletives. Was this Jessie?

He studied her figure and form. She did have a thick

mass of black curls, but it was tied neatly back and up, most of it hidden under a gray hat. His gaze strayed lower. Her shoulders were narrow and softly rounded, her waist so tiny he could probably span it with his hands, but her hips flared provocatively within the fitted gray suit she wore. A purely animal jolt of awareness suddenly shot through him. This couldn't be little Jessie Braddock.

Stepping closer, he waited for her to turn around. Was she afraid to face him, he wondered? Had she already realized the folly of her trip here? Moving closer still, he could hear her breathing, a soft sound that floated across his nerve endings like the down of a newborn chick. It was then he noticed a single tear slip silently down the curved plane of her cheek. She was crying and he felt a stab of pity shoot through him, twisting toward his heart like an arrow. Then, narrowing his eyes, he fought the emotion, trying to harden his heart against it. He wouldn't let himself feel sorry for her. He'd worked too hard in the past years turning the Triple X into what he wanted it to be to let himself be swayed by silly emotions. Determination pushing him forward, he was now standing only inches from her.

Jessie let her mind wander back through the days she'd roamed the ranch freely, wildly. She had been full of high-spirited energy and an overwhelming love of the open spaces. How could she have forgotten all this? How could she have been content in Charleston? This question brought her back to the present. She could once again smell the horses and the leather around her. She could hear the foal suckling its mother, she could hear—
The hair on the back of her neck stood on end. Something or someone was very near. Her heart seemed to stop beating as an alarming tingle of fear swept through her. She listened. She thought she could hear breathing. Anyone up to any good would have announced his presence, so who or what was behind her probably didn't have her best interests at heart. With every nerve standing at attention, she decided the most logical course of

action was to confront the intruder quickly, perhaps giving herself a slight advantage by way of surprise. Turning as quickly as she could, she stepped forward to demand an explanation only to find herself walking directly into the muscular chest of a very large man. "Oh!" she cried as strong arms closed around her.

James wasn't expecting the woman to turn so quickly. He certainly hadn't expected to find her in his arms a split second later. He was also unprepared for the sudden and overwhelming bolt of sizzling heat that coursed through him as the soft, full curves of her body made contact with the muscles of his chest. Instinctively, his hold on her tightened, bringing her flush with the length of his body.

Jessie gasped in shocked surprise as she found herself in an embrace like no other she'd ever experienced. She'd never been held like this by a man before, never felt the muscles of a man's stomach rippling against her rib cage, never known the sensation of strong thighs holding them both up. She had never, ever, felt the length of a man's passion pressing into her abdomen. She'd been ready to confront whoever had joined her in the barn unannounced, but to find herself flush with the hot, muscular body of a man, a very large man, shook her to her toes.

Struggling immediately to free herself, she looked up to see the face of the stranger holding her so intimately. The dark brown eyes that met her glance were familiar, the face itself was familiar. No, he couldn't have changed so much in just six years, could he? She'd met Jamie when she was just twelve years old and had run away to join her sister's cattle drive north. Her memories of him were few but, she'd thought, clear. Jamie had been handsome as a boy of nineteen, whereas this man holding her now had the power to take her breath away, was in fact, causing her to stop her struggles just to look at him. "Jamie?" she breathed softly.

James stared, stunned, into the emerald green eyes he remembered so well. The eyes, though, were in a face that barely resembled the one in his memory of a wild, little girl. And the body he held was in no way immature. The full, ripe mounds of her breasts were pressing into his chest, giving evidence that Jessie Braddock had grown up, though he noticed she wasn't much taller than he remembered. She was so petite he could have picked her up with one hand—or laid her down with one, his mind said wickedly. A surge of blood pounded downward through his body at this thought. Attempting to squelch the desire that coursed through him, he began to push her away.

Jessie felt herself being released and nearly swayed back into his arms, not wanting the startling emotions she was feeling to stop, but she caught herself at the last second, stepping just far enough from him to break contact. She continued to stare up into his dark eyes, blinking several times to be sure she was seeing right. Jamie Bonner had become more attractive than she'd have thought possible. "Jamie, is it you?" she spoke again.

James swallowed hard, not answering for a moment, not trusting his voice to come out normally. How had Jessie become so beautiful? How in hell had she changed from the baby wildcat she'd been into the sophisticated lady that now stood before him? The only thing marring her perfect image was a few smudges of dust on her suit from her stage ride. "Jessie?" he finally ventured.

"Yes, it's me," she answered, noticing the uncertainty in his voice, a voice several tones lower than she remembered. The timbre of it vibrated warmly across her ears. "I'll bet you're surprised to see me," she added.

James was still having a hard time pulling the old image of Jessie into line with this woman before him. "Yes, I'm surprised," he answered. "Though your father wired me you were on your way."

"He did?" she asked, a little perplexed. She'd been afraid her parents would send out a posse after her, but she hadn't thought they'd notify Jamie she was coming.

She suddenly felt at a disadvantage. "Did he say anything else?" she asked.

James raised his jaw a bit. "He did," he answered.

Jessie's heart began an angry pounding in her chest. She could tell by Jamie's answer he'd been warned about her reason for being here and had already made up his mind before he even heard her out. "What did he tell you?" she asked, her head tilted defiantly to the right.

Watching the emotions sparking in her green eyes, he was reminded of the little girl she'd been. He remembered how stubborn she'd been, how determined she'd been to have her own way. "I'm not selling the Triple X back to you or your folks, Jessie. I bought it and I'm keeping it. So you made this trip for nothing," he stated bluntly.

Jessie stared up into the handsome face above her and realized that not only his looks had changed during the years. The leaner, harder angles of his face and body were matched by a harder personality than she remembered. At a loss for a moment, she finally began to notice other things about him. His clothes were covered with dust from a hard day's work. He smelled of sweat and horses and looked as though he hadn't shaved that morning, a short stubble of beard showing along his jaw. He wore a Colt .45 strapped low on his right hip and a bowie knife sheathed on his left. His hat was pulled down to shade, or hide, his eyes. He looked dangerous, though she hadn't felt threatened when he'd held her. She'd felt excited. A surprising increase in her pulse as she studied him caused her to flush a little. *It's too bad he's my adversary,* she thought. "It is warm here, isn't it?" she asked, bringing one hand up to fan herself, buying herself some time.

James's eyes narrowed at her words. Was she going to ignore what he'd just told her? "Did you hear me, Jessie?" he asked.

"Of course I did," she answered, continuing to fan herself.

"I said I'm not selling," he repeated to make sure she understood him. He shifted his weight from one foot to the other in emphasis of his words.

Jessie thought fast. Her father's warning had ruined her plan of surprising Jamie. He'd been given time to think about her reason for being here and he'd made up his mind. He was obviously ready for a fight. His tone of voice and belligerent stance indicated his determination. But a person concentrating on defending a frontal attack rarely saw an enemy coming in from a different direction. If Jamie was expecting a fight, he might not be ready for a little sugar instead. "Well, it's obvious you've made up your mind," she said, lowering her eyes demurely. "I suppose there's no point in my trying to change it."

James stood stock still at her words. This wasn't what he was expecting. The Jessie he remembered would have cussed a blue streak at him. Narrowing his eyes at her, he spoke. "I mean it, Jessie. I'm not selling."

Jessie raised her eyes to gaze innocently up at him. "I understand you, Jamie." She lowered her eyes once more. "Now I feel foolish coming all this way for nothing," she said, managing to look flustered.

Jessie's attitude was completely perplexing to James. A person couldn't change her entire personality could she? Where was the feisty, hotheaded, foulmouthed urchin that Jessie had been? "You really do understand?" he asked.

Her glance darted upward at his words. "Of course," she said. "You've made yourself quite clear. I only wish I'd known how strongly you felt about it before I traveled that horrid distance to speak to you. I suppose I should have wired you instead. I always have been too impulsive." She let her gaze hold his a second longer than was considered proper, then lowered her eyes and tilted her head downward for a moment, letting her thick black lashes shadow her cheeks in the way she'd seen her friends do. "I won't trouble you further, Jamie. I'll go on back to town and catch the next stage for home." Raising her hand expectantly and once more meeting his gaze, she smiled. "It was good to see you again, anyway. Even if it was for so brief a period. Good-bye."

James's senses reeled at the sight of her smile and he was suddenly frustrated that she was going to leave so soon. "You don't have to go. As long as you're here you might as well stay for a visit," he heard himself saying.

"Do you really mean it?" she asked. "I'd love to," she answered before he could change his mind and rescind the invitation. "How wonderful of you to offer." She artfully looped her hand through his arm and began leading him toward the open doors of the barn.

"I . . . Yes, well," James stammered, suddenly not sure how this had happened.

Jessie smiled up at him and allowed her breast to gently brush his arm as they walked, a trick she'd learned from Mary. Mary had said it drove men wild to think they were touching a breast without the girl being aware of it. Jessie had tried it on several young men of their acquaintance, just to see what the reaction would be, and she'd had to admit Mary had been correct. The men had stammered and blushed and been ready to do anything she asked. She'd felt almost guilty about how easy it was to have her own way by using her femininity as a weapon, but now, with Jamie, she felt she was going to need to use every weapon at her disposal to get what she wanted.

Something was different with Jamie, though. As she let her breast touch his arm she felt as though she were being burned by the contact. Her insides were turning to mush and she felt as if the temperature around her had increased at least ten degrees. Glancing up from the corner of her eyes, she studied his handsome face and saw just the shadow of a smile turning up the corners of his mouth. What was there about him that was different from the other men she'd flirted innocently with? She'd certainly never felt anything like this with anyone else.

She was glad when they reached the buggy. "Just let me get my valise and we can go to the house," she said, her voice surprising her by coming out a breathy facsimile of her normal tone.

"We'll take the buggy over to the house. I'll have one of the hands take it back to town for you after supper," James responded.

Jessie glanced at the buggy. "Help me up?" she asked demurely.

James looked curiously down at her, searching her face for the little girl he'd known. This woman she'd become had his pulse racing like a well ridden horse's. His flesh burned where his arm had touched her, but something was missing, something that had been a vital part of the Jessie he remembered. And he wondered about her obvious attempt at flirtation. He'd known since he was sixteen that a woman was well aware of which parts of her body touched a man as she walked beside him. What was she up to? Why was she now asking for assistance to climb into a buggy? The Jessie of his memories wouldn't have asked for help climbing a sheer cliff, even if both her legs were broken. Staring into the cool depths of her eyes, he held her emerald gaze with his own. He saw a spark of emotion there, but what emotion? She was too well in control of her feelings now.

Jessie fought hard to keep her face a mask of calm, but with the heated stare of Jamie's dark eyes boring into hers it was difficult. He seemed to be searching for something in her face, testing her somehow. She couldn't fail. If she did, she'd never get her hands on the Triple X. "Please?" she asked, raising her hand for his assistance.

James responded by placing both hands around her waist, spanning it easily. Lifting her straight upward, he brought her face level with his. He pulled her to him for a second, allowing their bodies to touch as he set her in the buggy. The fire that flamed deeply within him at the touch, burned upward to his eyes. "Comfortable?" he asked.

Jessie was speechless. Her body throbbed from their contact and the heat emanating from the depths of his dark eyes frightened her a little. She suddenly wasn't so sure of herself or her plan of attack. It seemed he knew a few tricks of his own, and for a brief moment she thought about leaving after all. But no. This was her home, her birthright. She wasn't going to let herself be scared off by Jamie Bonner, no matter how unsettling he was. She would just have to best him at this game. She knew she could. She had to. Nodding at him, she settled her skirt around her.

James felt he'd won a small victory. He'd seen the flash of strong emotion in Jessie's eyes, and for just a second she reminded him of the little girl she'd been. Perhaps she wasn't as in control as she wanted him to believe. Perhaps, just perhaps, he could still get a rise out of her if he tried hard enough. Then, shaking himself mentally, he wondered why it mattered to him that she'd changed.

Rounding the buggy, he swung himself up into the seat. "Ready?" he asked.

"Whenever you are," she responded, glad when her voice once again sounded normal.

Letting his gaze roam her form from the top of her head to the tips of her toes, he realized she could get a rise out of him without even trying. "Damn it," he cursed under his breath.

"What's that?" Jessie asked.

"Nothing. I was just thinking out loud." He scanned her once more.

"Then I won't interrupt your train of thought, Jamie," she answered politely, smiling sweetly up at him.

James suddenly knew exactly what it was he missed about the child Jessie had been and why he'd been glad to see the emotion in her eyes. It had been her honesty. Whether she'd been sad or happy, calm or mad as hell, anyone within earshot of her knew it. She'd let the whole world know what she was thinking and feeling every minute. Somehow, that had changed. She was now what would be called a lady, and he didn't think of it as a compliment.

Twisting the corner of his mouth into a grimace as he flipped the reins, he got the horse and buggy moving the short distance to the house. "By the way, I'm not called Jamie any more, Jessie."

"Really?" She suddenly thought of a few things she could call him, but smiled at him instead. "What do I call you?"

"Uncle James! Uncle James!" screamed two tiny voices from not far away.

James jerked the horse to a stop and looked toward the voices. "What have you done?" he called as the twins ran from behind the barn as though the devil himself were after them.

"I didn't do it!" they yelled.

James gritted his teeth at their answer, then shouted, "What's wrong?"

The twosome ran on short legs as fast as they could go. "The horses got out!" they shouted.

"Which horses?"

"The big ones!"

"Damn it!" James cursed. "You two get in the buggy with your aunt Jessie while I go get those horses!" he yelled at them, jumping from the buggy seat to the ground in one leap. He knew which horses they meant. It had to be the last of the Thoroughbreds still on the ranch. The huge animals were due to be shipped to Sin and Rachel in Charleston at the end of the month, but now the twins had let them loose.

Pausing only a moment to see the boys made it safely into the buggy, he looked at Jessie, whose mouth was open in surprise. "Take care of them for me. I'll meet you in a while at the house." Running fast, he grabbed the reins of the horse he'd left tethered next to the barn, then swung up into the saddle. Jerking the leather straps to the side, he started his horse on a galloping path toward the other side of the barn.

Jessie watched him go, then looked down to see her small nephews sitting beside her. She was amazed at how much they still looked alike. She hadn't seen them since they were two, when Tish and Luke had visited Charleston during Christmas. "Hello," she said.

"Hello," they answered in unison. "Are you really our aunt?"

"Yes," she answered them, grinning down at their impish faces. "I think we should get acquainted. What do you think?"

They nodded like a pair of puppets.

"Why did you let the horses loose?" she asked, not giving them a chance to deny their crime.

The boys exchanged glances nervously. "They wanted to run in the field," Jeremy finally answered.

"Why?" Jessie asked.

"They didn't like their little corral," Jamie offered.

Jessie contemplated his words for a moment. "Well, the next time one of the animals tells you something, you come tell me. I'll go listen to what they have to say, and I'll decide if they're telling the truth. Animals are terrible liars, you know. And they love to get little boys in trouble."

"They do?" the boys asked, their eyes wide with wonder.

Jessie grinned and nodded knowingly. Picking up the reins James had dropped in his haste, she got the buggy moving once again. The boys began to talk a blue streak.

Just moments later they reached the house. As she pulled the reins, stopping the buggy next to the front porch, they were laughing together over the frog-in-the-pickle-barrel incident. "I told you animals are liars," chuckled Jessie.

The boys' heads bobbed in agreement.

"What did you two do now?" demanded an angry female voice as the screen door opened with a bang and a young, olive-skinned woman emerged in a flurry of brightly colored skirts, her long black hair swinging behind her. "Did you bother this lady?" She looked at

Jessie, not waiting for an answer from the boys. "I am sorry, Miss. These two are trouble. Did they ask you for a ride? I will tell their uncle to punish them." She let her dark eyes glance meaningfully back at the boys.

Jessie's hackles went up at the woman's tone and words. "These are my nephews and they won't be punished for spending time with me," she said coolly.

The woman was clearly taken aback by the statement, but only for a moment. Turning her head suspiciously, she let her eyes take in Jessie's appearance. "You are their aunt?" she asked, her tone implying she doubted the truth of Jessie's words.

Jessie did a quick appraisal of her own, then raised one brow with authority. "Yes. I'm Jessie Braddock. And you are?" she inquired.

The woman's eyes narrowed. This couldn't be Jessie Braddock. James had described her as an unruly child. This was no child. This was a woman fully grown. Her heart began to beat jealously in her chest. "I am Carmen," she answered shortly.

"And your position here?" Jessie inquired further.

Carmen's chin rose as she answered. "I am James's housekeeper."

Jessie felt a sudden tightening in her midsection at the implication in Carmen's tone as she described her place within the household. Her eyes scanned the woman again. She was very beautiful. Her skin was dark, her long hair and eyes the same coal-black color as the night. The white blouse she wore tucked into her colorful skirt was hanging loosely over one bare shoulder and it was obvious she wore no undergarment. The fullness of her breasts was apparent beneath the soft fabric. Her feet were clad only in sandals and a silver chain decorated one slender ankle. Jessie's gaze slid back up to Carmen's eyes. "I see," she finally answered.

The sound of approaching hoofbeats took Carmen's attention. The scowl that had contorted her features as she glared at Jessie lifted completely, changing her face from merely lovely to beautiful. She smiled widely at

James's arrival. "You are home," she said softly, her voice dropping to a low, sensuous purr.

Jessie's back stiffened at the sound. Swinging her gaze to James's face, she waited for him to respond.

James smiled at Carmen, but he felt the inner turmoil caused by what had happened only two weeks earlier, when he'd wakened to find her in his bed. He wished he could remember more, but he'd been drinking that night at a friend's bachelor party. When he discovered her, nude, curled up beside him, he nearly jumped out of his skin, and he had suffered bitter remorse ever since. She'd claimed he'd taken her to his bed in a drunken passion. He could remember none of it, and guiltily found himself doubting her story, even when she cried and confessed her love for him. He'd apologized and told her it would never happen again. He wasn't in love with her, and he certainly wasn't going to use her to satisfy his lust. She was the daughter of his ranch foreman and friend, Juan de Silva.

Since that night he'd been terribly uncomfortable around her but hadn't had the heart to let her go. Besides, with the boys visiting for the summer he really needed her help in the house. "Have you met Jessie?" he asked a little awkwardly.

Carmen's eyes swung briefly to where Jessie still sat in the buggy. "Yes. We've met," she said quickly, as though the meeting had been completely unimportant.

Jessie's gaze narrowed as she watched James. She could see he was uncomfortable. He deserves to be, she thought angrily. The nerve of him to keep his mistress under the same roof, especially in front of the twins. Does he actually believe people will be stupid enough to think this woman is his housekeeper? she thought.

James glanced from Carmen to Jessie. Jessie's green eyes seemed to dissect him, making him wonder what had been said before he'd ridden up. "Have you told Carmen you're staying for a while?" he asked.

Carmen's eyes flashed back to meet his, angry surprise on her face. "She is staying?" she asked incredulously.

James had raved for days how he would send Jessie packing the second she arrived to pester him about selling the ranch.

Jessie wouldn't let this opportunity pass. "Yes, I'm staying," she answered before James could speak. She began to climb from the buggy, reaching to help her nephews down. "I'll play with the boys while you get my room ready," she directed at Carmen. "And prepare me a bath, please. I feel quite in need of one after my journey." She then grasped the twins' hands and led them up onto the porch toward the door. Her back was straight, her head high, her demeanor every inch that of the perfect gentlewoman she'd been taught to be.

James rocked back in the saddle and sighed as he watched Jessie lead the boys into the house. He could hear Carmen swearing under her breath. How had things gotten so complicated?

❃ 3 ❃

Jessie watched James across the dinner table from beneath the thickness of her lashes. Eating delicately, she studied his every move, still astounded by how much he'd changed from the young man of her memories. His broad masculinity seemed to fill the room, and each time his eyes met hers she was reminded of the way he'd felt as he held her against his body earlier that day. Startling waves of heat coursed through her each time this happened, causing her to avoid looking directly at him too often.

After she'd bathed that afternoon, a shallow, cool experience thanks to Carmen, she'd taken a rather cursory look around the house and immediate area. Her parents hadn't moved all of their personal belongings from the ranch yet, so she recognized a lot of the things around the place. James had disappeared somewhere, leaving the boys to their own devices, and she'd found them sitting in the backyard up to their elbows in mud. It had taken her the rest of the late afternoon to get them clean again. It was amazing the places she'd found mud on their tiny bodies.

"Why do mice eat cheese, Aunt Jessie?" asked Jeremy, gazing up at her with adoring eyes.

Jessie turned her attention from her dinner plate to her nephew and smiled. "Because they know they're very small and they think that if they eat cheese it will make them big and strong." She pointed to Jeremy's glass. "Just like drinking your milk will make you big and strong," she answered.

Jeremy's eyes grew wide with wonder. Both boys reached for their glasses and took huge gulps. "Just like Uncle James?" Jamie asked with a white liquid mustache adorning his upper lip.

Jessie couldn't help darting her eyes to take in James's face. She was once more reminded of the ease with which he'd lifted her. "Yes," she answered quietly, "just like your uncle James."

James's dark eyes focused on Jessie's features and he felt a tingle of awareness shiver over his skin at the sound of her voice. Catching her gaze, he stared hard into the green depths of her eyes, only to have her look away. She became suddenly very interested in helping Jamie cut his steak, something the child had been doing just fine on his own. He frowned at her action. He'd been trying to figure her out since she'd arrived, certain there was something insincere about her behavior, but every time he'd made eye contact with her she'd managed to change the direction of her attention. "How do you like the place?" he ventured.

Jessie glanced nervously back up. "Everything is lovely," she answered softly, her eyes lowering immediately after the words left her lips.

"What do you think of the changes I've made to the house?" James tried again.

Jessie had noticed the addition to the house from a distance as she arrived. She learned later that the addition was made up of two new rooms, a master bedroom and a room that held a pool table. In her younger, wilder days she'd snuck into her family's small saloon, the Rosebud, but there had never been a pool table there to amuse the customers. It was a game she was sure she'd enjoy, but there had never been any opportunity to learn it while living in Charleston. Once more she felt a surge of anger at herself for succumbing so completely to the life-style forced upon her during the last four years. "Will you teach me to shoot pool?" she asked before she thought about what she was saying.

James's brows went up in surprise. Pool was considered a man's game. Was this a glimmer of the old Jessie? The Jessie he remembered so well? "Certainly," he responded, an amused rumble in his deep voice. "We can even start right after dinner tonight if you'd like."

"You can start what after dinner?" Carmen practically demanded as she entered the room carrying a coffee pot from the kitchen.

James looked up at her. "Jessie has asked me to teach her to shoot pool," he answered.

Carmen's dark eyes flashed their resentment at James first, then swung to take in Jessie's form. "James taught me," she stated coolly. "James has taught me many things," she added with emphasis.

Jessie clenched her jaw against the retort that threatened to erupt from her lips. This woman, though beautiful outwardly, was a wanton, and not a good influence on her nephews. Jessie could feel her heartbeat quicken in anger. Pointedly ignoring Carmen's gaze, she impaled James with a daggered look of her own. "I'm suddenly quite tired. Perhaps I'll let you show me the game of pool another time. I believe I'll read to the boys and retire early this evening." She glanced quickly at her plate. "In fact, I'm suddenly very full. Please excuse me," she said, her voice a cool monotone.

"But I—" began James.

"Good night," interrupted Carmen.

Jessie just nodded at the woman as she stood. "Boys, when you are ready for bed I'll be in my room. Bring along the book you'd like me to read to you," she directed to the two small faces looking up at her. Then, barely letting herself give James a glance, she left the room.

James watched Jessie leave. Seconds later he looked up

to Carmen's lovely features. She was smiling smugly. "Is there anything else I can do for you this evening, James?" she asked seductively.

James held back a disgusted sigh. "No thank you. I think I'll just go for a ride." He pushed himself away from the table, his chair scraping loudly as he went. "You boys finish eating, then go on up and get ready for bed."

"Yes, Uncle James," they replied as one.

James smiled down at them. They were such a precocious pair one couldn't help loving them. "Good night," he told them softly.

"Good night, Uncle James," they answered, this time their voices overlapped, slightly out of sync.

Walking toward the door, he heard them discussing what book to have Jessie read to them. Leaving the dining room he looked up the stairs, almost wishing he had a reason to go up and see her once more. Shaking his head slightly, he went out through the front door, letting the screen slam with a crash behind him. Leaving the porch, he set a straight course for the barn. He'd have to saddle his horse again, having already settled the animal for the night, but it didn't matter. He needed a drink, and he needed to get away from the house before he did something stupid. He was going to the Rosebud.

Minutes later, Jessie heard hoofbeats pass in the dirt below her window. She knew it was James without even looking, and sighed as he rode away. With him out of the house she could relax slightly.

Jessie lay awake in the pitch blackness of her room. Listening intently, she could hear night sounds in the house she'd grown up in. Mice scurried in the walls. An owl flapped its wings in the attic. Something else scratched under the foundation. These were all familiar, soothing noises that she knew had nothing to do with her insomnia.

Sitting up, she gave in to her wakefulness. Swinging her legs off the bed, she stood and walked to the window. She could see nothing below. Pressing her forehead against the warm glass, she thought about her reason for being here. She knew, now more than ever, now that she was here, that she wanted the Triple X to belong to her. It was home, it felt right. Even the quiet sounds of the house at night felt right. But what to do about James? Her parents' warning to him about her reason for this visit had nearly ruined everything, taking away the element of surprise. The quick decision she'd made to soften him up by using her femininity had seemed like a good idea at first, but the very maleness of him, the thing that should make him most susceptible to her plan, seemed to be working against her. It was causing her to feel a timidity she resented and at the same time couldn't help. "Oh, hell," she murmured. "I've got to get over it."

Turning away from the window, she went back to her bed and lay down. "I'll just take it one day at a time for a while. I'm sure I can convince James that the Triple X should belong to me. It's my home," she whispered.

James lay with his arms beneath his head, staring up into the darkness that filled his room. He couldn't sleep. He cursed himself for going to the Rosebud. All he'd managed to do was give himself a headache.

He thought about Jessie, upstairs now, sleeping under his roof. His mind emphasized the fact that it was his roof. The Triple X was his. Everything, from the house, barn, and other buildings, to the vast acres of land, and the Rosebud saloon belonged legally to him. He'd bought and paid for it. But more than that, he'd worked hard here the last four years. That made it his more than the deed did that was secured in the safe in his office.

When taking care of their Thoroughbred horse business had taken Rachel and Sin from the ranch more and more often, they'd hired him to be the manager of the Triple X. He'd taken over completely, and he'd begun hoping to own the ranch he was pouring his life into. After years of offering to buy and being turned down, he'd almost gotten used to the idea that all he'd ever be was someone else's employee, unless he left and started over on another ranch in another town.

Then recently he'd received the word from Sin that the Triple X was his if he still wanted it. If he still wanted it? He'd nearly shouted out loud with joy! And he'd sweated until the final papers had been signed, afraid something would happen to stop the sale. Nothing had. But now, Jessie Braddock had come to try and convince him to sell the ranch back to her. It would never happen. There was nothing she could do that would change his mind.

His eyes narrowed as he pictured her upstairs. He remembered the child she'd been, wild, willful, ornery, stubborn, and he could barely believe the beautiful woman under his roof was the same person. How could anyone change so much? Had he? No, he'd grown some, and he was certain he looked a little different, but he was the same person. He was sure of it. Jessie was not.

Letting his mind's eye focus on the memory of her in the barn earlier, he remembered the way she'd behaved when he'd told her he wasn't selling. She'd backed down immediately. The Jessie he remembered would have seen his decision as anything but final, as a challenge. She certainly wouldn't have acted . . . how? Embarrassed? Unsure of herself? He suddenly began to grin as a thought struck him. She'd been acting. No one's personality would change completely just because they'd lived in a city for four years.

He continued smiling and settled himself more comfortably against his pillows. Jessie had grown up. And she'd learned things. She'd learned new ways to get what she wanted, but she was still the hellion he knew under that cool exterior. He'd be willing to bet on it.

As sleep finally began to sneak up on him, he wondered what it would take to crack her facade.

Jessie heard men's voices as she descended the stairs early the next morning. Walking through the house to the large room off the kitchen where the crew was fed, she scanned the group quickly as she entered in hopes she might see a face she recognized. She didn't. But her entrance hadn't gone unnoticed by the hands. Everyone stopped eating and looked up expectantly.

James knew who'd walked in even though he had his back to the door. "Good morning, Jessie," he said as he swiveled round in his seat, his eyes instantly taking in the way the blue velvet of her riding habit hugged her curves, emphasizing her small waist. "Sleep well?" he asked.

"Yes, thank you, James," Jessie answered, instantly aware of her own femininity. "I heard voices," she added.

"Last night?" James asked, one dark brow raised curiously.

"What? No, of course not. I meant this morning. Now." She let her eyes scan the room as if in explanation.

"Won't you join us?" James inquired.

Jessie's gaze swung back to James. He was so damned good looking that it sent her heart racing just to look at him. But she'd made her resolve the night before to get over these foolish feelings. She had to in order to achieve her goal of owning the Triple X once more. "I'd love to," she answered coyly, dipping her chin slightly, fluttering her eyelashes ever so delicately.

Several men jumped up and pulled their chairs loudly around the table to make room for her. James stood and reached for an extra chair leaning against the wall. Bringing it to rest beside his, he motioned for her to sit down.

Jessie crossed the remaining distance to the table and lowered herself to the chair. "Thank you," she said softly. "Thank you, all of you," she added.

"You're welcome, Miss," came a many-voiced reply.

Before James sat down once more, he let his eyes meet the eyes of his men. "I'd like to introduce my guest. This is Jessie Braddock." He lowered one hand to rest lightly on her shoulder. "Her parents are Sin and Rachel Braddock," he explained. "Jessie, this is the Triple X crew. First, this is Juan de Silva and his son Marco. Juan is my foreman and friend, and no one breaks a bronc better than Marco. Next are Bobby and Tex, then . . ."

Jessie listened to litany of names and jobs the men did but barely heard a word. The feeling of James's hand, resting so innocently on her shoulder was setting her on fire. The touch of his fingers as he moved them slightly sent surprising little tingles to her middle and over her skin. How could a mere touch affect her so drastically?

"Do you think you'll remember all that?" James asked after a few minutes.

Jessie looked up at him and nodded. "I'll do my best," she answered.

"Good." He took his hand from her shoulder and sat down. "Then let's everyone finish eating. Carmen," he called toward the kitchen.

Carmen entered almost immediately, a smile brightening her already beautiful face. When she saw Jessie the smile turned into a frown. "What is she doing in here?" she rudely asked.

"Carmen," Juan de Silva warned before James could answer. "Remember your place."

Carmen immediately cast her eyes downward but kept the defiant tilt to her jaw.

Jessie looked from one to the other, perplexed.

"I'm sorry, Miss Braddock," Juan apologized. "Carmen sometimes forgets herself."

"Carmen is Juan's daughter," James explained.

"And a more willful daughter a man never had," Juan complained, though pride filled his voice.

"I see," Jessie commented, though things were still not completely clear. Why would Juan condone his daughter's relationship with James? Then it occurred to her. Perhaps Juan encouraged the relationship, seeing it as a way to insure his position on the ranch. Glancing at the man, she had a second thought. Juan might not even be aware of the relationship, though Carmen's attitude should have told him what was going on. Sometimes fathers were blind when it came to their children. James had called him his friend. Didn't men have ethics about such things? Weren't there unwritten rules about not sleeping with the daughter or sister of a friend? But maybe she'd jumped to the wrong conclusion about Carmen. Maybe the girl was just overly friendly with every one. Maybe it was her way.

She glanced at James and noticed he looked more than a little uncomfortable. Gritting her teeth, she knew her first assumption was correct, and she suddenly felt pity for Juan, a man with no apparent idea his daughter was sleeping with the boss and his so-called friend. She also let herself worry for just a moment that James might be so preoccupied by Carmen that he wouldn't even notice her own attempts at flirtation. She then remembered the way he'd held her while helping her into the buggy and was assured that his attentions were easily swayed.

"Bring Miss Braddock a plate and silverware," ordered Juan.

Carmen turned angrily on her heel and went back into the kitchen.

James sighed and turned his attention back to his plate. He wanted to confess to Juan what had happened between him and Carmen. He'd begun the conversation that would lead them to that confession at least a dozen times in the past three weeks, but every time he got to the place where he could say the words something stopped him. It wasn't the fear of losing Juan as an employee. It was the fear of losing the man's respect and friendship. "I guess I'm about finished eating," he said after a moment, the hot cakes and bacon he'd consumed sitting like a lead weight in his stomach.

"Do you ride, Miss Braddock?" asked Marco suddenly, glancing at her riding costume.

Jessie hadn't really looked at the young man when James had begun the introductions, and she was surprised to see he was as handsome as Carmen. The family resemblance was obvious in skin tone and eye and hair color. And he had the same high cheekbones and proud jaw that gave Carmen her beauty, but in him the features were purely masculine. When he smiled at her the stark white of his teeth was a lovely contrast to his darkness. "Yes, I ride, Marco. In fact, I was hoping to take a ride this morning," she glanced quickly at James. "If that's all right?"

"I'd be happy to be your escort," offered Marco enthusiastically.

Jessie heard several snickers from men in the room.

"You will be working this morning," Juan told his son.

Marco's expression fell. "Yes, Papa."

The cowboy James had identified as Tex reached up and messed Marco's hair. "This here kid thinks he's a real ladies' man," he said, laughter filling his words.

Marco pulled his head away, grinning once more. "Aw, leave me alone," he said to his friend.

Jessie looked again at James. "Will you accompany me, James?" she asked sweetly.

James, too, was smiling, enjoying the teasing among his hands. He turned this expression toward Jessie. "I have work to do this morning also," he told her.

Jessie lowered her eyes. "Oh, of course," she said disappointedly. "How silly of me. Well, I'll just borrow one of your mounts and take a look around the place by myself, if you don't mind."

James felt a sudden stab of guilt, then admonished himself mentally. Narrowing his eyes slightly, he studied Jessie. He had to admit she was good. She had her routine down really well. "I suppose I could take a little time to show you around," he offered quietly.

Jessie heard the reluctance in James's voice and had to fight the urge to decline his halfhearted offer. But she couldn't afford to give up even one opportunity to spend time with James. She had to show him how much owning the Triple X would mean to her. "I'd be so grateful for any time you could spare me," she said graciously, letting the corners of her mouth turn up in a provocative smile.

James felt the effects of her smile and heard a warning

bell go off in his head. "I'm sure it won't take too long to show you around the place."

"Shall we get started?" she asked.

"You haven't eaten," James observed.

"Marco, go tell your sister to get out here," Juan told his son.

"Never mind," Jessie told him. "I'm really not hungry. I'd rather get going." She smiled up at James once more, then stood.

James's eyes roamed her figure as she stood before him. The voluptuous curves under the tight blue velvet riding habit were going to be very distracting, and might make it difficult for him to keep in mind that he thought her a fraud. "Perhaps you should change clothes first?" he suggested.

Jessie looked down at herself. Although the velvet of the habit would probably prove to be a bit warmer than she'd like, she thought she was dressed appropriately. Besides, leaving in the middle of the night with only one valise had precluded packing much. The habit was the only garment she had with her suitable for riding. "I'm sorry. I have nothing else," she explained.

"Some of your old things are boxed in the attic," James said. He remembered the way Jessie had dressed in her youth in baggy old boy's clothes, and knew he'd find nothing about those clothes attractive.

"My old things?" Jessie asked.

"I think there are two boxes. Should I bring them down?" he offered.

Jessie thought about it for a moment. Most of her old clothes were atrocious, but wearing them might make her look as if she belonged here. "Certainly," she accepted his offer.

Twenty minutes later she was tucking a green plaid shirt into a pair of brown trousers. "Oh my," she whispered at her reflection in the mirror in her room. The clothes had stayed the same, she'd grown. The trousers fit snugly around her waist and over her hips and bottom, and the shirt pulled slightly across her breasts. "I didn't think I'd grown that much," she told herself. "Oh well," she murmured, shrugging her shoulders. "I guess these will have to do."

James groaned to himself as he watched Jessie descending the stairs a few minutes later. His plan to dress her unattractively had backfired in the worst way. Her figure was enhanced by the tight clothing, and the sight of her sent all sorts of sparks flying through his system. "I didn't think you'd grown that much," he said without thinking.

Jessie looked down at the clothing self-consciously. "I said the same thing up in my room," she told him.

"But you're no taller," he argued.

She raised her shoulders. "I guess I grew out," she offered.

It was all James could do not to roll his eyes at her statement. She'd grown out, all right. Out in all the right, or wrong, places, depending on how you looked at it. "Let's get going," he said gruffly, turning away from her.

Jessie followed silently, not sure why he was suddenly so angry.

The morning proved to be hot and trying for Jessie. She played the demure young lady with James until her face ached from all the smiling she'd done, and as they neared Leaver Creek and the swimming hole she had the urge to just push him in and forget the whole thing. If the ranch hadn't been at stake she might just have done it.

Pushing aside the long arms of the black willows that shrouded the swimming hole, Jessie guided her mount into the clearing near the water's edge. "It's been so long since I was here I'd almost forgotten how much cooler it is than out on the range," she said, lifting the weight of her heavy hair from the back of her neck where it rested in a sweat-dampened bun.

"Mmmm," James agreed, watching Jessie's every move. She'd played coy with him for nearly two hours already, but not once had she broached the subject of buying the ranch. He was certain she was acting, and he was getting tired of waiting for the real Jessie to emerge. Was there a chance he was wrong? Had she turned into this pale copy of what she used to be? "Want to swim?" he asked.

Jessie's heart skipped two full beats at his suggestion. "I'm sure that wouldn't be proper," she answered.

"So let's not be proper," he suggested, hoping to shock her into responding with some of the temper he remembered.

Jessie could feel her face redden. "I don't think that would be a good idea," she responded. "Maybe we could just sit beside the water and cool off for a moment?"

James grimaced at her tepid answer. Swinging down out of the saddle, he ground tethered his horse and walked to the bank. The creek was fairly deep and wide here, and turned on itself to form a perfect swimming hole. Standing with his back to her, he waited for Jessie to dismount and join him.

Jessie wondered whether this might be a good time to bring up buying the ranch. This was such a lovely spot, relaxing and tranquil, that he might be open to the discussion now. Swinging her right leg across the neck of her mount, she jumped to the ground. As her boot heels dug into the moist dirt, she was startled by how easily she'd dismounted this way. She hadn't jumped from a horse since she'd gone to live in Charleston. A small frisson of excitement coursed through her and brought a delighted smile to her lips.

James turned as he heard her dismount. The smile that brightened her face touched his heart. It was the first truly genuine smile he'd seen all morning. He felt himself smiling in return.

Jessie felt her pulse increase as James looked at her. He was the most attractive man she'd ever seen. He was tall and broad shouldered, narrow hipped and long legged, with a ruggedly handsome face she hadn't seen developing beneath the boyish exterior all those years ago. Of course, she'd been only twelve, much too young to see such things. But she had confided in her sister Tish that she was going to marry him someday. Foolish nonsense she knew, but standing here now the memory seemed fresh. Swallowing nervously, she looked away. She couldn't allow herself to be distracted.

James tipped his head downward, trying to catch her eye once more. He'd seen something in her expression. A flash of the old Jessie? "Come sit down," he said softly.

Jessie looked at the ground next to him. "It would feel good to relax for a minute," she admitted.

James lowered himself to the grass and waited for her to join him. When she did, she sat a way away from him. "Are you afraid of me?" he asked.

"Of course not," she defended.

"Then why sit way over there?"

James's voice vibrated across her skin. She moved a little closer. "Is that better?" she asked.

"I suppose," he responded. Lying back on the grass, he put one arm across his eyes. "What are you doing here?" he inquired.

Jessie wasn't expecting this question. "You already know. My father wired—"

"I know what your father's wire said. I want to know why you're still here."

"You invited me to stay," she told him.

James was silent for a moment. He had invited her, although he still wasn't sure how it had happened. "How long do you intend to stay?"

Jessie's pulse took another leap, but this time from nerves. Should she give him some feminine, flattering answer as she'd been doing all morning, or should she open her mouth and tell him she was moving in as soon as he'd sign the papers selling the ranch back to her? If she did the latter he'd just tell her he wasn't selling and ask her to leave. "I don't know," she finally answered.

James sat up again. She'd hesitated once more. She was thinking about her answers before giving them, a sure sign she wasn't being sincere. Staring hard into her green eyes, he wanted to reach out and shake some honesty from her. Just then a stray curl fell forward over her eyes. Watching her absentmindedly tuck it back behind her ear caused something to snap inside him. "Don't you carry a knife any more, Jessie?" he demanded.

"What?"

"Don't you carry your knife any more?" he repeated, leaning toward her.

"I don't know what you're talking about," she answered, unnerved by the emotion she saw in his eyes.

"Don't you? Your hair, Jessie. Don't you remember the way you used to cut your hair with your knife when it fell into your eyes."

Jessie thought for a moment. She had done what he'd said. "I was a child. I certainly wouldn't cut my hair with a knife now," she told him.

"Are you completely changed from that little girl, Jessie?"

"I grew up, if that's what you mean," she answered, her temper rising a bit.

"That's not what I mean. What I want to know is whether or not any of that little girl remains left inside you, Jessie." He leaned even closer to her. "Does she?" he demanded.

❊ 4 ❊

"I'm still the same person," Jessie responded.

"You don't seem to be. After your father's telegram arrived I expected you to ride in here like a thunder storm. I expected a tornado of emotion from you. I prepared myself to fight a bloody battle. Instead, you've smiled and simpered and flirted like some . . . Well, not like the Jessie I remember," he accused.

Jessie's jaw rose defiantly at his words. "I'm sorry I've disappointed you," she said stiffly, her temper building inside her. "And I'm sorry you're unhappy that I didn't come here carrying guns to force you off my land." Her voice had risen several decibels.

"Your land?" he nearly shouted. "This land is mine, and don't you forget it."

"You may have purchased the Triple X from my parents, without my knowledge I might add, but it will never really belong to you. I was born here. My grand-parents are buried here. And if you had any decency you'd sell it back to me right now." The temper she'd been trying to hold in check was suddenly breaking free and she scrambled to stand up.

"I told you yesterday that I'd never sell out, and I never will," James answered, also standing. Towering over her he began to smile. "It didn't take me long to figure out what you were up to with your little innocent act. And I'm glad it didn't take me too much time to get you to admit you still wanted the ranch. Now you can stop wasting your time and mine."

Jessie seethed with anger. Her eyes shot fiery sparks of emerald hatred and her breath was coming in heaving gasps. Her fists were balled up at her sides. "You bastard," she said furiously.

James's grin spread even wider at her show of temper. "And it's about time the old Jessie showed up," he added.

"I'll show you the old Jessie," she said through clenched teeth. Swinging her arm with all her might, she landed a hard punch across James's jaw. Pain shot through her hand and up her wrist, but she didn't care. Standing with her hands still in fists, she waited for him to retaliate.

James was shocked to feel Jessie's fist slam into his face. His head snapped from the blow, but the pain was minor, at least from the punch. Narrowing his eyes threateningly, he took a step toward her. "You do still act before thinking, don't you?" he said menacingly.

Jessie felt a sudden surge of panic. She hadn't behaved this way in years. She had planned to charm James into selling her the ranch, and somehow, instead, he'd goaded her into behaving exactly as he'd expected. "I'm sorry," she blurted. "I don't know what came over me," she explained, her words coming quickly.

James took another step toward her. "It's too late for that," he said. With the speed of a rattler he grabbed her arm and jerked her forward. "I can't punch you back, so I think I'll deal with you another way. You deserve a good, hard spanking."

Jessie pulled back on her arm but couldn't loosen the iron grip he had over her wrist. "No!" she protested. "You can't be serious!" She jerked hard on her arm and began swinging with her other fist to fight him off. She could tell her punches were going all but unnoticed and began to kick as well.

James fended off Jessie's attack with ease. She was so tiny he had no trouble wrapping his free arm around her waist and picking her up while she struggled. Her legs continued to kick aimlessly in the air and she tried to push away from him with her free arm. He only grinned at her attempts. "You should try picking on someone your own size," he told her.

"You horse's ass," she shouted. "I'll get even with you for this if it's the last thing I ever do!" Just then, James swung her a bit, causing her to feel as though he might throw her. A spark of fear flew through her and she grabbed him around the neck to keep from falling.

James swung Jessie slightly to get her to stop fighting him so hard, but he was unprepared for the feeling of her arm around his neck and her breasts flush with his chest. He felt as though his heart had suddenly dropped to his toes, then rushed back upward, sending blood pounding through his body. His arousal was instantaneous and complete. He stopped moving and released her wrist, wrapping his other arm around her waist, supporting her there.

When James stopped fighting with Jessie and let go of her wrist she reached up to hold on to him. It was that moment when she felt the change and became aware of the heat emanating from his body into hers. She suddenly felt the strong muscles of his chest pressed against her breasts, felt the rippled surface of his stomach flush against her abdomen, and most startling of all, the huge evidence of his arousal making a deep impression in her thigh. With a surprised intake of air, she raised her eyes to meet his gaze.

James stared down into the deep green of Jessie's eyes. Their usual emerald color had darkened, and he felt he was looking into the mysterious depths of some magical sea. His heart pounded in his ears and he could feel the rush of blood through his body, centering in his heated, throbbing shaft. Never before had he experienced such a powerful wanting. "Jessie?" he rasped.

Jessie was sensation. Her nerve endings hummed at

the sound of his voice. Her breasts burned where she touched him. Her stomach churned with excitement, and a strange, pulsing need seemed to be building inside her. She could feel her body changing, moistening, as she instinctively moved her thigh against the bulge between James's legs.

James shuddered as Jessie's thigh massaged his erection. His eyes darkened with purpose. Lowering his head, he saw the look of surprise in Jessie's eyes just before he claimed her lips in a devouring kiss. He kissed her possessively, completely, parting her lips with his tongue, probing the soft recesses of her mouth. He groaned against her mouth as his passion took control.

Jessie was stunned by the force of James's kiss. No one had ever kissed her this way. She was swamped by wild, unfamiliar emotions, lost on an ocean of feelings too powerful to fight. Opening herself to his kiss, she let her tongue mate with his, savoring the taste and texture of his mouth.

James sensed Jessie's surrender and felt an unbelievable rush of excitement pulse through him. Still holding her with one arm, he reached up with the other, sliding his hand along her side until he felt the swell of her breast. Moving his fingers over the full mound of womanly flesh, he found the hard bud of her nipple and massaged it gently, feeling her gasp into his mouth at his touch.

Jessie tried to breathe normally but found she couldn't. Spiraling waves of heat emanated from her breast as James touched her. Blindly, she pulled herself closer to him, needing to feel his body even more.

James's desire to possess Jessie completely brought him to his knees. Unbuckling his gun belt as quickly as he could, he let it fall to the ground behind him. Cradling her as they lay down in the soft grass, he covered her with his body, positioning his manhood over her thigh once more, moving himself against her in a rhythmic motion. Continuing to kiss her, he found the buttons of her shirt and began to release them one by one.

Jessie could feel the air touching her skin where her shirt gaped open. She suddenly felt the pressure of James unbuttoning her camisole and then the exquisite sensation of his work-roughened hands caressing her breasts. As his mouth left hers, she moaned in protest until she felt the tip of his tongue flick teasingly over her nipple. Lord, was it possible to feel so much? she wondered, gasping anew as he took her nipple wholly into his mouth to suckle her. "James," she breathed his name. "Oh, James."

James tantalized the two perfect breasts jutting upward to meet his touch. Jessie arched her back to give him freer access and he took advantage of it, holding her breasts with both hands, suckling one pouting, rosebud nipple and then the other, burying his face between them, tasting the light film of moisture he'd caused there with his passion. Shivering with emotion, he rocked his throbbing manhood against her thigh, needing more. "Jessie?" he groaned. Reaching for one of her hands, he raised his hips and placed her palm over the bulging mass of his arousal. "Touch me, Jessie," he whispered.

Jessie was shocked by the size of James's erection. She'd never touched a man before. She'd had no idea what a man's body was capable of, but the sensation of touching such a powerful part of James's body excited her beyond reason. Moving her hand over the length of his manhood, from the rounded tip just below his belt to the soft bulge between his legs, she explored.

James swallowed hard and took in several deep breaths as Jessie massaged him. Trying to maintain his control was taking practically all his concentration and he knew he would lose himself completely if he didn't do something. Unbuttoning the front of her trousers, he slid his hand inside and downward. The moistness he felt sent a new rush of heated blood pulsing through his arousal.

Jessie nearly cried out when James touched that part of her no man had touched before. He slid his fingers over her, caressing her, sending shock waves cascading through her body. Quivering with sensation, she clenched her jaw tight against the need to scream as he found the bud of her passion. "James, please," she breathed, almost choking on her words as his fingers slid deeply into her body.

James was crazed and blinded by the red haze of passion. He needed to complete this union. He needed to feel himself inside the dark, hot cavern of Jessie's body. Taking his hand from her trousers he looked at her beautiful face. Seeing the desire glazing her eyes, he reached to pull her boots off. Seconds later he tugged her trousers down around her hips and from her legs, tossing them away. Removing his shirt quickly, he dropped it to the ground. Pulling off his boots, he let them lie where they landed. Unbuckling his belt and unbuttoning his own trousers seemed to take only a fraction of a second, and a breath later he'd pushed the garment from his body, taking his undergarment with it. His erection sprang upward, throbbing with need, huge in its desire. Lowering himself over Jessie once more, he poised himself above her. "Jessie?" he murmured, not sure he could stop himself now if she said no.

Jessie had seen James's enormous manhood before he bent over her, but she was too far gone in her desire to fear it. Indeed, she felt she might die if he didn't join with her and put her out of the wonderful misery he'd caused. Her response was to grab him around the waist and pull him downward.

James let out his breath in relief and lowered his head to cover her mouth with his own. He wanted to taste her as he entered her. He wanted to swallow any passion sounds she might make. Pushing his hips downward, he felt the soft entrance to her body with the hot tip of his manhood. Stopping there for just a second, he savored the moment, then thrust forward in one swift motion. Surprise registered as he felt the tearing of her maidenhead and felt her cry out into his mouth. She writhed beneath him, sending him over the edge of his control. He pulled back and thrust once more, filling her even more. Again and again he moved inside her, pulling her along on the ride that would bring them shared ecstasy.

Jessie was unprepared for the pain that tore through her as James claimed her body. Her scream was muffled by his kiss, and her struggles were lost on him. Then the pain was gone, and she began to feel something else. Something that made her feel whole, yet incomplete. James's huge body joining with hers was causing spiraling waves to crash over her. A coiling heat began to build deep within her body, and she felt it growing tighter with each thrust of his manhood. She needed to release this tension. Wrapping her legs around James's hips, she began to meet his thrusts, rocking with him in perfect unison.

James felt Jessie's legs around him and kissed her more deeply. Grasping one of her breasts, he fondled her nipple as he continued to plunge himself completely into her body. The shudder of his release began so strongly that he had to tear his mouth from hers as he gasped for air.

Jessie felt the muscles of his body becoming tense as strong spasms vibrated from his manhood deep inside her. Her own body seemed to respond to his by exploding from within, the coiling knot of tension releasing all at once, sending wave upon wave of what seemed like pure white light washing over her. Shivering again and again in the throes of passion, she arched her back and clasped James to her with the strength of her legs.

James felt the fluid from his body mingle with Jessie's again and again. Over and over he shook with his release. Never before had he experienced such a powerful completion to this act, and he was filled with a sense of satisfaction that Jessie had gone over the edge with him. He'd seen and felt her shuddered climax at the same moment he'd enjoyed his own. As the spasms began to subside, he lowered himself over her, adjusting his arms to carry his weight.

Jessie lay in the warm cocoon of James's body. Her eyes were closed and her heart was beginning to beat at a more normal rate. Sighing, she realized she felt wonderful. Making love was incredible. No wonder men are so preoccupied with it, she mused. James shifted his weight a bit over her and she adjusted herself to fit more comfortably beneath him. Then, the seriousness of what she'd just done began to occur to her. Biting the inside of her lower lip, she wondered what James thought of her now? Had she just made a terrible mistake?

James let his breaths come slowly now that the maelstrom was past. Jessie was incredible. No woman had ever excited him the way she had. No one had ever brought him to such an incredibly high point before crashing downward with him the way she had. And to think she'd been an innocent, he thought. A cold hand of common sense seemed to come out of nowhere and touch his heart. Jessie had been a virgin, but she'd responded to him as though she couldn't get enough of him. Except for the moment he entered her, she'd been completely responsive to everything he'd done to her. That wasn't normal in a virgin. Virgins were timid and shy, afraid of the act they were about to participate in. James clenched his jaw against what he was thinking. Jessie wouldn't have had sex with him just to get the Triple X, would she? Giving a man your virginity was pretty powerful stuff, and it could certainly cause most men to feel indebted.

Pushing himself up, he gazed down at her face. She was frowning slightly. Did that mean she regretted what she'd done?

Jessie knew she was being studied and opened her eyes. Meeting James's dark stare while his body was still a part of hers felt like the most intimate thing she'd ever done. Even more so than making love had been. Now she'd have to face him and discuss it.

"I still won't sell you the ranch," James said firmly.

Jessie stared up at James, not believing she'd heard him correctly. Seconds passed and she felt herself begin to shake as she faced what he was thinking. Her heartbeat increased and she felt sick to her stomach. She'd done worse than she'd feared. She hadn't merely made a terrible mistake, she'd made the biggest mistake of her life, the biggest mistake she would ever make if she lived to be one hundred. And the worst part of it was that she could never prove to James he was wrong. She did want the ranch. Making love with him hadn't changed that. "Let me up," she said, her voice cracking traitorously. "Let me up!" she repeated angrily when he didn't move at once.

James felt a great disappointment when Jessie spoke. He realized he'd wanted her to deny what he'd been thinking. Instead, she got angry, proof he'd been correct in his assumption and called her on her actions. Rolling away from her, he lay back in the grass and let one arm fall across his eyes.

Jessie scrambled to her feet as soon as James's weight was lifted from her. Looking around, she found her clothes and grabbed them up in a bundle, taking them with her behind her horse. Pulling them on as quickly as she could, she fought the urge to cry, clenching her jaw so tightly it ached. She had to keep swallowing back the bile that threatened to erupt, and the sight of James lying on his back where they'd just made love caused her heart to ache unbelievably. As she buttoned her shirt, she noticed that one of the buttons had come off, leaving a gaping hole where the shirt wouldn't close. "Damn it," she whispered. Jumping on the back of her horse, she jerked the reins hard and spurred the animal to an immediate gallop. She had to pack and leave the Triple X before James returned.

James lay on his back in the grass and listened to the quiet sounds around him. Jessie had ridden away as if she were being chased by Comanches, and he hadn't had the desire to follow her. He knew if he waited long enough she'd be gone from the ranch before he got back to the house. A dark scowl crossed his face at the thought. "Well, it's what I wanted," he told himself.

Sitting up, he watched the water in Leaver Creek meandering by. Standing, he took the few steps to the water's edge and dove in. The water felt cool on his fevered skin, and the current tugged at his limbs as he swam. Making his way to the bank after a few moments, he sat in the shallow water and thought about Jessie. He was surprised her deceit meant so much to him. The memory of the little girl she'd been had shattered with the reality of the woman she'd become.

Jessie saw Carmen sitting on the porch as she rode up to the house. "Oh, hell," she cursed. Carmen was the last person she wanted to see now. Putting her horse in the corral she started for the house.

"You should cool off an animal when you get him so overheated," Carmen said as Jessie approached.

Jessie stopped at the bottom of the steps when she heard Carmen's words. "And what the hell would you know about it?" she fired back at the woman.

Carmen's eyes opened wide at Jessie's retort. She hadn't thought Jessie had it in her to argue. "I know how to take care of an animal," she answered, her voice rising a bit.

Jessie took the stairs slowly. "I'll bet you do," she said in an accusing tone. When she reached the level of the porch, she stared down at Carmen, who sat on the swing. "But since nothing I do is any of your business, I suggest you mind your own."

Carmen stood up and faced Jessie squarely. What had happened to this gringa? She then noticed the missing button on Jessie's shirt. Suspicion tore through her. Searching Jessie's face, she was certain she saw the telltale signs. Her lips were fuller and there were red marks along her jaw and down her neck and chest. Her eyes narrowed menacingly. "Where is James?" she asked determinedly.

Jessie would have liked nothing better than to tell Carmen exactly where James was. It would serve him right to feel the wrath of his whore, she thought. Then it struck her that she was no better than Carmen. "I don't know where he is, and I don't give a good God damn if I ever see him again," she finally said. Abruptly turning away from the woman, she entered the house and took the stairs two at a time to reach her room.

Once inside, she closed the door and pulled her valise from under the bed. It took her only a few minutes to pack her belongings and leave the room once more. As she started down the stairs she heard the sound of her nephews playing in their room. Sadness gripped her. She had to say good-bye to the two boys. Turning back up the stairs, she knocked on their door.

"Who is it?" Jamie yelled through some giggles.

"It's your aunt Jessie," she replied.

The door swung open and the two boys threw themselves at her. "Where were you all day? We missed you," they said together.

"I haven't been gone all day. It's only just a little past lunch time now," she said.

"It feels like all day. Will you read to us again?" Jeremy asked.

Jessie sighed. "I'm sorry. I can't. I have to leave."

"Leave?" they asked in unison. "Why? Don't you like it here with us?"

Jessie's heart lurched sadly. "Of course I like it here with you. I love you. But sometimes grown-ups have to do things they don't want to. And I have to leave here. Now give me big hugs and kisses good-bye, and be good boys for your uncle James. Don't listen to the animals, all right?" She knelt down to hug them properly.

Both boys threw their arms around her neck. "Where are you going?" asked Jamie.

"Back to Charleston," Jessie answered.

"We'll never see you again," whined Jeremy.

"Yes you will. I'm your aunt. My parents are your grandparents. When your mommy and daddy come back to fetch you tell them to bring you to see me," she told them.

"All right," they agreed, their faces downcast.

Jessie stood up again. "Let me see some smiles," she ordered them playfully.

Both boys did their best to smile.

"Bye," she said, and turned and left their room. Tears glistened on her lashes as she descended the stairs.

Once outside she retrieved her mount from the corral. James may be furious with me for taking one of his horses, she thought as she jumped into the saddle. "To hell with James," she said out loud.

Seconds later she was riding toward town. She didn't see James watching her from a ridge.

James saw Jessie leaving and sighed. It was too bad things had to work out this way, he thought. He could have really liked her under different circumstances. The memory of how she'd made love to him came unbidden to his mind. The instant rush of blood to his loins seemed to mock him. "Yeah, I could have liked her, all right," he admitted sourly.

Jessie scanned the town as she rode in. She knew there would be no stage for several days so she'd have to stay in the hotel while she waited. Guiding her mount to the Bartlett Hotel, she pulled the animal to a stop and dismounted. Pulling the reins with her, she tied them to the hitching post. "You wait here, fella," she said softly, rubbing his nose as she left.

It took only minutes to secure a room and to find out that another stage would arrive in four days. She asked the hotel clerk to have someone take care of her horse, then ordered a bath. She wanted to wash away every vestige of her lovemaking with James.

An hour later Jessie still sat in the rapidly cooling water of her bath. She'd been thinking about what she'd done and how it affected her life. Every time she thought about James her temperature would raise, sometimes with the memory of the things he'd done to her, and sometimes with anger at his stupidity. Slapping the water, sending some splashing out of the tub and across the floor, she cursed, "Damn you, James Bonner!"

James sat alone in the dining room long after the

dinner dishes had been cleared away. Carmen had been surly while serving the meal, and had left the house shortly after he and the boys had finished eating. He was grateful for her absence.

Standing up, he crossed to the buffet and opened one of the doors. Taking out a bottle of whiskey, he opened it and put it to his lips. The fiery liquid felt good sliding down his throat. It burned, and that's what he needed right now: something to take his mind off Jessie.

In the days that followed, Jessie fought with herself to keep from thinking about James. She wandered the streets of Mesa, exploring the town as she had in her youth, and, as she'd seen upon her arrival, some things had changed, others hadn't. One thing that hadn't changed was that it still felt like home.

On the second afternoon she ran into an old friend coming out of the general store. "Val? Val Harding?," she asked.

The young woman turned at the sound of her name being called. "Yes?" she asked after a moment.

"Val, it's me, Jessie Braddock," Jessie explained.

Val studied her for a moment. "My goodness, it is you, Jessie. You've changed so much I would never have recognized you. What are you doing here?" Val reached toward her.

Jessie stepped forward and took her friend's hands. "I just came for a visit," she lied.

"I'm so glad you did. You were going to call on me, weren't you?" Val asked.

"To be honest, I have no formal plans, but I'm glad I ran into you. Do you have time to grab a bite at the Shady Place with me so we can catch up on old times?"

Val looked around for a moment. "I'm supposed to meet my husband here in a few minutes," she hesitated for just a second, then laughed, "I'll leave a message with Mrs. Medley that I've run off with the circus. It'll do Ben good to worry about me for a while." She disappeared inside the store for a few minutes and was giggling when she returned. "Mrs. Medley refused to tell Ben I went with the circus. She's going to have him meet me at the Shady Place."

Jessie grinned at her friend as they began walking. "I didn't know you were married," she said.

Val smiled. "For a little over a year now. Are you?"

"No, not yet," Jessie replied, her eyes lowering as an image of James floated through her mind. "I don't think I'll ever get married."

"I used to think the same thing until I met Ben Richards. That's my new last name, Richards. Mrs. Val Richards. I still think it sounds wonderful."

Jessie nodded in agreement at they entered the restaurant.

A few minutes later they were settled at their table, sipping iced tea and digging into fresh apple pie.

"Do you know that Mary Mills has three children already? Of course, she is two years older than I am, and I'm a year older than you are, but still . . ."

Jessie listened to Val prattle on about who married whom and how many children they had for the better part of half an hour. Most of what was said went past her, as she couldn't remember the people Val was talking about, but the conversation was light and just what she needed to get her mind off her troubles. Then her mind snapped to attention when she heard James's name mentioned. "What was that?"

"I asked you whether you'd been out to your family's old place and seen that gorgeous James Bonner yet."

Jessie felt herself flush. "Ah, yes . . ." she stammered. "I stopped by there my first day here."

"Well?"

Jessie looked curiously at Val.

"What did you think of him? He's so good looking half the women in town are in love with him," Val confided.

"Yes, he is rather handsome," Jessie agreed.

Val raised her eyebrows. "Rather handsome? You're a

cool one, Jessie. If I weren't madly in love with my Ben I'd be after Mr. Bonner myself. Speak of the devil," Val whispered, grinning.

Jessie's heart skipped a beat at the sound of footsteps behind her. She didn't want to see James again ever.

"What are you up to, Val? Mrs. Medley said something about the circus."

Jessie let out a sigh of relief at the strange but friendly voice behind her. Turning in her chair, she looked up at Val's husband, Ben.

Val was laughing out loud. "Ben, this is my friend, Jessie Braddock. Jessie, this is my husband, Ben."

Jessie stood up to meet the man who'd stolen her friend's heart. Ben was tall and stocky, with a bristle of short red hair on the top of his head and two of the most startlingly blue eyes she'd ever seen. "Nice to meet you, Ben," she said, holding out her hand.

"Nice to meet you, too, Miss Braddock." He slipped his arm possessively around Val's waist. "What secrets has my wife been telling you?" he asked.

"Oh, Ben," Val protested. "You'll have Jessie thinking I'm untrustworthy."

"Not untrustworthy." He leaned a little closer to Jessie. "She just loves to gossip," he whispered.

Val immediately punched him playfully on the arm.

Jessie saw how happy Val and Ben were together and felt a small pang of jealousy. Pushing the silly emotion from her mind, she grinned at them both. "Ben, would you like to join us for pie and gossip?" she asked.

✤ 5 ✤

Jessie ended up having dinner with Val and Ben that night. The couple invited several other people Jessie had known as a child, one who played the fiddle, and they sang and danced until late into the evening. When she finally said her good-byes and left for the hotel, she had a warm, contented feeling in her heart.

The following morning she decided to go for a ride and donned her riding habit. As she saddled her horse in the livery, she felt a small twinge of guilt. "I suppose I should send you back to James," she told the animal. Rubbing its velvety nose, she looked into the large, gentle eyes that watched her. "I wonder if you have a name?" she asked. "I suppose I can call you whatever I choose for the time being." Looking the animal over, she decided he was too sweet to be given a name like Tornado, her horse in Charleston. "I think I'll call you Henry," she finally said, smiling. She quickly finished saddling him, then led him out of the livery. "Come on, Henry. We're going for a little ride."

Some time later, Jessie pulled Henry to a stop on a ridge overlooking one of the valleys that surrounded Mesa City. The wind was hot against her skin and perspiration glistened on her upper lip and trickled down her chest between her breasts. Breathing deeply, she inhaled the fragrance of the range: sage, pinion, wild flowers. "How could I have stayed away so long?" she asked herself. "I'll miss this so much when I go back." Tears misted her eyes at the thought of going back to Charleston. "Oh, Henry, what am I going to do? I miss mother and father, of course, but I don't want to go back." She let her eyes scan the beautiful, rugged land around her. This was where she'd been born and raised. This is where I belong, she thought. "But I've mucked things up so badly with James," she whispered. Thoughts of how she'd given herself to him caused a blush to turn her face crimson. She then remembered he'd thought she'd done it to convince him to sell her the ranch. Anger filled her heart and caused her to raise her chin defiantly. "How can a man be so thick headed?" she hissed into the wind.

Nudging Henry forward, she guided him down the ridge and on to flat land. The urge to go faster prodded her to slap the reins against his neck. He responded instantly by breaking into a trot. "Not fast enough, yet, Henry," she said. Bumping him gently with her heels, she grinned when he broke into a full gallop. Letting her head fall back, she closed her eyes, trusting the horse to run safely. This was still not enough. Putting the reins in her teeth, she pulled the pins from her hair and shook it free to fly wildly behind her. Then, spreading her arms wide, she closed her eyes again and let Henry have his head.

The sensation was extraordinary. She felt as if she were flying. The hot wind whipped her hair around behind her and dried the sweat on her face, feeling almost cool. "This is wonderful, Henry!" she shouted.

James was some distance away when he saw the horse and rider galloping hard across the open range. At first he thought someone might be in trouble, then his senses took a crazy leap when he realized it was Jessie. The sight of her on horseback, her long black hair blowing freely in the wind, sent his heart racing in his chest and caused a distinct response in a lower part of his body.

"Damn," he breathed. Sighing heavily, he watched her for a while. He'd wanted her to revert back to the girl he remembered and it certainly seemed she had. Sighing, he turned and headed back to the Triple X. He'd wait until he knew she'd left town, then he'd retrieve the horse she'd borrowed.

"I can't believe there's only one place for sale around Mesa City, Mr. Stilwell," Jessie complained to the banker.

"And as I said, it needs a lot of work."

Jessie looked at the man behind the desk. He was round and appeared to be nearing fifty, with a bald head and gray mustache. Tiny spectacles rested on his nose, and she had to wonder why since he never appeared to look through them. "Well, if the old Baker place is all that's available, I suppose I should go look at it," she said. Standing, she pulled on her new leather gloves and picked up her, also new, hat, placing it levelly on her head, tugging the brim down just a bit to shade her eyes. "I'll wait for you outside," she told him.

"Oh, well, yes," said Mr. Stilwell. "I'll only be a minute."

Jessie stepped out of Stilwell's office and walked through the bank. Moments later she was waiting on horseback. Swinging her eyes from side to side as she surveyed the town, she smiled, still pleased with the decision she'd made in the wee hours of the morning. She was staying in Mesa City. She knew she couldn't have the Triple X. James would never sell out to her, but she could buy another ranch and make a life for herself here, where she felt most at home.

"Remember, I told you it needs a lot of repairs," Mr. Stilwell told her again as he emerged from the bank. He climbed into a small buggy and flipped the reins over the horse's rump, starting them on their way.

Jessie followed along on Henry. She knew she was going to have to send Henry back to the Triple X soon, but she liked him so well. She was a little surprised

James hadn't come for him yet, or at least sent someone to fetch the animal. She supposed he'd decided to let her use him until she left town. Well, the stage had come and gone and she still had Henry. Mentally shrugging her shoulders, she pondered offering to buy the horse. Grimacing at the thought, she realized she didn't want to see James again. She'd given him her virginity and he'd assumed she had done it as a ploy to get the Triple X. She sighed deeply. He was a stubborn, stupid man.

A while later she saw the first signs they were approaching a ranch. A rickety wooden fence marked the property line and a piece of wood from a fallen gate had the letters *B A K* carved onto it.

"Remember, it needs some repairs," Stilwell repeated.

Jessie nodded. The man had said virtually the same thing at least twenty times on their ride out to see the property. Minutes later, she had to agree with him. The silo had toppled over, its open end pointing at them like the mouth of a huge cave. The barn was leaning to one side and had a large hole broken out of the wall up in the hayloft. The corral fence was missing several sections and the buildings she assumed were the chicken coop and pig pen were standing by will alone. Biting the inside of her lower lip, she turned her gaze to take in the house. It at least looked as if it wasn't about to fall over, but most of the windows had been broken and there were boards missing from the front porch. She also noticed a hole about the size of a pie in the roof and another identical hole in one wall.

"Mr. Stilwell?" she asked, letting her eyes convey the question.

"Shotgun," he answered. "Mr. Baker was prone to shooting in the house when he got drunk," he explained further.

Jessie raised her brows. "Well, he got drunk at least twice that we know of," she said, her mouth turned up into a half smile.

After inspecting the outbuildings and estimating the cost of repairing them, Jessie knew it would take practically every penny she had to fix the place up and stock it with cattle. She'd have almost no operating money left. She wondered whether or not she could do it. "Are you sure there are no other places for sale?" she asked hopefully.

Mr. Stilwell shook his head. "I'm sorry," he said.

Jessie sighed. "I suppose we should look at the house."

James rode into town and directly to the livery. He knew the stage had been through town. That meant Jessie was on her way back to Charleston. Tightening his jaw at the thought, he pulled his mount to a stop outside the large structure. "Willie," he called as he dismounted. "I've come for my horse."

Entering the dark building, he felt the heat from the pit and bellows. "Willie, are you in here?" he called again.

A sinewy man in blackened overalls came from the back of the livery. "James, is that you? What'd you say? You've come for what horse?"

James frowned uncertainly. Jessie wouldn't have taken the horse with her, would she? he wondered. "Jessie Braddock rode one of my horses to town a few days ago. I was sure she'd leave it here," he explained.

"Miss Braddock has been leavin' a horse here. It does have the Triple X brand. I thought you sold it to her. If I'd a'known—" Willie tried to explain nervously.

James raised his hand as he interrupted. "It's all right, Willie. I let her use the horse. But now that she's left town I've come to get it."

Willie looked perplexed. "But Miss Braddock took the horse out this morning," he said.

"This morning?" James studied Willie for a moment. "Didn't the stage come through?"

"Yes sir," Willie answered.

James's gaze fell to the ground as he thought. She wouldn't have taken the animal just for spite, would she? His eyes narrowed. Maybe she didn't leave on the stage. Raising his eyes and piercing Willie with a hard stare, he asked, "What was she wearing when she came for the horse?"

Willie blinked a few times in surprise. "Gosh, I don't know. I don't usually notice such things," he stammered.

"Try to remember," James urged.

Willie thought for a moment, his brow furrowed with the effort. "She was wearin' trousers and a shirt."

Not the clothes she'd wear for travel, James surmised.

"And a new hat," Willie added proudly.

"A new hat?"

"Yep. I know 'coz it was a hat I had an eye on myself," he said.

"A man's hat?" James asked.

"I guess so," answered Willie.

"She hasn't left town," James said between clenched teeth.

"No sir."

"Did she say where she was going when she left here this morning?" James asked.

Willie thought again. "I think she said something about the bank."

James lowered his dark brows into a frown. What would she be up to at the bank? Trying to check my accounts? he wondered. "Thanks, Willie," he said as he quickly turned and headed for the door.

Minutes later he was striding purposefully up to the teller's window in the bank. "Was Jessie Braddock in here this morning?" he demanded.

The man behind the counter looked at James in surprise. "Yes sir."

"What was she doing? Did she ask about anyone's accounts?"

The clerk stepped back from the counter a little. "I'm sorry, sir. I can't give out information about our clients."

"What seems to be the problem here?" Manda Banks, Mr. Stilwell's secretary, asked, walking up behind the counter.

"I was asking about Jessie Braddock," explained James.

"And?"

"And I want to know what she was doing here. Whether or not she inquired about my accounts."

The secretary nodded to excuse the teller. "I can't tell you the nature of Miss Braddock's business, but I can tell you it had nothing to do with you, Mr. Bonner. She had a meeting with Mr. Stilwell."

James frowned at this piece of information. Stilwell handled the business of bank loans. Why would Jessie need to borrow money? Then it occurred to him. Stilwell also dealt with the disposition of property after the bank had to foreclose. Relaxing his stance, he looked directly at Manda. "Is Mr. Stilwell here? May I see him?"

"I'm sorry. Mr. Stilwell has left the bank on some business. He should return in about an hour," Manda answered.

James sighed. "I need some information," he said.

"Perhaps I can help you?" she offered.

"Perhaps you can," he said. "I've been thinking about buying some property . . ."

Jessie looked around the filthy kitchen of the ramshackle house one more time. Dirt covered everything. It would take her a week just to get the place clean, let alone repaired. The cupboards hung from the walls by their nails. The heavy iron stove was missing one leg and leaned precariously, held up by a whiskey bottle wedged under the broken stump. The pump wouldn't pump, and a flock of wrens had decided to nest under one counter, the shotgun hole in the wall their entrance.

Shaking her head, she crossed the room and went outside to the porch where Mr. Stilwell waited. "You were right about it needing repairs," she said.

"There are skunks under the house." He spoke quietly, holding his finger to his lips to tell her to do the same.

"And birds in the kitchen, bees in the bedroom, and a snake in the fireplace," she said about the family of creatures she'd found inhabiting the house.

Stilwell shrugged. "I told you—"

"I know," Jessie interrupted. "The place is a wreck, Mr. Stilwell. I'd be crazy to buy it." She looked around the yard and out toward the barn. But it would be mine, she thought. And no one could ever take it away from me. "Do you think you could be a little flexible on the price?" she asked.

Stilwell's eyes lit up and he actually looked at her through his spectacles. "I'm sure we could work something out," he said, beaming.

"All right, then. I'll take it," Jessie heard herself saying. "And heaven help me," she added.

James had taken a more direct route to the Baker place, not having to use the road, as Stilwell had in his buggy, and he came up to the house from behind. As he rode around to the front he heard voices. Then he saw Jessie. She was wearing new clothes. Trousers and a soft green shirt that reminded him of the color of her eyes. These new duds weren't as tight as her old clothes had been, but they still emphasized her amazing figure. "Hello, Jessie," he said as he neared.

Jessie's heart slammed against the inner wall of her chest at the sight of him. He was all good looks and masculinity sitting on that horse. His hat was pulled low over his dark eyes. His shoulders and chest filled out his shirt in a way that should have been against the law, and the strong muscles of his legs stretched the fabric of his trousers as he controlled his horse with his knees. Memories of what they'd done together took her breath away. And the memory of his words and his refusal to sell her the Triple X sent the heat of anger rolling through her body. She set her jaw and looked at him silently.

"Hello, Mr. Stilwell," James said, not taking his eyes off Jessie.

"Hello yourself, Mr. Bonner," Stilwell said jovially, still basking in the glow of making a sale. "What brings you out here?"

"I heard Jessie was here and just thought I'd stop by and say hello."

Jessie rolled her eyes at his inane excuse. "Humph," she grunted.

"You don't believe me? Well, how about, I came to get my horse?" he said firmly.

Jessie's eyes opened wider at that. She knew she was in the wrong where Henry was concerned. "I meant to get him back to you," she started, "but I've grown attached to Henry. I'd like to buy him from you if I could."

James raised one brow. "Henry?" he asked, amused.

Jessie raised her jaw. "Yes, Henry. I named him."

"He's already got a name. It's Bouncer," James told her.

Jessie looked at the gentle horse munching weeds in the yard. "Bouncer? Henry suits him better. Anyway, will you sell him to me?"

"No," James answered.

"But, I—" Jessie began to argue.

"I'll give him to you," James interrupted.

Jessie leveled her gaze at him. "Why? You don't owe me anything," she stated.

James thought about their lovemaking. He certainly didn't feel indebted to her, but he felt something. "I'm not trying to pay you off. You like the horse. You can have him."

"I'd rather buy him," Jessie said determinedly.

James sighed. "Fine, have it your way," he said.

"Fine," she retorted.

Moments of heavy tension passed.

Mr. Stilwell cleared his throat. "Miss Braddock, perhaps we could get started back to my office? There are a lot of papers to sign."

James turned surprised eyes on Stilwell. "Papers?" he asked.

"What are you still doing here?" Jessie snapped at James.

"What papers? You aren't actually thinking about buying this dump, are you?" he asked incredulously.

Jessie took offense. "And what if I am? What business is it of yours?"

"None, sweetheart, but I can't believe you'd do something so stupid," he returned.

"You should be used to me doing stupid things by now," she answered, hotly.

James knew she was referring to their lovemaking. "I could get used to one of the stupid things you do," he said quietly, his tone becoming suggestive.

"You're disgusting," she snapped.

"You didn't think so once," he accused.

Jessie sent a horrified glance toward Mr. Stilwell and saw the look of curiosity on his face. "I will not discuss this with you," she said to James.

"Then will you discuss this?" he asked, waving his arm to indicate the ranch.

"There's nothing to discuss. I'm buying the place and that's final."

"Why would you want to buy this?" he exclaimed.

Jessie narrowed her eyes. "Because someone else now owns my home," she accused.

"And I'm going to keep it, Jessie," he said firmly.

"If you were any kind of a gentleman you'd sell it back to me," she said.

"Then I guess I'm no gentleman. I've worked too hard to make the Triple X mine just to sell it back to you for sentimental reasons."

"It's more than sentiment that makes me want it. It's my home."

"It's my home," he replied sternly.

Jessie's heart fluttered at his words. She knew he meant what he said. "Mr. Stilwell, let's get going, shall we?" she said. Leaving the porch, she grabbed Henry's reins and swung up into the saddle. She watched the banker climb into his buggy. "I'll leave a draft for you at the bank for Henry. How much do you want?" she asked James, her voice coming in clipped tones.

James studied her. "Twenty dollars should do it," he finally said.

"That's not nearly enough," Jessie argued.

"Take it or leave it," James responded.

"Fine," Jessie sighed, then addressed the banker. "Mr. Stilwell?" She nudged Henry and started them away from her new home.

James scanned the dilapidated structures of the Baker place. "Jessie," he called at her back. "You'll never make it here," he yelled.

Jessie gritted her teeth and refused to turn around.

"You don't know how hard ranching is. You'll fall flat on your face," he tried again.

Still Jessie ignored him, but she'd heard his words and anger burned hotly in her middle. She'd show him. She'd make a go of this ranch if it was the last thing she did.

James watched Jessie until she was no more than a speck on the horizon. He couldn't help admiring the way she sat straight in the saddle, her long hair flowing down her back and tied loosely at the nape of her neck with a leather strap. She was beautiful, more beautiful than any woman he'd ever known. And she was unattainable. The problems between them were too great to overcome. "Hell," he cursed as he started for home.

Jessie thought about James on the ride back to town. Mr. Stilwell talked constantly, but she barely heard him. She knew she had her work cut out for her. The ranch would take nearly all her money and certainly all her time. The only thing her traitorous mind would think about, however, was the way James had looked, the way he'd sat his horse, the tone of his voice, and the sensual look in his eyes when he'd referred to their lovemaking. Her blood boiled at the memory of his hands and mouth on her body, at the way he'd filled her, bringing her more pleasure in that short time than she'd known her whole life. Gripping the reins more tightly, she fought against these thoughts, trying to concentrate on the business at hand. "How many acres did you say I'm buying?" she asked Stilwell.

"There now, one more signature and we'll be finished," said Mr. Stilwell, pointing to a line at the bottom of the last page of the contract.

Jessie held the pen tightly in her hand. Leaning forward, she signed her name. "Is that it?" she asked.

Stilwell picked up the papers and blew on the ink, nodding and smiling at the same time.

It had taken three days to have her money wired from Charleston, but everything was now final. She was the owner of the old Baker place. It occurred to her that it would no longer be the Baker place. It was now the Braddock ranch and she'd have to come up with a name for it. But that was something that could wait for a while. There were other concerns more pressing.

She'd managed to hire two men to help out at the ranch, an old gentleman who'd worked for the Bakers and a younger man who claimed he knew all there was to know about cattle. She was willing to let him prove it. "I was wondering, Mr. Stilwell, if you could help me again?"

The banker looked across his desk at Jessie. "Yes, I'll try," he answered.

"I've hired a couple of men to work for me but I still have to stock the place. Can you tell me where to go to buy the cattle?"

"Certainly, Miss Braddock. And it should be easy for you to attain a good price as you already know the man in question."

Suspicion caused Jessie's nerves to stand on end. "Yes?" she asked quietly.

"James Bonner of the Triple X is the man to see."

Jessie took a deep breath and let it out slowly. She'd done her best to erase James from her mind and only succeeded in pushing him from her thoughts for short periods of time. "Isn't there anyone else around here who's selling cattle?" she asked, an urgent tone in her voice.

The banker tilted his head and looked at her through his spectacles. "I'm afraid not. The Triple X has become the biggest spread in this area. The other ranchers don't sell cattle until they're ready to drive them to market. Is this a problem for you?"

Jessie lowered her eyes. She wouldn't let Mr. Stilwell see her discomfort. Looking up again, she smiled. "Of course not. I was just curious," she said.

Rising, Jessie leaned over the desk and offered her hand. "Thank you for all your help, Mr. Stilwell."

"You're welcome, Miss Braddock," he replied taking her hand. "And now that you're a resident of Mesa City, let me be the first to say how happy I am to have you as a neighbor."

"I have lived here before, Mr. Stilwell. I grew up here," she told him.

"I know that, but now you own property."

"Yes I do." Jessie thanked him again and left his office.

Once outside the bank she mounted Henry and tugged his reins to the side. "Can you believe my luck, Henry?" she fumed. "The only place to buy cattle in this whole damned town is the Triple X. I have to buy cows from James."

The next several days Jessie had little time to think about cattle or James. She spent every day cleaning and fixing and convincing birds, bees, skunks, and snakes that they no longer lived in her house. Each morning she would rise with enthusiasm and each evening she would fall into bed exhausted. After nearly a week she could say the house was livable.

Stepping out on the porch early on the sixth day, she scouted the yard for her hired hands. "Tinker, Johnny," she called. Pulling on her gloves, she waited.

Johnny appeared from inside the barn. Tinker stepped slowly from behind the pig pen.

"Yes'm?" Johnny responded.

"I'm going to the Triple X. I don't know how long I'll be gone," she informed them.

"Yes'm," Johnny said again, lowering his eyes when he spoke.

Jessie studied the young man for a moment. He was tall and lanky, with long blond hair and blue eyes, and she'd put his age at nineteen or twenty. "If I'm not back by lunch time there's bread and jelly in the kitchen. Help yourself." She looked at the older man. "And there's a bottle of whiskey under the sink. But only one drink, Tinker," she told him.

"Yes, Miss," Tinker replied, grinning a toothless grin.

Jessie smiled back at him. It hadn't taken her long to discover that Tinker liked his whiskey, and as long as she allowed him only one drink with each meal, work continued to get done around the place.

Jessie rode Henry to the Triple X with trepidation. Would James sell cattle to her? Of course he would, she reasoned. But would she have to put up with more snide remarks? Probably. It galled her to remember he thought she'd fail in her attempt at ranching.

Getting closer to the ranch, she had to admit it wasn't only dealing with James's attitude that she was dreading. She was also dreading her own body's reaction to him physically. Just thinking about him sent her pulse rate soaring. "I'll just have to keep things on a business level," she said out loud. Henry snorted as though in answer.

Riding onto Triple X land brought a lump to her throat. This would never be her home again, she realized. Swallowing her sadness, she raised her chin. "I have a new home," she said defiantly. "And I'm still in Texas."

Entering the yard, Jessie didn't know where to start looking for James. She supposed she might as well start at the house. Riding up and dismounting, she tied Henry to the hitching post and climbed the porch stairs. As she reached the door it swung open and Carmen stood in her way.

"What do you want here?" Carmen asked.

Jessie could feel the woman's hatred like a tangible thing. "I've come to see James," she explained.

"He's not here, and he doesn't want to see you," Carmen said with venom in her voice.

"I need to see him on business," Jessie told her.

"I know what business you have with James," Carmen

said snidely. "He told me all about it and he wants no more of it."

Jessie felt the heat in her face and heard the blood pounding in her ears. Could James really have told this woman about their lovemaking? Would he do such a thing? She pictured James in Carmen's arms. Pictured them whispering together in the intimate darkness of his bedroom. She looked at Carmen's beautiful face, her voluptuous body, and she knew she was telling the truth. James had told her, and they'd probably laughed together about it.

Jessie swallowed the bitter taste of bile in her mouth. "I . . . I have to leave," she stammered. Turning around, she started down the stairs. As she untied the reins from the hitching post, she heard the happy, squealing voices of her nephews.

"Aunt Jessie!" they yelled. "We've missed you!" They came running from behind the house, their hands, faces, and backsides covered with mud.

Jessie put a smile on her face and knelt down to catch them as they ran into her arms. "You found that mud-hole again, didn't you?" she asked them.

"I told you not to play in the mud!" shouted Carmen at the boys as she stepped out onto the porch. "You will be punished for this," she threatened. "You will be spanked."

Jessie's blood ran cold at Carmen's words. Standing slowly, she turned back around to face her. "You will do nothing to these boys," she said menacingly. "If you so much as lay one hand on either of them you'll have to answer to me. Is that clear?"

Carmen's jaw rose insolently. "James wants me to—"

"I don't give a damn what James wants you to do. If I ever hear that you spanked these children or that he spanked these children, you'll both think the wrath of God has been set loose on you!"

"I . . ." Carmen began again, then stopped.

Jessie was fueled by her anger. "Now that I've made

myself clear on this subject, where is James? I have business with him."

Jessie felt Jeremy tugging on her arm. Turning around, she saw James walking toward her and her heart fell to her feet.

❋ 6 ❋

Jessie saw that James was drying his hands on a piece of toweling. His hair was damp and messy, as though he'd wet it and combed it with his fingers, and a dark curl had fallen over his forehead. His shirt was open nearly to his waist and she could see the black hair covering his chest. She took a deep breath and tried to calm the wild emotions running rampant through her body from the sight of him. "Hello, James," she said as he neared.

James noticed that Jessie's color heightened when she saw him. She must still be angry with me, he thought. He'd been meaning to call on her, to deliver a telegram that had come from her parents, but he hadn't been sure of the welcome he'd get. "Jessie? What are you doing here?" he asked, his surprise evident in his tone.

"I came to see you on business," she answered coolly. "I was told you didn't want to see me."

James's eyes focused briefly on Carmen before he answered Jessie. "I don't know why anyone would think that," he responded.

Jessie could see the scowl on Carmen's pretty face in her peripheral vision. "Maybe something you said?" she directed back at James. She was still seething from the knowledge he'd discussed her with Carmen. She hoped he wouldn't make things worse by trying to make excuses for his actions. "But it doesn't really matter," she continued before James could answer. "I've come on business. Perhaps we could get right to it?"

James was perplexed by Jessie's words. He knew Carmen was jealous. He also knew she'd guessed what had happened between him and Jessie, but that didn't give her the right to say things that weren't true. He'd be sure to speak to her about it later. Right now he wanted to know what Jessie was here for. "You've made me curious, Jessie. What can I do for you?"

Jessie looked directly at Carmen's indignant expression, then at the two impish, grinning faces staring up at her. "You two go wash up. I promise to say good-bye before I leave."

"Okay, all right," the boys answered and started running back around the house.

"They sure do get dirty," commented James, grinning.

Jessie raised one brow. "Yes, they do," she agreed. "Can we go someplace private to talk?" she asked.

James studied Jessie for a moment, his curiosity growing. Was she once again going to try to convince him to sell her the Triple X? Or did she want to discuss what had happened between them? "Whatever you say," he told her.

Jessie started walking toward the barn. She could feel James following her and she heard the door to the house slam behind them.

Once they were inside the barn, James stopped and waited for Jessie to say what was on her mind. He allowed himself the pleasure of studying her frame. She was so tiny that he felt huge beside her. Her dark, curling hair fell down her back to her waist. The sweet curve of her bottom encased in the snug fabric of her trousers was causing him to feel a heat that centered below his belt.

Jessie stood with her back to James while she tried to calm her nerves enough to discuss business with him. When she finally turned to face him she knew she'd wasted the time. As soon as her eyes met his she felt as though she'd been touched by a hot poker. Her temperature went up and her heart beat an unsteady rhythm beneath her breasts. Taking a deep breath, she blew it out slowly. "So," she said.

James raised one dark brow. "Yes?"

Jessie's nerves tingled at the sound of his voice. Gritting her teeth together for a moment, she mentally admonished herself for her hesitance. "I want to buy some cattle from you," she blurted.

James looked at her in surprise. "You needed privacy to tell me that?"

"No. I just . . ." She couldn't explain that she didn't want to talk in front of his lover. He'd only laugh at her. She supposed now it wouldn't matter anyway. He was sure to tell Carmen everything she said. She then remembered the twins. "I don't want you spanking the twins," she announced.

James was more than surprised by her words this time. "What?" he asked incredulously.

"You heard me. I don't want you spanking the twins. And if I ever hear of Carmen laying a hand on them I'll shoot her on sight. If they're too much trouble for you here they can come spend the rest of their visit with me," she finished.

James took a moment to digest what she'd said. Obviously, something had happened around here that he didn't know about. "First of all, I have never and will never spank those boys, though there have been times I wanted to tie them to their beds to keep them out of mischief. Second, as for Carmen spanking them, well," he paused for a moment as he thought about this. Had she spanked them? He found it hard to believe they wouldn't have told him if she had. "As far as I know, she's never struck them. But I'll talk to her and the boys to be sure. If it has happened, it'll never happen again. You have my word on it."

Jessie heard the ring of truth in James's words. "All right. I'll accept that." She dropped her eyes for just a moment. Now for business, she thought. Looking back up, she tried to use her most businesslike tone. "I want to buy fifty head of your best cattle. And I want to pay full price for them," she added, remembering the Henry incident.

James chuckled, a grin splitting his face. "Most people come here trying to bargain for a good deal. You come in here demanding to pay top dollar."

Jessie raised her jaw. "I only want what's fair. I don't want any special treatment because—"

"Because I made love to you?" he interrupted, his voice becoming a graveled growl.

James's voice rolled along Jessie's nerve endings and sent a shiver down her spine. His question set off a whirling chain reaction, starting in the pit of her stomach and emanating outward, targeting the most sensitive parts of her body. She felt her breasts tingle and her nipples harden, and the sensation of warmth between her legs caused her to take a quick breath before speaking. "You interrupted me. I was going to say I wanted no special treatment because of who I am."

James's eyelids lowered as he watched her. He felt himself growing within his trousers, a reaction that didn't surprise him. Every time he thought of Jessie, and it was often that he did, he became aroused. With her standing right here in front of him it was inevitable. "And who are you?" he inquired suggestively.

Jessie heaved a heavy breath. "A relative, sort of," she answered.

"I see," he responded. "And do you want to pick out the cattle yourself, or do you trust me to do it?"

Jessie blinked uncertainly several times. "I trust you to do it," she finally answered.

"Good. Then I'll start on it first thing in the morning and I'll have some of my men drive them over to your place in a few days. I'll let you know much you owe me then."

Jessie nodded. "That will work." She paused, uncertain what to say next. "I guess our business is finished," she said.

"I guess so," James agreed. Then, "I almost forgot. I

received a telegram from your parents a couple of days ago."

"From Mother and Father? What did they want? Are they all right?" she questioned hurriedly.

James held up his hands. "Whoa. Slow down. They're fine, but they wanted to know the same thing about you. Haven't you wired them since you arrived?"

Jessie felt a tremendous guilt. "No. I've been so busy, first here and now at my place, that I didn't think . . ." she trailed off.

"I answered their telegram. I told them you were fine. But I didn't tell them what you were up to."

Jessie bit the inside of her lower lip. Her parents were completely in the dark about her plans. They were still expecting her to come back to Charleston. "I've got to write to them," she said under her breath. She looked up at James then. "I wonder how they're going to take the news that I'm staying here in Texas?" she said.

James shrugged one shoulder. "Probably not very well," he commented.

Deep in thought about her parents, Jessie walked in James's direction, stopping just short of where he was standing, and leaned against a stall rail. "You're probably right," she sighed.

James felt the affect of Jessie standing so close to him. He could smell her soft scent and suffered for it. Looking down on her, he visualized himself running his hands through her glorious hair, losing himself in its thick mass. "I like your hair down this way," he said softly, stepping in front of her. "It's beautiful."

Jessie's eyes darted upward, her gaze meeting his. "Thank you," she said breathlessly. Nervously, she tried to step back but felt the rail behind her. Her eyes widened as James took another step toward her, bringing him to within inches of her.

James knew Jessie still resented his ownership of the Triple X. He knew she'd given him her virginity in hopes of influencing his decision to sell. He also knew she'd probably fight any other advances he made. None of this mattered. He needed to kiss her, needed to taste her, to feel the fullness of her breasts against his chest as he pillaged the sweet cavern of her mouth with his tongue. Reaching down, he slipped his hand behind her neck and wound his fingers in her hair. Making a fist, he pulled her forward.

Jessie felt herself being drawn to James and couldn't fight it. The feeling of his firm, demanding lips over hers sent white hot ripples through her body. She opened her mouth to his tongue and let her own join in this mating ritual. A moan escaped her throat as she leaned into him, needing to experience the sensual feel of his powerful body next to hers. She spread her fingers across his naked chest in the V of his open shirt and felt his rapid heart pounding beneath the muscled flesh and coarse hair that covered his breastbone. Sliding her hands upward, she arched more fully into him.

James was surprised when Jessie didn't try to pull away from him but instead began to participate in their kiss in an aggressive way. She wound her arms up around his neck and pulled herself closer to him, spearing him with her passion-hardened nipples. Loosening his grip on the hair at the nape of her neck, he moved both hands downward through the length of her soft, black curls. Then cupping her bottom, he lifted her up against the firm bulge of his arousal. His senses soared as she immediately began to sway her hips against him. "Jessie, Jessie," he groaned against her mouth.

Jessie heard James growl her name. She felt the timbre of his voice vibrating through and over her skin, and she experienced an overpowering, instinctive need to move against his engorged manhood, rocking with a rhythm as old as time. Letting her head fall back, she exposed her throat to his kisses.

James took his cue and let his mouth move from her lips to explore the tender flesh of Jessie's throat and the soft area behind her ear. Kissing and nibbling his way downward, he found the hollow at the base of her neck. Bringing one hand up, he unbuttoned her shirt, impatiently slipping his hand inside to feel the hot, pouting peak of her breast. Tugging her shirt to the side, he let his mouth follow the curve of her breast to its tip, then let his tongue move teasingly over it to tantalize her. A low moan escaped her throat as she shuddered against him.

Jessie was seeing white lights dancing behind her eyes. She was hot and ready to open herself to James's passion. The strength of his arousal was astounding, and she continued to push herself against him, the friction of the movements driving her wild.

James pulled Jessie's nipple into his mouth and suckled her tenderly. Just then something crashed in the tack room. James jerked his head up and released his hold on Jessie. "What the—Who's there?" he demanded.

Jessie nearly fell when James let go of her. She had to grasp the stall rail to steady herself, and she looked in frightened embarrassment toward the tack room, waiting to see who would emerge.

"Whoever's in there better come out now," James ordered. He could feel his erection falling, but the loss of such fever-pitch emotion was going to take some time to get over.

A huge black and yellow cat sauntered out of the tack room, a fat gray mouse in its mouth.

Jessie let out a sigh of relief. No one had seen them. She closed her eyes gratefully for a moment, then realized her shirt was still gaping open. Reaching for the buttons, she began to close the shirt as fast as she could. As she was doing this she gazed at the dirt floor and could see James's boots as he stood before her. Oh, God, she thought to herself. What have I done, or nearly done, again? How can I be so stupid? she thought angrily. Slowly raising her eyes, she followed his body from the ground up. When she finally looked at his face the emotion there angered her further.

"I think we need to finish this somewhere else," he said.

Jessie's heart was pounding wildly. She didn't understand why this man had the power to turn her to jelly, and right now she didn't care. She only knew she was furious with herself for giving in to him again. He was the one person keeping her from owning her family's ranch, her home. And he was involved with another woman! "I don't think so," she said vehemently. "This was a mistake."

James narrowed his eyes and took a step toward her. "I don't agree."

Jessie darted to the side and escaped his advance. She remembered that he'd told Carmen about their last time together and her temper grew. "I won't do this again, James. I won't be the stuff of gossip."

James looked at her perplexed. "Do you think the cat is going to tell someone?"

Jessie's eyes snapped with green fire. "No, I don't think the cat is going to tell someone," she answered with a sneer.

"You don't think I'm going to tell someone?"

Jessie raised her chin. She wasn't going to give him the opportunity to deny he'd told Carmen. Carmen knew and he was the only one who could have told her. "I'm leaving now. I'll be expecting the cattle in a few days," she stated flatly. Turning her back on him, she left the barn as quickly as she could, her back straight, her head high. She crossed the yard and mounted Henry. As she flipped his reins she remembered she'd promised the twins she'd say good-bye. "Oh well, they'll just have to forgive me," she said out loud. "Come on, Henry. Let's go home."

James remained in the barn for a long while after Jessie left. His emotions were running out of control and he needed the time to compose himself before anyone saw him. What the hell was wrong with Jessie, anyway? She'd responded to his lovemaking like a starved person, then resented him all the more for it afterward. Shaking his head, he realized he knew the answer. He owned the Triple X, and as long as he did she wouldn't let herself admit she wanted him. "I'm not going to sell you the

Triple X just to get you into my bed, Jessie," he asserted into the quiet of the barn.

Running his fingers through his hair in frustration, he inhaled deeply, remembering the way she'd felt and tasted, the way she'd arched into him, wanting him as much as he wanted her. "Damn it!" he shouted.

During the ride back to her ranch, Jessie fumed and mumbled to herself about her own stupidity. How could she let herself get involved with James Bonner? It shouldn't matter that just looking at him made her melt from the inside. It shouldn't matter that when he touched her she felt on fire. It was bad enough that he owned the Triple X and refused to sell, but he'd made love to her when he was involved with another woman and then told that woman about it. The image of him lying with Carmen in his arms, laughing at her own inexperience, caused her to grip the reins so tightly her fingers ached. "Never again, James Bonner. Never again!" she vowed.

"You told her what?" James bellowed at Carmen. "How could you do such a thing?"

Carmen stared hard at James. "Because I won't let her have you," she said.

James rubbed his eyes tiredly. He thought about Jessie. "Don't worry about Jessie having me. She wouldn't touch me now with a twelve-foot willow branch."

Carmen stood up from the dining table where they'd sat to have their talk and looked down at James. "She wants you, all right, but you're mine. Ever since that night." She leaned over and ran her hand along his shoulder.

James jerked back away from her. "I was drunk, Carmen. I don't even remember what happened." He searched his mind for some small fragment of memory of that night, some tiny glimpse that could convince him he'd actually done what she accused him of.

"You made love to me."

"So you say," he answered her.

Carmen glared down at him, her breasts heaving with each breath. "We made love," she repeated angrily.

James looked at her with regret. "I'm sorry, Carmen. I just don't remember, and under the circumstances, I think it would be best if you didn't work for me any longer. You can tell everyone it was your idea to quit."

Carmen scowled blackly at him. "You can't do this to me. I won't leave you."

"You're fired, Carmen."

"I'll tell my father what happened between us," she threatened angrily.

"Go ahead. I should have told him, myself, long ago."

Carmen's face contorted with her rage. He was ruining all her plans. "You'll be sorry for this, James Bonner, and so will that slut, Jessie Braddock. She thinks she can just ride in here and take what's mine, but she'll learn she can't!" Her fists were clenched against her breasts and a tiny line of spittle fell from the corner of her mouth. Swiping at it, she turned and stomped from the room. She pushed the kitchen door open with such force that it banged against the cupboard behind it loudly enough to wake the twins upstairs.

James sighed and listened for two little voices to call him from the top of the stairs. A few minutes later he said a prayer of thanks that the boys had slept through Carmen's tantrum. Now he'd have to hire another woman to be his housekeeper and take care of the twins. He thought about Jessie. She'd offered to take the boys if they were too much for him. His eyes narrowed. If the boys were on her ranch she'd have no reason to come to the Triple X.

Shaking his head in disgust, he realized what he was doing. "Jessie doesn't want anything to do with you, you fool," he said to himself.

In the days that followed Jessie threw herself into the task of getting her ranch ready for the cattle that would soon be delivered. With the help of Johnny and Tinker, she mended the fences and repaired the barn as well as she could, seeing to it the stalls were clean and free of manure, which she piled outside to use on the garden she was going to plant. It was late to plant, but with a little luck they'd have an Indian summer and she'd be able to harvest enough vegetables to get herself through the winter.

As she bent over the outside pump, splashing cool water over her head and hair, she heard someone approaching her. Her heart skipped a beat in fear it might be James.

"Miss Jessie?" Johnny said.

Jessie flipped the wet length of her hair up over her head and began pushing the water from it, starting at her hairline and working it through to the ends. "Yes, Johnny?"

"Well, I don't know if it's my place . . ." he stammered.

Jessie studied him more closely. He held his hat in his hand and was shifting his weight nervously from one foot to the other. "Yes, what is it?"

"Well, me and Tinker was talkin'," he paused again and looked over his shoulder for the older man. "And we think you're workin' yourself too hard."

Jessie let out the breath she'd been holding. "How sweet of you both," she said. "But I'm fine. Really," she added when she saw the look of disbelief in his eyes.

Johnny leaned forward and reached for her hand. Taking it in his own, he turned it palm side up.

Jessie had the urge to close her hand but didn't. Angry red blisters glared up at her. "I'm just not used to this kind of work," she explained.

Johnny nodded. "That's why me and Tinker think you should slow down a little. Your hurtin' yourself."

Jessie gently took her hand from Johnny's. "I'll be fine." She began walking away. "I'm going to go put dinner on the table. You go get Tinker and wash up."

Inside her house, she felt tears spring to her eyes at the

thoughtfulness of the men. It was nice having someone care about her.

Wiping the moisture from her eyes, she put plates and silverware on the table, then went to the stove for the large pot of ham stew she'd put on early in the afternoon. Lifting the lid, she sniffed the aroma coming from the pot. "Mmmm," she breathed. The combination of ham, potatoes, carrots, and cabbage, was heavenly. "I'm going to eat like a pig tonight," she mused.

Tinker and Johnny came through the door just as she set the pot on the table. "I think you're going to like this," she told them. "It's one of my mother's best recipes."

Tinker slid onto his chair and removed his hat, letting it fall to the floor beside him. Johnny sat down after hanging his hat on the back of his chair. "Sure smells good," he offered.

Jessie took her place at the head of the table and lowered her eyes to say the usual grace. She was beginning to feel as if she had a lot to be grateful for.

The meal was as delicious as she'd expected and she basked in the praise of the two men who were fast becoming her friends.

As Jessie entered the general store early the next morning she was feeling quite happy, but the happiness faded when she saw Carmen standing at the counter. She nearly gave in to the urge to leave, but decided against it. She couldn't live in this town and be afraid to face this woman. As ill tempered as Carmen was, she couldn't blame her. If she, herself, were in love with a man and found out he'd slept with another woman she was sure she wouldn't be exactly pleasant, either. "Good morning, Carmen," she said as she neared the counter.

Carmen turned cold eyes on Jessie. "Good morning, Miss Braddock."

At least she's speaking to me, Jessie thought. It's too bad I can't convince her she has nothing to fear from me where James is concerned. "Lovely day," she offered.

Carmen nodded, wondering whether Jessie had come in to gloat.

"How are my nephews?" she asked.

Carmen studied her carefully. Was it possible Jessie didn't know about her change in status on the Triple X? "The boys are fine. They helped me make pies yesterday," she lied.

"That must have been fun for them. I'll bet they made quite a mess." Jessie smiled at the picture of her nephews covered in flour instead of mud.

"Not too bad. They helped me clean up afterward," Carmen continued lying, testing Jessie.

"Here is your fabric, Carmen," said Mrs. Medley, carrying a bolt of brilliant red satin from the back room.

"Ohhh, it is beautiful!" Carmen exclaimed, touching the fabric gingerly with her fingertips.

"My goodness, that's lovely," offered Jessie. "What's it for?"

Carmen turned a smug expression to Jessie. "James ordered it for me. I am going to make a dress for the dance."

Jessie felt the intended stab of Carmen's barb, but chose to ignore it. "What dance?" she asked.

"Goodness," exclaimed Mrs. Medley. "You haven't been told about the dance? It's a switch dance. You know, the women ask the men to attend and to dance," she explained. "It's all very exciting, and quite funny for us old married ladies. We get such a kick out of seeing the girls squabble over the single men. One year we had an actual knock-down-drag-out between two girls over one young fellow." She chuckled at the memory.

"When is it?" Jessie asked.

"Friday next," answered Mrs. Medley. "You will be going won't you? It's held out behind the church. Everyone attends. And there's always a lot of good food."

Jessie glanced at Carmen. There was no doubt about who she'd be bringing to the dance. "I probably won't be going," she said. "I have a lot to do out at my place."

Carmen smiled victoriously. "Too bad. You might

have met someone there you could fall in love with," she said.

"Oh posh," said Mrs. Medley. "I just think she'd have some fun. I hear you've been working too hard out at that ranch of yours. You probably need a night out more than anyone."

Jessie lowered her eyes. There was no one she was going to fall in love with at the dance. "I'll think about it, Mrs. Medley. Thank you for telling me."

Carmen reached inside her handbag and pulled out some bills. "James asked me to pay you for the fabric," she said.

Mrs. Medley took the money, then handed back her change. "That satin is going to make up into a beautiful dress," she commented.

"Yes it will," cooed Carmen, picking up the bolt. "See you at the dance," she said as she swished out the door.

"Now what can I do for you?" Mrs. Medley asked Jessie in a more businesslike tone.

Jessie had watched Carmen's exit and could still see her walking across the street. "I need some molasses and some soap and some coffee. Here's my list," she said, pulling a folded piece of paper from her pocket and handing it to Mrs. Medley.

"Looks like you're stocking up," the storekeeper said.

"Yes." The sway of Carmen's hips was drawing attention from several male passersby.

"Did you bring a wagon?"

"Yes. It's just outside." A wagon was one of the first things she'd purchased after buying the ranch. It had already been more useful than she could have imagined, hauling everything from hay and lumber to these grocery items now.

"Will you need help loading?" Mrs. Medley asked.

Jessie had lost sight of Carmen. "No, I can manage," she answered, turning her full attention once more to the matters at hand.

"Do you have a dress to wear to the dance?" the woman inquired.

"What? No. I don't think I'm going," Jessie said.

"Wait here a moment." Mrs. Medley disappeared into the back room again. When she returned she was carrying a second bolt of satin, this time in the most beautiful shade of pale green Jessie had ever seen. "I didn't order this, and I was going to send it back. It came in with the red. A mistake at the factory, I'm sure. But I'm a strong believer that mistakes happen for a reason."

Jessie leaned toward the fabric, her breath in her throat. "It's so—"

"Isn't it? I dare say I've never seen a color like it. And it would be beautiful on you, what with your eyes and all."

Jessie was tempted. A dress made of this fabric would look wonderful on her. "But I don't have a pattern," she said.

"Heck, I've got lots of patterns."

"But who would I go to the dance with?"

Mrs. Medley pondered this for a moment. "I heard you have a young man working for you. Would he do?"

Jessie thought for a moment. Johnny was nice and a hard worker, and he was becoming a friend. She didn't want to ruin that by asking him to a dance. She shook her head.

"Then why don't you go alone? Lots of girls do. All the single men who haven't been asked show up to let the girls fight over them."

"I certainly wouldn't fight for someone," said Jessie.

Mrs. Medley fingered the fabric and looked at Jessie. "I don't think you'd have to."

❈ 7 ❈

Jessie was nearly home when she reached behind the wagon seat and stuck her fingers inside the paper that held the green satin. "I can't believe I bought this stuff," she said out loud. She pulled out the pattern Mrs. Medley had insisted she buy. Looking at the drawing on the front of the package, she grimaced. It was too low in the front; the tight waistline fit snugly over the hips and a small bustle pulled the skirt from the front, which caused it to curve over the abdomen and caress the woman's thighs in a most indiscreet way. It definitely wasn't the demure white dress she'd worn to the party such a short time before. "This is the dress of a woman with one thing on her mind," she murmured. "Oh, why did I let Mrs. Medley talk me in to this?" she moaned.

Stuffing the pattern back behind the seat, she let out her breath in a puff. "Maybe I can change the pattern," she commented, then sighed, knowing her sewing abilities were limited. "I'll be lucky if I can even follow the pattern and make the damn dress at all," she admitted to herself.

A sound up ahead took her mind off the dress. "My cattle," she breathed excitedly. "Come on, boy," she said, slapping the reins to speed them up. A few minutes later her ranch was in view and she could see fifty head of cattle meandering around their new home. She could also see James on horseback. "Damn," she fumed.

"I thought you were going to have some of your hands deliver the cattle," Jessie called angrily as she stopped the wagon in front of the house. Jumping down, she walked toward the herd.

"I was, but two small people wanted to see their aunt," James said. At that moment the twins burst from the barn at a dead run.

"Aunt Jessie!" they squealed.

Jessie knelt and grinned from ear to ear as the wiggly little boys leapt into her arms, nearly knocking her down with their enthusiasm. "Oh, I missed you two," she said.

"We missed you. And we have so much to tell you," said Jeremy.

"You do?" she laughed.

They nodded together.

Jessie smiled at them. "Let me look at my cattle, then we'll go into the house. I have some pie left over from dinner last night. Would you two like some?" she asked.

"Yes! Yes!" they answered, excitedly jumping up and down.

The twins followed Jessie like two tiny shadows as she inspected the cattle James was selling her. "They look like good stock," she said as he walked toward her.

"They'll do, then?" he asked.

"They'll do," she replied coolly. "Come into the house so I can pay you," she said.

"All right, just give me a minute to send my hands back to the Triple X."

Jessie watched him walk toward the men who'd helped him with the herd. Seconds later the men were riding away and James was returning. Not waiting for him to catch up with her, she headed for the house, the twins on her heels.

James followed the three toward the house. As they neared the porch he noticed that the wagon was still loaded. "Come on, boys," he called to the twins. "Let's help your aunt Jessie unload the wagon."

"Okay!" the boys answered happily, running from Jessie's side.

"That won't be necessary," Jessie protested. "I can do it later with Tinker and Johnny's help," she said.

"They're going to be busy for a while," observed James.

Jessie glanced back to where her hands were tending the cattle. James was right. It would be a while before the cattle got used to their new surroundings and settled down. But she still didn't want his help unloading. She didn't want anything from James Bonner, at least nothing but the Triple X. Frowning, she saw it was too late. He'd already loaded the twins' little arms down with packages they could handle and had a huge sack of flour over his shoulder and a bag of sugar under his arm. The sight of his muscles bulging under the fabric of his shirt took her breath away. "Hell," she murmured.

"Where do you want these?" James asked.

Jessie tore her eyes from his body and charged ahead into the house. "Boys, just put your things on the table. James, you can set those down on the floor."

"You got it," he answered jovially.

"You got it," the boys mimicked.

Jessie grinned at the twins.

"Come on, boys, we're not finished yet," James told his helpers.

Jessie dashed outside behind them. This time she grabbed an armload of supplies, too. Back and forth they went several more times.

"This looks like the last load," James announced as he reached behind the seat for a large, paper-wrapped package.

Jessie's eyes grew wide. It was the fabric. "I'll get that," she said quickly. It was too late. James picked up the package and she watched as the paper gave way where she'd pulled it open on the way home. The bolt of cloth slipped from the paper, the pattern on top of it. He grabbed at the package, trying to save the contents, and ended up with slippery green satin in one hand, the pattern in the other.

James raised the pattern to look at what he'd nearly dropped in the dirt. His brows rose when he saw the picture on the front of the pattern. Glancing from the picture to the fabric, then to Jessie, he grinned. "Planning on making some curtains, are you?" he teased.

How dare he tease her? Jessie stomped up to him. Grabbing the pattern and the bolt of cloth, she jerked them from his grasp. "It's none of your business what I'm doing," she snapped, her face becoming crimson with embarrassment.

"Aunt Jessie, Aunt Jessie, we're ready for pie," the twins announced, running back outside after depositing their last load.

"Fine, I'll just put this away and cut you some," she said. Not meeting James's gaze, she hurried into the house.

James followed her inside.

Some time later, Jessie sat at the table with Jamie, Jeremy, and James. She'd paid James and now they were all eating the leftover apple pie she'd promised the twins. She'd managed to curb her temper for the boys' sake.

"Do chickens like to swim?" Jeremy asked innocently.

"Do chickens like to what?" Jessie asked. James started to laugh behind his hand. She glanced at him, but he wouldn't meet her eyes.

"Like to swim?" Jamie repeated for his brother.

"Did the chickens tell you that?" she asked.

"The rooster told us," said Jamie.

Jessie lowered one brow. "And what did you do about it?"

The boys exchanged glances. "We took one in the bathtub with us," Jeremy said.

"And?"

"She didn't seem to like it much," Jamie observed solemnly.

Jessie tried not to laugh.

"Especially when I made her dive," added Jeremy thoughtfully.

Jessie couldn't help giggling. She bit her lower lip and tried to look at the boys seriously. "I told you not to believe anything the animals told you without checking with me first."

"We know. But you weren't there," said Jamie, wiping a sugary drip from his chin.

"Yeah, and you live so far away," said Jeremy.

Jessie looked at one tiny face and then the other. She didn't live far from the Triple X at all. In fact, one corner of her property touched Triple X land, but to two little boys it probably seemed like a great distance. "That can't be helped," she told them. "You'll just have to tell your uncle to bring you over to see me more often," she said without thinking.

James felt a warmth spreading through his body at her words. "I can do that," he said softly, his tone dropping playfully.

Jessie's eyes snapped up to meet James's dark gaze. There had definitely been a suggestive note in his voice, and the burning light in his eyes confirmed what she'd heard. She felt her traitorous heart take a leap in speed, but she wanted to tell him he was wasting his time. Clenching her jaw, she glared at him.

"And you should come see us more, too," said Jamie, a little accusation in his voice.

"Yeah," agreed Jeremy.

"You should come every day," said Jamie.

"Yeah," agreed Jeremy once more. "We don't have anyone to play with," he added.

Jessie felt as though she were being ganged up on and it wasn't fair. The twins didn't understand why she couldn't come to the Triple X every day. But she did feel sorry for them. James worked all day every day, and Carmen . . . well Carmen wasn't the playful type. At least she didn't play with children. "I'm sorry boys. I can't come to the Triple X every day, but I'll try to come more often, all right?"

The twins looked at one another and communicated silently. "All right," they agreed in unison. "And we'll have Uncle James bring us all the time."

Jessie let the fire in her green eyes tell James he wasn't welcome. "Yes, well . . . we'll see," she answered.

After the pie was devoured, the boys ran out the front door to play. Jessie instantly felt nervous being alone in her house with James. Rising, she gathered the plates and silverware and set them in the sink, pumping water over them to let them soak.

"Those two are sure a handful," James said, studying Jessie's every move.

"I'm sure they are," she said, pushing down on the pump handle.

"They get into a lot of mischief," he said. "The chicken episode was only one of many this past week."

"I'll bet." Jessie wondered how long he thought he was going to sit there and make small talk.

"I don't know how Tish and Luke handle them all the time," he said.

"I suppose people know what to do with their own children," she commented. The dishes were rinsed and soaking in cool water. There was nothing to keep her at the sink. "You probably have a lot to do at the Triple X so I won't keep you any longer," she said, turning to face him. "Thank you for bringing the cattle—and the boys—and for helping me unload the wagon," she said.

"Thank you for the pie," James said, standing. He then remembered the fabric. "You'll be beautiful in that dress," he told her, his eyes narrowing as he pictured her in the gown. "Something that beautiful must be for a special occasion."

"Not really. I'm not sure I'm even going to the dance," she said, regretting her words the second they left her mouth.

James frowned curiously for a moment. He remembered Carmen had asked him to a dance about a fortnight earlier and he'd turned her down. Was this the dance she meant? It had to be. And now Jessie was thinking about attending? "Carmen mentioned a dance a while ago," he commented, suddenly more interested in the event.

"Yes," Jessie allowed herself the one word. His coyness was just too much.

"You should go, Jessie. I'm sure you'd enjoy yourself." He suddenly decided that if Jessie went, he'd be going.

"I don't know," she said, glancing at the floor. She didn't want to see him at the dance with Carmen, her red dress outshining all the others in the room including her own.

James could tell she wanted to be finished talking but was reluctant to leave. "The place looks a lot better than when you bought it," he commented.

"I've worked hard."

He nodded. "It shows." He looked around again. "You've still got a long way to go, though."

Jessie raised her chin, taking offense at his words. "I'm doing fine," she said shortly.

"I'm sure you are," he assured her.

Jessie remembered he'd predicted she'd fail. She wondered if he still believed it. "I'm going to make it here, James," she said.

James didn't say anything for a moment. He'd delivered cattle to her. He'd seen the repairs she'd already made and the ones in progress. It was true she was working hard, and he found he honestly hoped she'd be a success. He just didn't believe she would. "You probably will," he agreed with her as convincingly as he could.

Jessie heard the doubt in his voice and a small knot of anger grew in her chest. She was about to tell him to go to hell when the door flew open.

"Uncle James! Aunt Jessie!" Jamie ran in yelling. "Jeremy found a beehive!"

"Oh dear!" Jessie said as she ran for the door.

James ran after her, everything else forgotten for the time being.

* * *

"You have to go," urged Val. "If you don't I'll be so disappointed. And what about this fabric. It's too beautiful to waste."

Jessie looked at her friend and sighed. It had been two days since James and the twins had been there, and after she'd gotten over her anger at James, she'd let herself think about the dance. When Val stopped by to see the ranch, she decided to ask her opinion. Val had been insisting she attend since then. "I'm just not sure I want to go," she said.

"But why not? This is one of the biggest events this town has. It started right after you left, and it was so much fun that first year we've been doing it ever since."

"I just feel funny about going. I don't have an escort and I have no one to ask."

"But that's the best part. You'll be so beautiful in this dress, if you ever get it made, that you'll start a regular ruckus."

Jessie couldn't help laughing at her friend. "I don't want to start a ruckus," she said.

"Oh pooh," Val admonished. "Don't tell me it wouldn't do your ego a world of good to have men fighting over you."

"Mrs. Medley thinks it'll more likely be the women doing the fighting."

Val let her head fall back as she started to giggle. "She might be right. Two years ago a couple of girls actually got into a fistfight over one of the young men at the dance. It was so funny."

"Well, I'm certainly not fighting over some man," Jessie announced haughtily.

"Of course not," said Val. "But wouldn't it be funny to watch someone else do it? Please go, Jessie. I want you there."

Jessie sighed. "All right. I'll go. But you have to promise me I can sit with you and Ben all night."

"Certainly, but I doubt if you'll be sitting much."

"I will if I don't ask anyone to dance."

* * *

Hours later, Jessie's dream began with a bright light in her eyes. The light turned into a bonfire with people dancing around it, singing and laughing. She smiled as she watched from a distance. This must be the dance, she thought. Looking down, she saw the green dress, pleased it had turned out so well. Scanning the crowd, she looked for James but couldn't find him. She noticed the fire was getting larger and she could smell the smoke getting stronger and stronger as she watched the people. The circle of dancers grew wider while she observed. Squinting her eyes, she wrinkled her nose against the acrid smoke that was growing more offensive with each passing minute.

Jessie turned in her bed and put her face into her pillow to filter the smoke. Suddenly she was awake. The smoke wasn't in her dream. It was in her room! Jumping from her bed, she looked around frantically, terrified she'd find the room in flames. A glow from outside drew her to the open window. Pushing back the cotton curtains, she peered out into the night. The smoke was thick in the air and she could see flames licking up the side of the pigpen. "Johnny!" she screamed. "Tinker!"

Running from the room, she dashed outside and grabbed a bucket. Filling it from a trough, she ran as fast as she could to the pigpen. She splashed the water over one section of the outside wall and heard it sizzle. "Johnny! Tinker!" she screamed again.

"We're here, Miss. What's happened?" yelled Johnny.

"I don't know. Help me save it," she replied, running back to the trough for more water.

Johnny followed her, picking up another bucket on the way.

Tinker came running with a burlap sack soaked in water and began slapping it against the flames. Again and again he struck at the fire while Jessie and Johnny threw water into the battle. After a bit he let the sack hang limply at his side. "It's no use, Miss Jessie." We can't fight this any more."

Jessie stopped running, a full bucket in her hands. She

could see Tinker was right. The pigpen was a loss. She lowered herself to sit in the dirt. Tears of anger and frustration coursed down her dirty cheeks in white trails. "What happened?" she asked, sniffing.

Johnny sat down beside her and shrugged his shoulders. Tinker shuffled to where they were sitting and sank to the ground. "Somebody set the pigpen on fire," he said between tired gasps.

Jessie looked at him with incredulous eyes. It hadn't occurred to her this fire had been man-made. She'd assumed something natural had caused it. Lightning or . . . She scanned the cloudless skies. "Who would do such a thing?" she asked.

Tinker just raised his shoulders.

"But you said someone set the pigpen on fire," Jessie said, swiping at her tears.

"Couldn't o' started any other way. But I didn't say I knew who done it," answered the old man.

Jessie stared at him for a moment. Maybe he was wrong. Maybe it did start by some natural means. A loud crash startled her into turning her gaze toward the fire. The roof had just fallen in. Sighing, she watched her building burn to ashes. "I guess I'm lucky I had no pigs yet," she said quietly. The thought of innocent animals losing their lives in a fire caused her to cringe and reminded her of the cattle. "How's the herd?" she directed at Johnny.

"They're fine, Miss Jessie. They settled down real good."

"Thank God the fire didn't spook them," she said.

Johnny just nodded.

As the fire burned brightly, Jessie realized she was sitting in the dirt in her nightgown. She'd run from the house so quickly she hadn't even noticed what she was wearing. "I suppose I should go put on my robe," she commented. "I think I'll start a pot of coffee, too. I don't want to go back to bed until this burns itself out. Would you like some?" she offered.

"I could use something a little stronger, Miss Jessie, if you don't mind," said Tinker.

Jessie grinned affectionately at the old man. "I may join you, Tinker. A shot of whiskey in my coffee might just hit the spot." Standing up, she started for the house. "I'll call you when it's ready."

When Jessie entered her room moments later, she began to feel angry again. Why would someone set her pigpen on fire? Gritting her teeth, she splashed water on her face from the basin and washed up as well as she could. Grabbing her robe, she pulled it on as she headed for the kitchen. Dumping the used coffee grounds from dinner into a can to save them for her garden, she poured fresh grounds into the pot and filled it with water. Setting it on the stove, she bent and opened the grate, stirring up the coals to get a fire going, throwing a new log in and closing the grate. All the time she was doing these mundane tasks she was trying to think of who might want to burn her pigpen.

It was a mystery she couldn't solve. No one had anything to gain from causing her a hardship such as this. And that's all this would prove to be, a hardship, albeit a frightening one while the fire burned. A niggling little thought began in the back of her mind and tried to push its way forward. She fought it. She didn't want to think what she was thinking. James wouldn't have set the fire. He didn't want her to fail badly enough to do something so underhanded. He had never actually said he wanted her to fail, only that he thought she would.

Lowering herself onto one of the kitchen chairs, she covered her face with her hands. He wouldn't do it, would he? Her heart pounded with the thought. Did her presence here irritate him so much he'd do something like this? No, she told herself. Absolutely not. James was not the type to be so deceitful and destructive. But did she really know him? She'd met him once when she was twelve, for heaven's sake. How good a judge of character was she at twelve? Her parents trusted him, she argued. But did her parents really know him either? They'd turned over the manager's job of the ranch to him, and he'd apparently done a good job, but he'd obviously always felt he was working toward owning the Triple X himself. He certainly would never have done anything to jeopardize that.

Rubbing her eyes, trying to wipe away these thoughts, she groaned, "And now I show up. A thorn in his side." Sliding her fingers down to cover her mouth, she looked around her small kitchen without actually seeing it. "I made love with this man. This total stranger," she said, her voice strangled in her throat. "I gave him my virginity." Closing her eyes, tears began to slip once more down her cheeks.

"Are you all right, Miss?" asked Johnny a few minutes later.

Jessie looked up, startled. "I didn't hear you two come in," she said, sniffing.

"Do you want to be alone?" asked Tinker.

Jessie quickly wiped her eyes. "No, of course not. Have a seat." She stood up and checked the coffee. "It's done," she announced. Getting three cups, she set them on the table. Then she got the whiskey and poured a good amount in each cup. She poured the coffee on top of that. Seconds later, the hot liquid burned its way down her throat. "This is exactly what I needed," she said hoarsely.

"So, did you think of anyone who might a' done it?" asked Tinker, sipping his brew.

Jessie lowered her eyes. "No, I can't think of a soul who'd do such a thing," she said, not yet ready to point the finger at James, or at anyone else, for that matter. Getting up from the table, she walked outside to stare at the burning building. The flames had died down, licking skyward only occasionally, and brilliant gold and orange embers glowed in the dark. "It sure went up fast," she said softly.

"Sure did."

"Oh! You startled me," she said to Tinker, who'd come up behind her. "I didn't hear you."

"Sorry, Miss Jessie. I just wanted to make sure you was all right. You seemed awful upset 'bout this."

Jessie smiled warmly at him. "Thank you for worrying about me, but I'm fine, really," she said.

"Good. 'Coz me and Johnny was talkin' inside. We think one of us should stand watch at night for a while," he suggested.

"Stand watch?" she said. "But why would—" She stopped, reading Tinker's thoughts. "You think this might happen again?" she asked.

Tinker shrugged. "Probably won't. But it don't hurt to be ready, just in case."

"I suppose you're right," she said. "But I hate to think one of you will be loosing sleep over this. I should be the one to stand watch."

Tinker looked at her with surprise in his eyes. "We couldn't let you do that, Miss Jessie."

Jessie raised her eyebrows. "You can't let me do that? Tinker, I sort of recall that I'm the boss around here," she said in an affectionate tone.

"Yes'm, but you're a gal," he said as if that should explain everything.

Jessie shook her head. This kind of male attitude was something she'd grown up with. She'd dealt harshly with it in her youth, but during her years in Charleston had learned to be patient with the male sex. "I'll make you a deal, Tinker. You and Johnny and I will sleep in shifts, each one of us taking our turn at watch. How does that sound?" she asked.

Tinker rubbed his whiskered chin as he thought about it. "I'm not sure I like it altogether," he finally said.

"I insist," she said firmly. She hated the fact that she agreed they needed a watch. If the person who started the fire had wanted to, he could just as easily have set the house ablaze, and she might not be standing here having this conversation.

"All right," Tinker agreed, nodding. "I'll go tell Johnny. We'll start tonight. I'll take the first watch."

Jessie knew she wouldn't sleep a wink the rest of the

night regardless of which watch she took. "Fine with me," she told him.

Night passed slowly. Jessie lay in bed and listened intently. At first she tried to analyze every sound she heard, and was soon driving herself crazy imagining all sorts of frightening scenarios. When she managed to stop herself from listening to the night sounds, her mind once again went round and round with the possibility that James might have had something to do with the fire. "Damn it, I've got to stop this," she fumed. Sitting up, she stared at the moonlight streaming in through her window. I've got to do something to get my mind off my troubles, she thought. Leaning to the bedside table, she lit a small lamp, blinking as her eyes adjusted to the light.

Swinging her legs off the bed, she reached beneath it and pulled out the green satin fabric and pattern. Opening the pattern package, she turned it over and dumped the papers on the bed. Then, one by one she unfolded them. She could tell the dress was difficult to make, but not so difficult that she thought she couldn't do it. If she took her time and was very careful, the dress might just turn out all right after all.

❈ 8 ❈

It took three days for Jessie, Tinker, and Johnny to rebuild the pigpen. When they were done, Jessie surveyed their work. "Looks great," she said, smiling happily at their accomplishment.

"It does at that," agreed Tinker. Johnny grinned and nodded, wiping sweat from his brow.

"Now I'm going to go buy some pigs," she announced.

"Now?"

"Yes, right now. Well, at least as soon as I go clean up," she told them, turning on her heel toward the house. Once in her room, she eyed the green dress lying in pieces on her bed. She'd been sewing on it every night since the fire. She hadn't been able to sleep much, even when it wasn't her turn to stand watch, and figured she might as well put her insomnia to good use. She was tempted now to pick it up and finish the seam she'd begun the night before, but if she wanted to get to town and back before dinnertime she'd have to get moving.

She'd also done a lot of thinking during those long quiet hours of the night. She couldn't quite believe James had anything to do with starting the fire. He might find her a nuisance and want her to pack it in and go back to Charleston, but she didn't really think he would resort to arson to get her to go. No, she'd nearly

114

convinced herself the fire had to have started by natural causes, though Tinker was adamant that someone had started it.

Stretching and yawning, she picked up a washcloth and began to clean up.

The ride to town was peaceful and a little lonely. Loneliness was a new emotion for her. As a child she'd been so tuned into the animals and nature around her that she'd never felt alone, and she'd had a few friends, such as Val, whom she could call on when the need for companionship arose. Later, in Charleston, she'd rarely been alone. But out here, riding over the stark and quiet terrain of the Texas range, she felt the melancholy of loneliness. "What do you think, Henry?" she asked. "Do you ever get lonely?"

Henry ignored her.

Chuckling slightly, she let her eyes scan the vastness around her. "I'd rather be a little lonely here than surrounded by people in the city. This is so beautiful it sometimes makes me want to cry," she said quietly to the horse. "I still don't know how I allowed myself to become so contented in Charleston. Oh, don't get me wrong, Henry. I had a nice life there, but it wasn't really home. It's strange how it took the sale of the Triple X to remind me how much the land means to me." She took a deep breath and blew it out slowly, her brows knitting into a frown. "The Triple X was always home to me. But it will never be mine again," she whispered, her heart filling with emotion. "I suppose I shouldn't blame James for not wanting to sell it, but I do. If I found out tomorrow that one of the Bakers had returned to town and wanted his family's home back, I'd sell it to him. Home is very important." She flicked the reins over Henry's rump, speeding him up a bit. Mesa City was coming into view.

Jessie asked in town where she needed to go to buy pigs and chickens and was soon guiding her wagon onto the property of a Mr. Hank Webber. "This looks like a prosperous little place," she observed. The house appeared to be wearing a new coat of whitewash, and all the outbuildings were well kept and painted bright red. The yard and grounds were neatly tended, with grass, hedges, and flower beds in abundance. Mature fruit trees grew in straight rows along one side of the house. "Our ranch will look like this some day," she said.

She saw several men working around the place but they looked at her with the indifference of employees. She then noticed a huge dog chained to a tree in the front yard. Three large, clumsy looking puppies played nearby. Pulling Henry to a stop, she jumped from the wagon and studied the canines. "Oh, the puppies are adorable," she crooned. Walking toward them, she watched the mother, making sure she wasn't going to object to a stranger getting close to her offspring. As she neared, the large female rolled to her back and whined to be patted. Jessie laughed. "Some guard dog you are," she mused. "I wonder why they have you chained like this? Do you roam?" She lowered herself to her knees beside the huge, silver-grey animal and began to scratch her furry stomach with both hands. The puppies came bounding over immediately, demanding attention. "Just a minute, you guys. Let your mama have some attention," she said as the puppies tried to lick her face. A low, almost moaning sound of pure pleasure rolled from the female. Jessie giggled in delight.

"What the hell do you think you're doing!"

Jessie started at the cross voice coming toward her. Jumping up, she whirled to see a big, burly man walking toward her. "I'm sorry," she tried.

"You will be sorry if you don't get out of there quick. That wolf is a killer. Why the hell do you think I keep her chained like that?" the angry man demanded.

Jessie blinked several times, then looked down at the gentle animal still lying on her back and whining for attention. "You're talking about her?" she asked incredulously.

"Of course I'm talking about her," he said as he neared.

Jessie looked down at the female again. "But she seems harmless. We were just getting acquainted." The wolf finally gave up her whining and stood up, her back almost reaching Jessie's waist, and leaned into her, putting her head in her hand. "See?" Jessie giggled, scratching her behind one ear.

"Well I'll be damned," the man said as he reached them. Rubbing the top of his bald head, he watched the exchange. "I ain't never seen anything like it. Lady hates everyone but me and my wife, and she only tolerates Matilda because she feeds her. I've had to buy bigger and bigger chains because she keeps breaking them. She nearly killed one of my hands a couple of months ago," he said.

Jessie looked down at the wolf as she continued to pat her. "She doesn't seem so scary to me," she commented.

The man continued to rub his head in bewilderment. "Like I said, I ain't seen nothin' like it." He paused for a moment, then asked. "What can I do for you, little lady?"

Jessie looked at him again. "Are you Mr. Webber?"

"That I am."

"Glad to meet you, Mr. Webber. I'm Jessie Braddock, and I need to buy some pigs and chickens. I heard in town you were the person to see," she said, holding out her hand in friendship.

Webber shook her proffered hand and smiled. "I've got the best pigs in the area," he said proudly. "And chickens, too. I see you brought your wagon. You planning on taking them with you now?"

"If I can."

"You bet. Let's go look at the chickens first."

As Jessie began to walk away from Lady, the wolf started to whine. "It's okay girl, I'll come back and pat you some more before I leave," she promised. "She sure is a sweet thing," she said to Mr. Webber. The man just laughed in disbelief.

As Jessie surveyed the chickens and made her choices she heard Lady crying. While she made her decision over the pigs, she listened to the low whine Lady kept up. "Does she always cry like that?" she finally asked.

Mr. Webber shook his head. "Nope. Usually only when the missus and me go to town. She sure took a liking to you."

Jessie had started to get an idea. "And you say she's usually pretty mean?"

"Mean ain't the word for it."

"Do you ever let her loose?"

"Of course. It wouldn't be right to keep her chained up all the time. She's too much of a wild creature yet. My wife and I have gotten a real kick out of her. She changes color with the seasons, and it's wonderful watching her trying to teach her puppies how to hunt. Some of the little runts are real good at it. Others couldn't care less what she's doing. I suppose it has something to do with who their fathers were. Of course we never know which dog around here sires the litters. Whenever she comes into season she takes off for sometimes two weeks at a time. When she comes home she's half starved and exhausted."

Jessie had been thinking while Mr. Webber talked. "But most of the time she's a good watch dog—or watch wolf," she corrected.

"Lady a watch wolf? I couldn't ask for better."

"You wouldn't happen to be thinking about selling any of those puppies, would you?" she asked.

Mr. Webber started to laugh. "Little lady, I've been trying to get rid of puppies for three months now. We started with a litter of twelve. Those three are all that's left, and I was beginning to think I'd be stuck with the little cusses forever."

Jessie grinned. "How much do you want for them?" she asked.

Mr. Webber continued to laugh. "Nothing. If you take one of them off my hands I'll throw in a sack of food. If you take all three I'll make you my heir," he teased.

Jessie smiled broadly. "I only need one," she said.

"Well it was worth a try," he replied. "You're all set

with the chickens and pigs. I'll have one of my hands load everything up for you. Let's go pick out your puppy."

Jessie practically ran back to the puppies. Now that she was taking one of them she studied them more closely. They were all about the same size, their markings similar in color and design, so she tried to see if there was a difference in personality and temperament. Lowering herself to sit beside Lady, she asked, "May I just sit here until I decide, Mr. Webber?"

"Sure. I'll go tell the missus we're going to have one less mouth to feed around here."

At first all three puppies ran to Jessie, licking her face and biting her hands when she tried to pat them. They seemed nearly identical. After a while one of the puppies lay down next to its mother. Another of the puppies began to torment the first one, chewing on its ears and tail, tugging on its feet, and generally being a nuisance. Jessie giggled at the scene. But it was the third puppy that began to stand out to her. While his siblings were content to play close to their mother, he went off on his own, sniffing everything in sight and biting anything that got in his way. She called him back once, and he came happily enough, but was soon off exploring again. "I think you're the one," Jessie said quietly. "I want a dog that's not afraid of anything. You seem to be headed in that direction."

Standing up, she swiped at the dirt on her backside. Crossing the yard to where her puppy was digging up one of the flower beds, she picked him up and received a short, very tiny growl for her trouble. "Oh yes, you'll do," she told him, burying her face in his soft coat. "You need a bath," she said, wrinkling up her nose. The puppy shook his head as though he understood what she'd said.

"Is that the one?" Mr. Webber asked as he stepped outside onto the porch.

Jessie looked up at him. A small blond woman stood smiling at his side. "Yes, this is him," she answered.

"I'm so glad you're taking that one," said the woman.

"Matilda," scolded Mr. Webber affectionately, "you're going to have Miss Braddock thinking there's something wrong with him."

"There's nothing wrong with him," said the woman. "I'm just tired of him digging up my flower beds."

Jessie laughed. "I don't have any flowers yet, so we're perfect for each other."

"Miss Braddock, this is my wife, Matilda," introduced Mr. Webber.

"I guessed as much," said Jessie. "It's very nice to meet you."

Matilda nodded at her. "It's nice to meet you too, dear. Did my husband give you some dog food for that little guy?"

"Yes ma'am, he did."

"Good, then the only other thing he needs is love, and by the look of the way you're holding him, I think he'll get that."

Jessie had cradled the puppy in her arms like a baby and was absentmindedly patting his soft tummy. She looked down at him. His eyes were glassy and his mouth was open, his little pink tongue hanging out the side. "He looks comfy, doesn't he?"

"He'll get used to that real fast," observed Mr. Webber. He looked past her to her wagon. "Looks like the boys are finished loading for you."

Jessie turned and saw the chicken crates piled on the wagon. The three pigs she'd purchased were tied to the back. Leading them all the way home was going to take some time. "I'd better get going. I still have to make dinner for my hands," she said. "Thank you for everything, Mr. Webber, Mrs. Webber. Especially for this little guy."

"You're very welcome, Miss Braddock. And thank you for taking him," Mr. Webber responded, a twinkle in his eye.

Moments later Jessie settled herself and the puppy in the wagon. "What am I going to name you?" she asked him. "How about Smokey?"

The puppy yapped in response.

Tinker and Johnny met Jessie as she came into the yard some time later. Smokey barked at the strangers. "Good job, boy, but you're barking at the wrong people," Jessie giggled.

"Who's this?" asked Tinker, smiling at the small grey face peering over the side of the wagon.

"This is Smokey," Jessie answered. "And I don't think it'll be too much longer that we have to stand guard at night."

"I think you're right," said Johnny. "Come on, little fella," he crooned, reaching in the wagon to pull him out.

Smokey barked again and tried to bite the hand coming toward him.

"Feisty little guy," said Johnny as he lifted Smokey and brought him to his chest.

"He seems to be. Put him down so he can go exploring his new home," said Jessie with a grin.

Johnny bent to lower Smokey to the ground. As soon as his feet hit the dirt the puppy was off and running, sniffing everything in sight and barking at bugs and leaves.

Jessie, Tinker, and Johnny laughed at his antics the whole time they unloaded the wagon.

The next day Jessie put the final touches on her dress. It had turned out better than she could have hoped and it fit like a glove. When she tried it on for the first time she was a little embarrassed by how low the neckline was, but the color suited her so well she decided no one would probably notice.

The afternoon of the dance she told Johnny and Tinker they were all going to quit work early because she had to get ready.

"I was hoping you'd say that," said Johnny. "I've got to pick up Milly Watson by six thirty. If I don't she might go with someone else."

Jessie looked at Johnny with surprise. "I didn't know you were going to the dance. You never mentioned it."

"Yeah," he said sheepishly. "Milly asked me a long time ago."

"Then I doubt that she'd go with someone else," Jessie assured him.

Johnny shook his head. "You don't know Milly. Gals that pretty don't have to wait around."

"If Milly is even half as smart as Smokey she knows you're worth waiting for. Besides, you're not going to be late. Go on and start getting ready," she said with affectionate gruffness to her voice. She looked at Tinker. "Are you going, too?" she asked, afraid he'd say no.

"Certainly," he answered as though surprised she'd even asked. "Three of the town's matrons asked me, but I turned 'em all down. I want to play the field. Maybe I'll get a couple of them to fight over me," he said.

Jessie laughed and shook her head at the old man. "I'm sure if there's any fighting going on tonight it'll be over you," she said kindly.

Three hours later, Jessie guided Henry through the streets of Mesa City. Many people were out and about and she could hear the musicians tuning up their instruments. Heavenly smells of barbecued meat drifted on the evening air, and the sounds of laughter in the distance filled her heart with gladness. She loved this town and its people.

"Jessie!" squealed Val from not too far away.

"Val!" Jessie called in return. "I was hoping I wouldn't have to look too hard to find you."

"Give me a ride the rest of the way, will you? Ben went with some of the other men to help haul a keg of beer over from the Wagonwheel."

Jessie pulled the wagon to a halt and waited for her friend to climb on board. "Val, you look so pretty," she said, taking in the dark blue dress she was wearing.

Val settled herself in the wagon and turned to face Jessie. "Thank you. Oh my God!" she exclaimed.

"What?" Jessie asked nervously. "What's wrong?"

"Nothing's wrong. You look absolutely gorgeous!" Val gushed.

Jessie looked down at the dress she was wearing. "It did turn out nicely, didn't it?"

"Nicely? Are you kidding? You'll have every man in town falling in love with you. Even my Ben," she added for emphasis.

"I don't think you have to worry much about Ben. He's head over heels in love with you."

"Maybe so, but if he was single I'd have a fight on my hands."

Jessie laughed. "I doubt it," she said.

"I don't. Are you just being modest, or do you really not know how beautiful you are?" asked Val.

Jessie glanced down at the dress again. "I know the dress turned out pretty, though it is a little too low in the neckline."

Val sighed. "It's not just the dress, Jessie. It's you."

Jessie found it hard to believe Val. She'd spent the better part of her life in men's clothes and riding hell-bent for leather across the open range. She usually had more dirt on her than the animal she rode, and she smelled worse, too. Compliments she'd received in recent years were hard to accept as truth. "Thank you," she answered after a moment's hesitation.

Val shook her head. "You don't believe me, do you?"

Jessie just shrugged her shoulders.

"You're impossible," Val admonished. "Oh well, let's get going to the dance. I don't want Ben getting drunk before I can get him out on the dance floor."

Jessie flipped the reins and started them toward the sound of the music.

After parking the wagon and climbing down, Jessie followed Val through the crowd of people in search of Ben. She heard several comments and exclamations over her appearance as they made their way through the throng. Oh dear, she worried, maybe the neckline is too low.

Suddenly, they were no longer surrounded by people. They'd broken through to the wooden dance floor some of the men had built for the event. The floor was lifted off the ground by only about four inches, but it spanned an area of about forty feet by thirty feet. "This is wonderful," commented Jessie.

"Yes. It's bigger than last year. And see, the food tables are on the other side. That's where Ben and the others were going to set up the bar. There he is. Come on," Val said as she grabbed Jessie's arm.

Val pulled her up onto the dance floor. Jessie felt as though she were immediately on display and could feel many pairs of eyes on her. Nervous knots filled her stomach and she felt herself blushing. She definitely didn't like being the center of attention.

"Goodness, who's this?" a young man exclaimed as they neared.

Jessie looked up to see a pleasant face smiling down at her.

"This is Jessie Braddock," offered Ben. "She's a friend of my wife's," he explained. "Jessie, this is Richard Dean."

Richard's eyes narrowed slightly. "You're not Jessie Braddock from the Triple X, are you?" he asked cautiously.

"Yes, I am," she answered. "Or was," she amended.

"Not the Jessie Braddock who snuck into the Rosebud and smoked cigars?"

Jessie nodded, uncertain where this was leading.

"I don't believe it!" he said. "You beat up my little brother," he said with a huge grin of recollection.

Jessie tried to remember the incident he was referring to. She did recall beating up a boy once for kicking her horse. She just couldn't remember his name. "I'm sorry," she said.

Richard threw his head back and laughed out loud. "Don't apologize. The little shit was always doing something he deserved to get beat up for. You were the only person who had the nerve to do it. It's great to see you again, Jessie. And I have to say, you grew up real nice." This last he said with a lower tone to his voice.

"Thank you, Richard. It's nice to see you again, too," she said, though she honestly couldn't remember him from her past.

"May I have the first dance?" he asked.

"Richard, you know this is a switch dance," scolded Val.

"I know it, but if I wait she might ask someone else," Richard complained with a little boy whine.

Jessie laughed. "You may have the first dance," she said.

"Wonderful," he replied, smiling warmly at her.

The dancing began at precisely seven o'clock, and though not everyone had arrived yet, the dance floor was already crowded. "This is quite an event," commented Jessie as she twirled in Richard's arms.

"It's turning out to be. The ladies start asking the men at least two months in advance now," he answered.

"Why aren't you here with a lady?" she asked. "Or is that too personal?" she added, suddenly embarrassed by her question. What if he hadn't been asked by anyone?

Richard laughed when he recognized her expression. "Don't worry, Jessie. I was asked. I gently told the ladies, no thank you. A lot of us single men are doing that now. We still come to the dance and we get asked by a lot of different ladies to dance. It's a lot more fun this way." He pulled her a little closer to him. "If I'd accepted one of the ladies who asked me to the dance I wouldn't have been able to dance with you now," he said quietly down to her.

Jessie felt a short tingle of alarm shoot through her. She liked Richard, at least what little she knew of him, but she didn't want him getting any ideas about her. She wasn't interested in getting involved with anyone. She hadn't recovered emotionally from the mistake she'd made with James yet. She wasn't about to repeat her mistake with someone else.

By eight o'clock Jessie had danced every dance and

was already feeling tired. "I'm sorry, I've got to sit this one out," she apologized to yet another pursuer.

"I told you you wouldn't be sitting with Ben and me all evening," said Val beside her.

"I guess you were right. I didn't know there were this many single men living in Mesa City," she said. "Come on, let's sit down for a few minutes." She led the way to a bench just beyond the food table. As Jessie lowered herself to the bench she heard Val laughing. "What's so funny?"

"Some of the men you danced with weren't single."

"What?" Jessie's eyes opened wide in shock.

"Nope. Jim Field's wife is back East visiting her sister. And Wes's wife is at home, probably delivering their sixth child as we speak."

"The cads!" Jessie exclaimed. "Especially that Wes person!"

Val nodded. "Don't worry. Their wives will hear about them being here. Nothing happens in a small town that isn't eventually learned by everyone. They'll get their just desserts, wait and see."

"I hope so," groused Jessie. Another man bent toward her at that moment and begged for a dance. Jessie looked curiously at Val. "Is he?" she asked.

"He's single," Val answered.

James stood outside his house and looked at his pocket watch for at least the tenth time in as many minutes. Pacing back and forth, he fumed in frustration. "Damn it," he muttered. How had he allowed himself to be talked into giving Carmen a ride to the dance? He knew the answer. Her father had asked him. But why the hell was she so damned late? Looking at his watch again, he stomped down the porch steps and climbed into the wagon. "This is it, Carmen! I'm leaving now with or without you!" he shouted at the house.

He squinted at the house in frustration. Carmen hadn't yet moved her things out of the house. She continued to act as though he hadn't fired her, and he was loath to cause a scene by throwing her out bodily. He'd gone ahead and found a woman to replace her, a sweet, mature widow who needed the job, but he hadn't been able to let her move in yet because of Carmen. "Good-bye!" he yelled and flicked the reins to start his team on their way.

"Wait!" shouted Carmen, emerging from the house in a red flurry. "I'm ready," she said loudly. "What do you think?" She stopped on the porch and struck a seductive pose, her hands on her hips, her breasts jutting forward.

James raised his eyebrows. He had to admit she was beautiful. The red satin dress she'd made showed off her assets to their best advantage. It was so tight he was surprised she could breathe. The neckline of the gown drooped so far he thought her breasts might fall out if she moved wrong, and the skirt was slit nearly to her hip on one side, showing off her long legs. Yes, she was beautiful, but she didn't even pique his interest. He couldn't wait to get to the dance to see Jessie. "Come on!" he said crossly.

Carmen frowned at him and flounced down the stairs. "I need help up into the wagon," she complained.

James closed his eyes and counted to ten. Then, jumping from the wagon, he went around to her side and gave her his hand.

"That won't do, James. This dress is a little tight," she explained.

"What do you want me to do about it?" he asked.

"Lift me?" she replied.

Sighing heavily, he bent over and put one arm beneath her thighs, the other behind her back, and lifted. As she left the ground she wound her arms around his neck. "Damn it, Carmen, stop it," he told her angrily.

"I'm not doing anything," she said innocently.

Sighing again, he deposited her on the wagon seat. Why couldn't she get it through her head that he wanted nothing to do with her, that if he had, in fact, had sex with her, well, he just couldn't remember it. Walking around to the other side of the wagon, he once more climbed up onto the seat. He snapped the reins, and they were immediately on their way. He only hoped Jessie would still be at the dance when he arrived. He grimaced at his own foolishness. Jessie wanted nothing to do with him.

"Will you dance with me, James?" Carmen asked, leaning toward him.

James glanced at her. His initial urge was to give a flat no to her question. He didn't want to dance with her. He didn't want to be seen with her. But he didn't want her to cause a scene either, and he thought she might if he denied her completely. "I suppose I'll dance with you once," he agreed reluctantly.

"Only once?" she pouted.

"I don't know Carmen. We'll see how the evening goes, all right?" he asked.

Carmen gave him a sidelong glance. Yes, we'll see how the evening goes, she thought. Before this night was through she was determined to end up in James's bed.

Jessie sipped a glass of punch Ben had given her. "Having fun," he asked.

She nodded and swallowed. "More than I thought I would," she admitted. Sometime during the preceding hour she'd realized James and Carmen weren't showing up after all. A sense of relief had washed over her and she'd begun to enjoy herself even more. Many men had asked her to dance, and she'd seen Johnny and Tinker sweeping across the dance floor, their respective ladies in their arms. "Why don't you go ask your wife to dance?" she suggested.

"Because she told me to let her toes rest for a minute," he responded. "Would you like to dance?"

Jessie glanced toward Val and saw her nod in her direction. "I'd love to," she answered. "Are you really that hard on toes?" she asked, teasing.

Jessie let herself be turned in time to the music and felt like laughing. Ben was a wonderful dancer, leading her expertly across the floor. She closed her eyes for a moment, allowing Ben's arms and the music to guide her. When she opened them, the first thing she saw caused her to stumble, tripping over Ben's feet.

"Excuse me, Jessie. Are you all right?" Ben quickly asked, taking the blame for her slip.

"I'm fine, Ben. It was my fault. But do you mind if we sit the rest of this dance out?" she asked.

"Of course not. Is something wrong? You don't look well," he said, concern in his voice.

"I'm perfectly fine," she answered. "I just need to sit down for a moment." As she crossed the floor to reach the bench where Val waited she couldn't get the picture of James and Carmen out of her mind. They were beside his wagon and she was in his arms.

❊ 9 ❊

"What's wrong, Jessie?" asked Val with concern. "You look like you've seen a ghost."

Jessie couldn't explain why she was so affected by the sight of James and Carmen in one another's arms. She didn't understand it herself. She only knew a feeling of intense anger had pounded through her system when she saw them. "I just tripped over Ben's feet," she said.

Val studied her friend's face. "Are you sure?" she tried again.

"Positive," assured Jessie. She let her eyes scan the dancers, trying to see past them to where she'd seen James and Carmen. How could he be so careless about what his neighbors thought of his behavior? How could he put himself on display like that? Her eyes caught the flash of red satin on the far side of the dance floor. Following the brilliant color, she soon saw James guiding Carmen in a waltz. Turning quickly away, she looked at Val. "I could use a drink. How about you?" she asked.

Val raised her eyebrows. "Do you mean another glass of punch?" she asked.

"No, I mean a drink," she said.

"Do you drink, Jessie?" Val asked, her eyes wide with surprise.

Jessie let her eyes fall for a second, then raised them

again to look at her friend. "Well, not often, but I think this is the perfect time to have one," she said.

"Have one what?" asked Ben, returning from getting himself another beer.

"Jessie just told me she'd like a drink," Val said, incredulously.

Ben looked down on the two woman with surprise. "What would you like, Jessie?" he asked after a few seconds of silence.

Jessie thought about it. "I don't know, whiskey maybe. I'll leave it up to you. Just please bring me a drink of something strong," she said.

"You've got it," said Ben, turning to head back toward the bar.

"Are you sure about this, Jessie?" asked Val. "What's come over you?"

"I don't know," she answered honestly.

Ben returned in a few minutes with a short glass, amber liquid filling the bottom. "Whiskey, neat," he said as he handed Jessie the glass.

Jessie took it and sniffed the liquid. She'd had a small amount of whiskey in her coffee before, but she'd never drunk it straight.

"You don't have to do this," said Val.

"I want to," Jessie answered. Tipping the glass to her lips, she leaned her head back and let the whiskey fill her mouth. With one swallow it was gone. Then the fire hit. Her eyes began to water and her throat burned. "Oh— my—goodness!" she gasped between choking coughs.

Ben quickly took the glass from her hand and replaced it with a large one of water. "I figured you'd need this," he laughed.

Jessie gratefully accepted the water and immediately took a huge gulp of the cooling liquid.

Val looked on in concern. Something had happened that affected Jessie strongly. She just wished she knew what it was.

After a few large swallows of water, the burn in Jessie's throat began to cool. When it did she began to laugh. "I guess that was a pretty stupid thing to do," she said, wiping her eyes. "It's a lot stronger that way than in a cup of coffee."

Val was relieved to see Jessie returning to her old self. She started to chuckle. "I guess so," she agreed. "Why did you do it?" she asked.

Jessie shrugged her shoulders. "I don't even know myself," she replied. "Have you ever tried it?"

Val nodded. "On my wedding night. Ben insisted I have a few drinks to calm my nerves. Instead of calming me down it made me silly. I couldn't stop laughing, which did nothing for his mood, if you know what I mean, and we didn't . . . you know . . . for several days."

"Days?"

"I had a terrible hangover," Val clarified.

Jessie grinned at her friend. "How dreadful for you," she commiserated. "But I doubt if one drink is going to give me a hangover," she commented. "I doubt I'll even feel it," she added.

"You might be surprised," warned Val. "I know I felt the first one. If Ben hadn't made me drink several more our wedding night might have proved to be exactly what he'd wanted it to be. Besides, you've had punch, too."

Jessie listened to Val with a slight feeling of concern. Would she suddenly feel the alcohol? Then shaking herself mentally, she decided she wouldn't worry about it. It couldn't possibly affect her that much.

Several minutes later Jessie felt a warmth spreading through her limbs, and it seemed the colors of the evening were more intense and the music more beautiful.

James led Carmen off the dance floor. "I'm going to sit out several. Why don't you go ask someone else to dance?" he suggested.

Carmen looped her arm through James's. "I'll wait until you're ready again," she cooed.

James disentangled their arms. "That may be a while,"

he said. He'd danced with her once. That was enough. He thought he'd caught a glimpse of Jessie on the other side of the dance floor and he wanted to go find her. He couldn't do that with Carmen hanging all over him.

He thought about the stunt she'd pulled as he'd lifted her out of the wagon and frowned. Did she think he was an idiot? Did she really expect him to believe she'd slipped and conveniently ended up in his arms? He remembered the curious expressions on several of his neighbors' faces. He didn't want people thinking he and Carmen were involved in a relationship. "I'm going to go get a drink. I'll see you later."

"I'll go with you," she said quickly, falling into step beside him, once more looping her arm through his.

James's anger took a jump upward. Pulling away, he looked down on her. "Carmen, I am not your escort. I merely gave you a ride here. I see several of my friends at the bar and I'm going to go say hello to them and I'm going without you," he said firmly.

Carmen raised her chin angrily. "I did not think of you as my escort, simply as my friend. But if it's too much trouble for you to spend a few minutes with me while I search out some other friends, then go ahead and leave." She allowed her eyes to fill with tears as she spoke. She knew she'd have him again before the night was over.

James sighed. His anger was still warming him. He didn't want to spend time with her, but he didn't want to make her cry either. "All right, you can come with me to the bar," he gave in.

Carmen smiled beautifully at him. "You are a good man, James," she said, placing her hand on his arm.

He sighed. He didn't feel like a good man. He felt like a fool.

The bar was crowded with men, most of whom James knew well, and **who** said hello as he approached. All of them looked at Carmen with thinly veiled lust in their eyes. Her dress was so revealing and her demeanor so sensual that they couldn't help noticing her. Several raised their eyebrows at the way she was leaning into James, and he wished he'd been more adamant about her leaving him alone. "I'll have a whiskey, Pete," James said to the man behind the bar.

"And for the lady?" Pete asked.

"I wouldn't know. You'll have to ask her yourself," James responded rudely, his anger beginning to get the better of him.

Pete's face showed his surprise at James's words. "Yes, well," he stammered.

"Darling, you know I only drink red wine," Carmen scolded affectionately, laying her hand flat over James's chest.

James stood up straighter, pulling away from her slightly. "How would I know that?" he asked her.

Carmen laughed a deep, throaty rumble that brought even more attention from the people around them. Without responding to James's question she turned to Pete. "Do all men forget their ladies' drinks?" she asked, favoring him with a stunning smile.

"I . . . ah . . . A lot of them do," Pete answered, stumbling over his words.

"What a shame," she responded, still smiling.

James was speechless, mostly by choice. If he'd said what he was thinking he'd have definitely caused a scene. Watching while Pete poured Carmen's wine first, he waited for the opportunity to leave the bar. While he waited he noticed a flash of light green satin not far from him. Narrowing his eyes, he moved a bit to get a better view. It was Jessie. And she looked more beautiful than he'd have thought possible. At that moment he heard someone mention her name.

"I swear it's Jessie Braddock," said a voice behind him.

"It can't be. I remember Jessie. She was a dirty faced little brat," said another voice.

"Well, it's her all right. Ben Richards introduced me when I asked her to dance," said the first voice.

"Do tell," the second voice responded. "And you say

she came to the dance alone and is dancing with whoever asks her?"

"She danced with me."

"How did she feel?"

"Pretty damn good. She's so small it's easy to pull her close, and the view from above is something else. She's got great tits."

"That's for me. I'm going to go ask her to dance myself."

"You'll be getting in line."

"I can wait."

James felt himself getting stiff with rage. How dare those bastards talk that way about Jessie? Turning around, he tried to see who'd been doing the talking. His fists were clenched and ready to smash someone's face. But when he turned around he saw several men behind him and didn't know who'd been involved in the conversation. Looking toward Jessie, he watched for someone to approach her. "Damn," he fumed when three men walked up to her at the same time. He couldn't beat up everyone in hopes he'd gotten the right one.

"Your drink, James," Carmen said, holding a glass out to him.

Taking the drink from her, he knocked it back in one swallow. "I'll have another, Pete," he said gruffly.

Carmen smiled, a sly, self-satisfied turn of her lips. The more James drank, the easier it would be to end up in his bed.

Jessie looked up at the handsome face smiling down at her. "Marco?" she said, recognizing Carmen's brother.

"Yes, Miss Braddock, it's me. I was hoping to have the honor of this dance," he said, grinning down at her, his startlingly white teeth in sharp contrast with the dark tan of his skin. He held out his hand to her.

Jessie smiled in return and lifted her hand to his. "I'd be delighted," she answered, standing. As she stood, she felt a wave of dizziness wash over her. "Oh my," she breathed.

"Are you all right?" Marco asked, concern knitting his black brows.

Jessie took a deep breath. "I'm fine," she said. "I think I had a little too much to drink," she admitted.

Marco laughed delightedly. "Then you need this dance," he teased. "And you are lucky it's to be with me."

"Oh really?" Jessie asked.

"Yes, because I am the best dancer here, and I'll not step on your pretty feet if you stumble." He leaned a little closer to her and whispered, "And I would not mind holding you up if it becomes necessary."

"I'm sure it won't become necessary," she answered.

Marco touched his heart. "How sad for me," he told her.

Jessie giggled at his manner. He was so young, about seventeen she'd guess, yet so charming. Some day his charm would prove to be quite lethal, she was sure, but for now she saw only the boy standing before her. "Shall we?" she directed.

Marco bowed low, then led her out onto the dance floor.

Once in Marco's arms, she had to admit he was, indeed, an accomplished dancer. "Where did you learn to dance like this?" she asked as he led her through a series of intricate steps.

A small cloud of emotion crossed Marco's face. "From my mother. She was a wonderful dancer," he answered.

"Was?" she asked gently.

"She died several years ago," he responded.

"I'm so sorry, Marco."

"It's all right. We were very close, so I feel grateful for her life. I don't feel cheated by her death."

Jessie thought about his words. "What a wonderful sentiment," she said. "I adore my own mother, but there have been times when I've wished we were closer," she said introspectively.

"You are not close to your mother?"

Jessie didn't know how to explain her feelings. "I'm

close to her in some ways. She and my father sent me to Charleston when I was younger. They thought it was in my best interests, but—"

"It wasn't," he said.

"I learned a lot, but looking around me now, I think I also lost a lot."

"And your mother doesn't understand this?"

"She doesn't even know it."

"You have not told her?"

"I've tried." Jessie suddenly shook her head. "Let's not ruin the dance with this kind of talk. I'm here now, and that's what matters," she said, smiling up at him.

"You are right. This is a time for gaiety. Hold on," he warned, grinning as he began to turn her round and round.

Jessie threw back her head and laughed as she felt the dizzying effects of the whiskey and the dance taking hold of her.

Carmen seethed at the side of the dance floor as she watched her little brother dancing with the woman she hated so much. He knew how she felt about the gringa. How could he be such a traitor? He was going to have to pay for his disloyalty. She then heard James's deep intake of air and looked up to see what was wrong. The direction of his gaze brought jealous fire to beat beneath her breasts.

James's eyes were focused on Jessie. He watched as she spun around the dance floor in Marco's arms, the green satin of her gown emphasizing the shape of her legs as she moved. Narrowing his eyes, he felt a heat below his belt and cursed under his breath.

"Dance with me, James?" Carmen asked, her voice soft and pleading.

James tore his eyes from Jessie and stared down at Carmen. She hadn't left his side since they'd arrived and it didn't look as if she was going to unless he did something just short of picking her up and throwing her into a horse trough. Appealing as the idea was, it wasn't something he could do. Glancing briefly back at Jessie, he suddenly got another idea. "Yes, Carmen, I'd like very much to dance," he responded.

Carmen was surprised when James gave in so easily. Perhaps her plans would come to fruition without as much resistance as she'd thought. Linking her arm with his, she smiled up at him.

James led Carmen out onto the dance floor. Taking her in his arms, he began to turn her around, maneuvering his way across the floor. It took several minutes to accomplish the trip, but soon they were dancing next to Jessie and Marco.

Jessie saw James and Carmen dancing toward her and felt a swell of anger once more in her chest. Carmen danced as close to James as she could, her breasts touching the front of his shirt, her long legs practically tangling with his. "Disgusting," she muttered.

"Yes?" Marco asked, not hearing her word.

"It's nothing important," Jessie responded.

"Marco, Jessie, what a nice surprise," James said when they were close enough to start a conversation.

Marco stopped dancing and bowed to his boss. "Good evening, Mr. Bonner. Carmen."

Carmen glared at her brother, then pinpointed Jessie with her angry stare.

Jessie raised her chin and met Carmen's glare with one of her own.

"Are you two having fun tonight?" James asked.

"Yes, sir," responded Marco.

James looked expectantly at Jessie, waiting for a reply.

Jessie moved her glare from Carmen to him. "Marco is a delightful partner," she responded coolly. "He's a wonderful dancer."

"So I see. Carmen is very good also. I'll bet it'd be something to see the two of them dancing together. Here," he said, handing Carmen over to her brother before she could protest.

"I . . . Certainly, Mr. Bonner," said a very startled Marco.

"But I don't—" sputtered Carmen, suddenly aware that this had been James's plan from the start.

"Carmen," warned Marco.

"Fine," she said through clenched teeth. Now she'd have to work all the harder to get James where she wanted him. Narrowing her eyes, she let her brother lead her into a dance.

Jessie watched them go. They did dance beautifully together, but she had no intention of standing in the middle of the dance floor as Carmen drew a crowd of observers. She began to turn away from the sight, intent on going back to where Val and Ben were sitting, when she felt James's strong hand on her arm. "Shall we?" he asked, drawing her to him.

Trying to pull away from James was no use. He was too strong, and apparently determined to dance with her. Jessie looked up at him. "You know I don't want to dance with you," she stated flatly.

"I know that," he responded, looking down into her beautiful green eyes.

"Then why do this? You'll only upset Carmen," she said.

James glanced in Carmen's direction and shrugged. "It doesn't matter."

Jessie felt her emotions take a dive. How could he be so cold about hurting someone's feelings? Granted, she didn't like Carmen, but no one deserved to be treated so callously. She remembered how he'd made love with her while being involved with Carmen. He obviously fought no moral battles within himself. "If you'll excuse me?" she said, trying to free herself from his arms. She clenched her jaw and refused to look at him when he wouldn't release her.

James held on tightly to her. He'd been wanting to dance with her since he'd arrived and he wasn't giving her up so soon, especially not when holding her was wreaking such a wonderful havoc in his system. His hands felt on fire where he touched her. His pulse rate had gone through the roof, and the sensation of fullness between his legs was making him crazy. Letting his eyes study the beauty of her face, he remembered the way she'd opened for him and wanted to feel the softness of her kiss again. He knew the dance floor wasn't the place for it, but, he promised himself, soon. He lowered his gaze to her throat and her chest, then lower, to the firm swelling of her breasts above the neckline of her gown. He discovered the words the men had spoken near the bar were true. With only a slight adjustment of his position he could look down the front of her bodice, glimpsing the rosy color of a softly protruding nipple. He felt a swift and shocking surge of blood to his manhood. Taking a deep breath, he tried to cool the fire that raged out of control in his body.

Jessie heard James's swift intake of air and looked angrily up at his face. When her eyes met his she was stunned by the amount of emotion she saw there. Raw passion burned in his dark eyes, stark and real. Her own breathing became erratic and she felt a momentary fear of him. She missed a dance step and was pulled more tightly against him. Her heart rushed blood to her most tender parts. She felt the pulsing between her legs and in her nipples. A blush colored her creamy complexion. "James, please let me go," she said breathlessly.

"The dance is almost over," he told her. He was mesmerized by the pink glow that had touched her skin. He could see she was breathing more deeply and could feel the hardened buds of her nipples against his chest. She was just as aroused as he was, and the realization made him bold. Lowering his head, he touched her hairline with the tip of his tongue, tasting the sweet sheen of perspiration that glistened there.

Jessie was stunned by the feel of James's tongue on her skin. Stumbling again, she was grateful that the music had stopped. Straightening herself, she pushed her way out of his arms and began a retreat back to the safety of Val and Ben's company.

"Jessie," James called after her, only to be ignored.

Pushing his fists into his pockets, he headed toward the bar.

"What's wrong?" asked Val as Jessie neared.

Jessie couldn't explain to her friend that James Bonner had tried to seduce her on the dance floor. "I think you were right about that whiskey," she lied. "I'm feeling quite flushed."

Val giggled. "I told you so. You do look a little red. Should I get you anything?" she asked.

"No. I'll just sit here and rest for a while," she said. "I think I'm about ready to go home, anyway."

"May I dance with my beautiful wife?" asked Ben.

Val gave her husband a wide smile. "I'd love to dance with my handsome husband," she said. She glanced quickly at Jessie. "Will you be all right alone?"

Jessie waved her hands at her friends. "I'm fine. You two go have fun," she urged and winked at Val. A second later she watched as they danced away. Sighing, she closed her eyes and tried to stop the turmoil in her heart.

"May I have this dance?"

Jessie opened her eyes and looked up. A strange face leered down on her. "I'm sorry. I'm feeling a little indisposed," she apologized. "Perhaps later." She smiled weakly.

"Sure. That'd be fine," the man said.

As he left, Jessie saw another potential dance partner heading her way. She had to get away from this for a while. Standing, she walked around the bench and past the food tables. Moments later she was passing the outhouse behind the church. There was a long line of people waiting to use it and she walked on beyond them into the dark.

James had swallowed another strong drink of whiskey and was arguing with himself over the folly of pursuing Jessie when she so obviously wanted nothing to do with him. Then why does she get so hot and responsive when I touch her? he asked himself. Why did she give me her virginity? Because she wants the Triple X, but that doesn't explain why she breaks out in a sweat whenever

I'm close to her, he justified. You're a fool, he told himself. "I know it," he said aloud.

"What's that, Mr. Bonner?" Pete asked.

"Nothing, Pete. Just a fool talking to a fool," he answered. Pushing himself from the bar, he headed toward the outhouse. He needed to relieve himself.

The path to the outhouse was short, the waiting line was long. There was no way he could wait that long. The whiskey he'd drunk had begun to go through him and he needed to remedy the situation now. Looking into the darkness beyond the outhouse, he decided a tree would work just as well. Passing the tiny structure, he walked out into the night.

Jessie had found a tree stump and was seated comfortably, letting soft moonlight wash over her, relaxing her. Gazing skyward, she was surprised to see a full moon gleaming down on her. The lamps and lanterns at the dance had drowned out the moonlight completely. But out here in the dark, away from the brightness of the party, she reveled in the silver glow from above. "A Texas moon," she breathed.

James walked a good distance from the crowd of people at the dance before he opened the front of his trousers and relieved himself. He wasn't particularly modest, he just didn't want to frighten anyone who might have had the same idea he'd had about avoiding the long line at the outhouse. Once finished, he refastened his trousers and began to walk slowly back to the dance. He wasn't in any hurry. Jessie was angry with him. Carmen would track him down again, he was sure. And it was peaceful out here.

Carmen stared off into the dark. She'd given Marco a good piece of her mind, then started looking for James again. She'd seen him walk out this way. She would wait a little while for him, but if he didn't come back soon, she'd go out and find him.

James wandered through the darkness in an indirect route toward the dance. The night air had cooled and the moon turned the surrounding landmarks a soft, silvery grey. His nerves began to calm and he took deep, cleansing breaths as he walked. He smiled as he listened to the sounds around him: the breeze through the treetops nearby, the chitter of some tiny night creature, the twigs snapping beneath his feet.

Jessie heard someone, or something, coming through the darkness toward her. Standing, she waited, poised to flee should she be in danger. After a few seconds, she saw the gray outline of a man walking toward her. "Who's there?" she called.

James stopped in mid stride. "Jessie?" he asked, all his senses once more coming to life. "Is that you?"

Jessie felt her stomach drop. "Did you follow me out here?" she demanded, putting her hands on her hips.

"No. I came out here because the line to the outhouse was too long. I was just heading back," he explained honestly.

"Oh. All right. Well, you can just keep going. I want to be alone," she said firmly.

James glanced around them. They were indeed alone. Stepping closer to her, he tried to read her expression but realized the moon had slipped behind a small cloud. "Are you sure you want to be all alone, Jessie?" he asked softly.

Jessie backed up a step. "I'm sure," she replied, her pulse racing wildly. James had an effect on her that wasn't fair. Even when her common sense screamed out a warning against him she felt drawn to him. Even while dancing with him, her anger about his crude, boorish behavior couldn't stop the desire from rolling over her like a great wave. And now, while she was able to tell him to leave, her heart was going crazy and she felt her body readying itself for lovemaking. "Please go," she told him, her voice coming out thick with emotion.

James couldn't let this opportunity pass by. He knew what he wanted was wrong, but since he'd made love to her beside Leaver Creek he had found himself thinking of her more and more often. Stepping closer still, he reached out to her with both hands. Taking her by the waist, he pulled her to him, his lips covering her passionately. The sudden contact of his body with hers made everything else around them disappear.

Jessie knew she was lost the second James touched her. Her mouth opened to his kiss and her arms went around his neck of their own accord. The heat in his body was so intense she was consumed by it, lost in the swirling, molten sea of desire that was James.

❃ 10 ❃

Carmen folded her arms angrily across her chest. She studied the people coming back from the outhouse. James wasn't among them. What was he up to? she wondered. A feeling of suspicion wormed its way through her. Turning back toward the dance, she began to scan the crowd, looking for a green satin dress.

James reveled in the feeling of Jessie's sweet lips under his. He caressed her waist, her back, her buttocks, pulling her closer to him with each passing second. Tilting his hips forward, he pressed his arousal into her abdomen, wanting her to feel what she did to him.

Jessie couldn't think, could barely breathe, and felt as though she was caught in a sensual tidal wave. She was being touched by James everywhere at the same time. She formed her body to his, to the length and strength of his manhood, huge in its desire. She shivered as she remembered how it filled her, and she felt empty, anticipating what was to come.

James lifted his head and looked down into Jessie's fiery green eyes. She was the most beautiful woman he'd ever known, and to possess her now was what he needed. Reaching up with his hands, he found the full globes of her breasts and covered them with his palms, massaging them firmly, bringing them together in his grasp. Letting his head fall forward, he nuzzled her deep cleavage. Her heavenly scent was an aphrodisiac to him, and he let his tongue trace the curve of one breast and then the other. He heard her gasp at this touch and felt his manhood jerk and pulse against her in response. Finding the edge of her neckline, he tugged it downward, freeing her breasts completely to his view, letting the jutting peaks of her passion-hardened nipples point upward to him as though begging for his attention. He bent his head and kissed the smooth skin of her throat, then began a slow and languorous journey of wet exploration downward. When he reached the peak of one breast, he sucked it into his mouth almost roughly, taking it deeply, rubbing it with the tip of his tongue.

Jessie groaned and arched upward to meet James's kisses. She reached up and grasped the underside of her breasts and lifted them to his mouth. He responded by removing one of her hands and guided it to cover the head of his throbbing manhood. Touching it was like touching white-hot coals and she shuddered as she began to stroke him.

James rocked his hips, moving his erection against Jessie's hand in a motion he would soon repeat within her body. Groaning against her flesh, he shuddered, biting down on the soft skin of her breast.

Jessie shivered and cried out as James branded her. He'd bitten her gently, but with enough pressure to mark the white skin over her breast. Closing her eyes, her breaths came quickly and she increased the pressure and rhythm over his engorged manhood.

Carmen stomped around the perimeter of the dance floor. James was still missing and so was that little bitch, Jessie. "I'll show them they can't do this to me," she muttered. Storming out toward the outhouse, she passed people without even seeing them. She was going to find James if it was the last thing she did.

Jessie was getting weak with desire. She needed to feel James inside her. She needed to explode from within as he rocked against her. Moving her hand from his erection, she reached behind him and pulled him close again. "James," she moaned her need.

James was nearly mad with wanting her. Sliding his hand down between them, he found the V of her legs and pressed his palm over her, cupping the mound of moist heat he needed so desperately.

"I knew it!" Carmen screamed. "I knew I'd find you with her!"

James raised his head at the sound of Carmen's hysterical voice. "Oh God," he moaned, his desire falling like his manhood.

Jessie turned her head and saw the furious woman standing not five feet from them, her teeth bared in a feral snarl. "Oh Lord," she echoed James. Pushing away from him, she tugged on the bodice of her gown, trying to pull it into place.

"Don't bother," Carmen spat. "You've already shown the world what you've got. Don't try to be modest now!"

James saw Jessie's dilemma and moved to stand in front of her, shielding her while she put herself back together. "What are you doing here?" he demanded of Carmen.

"What am I doing here? You have a lot of nerve asking me that when you're the one in the wrong. As soon as my back was turned you took off after this little slut."

James narrowed his eyes dangerously. "Be careful what you say, Carmen. You have no right to call anyone names."

Carmen burst into tears. "I know you think so, but," she sobbed, "how can I help how I feel when you made love to me the way you did? What am I to think?"

Jessie closed her eyes and clenched her teeth in disgust. She didn't want to hear this. She didn't want to be a part of a lovers' triangle. Now that her ardor had been so effectively cooled and she was thinking more clearly, she wanted to shoot herself for giving into James's brand of seduction, again. "I'm going home," she announced loudly. She pushed past James and didn't give Carmen a glance as she left.

"Wait, Jessie," James called after her, but he saw that he was being ignored. He turned his eyes back to Carmen, still sobbing in front of him. His blood ran cold at the sight of her. "You had no right to do that," he said in a menacing tone.

"I had every right. I love you, James. I know you don't love me, but you should at least consider my feelings. I came to this dance with you. What would people say if they found out you were out here screwing that little whore?"

James took a threatening step toward her. "If you ever call Jessie a name like that again I'll—"

Carmen raised her chin. "Go ahead, hit me. I don't care," she said.

James sighed in disgust. "I won't hit you, and you know it. Though it's exactly what you deserve. I'm going home now. Alone. You can get a ride from Marco."

"But Marco rode his horse," she complained. "I can't very well ride a horse in this dress."

"Then I'll take Marco's horse and he can take you home in the wagon," he said.

"You bastard," she cursed him. "You'll regret this, I promise you."

James ignored her threat and walked away. He was suddenly very tired. Once back at the dance, he found Marco easily and told him of the change. He scanned the crowd once to see if he could find Jessie, but she was nowhere to be seen. Moments later he was spurring his mount to a gallop, determined to get home quickly.

Jessie wiped her face with a damp towel Val had found for her.

"That whiskey really got to you, didn't it?" questioned Val.

Jessie nodded. When she came back looking so upset and disheveled she'd had to come up with an excuse. She'd lied and said she was ill, that she'd vomited her dinner and had waited until she felt better to return to the party. Val had whisked her into the church through a back door and made her lie down on one of the pews. "I didn't know anything could affect me so," she answered, thinking about James.

"Well, you just lie here for a few more minutes, then Ben and I will see you get home safe."

Jessie looked up startled. "I can't let you and Ben take me home. It's too far. It's too much of an inconvenience."

"I won't let you go home alone. Not ill like you are," insisted Val.

"But—"

"I know. You can come home with us for tonight," Val interrupted.

"I couldn't." Jessie tried to protest. She'd gotten herself into this, now all she wanted to do was go home and lick her wounds.

"I insist," Val said. "And I know Ben will feel the same. You stay here for a while longer and I'll go tell him."

"But—" Jessie watched her friend hustle out of the church and fell back against the seat. How had she gotten herself into this? "Damn," she whispered. Then, glancing at the cross over the pulpit, she bit her lower lip. "Sorry," she said looking upward.

After a few minutes passed, she didn't want to remain in the church alone. There was no reason for it. She wasn't, in fact, ill. Taking the damp cloth with her, she stood up and left the church. Placing the cloth on a bench just outside the door, she looked around. She could see the crowd was beginning to thin out a bit, and was grateful the evening was at an end.

"You think you'll get James and the ranch just because he has sex with you," said Carmen from the shadows beside the church.

Jessie whirled around, looking for Carmen. "Where are you?"

"I'm here," Carmen replied, stepping out into the light. "Don't think that because James went home without me that I won't be in his bed tonight," she added.

Jessie felt a tightening in her gut. "I don't care what you and James do," she said.

"Hah! You think you'll convince him to sell you the Triple X by giving him sex."

"I've never thought that," denied Jessie.

"Then you think he'll marry you and the ranch will be yours that way."

Jessie actually laughed out loud at the wild suggestion.

"Don't laugh at me, slut!" said Carmen.

Jessie's eyes narrowed. "You're in no position to call anyone a slut, Carmen. You flaunt the kind of relationship you have with James, yet I see no ring on your finger. Now if you'll excuse me, I'm going home," she said with as much dignity as she could muster. Turning her back on the angry woman, she headed toward the crowd.

"You bitch!" Carmen shrieked, her hands coming up like claws in front of her. "I'll—" She reached for Jessie and grabbed her by the hair, jerking her to a sudden, vicious stop.

Jessie felt the violent jerk on her hair and tears stung her eyes as the sharp pain of Carmen's assault stopped her in her tracks. Turning, she pulled her hair from the woman's grasp. "Are you out of your mind?" she demanded.

"Not so much as you, I think," returned Carmen. "You deny that you want James, and this may be true. You may only want the ranch. But I am warning you to stay away from him. If I ever find out you've had sex with him again I'll—"

"You'll what!" demanded Jessie, her temper flaring at the beginning of the threat. Straightening her back and raising her chin, she looked down on Carmen as well as she could though she was shorter than the woman by inches. "Go ahead. Finish what you were going to say, but remember one thing, Carmen. I don't frighten easily. I was born and raised in this country, and though I've been away for a while, I haven't forgotten how to take care of vermin." By now her fists were clenched at her sides and she could see a crowd had gathered, listening to their words. Then she saw Mrs. Medley standing among the observers and remembered the woman's story about the scene two women had caused a few years earlier when their argument ended in a fistfight. Something in her rebelled against causing such a scene with Carmen. She couldn't deny she felt a nearly overwhelming urge to smash her fist through the sneering face of her adversary, but she had apparently absorbed more in Charleston than she'd realized. She simply couldn't lower herself to fistfighting in the dirt for any reason, least of all over a man.

"You threaten me?" Carmen snarled, taking a step closer.

"I don't think I have to threaten you, Carmen. We have nothing to fight about."

"What I just saw—you and James—you can't deny it!" she sputtered, her face crimson with anger.

Jessie thought for a moment. She couldn't deny the way her body responded to James's touch, but it wasn't something she was proud of. "It was a mistake. And I promise you it won't happen again."

Carmen spit on the hem of Jessie's gown. "That is what I think of your promise," she sneered.

A buzz passed through the crowd at Carmen's action. Jessie clenched her fists tighter at her sides and raised her chin even higher. "You're a pathetic woman, Carmen. You love a man who obviously doesn't love you in return. You're even willing to embarrass yourself and me in front of the whole town because of him. I'm actually sorry for you."

Carmen's face went white at Jessie's words. Her eyes blazing like black coals, she swung her arm with all her might and slapped Jessie across the face, the sound like the crack of a bullwhip.

Jessie's head snapped with the force of Carmen's blow. Her cheek stung like fire and her eyes filled with tears. She wavered a bit on her feet, blinking back the stunned emotions that jolted through her. Then, clenching her jaw and steeling herself against the pain, she raised her head again and leveled her gaze evenly on Carmen once more, staring defiantly.

"How dare you!" screamed Val, breaking through the ring of people watching the heated exchange. "How dare you strike her you—you—Jessie's ill!" She raced to put herself between the women.

"Val, get out of there," called Ben as he ran toward them, following his wife. "This is none of your business," he said.

"He's right, Val," Jessie said quietly to Val's back, though her heart lurched with affection at her friend's attempt to protect her. "This is between Carmen and me."

"Not while you're ill," Val responded strongly, staring Carmen in the eye. "If you have a bone to pick, Carmen de Silva, I suggest you pick it with me, or wait until Jessie is quite herself."

"Val—" Ben began to protest.

"Hush, Ben," Val said, her hand raised to silence her husband.

Carmen's eyes narrowed as she looked into the blue eyes of Jessie's defender. "I have no argument with you," she said.

"Then you have no argument with anyone this evening. Jessie is ill and going home with us," Val told her sternly.

Carmen let her gaze pass Val and pierce Jessie's eyes. "That is fine, for tonight. There will be another time. Another time when this gringa will feel my anger." With that, she turned and walked back into the shadows.

Val instantly turned and faced Jessie, taking in the bright red welt that covered her cheek. "That bitch," she whispered. Running the few steps to the bench where Jessie had left the damp cloth, she returned with it in seconds and applied it to the inflamed area. "You poor thing. How could that woman do such a thing. Well, it's certainly obvious she's no lady. I swear, her mother, good woman that she was, will be turning in her grave this evening, I can tell you . . ."

Jessie blinked a few times as Val rattled on about Carmen's behavior. She glanced past her to where Ben stood with his mouth open, still stunned that his meek wife had taken such bold control of the situation, even shushing him. Suddenly, Jessie felt an overwhelming urge to giggle. Biting her lower lip as it began to tremble, she tried to stop the laughter that welled up inside her. Finally, as Val continued her diatribe, she burst out laughing. Ben followed suit immediately.

Val stopped her tirade and her ministrations to Jessie's face and stared at them both. "What's so funny?"

Jessie just shook her head helplessly as she grasped her stomach, laughing.

Ben covered the several steps to his wife's side and put his hands on her shoulders. "You're what's so funny," he managed to say through his mirth. "You were ready to do battle in the dirt with Carmen for Jessie. You very nearly caused a scene this town would talk about for years."

Val thought for a moment. "I suppose I did," she responded with contrition. "But I couldn't let Jessie be assaulted by that horrid woman," she defended.

Jessie took a deep breath, breaking the chain of laughter that had controlled her for a moment. Taking Val's hands in her own, she smiled up into her face. "I don't deserve a friend like you," she said affectionately.

"I'd argue that point," said Val.

Jessie threw up her hands in mock defeat. "I won't," she responded.

"Somebody start up the music again. I feel like dancing some more," a voice came up from the crowd.

"Yeah, watching those women gave me a second wind," came another.

"These dances just seem to invite trouble," a woman's voice was heard.

"We should stop having them," another added her opinion.

"Wait until James hears those two were fighting over him. It's a shame he already left and didn't see it for himself. He'd 'a' gotten a real kick out of it."

Jessie heard the comments and felt as though her heart had suddenly stopped beating. James was going to think she was fighting Carmen for him. "Damn," she whispered.

"Jessie?" inquired Val.

Jessie looked at her friend and sighed. "It's nothing," she responded, not wanting to elaborate on her relationship with James.

"Are you ready to go?" she asked.

Jessie remembered she was supposed to spend the night with them. "I really feel fine. I'm sure I'll be all right going home."

"We won't hear it, will we, Ben?" Val said, glancing at her husband for confirmation.

"No, Jessie. Val's right. I'd feel better if you stayed with us."

Jessie could see the determined expressions on her friends' faces. Sighing, she gave in. "All right. And thank you."

A short while later, Jessie stood in Ben and Val's extra bedroom with one of Val's cotton nightgowns in her hand. "Thanks again, Val. I appreciate you letting me stay," she said, realizing she was beginning to mean it. Her head had begun to pound. Reaching up with one hand, she rubbed her temple with her fingertips, flinching slightly as her hand brushed the tender welt left by Carmen's slap.

"Are you all right?" inquired Val, concern wrinkling her brow.

"I seem to be getting a headache," Jessie answered.

"I'm not surprised," said Val. "Wait here a moment." She turned quickly and left the room. Seconds later she returned with a small brown medicine bottle. "Just a couple of drops of this and you'll feel wonderful and sleep like a baby," she said.

"Laudanum?" Jessie asked.

"The doctor gave it to me last year when I sprained my ankle stepping off the porch."

"I've never taken laudanum."

"Just don't take too much. It'll make you loopy," said Val.

Jessie grinned at her friend. "Loopy?"

Val nodded, smiling. "Just a couple of drops in a glass of water should help you sleep and take care of that headache. Good night," she said, backing out of the room. Raising her hand in farewell, she closed the door behind her.

"Good night," responded Jessie as she watched Val leave. Standing still for a moment, she stared at the small bottle in her hand. Loopy sounded nice, but she'd take Val's advice and allow herself only a tiny bit. She just wanted to get rid of this darned headache.

James sat in the dark on the porch. He heard a wagon approaching and knew it would be Marco and Carmen. He'd made a decision tonight. He was going to tell Carmen to move her things from the house this very night. If she refused he was going to throw her out, even if it meant losing Juan and Marco both.

As the wagon grew closer he heard weeping through the darkness. Carmen couldn't still be crying over finding him with Jessie, could she? It had been hours since he'd left the dance. "Marco, is that you?" he called into the darkness.

"Mr. Bonner? You are still awake? Come help me, please."

"Marco? What's wrong?" he asked, his voice rising in concern. Had something happened he didn't know about? Had there been an accident? He left the porch and quickly went to the side of the wagon.

"It's Carmen. She's very upset. She cried all the way home," Marco answered.

James frowned. "Really?" he said in a sarcastic tone. She's certainly playing this up, he thought, listening to her whimpering at her brother's side.

"Yes. She and Miss Braddock got into a terrible argument after you left."

James felt a jolt of alarm burn through him. "Jessie?"

"Yes, sir."

The blood rushed through James's body as he wondered how Jessie had fared in this argument.

"I have been trying to calm her down, but she refuses to be comforted," Marco told him.

Carmen sobbed more loudly as her brother spoke.

James was irritated by the sound. Then he realized that if Carmen was this upset, Jessie must have made a few good points for herself.

"Will you help me get her to her room, sir?" Marco asked.

James contemplated his desire to be rid of Carmen once and for all. He decided this was probably not the perfect moment to tell her to leave. "All right, Marco. I'll give you a hand. Come on, Carmen. Let's put you to bed."

Carmen slid across the seat of the wagon and let herself be lifted to the ground. Slipping one arm around James's waist, she clung to him for support, burying her damp face in his shoulder. "She said such hateful things to me," she sobbed.

James was more concerned about what Carmen had said to Jessie, but he thought better of questioning her about this. "You'll feel better in the morning," he told her.

"I told her this, too," said Marco, walking on Carmen's opposite side.

A few minutes later, James stood in the doorway to Carmen's room. "I'll let your brother help you get ready for bed. Good night," he said. Watching her sniffle as she sat on the edge of the bed while Marco removed her shoes, he was filled with regret—regret that she'd fallen in love with him, regret that he couldn't even remember making love to her, if, in fact, he had, and regret that he would have to hurt her even more in the morning. "I'll want to speak to you first thing tomorrow, Carmen," he said.

Raising her swollen eyes to meet James's, she took a deep, sob-racked breath. "Yes James, I think you should know what that slut said to me," she breathed.

James's jaw clenched at her words and the regret was replaced by another emotion, anger. "I told you earlier this evening not to call Jessie such names," he said stonily.

Carmen raised her chin. "When I tell you what she said you may feel differently about her," she said.

Sighing disgustedly, James turned his back to her and left the doorway. He didn't want to listen to her any longer, and he found he didn't particularly want to know what Jessie had said.

"Are you awake yet?" asked Val quietly, poking her head in the door.

Jessie woke at the sound of Val's voice, but she felt as though she had to fight to stay awake. "Yes," she mumbled. "I'm awake."

Val stepped into the room. "How are you feeling?"

Jessie pushed herself up to a sitting position and looked groggily around the room. "I'm fine, I think. What time is it?"

"Nearly noon. I was beginning to get worried about you, so I thought I'd better check—"

"Noon!" Jessie exclaimed. "How did I sleep until noon?" She hurriedly swung her legs off the bed and stood up. "The day's nearly gone." It was then a wave of light-headedness washed over her. "Ohhh," she said, lowering herself to the bed once more.

"Jessie?" Val said with concern.

"I think I just stood up too fast," Jessie explained.

"It might be the laudanum," Val suggested.

Jessie tried to clear her head by shaking it slightly. "I only took a few drops."

"It doesn't take much to make you loopy," said Val.

Jessie continued to move her head, blinking as she tried to clarify her thinking. "I don't feel loopy . . . I don't think. I just feel a little dizzy." She glanced up at Val. "And like I could sleep for about thirty more hours."

Val nodded. "That's the laudanum," she confirmed. "You may be especially sensitive to it. Just sit there for a while and I'll get you a slice of bread and butter and some coffee. Food should make you feel better."

"I hate to be so much trouble," said Jessie.

Val smiled. "I don't think getting a slice of bread and a cup of coffee will wear me out too tremendously," she giggled.

Jessie grinned as her friend left the room, then once more focused on waking up. She had to get rid of this dizziness so she could get home. She had work to do today.

✸ 11 ✸

James sat at his desk waiting for Carmen to join him. He'd let her sleep in, but was now ready to confront her. The door swung open slowly. "Come in, Carmen. Have a seat," he said, gesturing to one of the chairs facing his desk.

Carmen glowered at him. The memory of finding him in the dark with Jessie Braddock still burned in her brain, and she was going to find a way to make them both pay. "What do you want to speak to me about?" she asked somberly as she lowered herself to one of the seats offered.

"It's about your employment here, Carmen. I already told you your services were no longer required. I've found a woman to replace you. I want you to pack your things and move out today. You can go back and live with your father."

Carmen sat very still, listening to what she'd guessed had been coming. "It's because of Jessie you're doing this," she began. "If she hadn't shown up, you'd have remembered what I meant to you once."

James clenched his jaw and tried to steel himself for her recriminations. He'd known she wasn't going to make this easy. "This has nothing to do with Jessie," he said.

"Liar! And to think I defended you last night when she said all those horrible things about you," Carmen said, her voice shaking with emotion.

James raised a brow. He hadn't wanted to know what the two women had argued about. He'd already guessed Carmen had caused a scene because she'd found him with Jessie. Carmen's words, though, were implying Jessie had been the one to start the argument. "You defended me?" he said doubtfully.

Carmen raised her jaw. "I know you won't believe me, so I don't know why I bother, but yes, I defended you. I couldn't bear to hear the things she was saying about you. When she said she cared nothing for you, that she was only trying to make you fall in love with her so you'd sell her the Triple X, I had to say something." Her voice cracked at her last word.

James felt anger close over his heart at Carmen's words. She'd only verbalized what he'd been thinking all along, but to hear that Jessie had admitted it caused his emotions to run cold. "She actually said this to you?" he asked.

Carmen nodded, satisfaction burning through her. "Yes," she managed to say in a soft, wavering voice. "I love you, James. I couldn't stand to hear her speak of you in that way." A tear slipped from her eye. Looking down, as though in defeat, she began to stand. "I'll go start packing my things. Papa will have to give up his workroom for me."

James felt a stab of guilt. Had he judged her unfairly? She was a nuisance, and her infatuation with him had caused him a good deal of discomfort, but perhaps he was being too hasty. "Maybe—" he paused. Did he want her to continue in the house? Could he put up with her jealous, possessive ways? "If I let you stay, there would have to be an understanding between us."

"Yes, James?" she said hopefully. "Anything."

The look in her eyes gave him a moment's hesitation. Would she agree to his terms? "You must understand that I don't love you, Carmen."

"But that night—"

"I've told you, I don't remember making love to you, and, as harsh as this may sound to you, if I hadn't been drunk that night it never would have happened." He didn't want to confront her with the fact that he still doubted he'd been able to perform that night. He just couldn't believe he'd made love to her and not been able to remember even one tiny detail of the event. "If you wish to remain in my employ you must accept my feelings and realize you are my housekeeper, nothing more. I'm sorry," he finished.

Carmen sank back down into the chair, her head down. She couldn't look at him yet. If she did, he'd be sure to see the smugly victorious glow in her eyes. She hadn't lost yet. He might think she would only be his housekeeper, but in time things would change and she'd be mistress of the Triple X. Her only obstacle was Jessie Braddock, and she meant to rid herself of the woman as soon as possible.

"Carmen, do you understand me?" James asked after a few moments of silence had passed.

Carmen raised tear-filled eyes and smiled gratefully at him. "Yes, James. I understand. And I will be your housekeeper, but you must understand that I can't help how I feel about you. In time . . ." she let her voice trail off and her eyes lower once more.

James stifled a sigh. He felt bad about the girl's feelings, but she was right. In time she would fall in love with another. "Very well then, we have an agreement."

Carmen stood once more, wiping her eyes on the apron she wore. "I'll go start lunch," she said, heading for the door.

"One more thing," James stopped her.

"Yes?"

"While the twins are here I would like to be able to count on your continued assistance with them. They're a real handful." He smiled at her.

"Of course I'll help watch the boys. They're really no trouble at all," she said. She turned and left the room, grimacing when she was safely out of his sight. "Those two brats aren't going to come between me and what I want," she whispered to herself as she walked to the kitchen.

Moments later, Juan entered James's office. "James, one of the young bulls has wandered off," he announced.

James frowned at the news. Bulls could be dangerous under certain circumstances. "All right, Juan. Let's go find him."

The ride home was long and uncomfortable for Jessie. The bread and coffee Val had given her had helped, but she still felt the effects of the laudanum. She knew some people became addicted to the drug and she couldn't imagine why anyone would want to feel this way on purpose.

Rolling into the yard, she heard Smokey yapping playfully in the barn. When he sensed her arrival he came running from the building, his long pink tongue hanging from the side of his mouth, making him look as if he were smiling sideways at her. Tugging on Henry's reins, she stopped the wagon in front of the house. "Hey, boy, did you miss me?" she asked the jumping puppy.

Tinker emerged from the barn, a hammer in his hand, and walked toward her. "I'm glad you're back. Me and Johnny was gettin' worried."

"I'm sorry," said Jessie. "I spent the night with Val and Ben Richards." She felt guilty she hadn't thought her hands might worry about her.

"We knew that. Ben told us last night you weren't feeling well."

"Oh good," she said.

"But it was gettin' so late in the day that we was afraid somthin' might o' happened to you on the way home."

"I just overslept," she said, stepping down from the wagon. As her foot hit the ground she felt the dizziness again and wavered, grabbing for a safe hold.

"Whoa, there," said Tinker, dropping the hammer and reaching out to steady Jessie. "You ain't all right."

Jessie shook her head again. "I'm fine, really. Val gave me some laudanum for my headache last night and I can't seem to shake it completely." She smiled at the old man. "It's getting better, though. I'm steady now. Thank you," she said, taking a deep breath and starting for the house.

Tinker bent to pick up the hammer. "Maybe you should go lie down," he suggested.

Jessie glanced at him over her shoulder. "I have too much to do to lie down. I just have to go inside and change clothes first, then I'll be back." She glanced down at the serviceable dress Val had loaned her for the ride home. It was light blue cotton and at least four sizes too big.

Tinker rubbed his chin whiskers. "I sort o' wondered what'cha were wearin', but I didn't want to say nothin' in case you were lookin' that way on purpose."

Jessie giggled at him as she entered the house.

An hour later, Jessie was dressed in her trousers, shirt, and boots, her hat sitting level on her head to shade her eyes. "Tinker, I'm going to ride fence for a couple of hours. I'll see you around dinnertime."

Tinker nodded in her direction.

Smokey began to follow her.

"You mind if'n he goes along?" asked Tinker. "He's helped me about all I can stand for one day," he laughed as the puppy started jumping under Henry's feet.

Jessie laughed as Henry sidestepped beneath her to avoid the busy puppy. "Sure, he can come along. The run will do him good. Maybe use up some of that energy."

Jessie enjoyed her ride. Checking fences was one of the least exciting chores on a cattle ranch, but it was very necessary, and she sometimes looked forward to it. The peace and quiet on the range always gave her spirits the time to calm. It seemed as though the stillness of the earth seeped into her soul as she rode.

At first, Smokey ran along ahead of her, chasing bits of blowing sagebrush or tumbleweed, disappearing behind rocks and trees, and keeping himself thoroughly busy. He barked at anything that moved and seemed afraid of nothing they encountered, though the most threatening thing in their path had been a large jackrabbit. "Hey, Smokey, you think you can take him?" asked Jessie when the animal appeared, then disappeared in the blink of an eye.

Smokey yapped and growled after the rabbit, and even chased it for a while, but soon discovered the rabbit was much too quick for him. Jessie giggled at the puppy. "Some day things will be different," she said. "When you're grown that jackrabbit will have to worry in earnest."

The ride continued peacefully for a long while. Then, as they neared the border of her land that butted up to the Triple X, Jessie heard a strange sound coming from behind an outcropping of rock where it jutted from the side of a ridge. Smokey stopped in his tracks and began to growl deep in his chest.

"What is it, boy?" Jessie whispered, slowing Henry with a gentle tug on the reins. The puppy continued to growl.

Riding closer to the outcropping, she steered them around the point of rocks that obscured her vision. When she rounded the corner, she saw what the problem was. A bull, it looked like a yearling, was cornered in the rocks by a rattlesnake. The rattler hissed and shook its rattles threateningly while the bull pawed the ground, snorted, and looked wildly around him for a way past the dangerous, scaly creature.

"Damn," breathed Jessie. Pulling her gun from its holster, she aimed with a deadly eye at the head of the snake. Just then, Smokey decided to assist her, rushing toward the snake, barking. "No!" shouted Jessie, lowering her gun. "Smokey, get the hell out of there!"

Smokey continued barking and charging the snake, the creature striking at him and missing by only inches. "Damn it, Smokey! Didn't you hear me?" she yelled at her puppy. "That snake could kill you, you idiot. Get away from him!" But Smokey kept up his attack. The bull pawed the ground with even more frenzied movements and Jessie could see he was angry and frightened, a dangerous combination. Raising her gun once more, she tried to aim for the snake, but Smokey's aggressive actions kept putting him in the line of her fire. Then her eyes narrowed slightly in satisfaction as the puppy began to move around the snake, positioning himself on the opposite side. "Just a little farther," she whispered, pinpointing her aim on the snake once more. The snake struck out again and Smokey jumped back out of its reach. It was that moment the bull charged.

Jessie screamed as the bull came at her and Henry with all the vicious force of a grizzly, its horns slashing left and right as it tried to find an opponent. Henry reared as the mighty animal thundered past, and Jessie grabbed at the saddle horn trying to remain astride her mount. "No!" she shouted as she felt herself slipping. She could see the bull turning to charge again and fought to hang on, dropping her gun. Smokey barked loudly at the snake, then at the bull, jumping around on his back legs, uncertain where his attention should be focused when so much was going on.

Henry bucked again. This time his back legs left the ground at the same time his front ones did, and Jessie guessed where he'd gotten the name Bouncer. This time she couldn't hold on. "Damnnnnn!" she shouted as she flew from the saddle. The ground came up hard to meet her. She landed on her right side, her arm taking a lot of her weight, and she felt faint as she heard the bones in her wrist snap. Blackness teased the fringes of her consciousness, and a sudden chill shot through her in the form of a cold sweat. "Oh, God," she moaned, trying to sit up, fighting to stay aware of the danger around her.

James heard the barking of a dog and decided to follow the sound. Riding to the top of a small ridge, he felt his heart rise to his throat as he watched Jessie fly from the back of her horse. He could see the bull readying to charge once more, and the puppy standing between Jessie and the bull. "Jesus Christ," he mouthed as he spurred his mount, guiding it straight down the side of the ridge.

Jessie didn't hear James arrive, but she did hear a gunshot. Trying to focus her eyes as she fought the pain in her wrist, she could see the bull backing away. Then she saw James on horseback, not far from her and between her and the bull. Smokey, too, was in front of her. She remembered their other danger. "James, a snake," she called weakly.

James could hear Jessie behind him, but he couldn't take his eyes off the bull yet. His gunshot had effectively stopped the bull's charge, but the animal's snorting and pawing behavior told him the danger hadn't passed yet. Riding toward the bull, he waved his arm, driving him even farther from Jessie. "Hee yah," he yelled like a drover. "Get a move on," he told the frightened animal, relieved when the large bull began to back away. Finally, when he saw the bull was calming, he turned back toward Jessie.

"A snake," Jessie tried again. James had dismounted and was running toward her. "A snake, James," she said once more.

James knelt beside Jessie, placing one arm behind her shoulders, and looked into her face. She was pale, with a sickly blue-gray tinge surrounding her mouth. She was covered with sweat, but shivered against his arm. "Jessie, my God. Where are you injured?" he murmured.

"There's a snake, James," she told him, glancing in the direction of the scaled creature.

James finally understood her words. Looking past her, he searched for a snake but couldn't see one. "He's gone, Jessie," he said softly.

"But Smokey . . ." she whispered weakly.

"He's right here." He whistled once, bringing the busy puppy to their sides. "See?"

Jessie smiled when she saw her pet. "Good," she said.

"Where are you hurt, Jessie?" James asked again.

Jessie tried to raise her arm, but winced as intense pain shot up from her wrist. "My wrist," she said through clenched teeth.

James looked down at the wrist she'd indicated. Shaking his head, he sighed. Her hand hung limply below the wrist she'd indicated, and at a somewhat odd angle. It was already turning a deep black and blue, and was swollen to nearly twice its size. "It's definitely broken," he told her.

Jessie nodded. "Thought so. I heard it crack when I hit the ground," she said.

James didn't like the color of her skin, nor the beads of sweat that formed on her upper lip. Her eyes also looked a little glassy. She was shocky, and they were quite a way from the house. "Are you hurt anywhere else?" he asked.

Jessie shook her head. "I don't think so. I landed on my arm."

"All right. Don't move. I'm going to find something to wrap that arm in," he instructed her.

Jessie watched as James used his bowie knife to cut two small branches from a nearby tree. He scraped the prickly bark away, making the branches as smooth as he could in a short period of time. He came back to kneel before her. Removing his neckerchief, he looked into her eyes. "This is going to hurt, Jessie," he said.

Jessie nodded her understanding.

James picked up Jessie's hand and arm as gently as he could. He heard her sharp intake of air as he touched her and felt a moment of guilt that he had to cause her more pain. Probing the broken area slightly, making sure no bones were protruding through the skin on the underside, he placed one stick on each side of her arm, then wrapped the kerchief around it, securing the sticks to her wrist, immobilizing it. He looked back up at her face. Her eyes looked even more glassy, their usual deep emerald color a pale green. "We've got to get you to a doctor, Jessie. That wrist needs to be set properly," he said, concern filling his voice.

Jessie only nodded. She'd nearly fainted while James had bandaged her wrist. She was cold and nauseated, and she felt as though she wanted to sleep for a week.

James put one arm behind her waist and the other under her broken wrist to steady it.

"My gun," Jessie whispered.

James glanced around them and found the revolver she'd dropped. Reaching for it, he placed it in her holster, then began to help her to her feet. "Can you ride?" he asked.

Jessie couldn't believe she felt so weak. "Yes, I think so," she answered. Looking around for Henry, she saw him standing about twenty feet from them.

James doubted her words, but began to help her toward her mount.

Jessie forced herself to put one foot in front of the other. I've only got a little way to go, she told herself. But the farther she went, the farther it seemed she had to go. When she'd covered about half the distance she started to get dizzy, her head bobbing as she came to a stop. "James, I don't think—"

James didn't wait for her to finish. He swung her up into his arms and started for his horse. "Don't try to be brave, Jessie. You'll ride with me." He crossed the ground to his horse in quick, long strides, and climbed into the saddle, Jessie still in his arms. He marveled at how light she was, barely weighing down his arms. "A sack of feed weighs more than you," he observed as he settled her in front of him.

"I'm not so light," Jessie responded breathily.

James just shook his head. He doubted she'd even remember these comments in the future. Nudging his mount forward, he rode abreast of Henry and took up his reins, slipping them over his saddle horn. "Now to get you to a doctor," he said. Whistling for Smokey, he began the journey toward town.

As he rode, James couldn't help noticing the sweet smell of Jessie's hair as she leaned back against his chest. She hadn't even tried to keep a distance between them.

She had just fallen back to be cradled by the cocoon of his arms and chest. The scent of her filled his nostrils, and memories flooded his brain, reminding him of how she'd made love to him, how she had responded to him every time he touched her. He then remembered Carmen's words earlier that day. Had Jessie really admitted she was attempting to make him fall for her just to get her hands on the Triple X? Was she capable of such behavior? She groaned in his arms and he felt a surge of protectiveness wash over him. "Damn," he murmured.

A little over an hour later, Jessie lay on the examination table in the doctor's office in town.

"You fell off your horse?" Dr. Wills commented.

Jessie nodded and winced as the doctor turned her wrist slightly.

"This is going to hurt, Jessie," he said.

James watched the proceedings from several feet away. He'd been going round with himself again and again over Carmen's words, and though he found himself believing what she'd said, he couldn't help wishing it was he on the exam table instead of Jessie. The plain truth was that she had gotten under his skin, and it didn't please him any to admit it. It still didn't change the fact that he wasn't about to sell her the ranch. Clenching his teeth, he watched as the doctor began to pull on the broken wrist.

Jessie felt white-hot pain shooting up her arm as the doctor began to set the break. Tears fell from the corners of her eyes and slipped down into her hair, and she gritted her teeth to keep from crying out. "James," she called through her teeth, holding out her uninjured hand.

James stepped forward and took her hand in his, letting her squeeze down on his fingers as the doctor did his work. Watching her suffer was killing him, but her wrist had to be set.

"This is a bad break, Jessie," Dr. Wills told her. "Both bones are fractured. But it's also a clean break and should heal well." He turned her wrist in his capable hands, satisfied when he felt the bones slide into place. "There. Now I'll bandage it."

James studied Jessie's face. Her eyes were closed against the pain and the sickly gray tinge of color still circled her mouth. "Is there anything you can give her, Doctor?"

"Certainly. I'll give her some laudanum now, and some to take home with her," the doctor replied.

Jessie groaned at the thought of taking more laudanum.

"Jessie?" James asked at her groan.

Jessie just shook her head, not sure she could trust her voice quite yet.

Half an hour later, Jessie let James lift her to his saddle once more. Her arm was set, the laudanum was taking effect, and it was time to go home.

"You be sure to have someone bring you back to see me in a few days," Dr. Wills instructed.

Jessie nodded and smiled weakly, her vision becoming slightly blurred. "Tinker or Johnny will bring me back in the wagon," she responded, her voice soft and slightly raspy.

"You see that they do. You're not to ride for at least two weeks," he further directed.

Jessie just nodded, blinking several times.

"I'll make sure her hands understand, Doctor, and thank you," James told him.

"You're welcome," the doctor replied.

James gently spurred his mount from the front of the doctor's office and began the ride back to Jessie's ranch. She once more leaned back into him, this time the laudanum taking away the pain but making her groggy. Sighing, he fought the emotions that filled his system as she rocked against him.

Jessie felt herself slipping in and out of consciousness as they rode toward home. James felt warm and solid behind her, and she was grateful he'd come along when he did. She shuddered to think what might have happened if he hadn't. "Thank you," she murmured.

James thought he heard Jessie speak. "What's that, Jessie? Are you all right?"

Jessie tilted her head so her face was pointing more in his direction. "I just wanted to say thank you," she said again.

James set his lips in a firm line. "You're welcome," he replied. The soft shape of her mouth as she'd spoken so quietly set off alarms in his body. A humming warmth spread through him, heating the area below his belt and making him want to kiss the words from her lips. He also felt a spark of anger that she had such a potent affect on him. She hadn't made him fall in love with her, but he definitely wanted her physically, and that was sometimes the first step toward love. Narrowing his eyes resentfully, he once more recalled Carmen's words. He believed her, and yet, it was hard to believe Jessie's responses to him weren't genuine. Wouldn't he be able to tell whether or not a woman truly wanted him? he wondered. It rankled his ego to think she'd been acting with a single goal in mind. He had to find a way to be sure.

Glancing down on her dark hair as her head bobbed forward, he thought, I can't do anything now while she's injured, but in a while . . .

❋ 12 ❋

Jessie did little but sleep the first three days she was home. Her arm throbbed horribly, so she did take some more of the laudanum the doctor had sent with her, but she took as little as possible. It didn't seem to matter, though, how little she took, it affected her very strongly.

On the morning of the fourth day, she opened her eyes to discover the pain in her wrist had dulled some, and she decided she wasn't going to take any more of the drugging medicine. She also realized she was starving, having eaten little in the past days. Swinging her feet to the floor, she sat very still at the edge of her bed for a few moments, waiting to make sure she was going to be able to remain standing once she tried.

Very slowly, she raised herself from the bed. She felt a slight dizziness, but was relieved that it passed quickly. Finding her robe, she carefully pushed her bandaged arm through one sleeve, then pulled on the other one. Tying the sash wasn't easy, but she managed, and was soon searching through her kitchen for something to eat.

"What'r you doin' out o' bed?" asked Tinker in an aggravated tone as he walked through the door.

"I'm hungry," responded Jessie.

"Then go set yourself down and I'll git you somthin'," he ordered her.

"Tinker, I'm perfectly capable of feeding myself," Jessie scoffed.

"Not while I'm around. Mr. Bonner said to see to it you didn't do nothin' for a spell, and that means nothin'," the old man warned. "You sit down and I'll fix you some breakfast. Then I'll drive you in to town. The doc wanted to see you in a couple o' days, and today will do just fine."

Jessie could see she'd make no progress in arguing with him, so she sank down into one of the kitchen chairs. She had to admit she was feeling a little weak yet. Maybe letting someone else do for her for a while longer would be nice, after all. "How about some coffee, a couple of fried eggs, and some toast?" she asked.

Tinker grinned. "You got it, long as you don't mind if'n the yolks is broke a little."

"I don't mind. While you cook, I'll go wash up and get dressed," she said.

Tinker just nodded, now busy preparing her breakfast.

Jessie went back to her room and removed her robe. She vaguely remembered getting into her nightgown the day James brought her home, and she'd been wearing the same one for the past three days and nights. She wrinkled her nose. "I probably smell pretty bad," she mused. Pouring water from the pitcher to the basin, she prepared to get good and clean.

James had ridden to Jessie's ranch to check on her the day after her accident, but she'd been in a deep, drug induced sleep. He'd peeked in on her anyway, and been relieved to see her color had returned to normal: her cheeks pink, her lips nearly ruby in hue. He'd watched her sleep for a few minutes and wished things could be different between them.

He'd thought again about Carmen's declaration, and became even more determined to test Jessie's emotions. He just couldn't believe her responses to him weren't real. She'd seemed as caught up in making love as he had. No, he knew he had to touch her again, had to see if the flames in her eyes were real. The next time he pulled her into his arms he'd be watching her very closely. He'd try to maintain enough control himself to read her. If only he could think of a way to test her motives as effectively.

Deciding it would be a while before she'd be well enough to approach, he set himself the task of waiting two weeks before he saw her again. He knew it would be a very long two weeks.

"Tinker, saddle Henry for me, will you?" Jessie called as she jumped down the porch steps.

"No, I won't," he groused as he exited the barn. "The doc said it'd be two weeks before you could ride ag'in."

Jessie put her left hand on her hip defiantly. "It's been two weeks," she said.

Tinker squinted at her. "Well . . . just," he argued. "Why would'ja want to push yourself?"

"Because I've been cooped up in this house for so long I'm ready to scream," she answered. "So, would you saddle him for me, pretty please?" she wheedled, smiling flirtatiously at him.

Tinker shook his head. "I don't like this none at all," he grumbled, turning from her toward the corral where Henry stood munching on some green grass Johnny had thrown in for him earlier that day.

Jessie grinned as Tinker neared the gate, then turned when Smokey began to bark, running down the road. Her grin turned into a frown when she saw James riding toward her.

"Guess I don't have t' saddle Henry after all," observed Tinker. "Looks like we got company."

Jessie heaved a sigh. "Looks like," she murmured. She could have gone a long time without seeing James again. Each time she'd thought about him in the past weeks, she was reminded of her argument with Carmen and the fact that he'd discussed her with the woman. But her animosity toward him couldn't stop the leap her pulse took as he rode closer and she could make out the muscles of his thighs beneath the taut fabric of his trousers. "Damn," she fumed as she recognized the familiar softening of her body at the sight of him.

"Hello," James called as he neared Jessie standing in her yard. "You're looking well."

"I'm feeling well," she answered. "Thank you for all you did for me," she added, remembering her manners.

"You're welcome," he answered.

"Hello, Mr. Bonner."

"Hello, Tinker. How are you?"

"Fine, sir. Just fine." He turned a smug grin toward Jessie. "I have some work to finish in the barn. I'll see you later."

James tipped his head in Tinker's direction, then glanced back to Jessie for a second before focusing his attention downward. Smokey yapped at his horse's feet. "Hey there, little fella. I'm one of the good guys," he said.

Jessie grimaced at his words. She'd call him a few different things if given the chance.

"May I get down?" James asked. He could tell Jessie was less than thrilled to see him, and it sent a shiver of apprehension through him. Had her responses been an act? he wondered again.

Jessie shrugged. "Certainly," she offered, wondering what he could want.

"Thanks, I was just taking a ride and somehow ended up near here. Decided to stop in for a minute or two and see how you were getting on." He swung down out of the saddle. "How's the arm?"

Jessie held up the bandaged limb. "Just fine."

James nodded. "Good. The doctor said it would heal well." Flipping his reins over the hitching rail, he took several steps toward the porch. "You wouldn't happen to have some coffee on, would you?" he asked.

Jessie just sighed and nodded yes, turning to lead the way up the porch and into the house.

Jessie suffered a long afternoon and evening with James. He watched her every move, made solicitous remarks about her arm, insisted on helping her with dinner, and the dishes afterward, and just generally made her very uncomfortable with his presence in her home. Several times she'd been tempted to tell him point blank that he'd overstayed his welcome, but each time she opened her mouth he'd do or say something to quickly change the subject or draw her attention elsewhere. By the time the dinner dishes were put away and she'd felt him accidentally brush against her for the tenth time, sending her senses reeling, she needed a breath of fresh air.

Glancing toward Johnny and Tinker, still sitting at the table with their coffee, she smiled. "You two don't mind keeping James company for a few minutes, do you? I need to step outside for a moment." She knew they'd all think she was going to the outhouse and not object.

Tinker just nodded in her direction, while Johnny asked James his fifth question about crossbreeding. Stifling a sigh of relief, she headed for the door.

James narrowed his eyes as he watched Jessie cross to the door and go outside, then he addressed Johnny's question. He'd spent the afternoon studying her actions and felt frustrated that he was no more certain about her now than he had been when he'd arrived. There had been several times when he'd felt she was becoming aroused by his nearness, but it may have just been an angry reaction to his unwelcome visit.

He suddenly felt very tired and somewhat foolish. "I should be going home now, Tinker, Johnny," he said, pushing himself away from the counter where he'd been leaning with his hips. "It was a real pleasure seeing you both again. I enjoyed our visit."

"Sure 'nough," said Tinker.

"Me, too," responded Johnny. "I'd like to talk to Jessie about my crossbreeding ideas. With the information you gave me tonight I'll be able to explain myself better."

James smiled at the younger man. "I'm glad I could

help. And you're always welcome to come on over to the Triple X to talk to me any time you like. I'd be happy to help you with your ideas."

"I might just do that," Johnny answered.

Jessie was relishing her stolen moments. The moon glowed overhead, turning her ranch into a stark portrait of light and dark, silver and black. Breathing deeply of the cool, night air, she walked in the direction of the barn. Glancing back toward the house as she passed the large structure, she tightened her jaw, picturing James inside her home. She was frustrated with herself. Even though she was angry with James for several very good reasons, the fact that he discussed her with Carmen being only one of them, she hadn't been able to stop the sizzling effect he'd had on her all afternoon. His smiles and concern for her arm had made her want to slap him silly, but they'd also sent ripples of awareness shooting through her. Why couldn't she just come to terms with the fact that he was a snake and get on with her life? she wondered. "Oh hell," she muttered.

Veering away from the barn and the dim yellow light shining through the house windows, her eyes became accustomed to the moonlight. She could make out every detail of the ground beneath her feet, the hills and gullies around her. Moving farther into the night, she found a small patch of grass beneath a tree and sat down. Pulling her knees up, she wrapped her arms around them and rested her chin on the thick bandage over her wrist. Breathing deeply, she closed her eyes and let her mind wander.

James stepped outside just in time to see Jessie disappearing into the dark behind the barn, and a thrill shot through him. Following her was his only choice.

Once beyond the ranch buildings, he squinted into the blackness of the night, pausing while his eyes adjusted. He saw her sitting beneath a tree. "Perfect," he murmured, moving toward her.

Jessie heard someone walking through the darkness. She didn't need to open her eyes to know it was James. Her body told her who it was by turning to liquid fire as he grew closer. Raising her eyes to him when he was standing directly in front of her, she asked, "What do you want?"

"I just wanted to talk to you for a while," he said, watching how the moonlight played in blue-black reflections over her hair.

Jessie nearly snorted. "You've been talking to me all afternoon," she said.

"Yes," he responded softly, "but I may have a few more things to say. Mind if I join you?" he asked already lowering himself to sit beside her.

Jessie's nerves were already on edge. His nearness was making her feel even more tense, but there was also something exciting about the way they seemed to be hidden by the darkness—exciting, yet dangerous. "I wish you'd go," she told him, attempting firmness. Her voice didn't sound as strong as she would have liked, but her words were clear.

James heard the uncertainty in Jessie's voice. Searching her face for the signs of passion, he reached out and touched her hair, taking a long black curl and wrapping it slowly around his finger. A frisson of elation coursed through him when he recognized the flare of emotion in her eyes. She was feeling his presence whether she'd admit it or not. "I won't ask you to do anything you don't want to do," he said.

Jessie heard alarms go off in her head. The sensual timbre of his voice touched her nerve endings like the caress of a warm breeze. "I want you to go, James," she said.

"I know you do," he whispered leaning forward.

Jessie looked at him as he got closer to her. A stray lock of dark hair had fallen over his forehead, his thickly arched brows were drawn into a slight frown of intense emotion. The moonlight glistened off the planes of his high cheekbones and along his jaw, and illuminated his lower lip. Meeting his gaze was like connecting with an electrical force. A force she couldn't control or escape from.

James saw the look of urgency in her green eyes. He loved her eyes. He was beginning to be able to tell what she was thinking by looking into her eyes. And right now she was thinking the same thing he was. Tugging gently on the curl around his finger, he pulled her toward him.

Jessie knew it was going to happen, but she was helpless to stop it. All good intentions evaporated like water over the desert and she let herself lean toward him. Had she known earlier today that this was going to happen? Is that why his visit had made her so nervous? Had she walked out here knowing he'd follow her? Did she want to make love to him in the moonlight? As she opened her mouth to meet his lips, she stopped asking herself questions. James's powerful presence blotted all thought from her mind.

James took Jessie's lips with his own, the feel and taste of her a heady combination. His mind reeled with desire. He'd wanted this the night of the dance, but Carmen had interrupted them. Tonight, nothing would stop him from completing their union. Releasing the single curl of hair, he reached up and wound both hands in the black mass of curls around her head, moaning his passion into her mouth. "Jessie, Jessie," he groaned against her lips. He wanted her so badly he ached. Kissing her feverishly, he leaned forward, pushing her back, cradling their fall, then covered her body with his own.

Jessie let James lead her. He kissed her lips, her eyes, her cheeks, her throat. She felt the soft, cool grass beneath her and the pressure of James's strong, hot body above her, his arousal huge and demanding between her legs. She was frantic with desire and filled with an urgency she couldn't contain. "James," she rasped. "Please make love to me."

James clenched his jaw against the startling rush of

blood that surged to his erection at her words. Reaching between them, he unfastened her trousers as rapidly as he could. He felt her kicking off her boots, and he tugged the trousers down, pushing them free of her body. He then unfastened his own, feeling relief as the pressure of fabric fell away from his throbbing manhood. Pushing them only down to his thighs, he quickly poised himself above her, just touching the moist heat between her legs with the tip of his arousal. "Jessie, look at me," he ordered her in a groan. He wanted to see her eyes when he entered her. He needed to know she wanted him.

Jessie was stunned by the wild passion that consumed her. She writhed beneath him, needing him to enter her, to fill her, to bring her the release she desired so greatly. When she heard his words she whimpered and opened her eyes, her lids feeling like lead weights. "Please," she whispered.

James was rocked to his soul by the look in Jessie's eyes. They were the color of pure emerald, glowing with a fire out of control, glazed and passion blinded. He entered her wholly with one swift movement, burying himself within her silken core. The heat from her body caused him to shudder as the urge to release his fluids became nearly overwhelming. "Jessie, Jessie," he groaned against her temple as he struggled to regain some control.

Jessie gasped as James entered her so deeply. She felt the strong tensing of his muscles and shivered as his manhood convulsed within her. "James," she whispered. "Take me there."

James responded to her plea, unable to restrain himself any longer, hoping she was truly ready. He pulled himself out of her until the head of his arousal once more rested against the opening to her body. Then he crashed against her, driving himself into her again and again. Faster and faster he moved within her, thrusting with every bit of strength he possessed.

Jessie arched into James's body. Reaching upward

with her hips, she met his forceful thrusts, matching his rhythm perfectly. Grasping his buttocks with her left hand, she pulled him to her even more tightly when he thrust inward, then curled upward reaching farther behind him. Stretching, she managed to maneuver herself so she could smooth her hand downward, finding the heat between his legs. She felt the raised mound at the base of his manhood, then the soft globes of his passion. She heard him gasp as she touched them.

"Jessie—I can't—" James breathed out of control. "I—" Brilliant lights began exploding behind his eyes as Jessie found that sensitive part of his body. A throbbing, overwhelming in its force, began between his legs and spread outward, tightening his muscles sporadically, sending him over the precipice and into ecstasy.

Jessie felt the powerful, rhythmic surges of James's body beneath her fingers. Deep within her the rhythm continued. White-hot sparks began to center in her womanhood and shoot outward, hurtling her along the same whirlwind path that James was following. She groaned as the uncontrollable spasms seemed to jump from his body to hers, encompassing them both, pulling her apart from within. She was in a million tiny pieces floating above the earth, swirling downward to become one again.

James tried to control his breathing as the maelstrom passed, but could only gasp as he lay over Jessie's writhing body. He looked down on her in amazement. She was passion incarnate. His perfect sexual partner. There was no way Carmen could convince him this had happened simply because Jessie wanted the Triple X. There had been too much emotion here for that. He closed his eyes and propped his head against his fist.

Jessie began to feel reality closing in around her. She'd done it again. She'd made love to the man who kept his mistress under his own roof and who blatantly flaunted that mistress in public. The man who would later tonight lie in that woman's arms and tell her all about this, probably laughing about it. The same man who refused to sell her the Triple X. Would she forever be so stupid? she wondered angrily. "Let me up," she said firmly through clenched teeth.

James's eyes flew open at her tone. "Jessie?" he said.

"I said, let me up," she repeated, this time pushing at him.

James rolled away from her and lay on his back in the grass. He watched as she scrambled to pull up her trousers, tucking her shirt in with forceful jabs. "Jessie, I think we need to talk about this," he tried.

Jessie stopped tucking in her shirt long enough to answer him. "There's nothing to talk about," she said.

"I think there is," he urged.

"You're wrong," she snapped. She didn't want to hear him say that what they'd just done didn't mean he'd sell her the Triple X. She already knew that. Standing up, she looked down at him. Why the hell did he have to be so damned good looking? No man had the right to look so handsome. The moon shone down on him as though he were a god, and, indeed, he looked like one. His shoulders were broad, his arms sinewy. The muscles of his chest and stomach rippled as he moved to his side, raising his head to rest on one hand as he watched her. His narrow waist was deceiving, masking a strength that traveled through his back and down his hips. His legs were straight, perfectly formed, and well muscled from years of hard work. Her eyes followed a traitorous path to the dark thatch of hair between his legs. His manhood hung thick and long, damp from their lovemaking. Tearing her eyes from it, she looked him in the face again. "I'm going back to the house. Don't feel you have to come in and say good-bye when you leave," she told him, trembling. Turning quickly, she started toward the house.

"But Jessie," he said, sitting up. "We should talk about this," he called after her. "Damn it, Jessie! Listen to me!" he shouted after her.

Jessie could hear the anger in James's voice, but she

wouldn't listen to him. She knew she was a fool. She didn't need to hear it from him.

James fell back against the grass in exasperation when he saw she wasn't going to talk to him. "I accomplished one thing," he said to himself after a moment. "There's no way Jessie could ever convince me her responses to me aren't real." He thought for a moment longer. "Now if I could only feel as sure of her motives," he sighed.

Jessie's nightmares were interrupted by Smokey's incessant yapping. "Shut up," she told him groggily. "You'll wake the dead."

The puppy kept on with the barking.

Jessie yelled at him again with the same results. Finally, she sat up and looked at him. He was facing her door and prancing anxiously, barking continuously. "Do you have to go out?" she asked, swinging her legs off the bed. "If you do, you must really have to go," she commented. Reaching for her robe, she pulled it on as she left her room and walked through the house. Picking up a length of rope she'd begun using as a leash for him, she tied it to his collar. "Come on. If you have to do this let's get it over quickly," she said.

The night was silent and pitch black when she led Smokey outside. The puppy growled and pulled against his leash. "Come on, Smokey, get your business done so I can go back to bed. Stop this nonsense," she ordered him.

Leading him down the steps and out into the yard, she waited for him to calm down and do what she'd brought him outside to do. He continued growling and barking, his tiny yaps echoing in the darkness. He began tugging in the direction of the barn. "Smokey, I'm not letting you go play with Johnny now. It's the middle of the night, for heaven's sake." She waited a few more seconds then began dragging him back toward the house. "Fine. You can just wait until morning," she scolded.

Once inside, the puppy continued his tantrum for at least twenty more minutes, barking and growling at the door. Jessie lay in her bed with a pillow over her head. "I swear, if you don't shut up I'm going to spank you," she blustered.

After a few more minutes, he finally began to settle down.

"It's about time," Jessie groaned. Removing the pillow from her head, she tried to relax once more. It had taken her over an hour to fall asleep the first time. She knew it would take at least that long again.

"What do you mean, some of the cows are missing?" Jessie asked incredulously.

Tinker looked sadly at the ground. "I'm sorry, Miss Jessie. It's my fault. I had the last watch last night and I fell asleep. As near as we can tell, about fifteen head are missing."

Jessie squinted against the sun and gazed out toward her herd. "Cattle just don't get missing," she said. "Either they wandered off and you just haven't found them yet, or someone took them."

Tinker looked up at her. "They was rustled," he said. "I'm so sorry, Miss Jessie," he apologized again.

Jessie couldn't be angry with the old man for falling asleep. They were all getting tired of the watches. She was more angry with herself for not listening to Smokey. The little dog had tried to tell her something was wrong, but because of his age she'd ignored him. "It's not your fault, Tinker." She put her hand affectionately on his shoulder. "I've dozed off on my watches, too," she lied to make him feel better. "This could have happened any time. We just have to get the cows back," she said.

"The rustlers tried to cover their tracks, but I think I know which way they went," Tinker said. "I sent Johnny to see if I'm right. He's supposed to come back and give us word when he knows for sure."

"Which way did they go?" she asked.

Tinker turned and pointed. "That way."

Jessie narrowed her eyes as she looked in the direction he'd indicated. "The Triple X," she breathed.

An hour later, she was riding toward the Triple X. Johnny had returned and confirmed Tinker's suspicions, and she'd saddled Henry immediately. She was furious with James for pulling such a stunt. He was angry with her for last night, but so what! Rustling her cattle to get even was just plain stupid. What if she hadn't decided to handle it herself? What if she'd gone and reported it to the sheriff instead? Rustling was a hanging offense.

James saw Jessie riding in and wondered why she'd decided to see him now, when last night she couldn't get away from him fast enough. Then he realized she might not have come to see him, at all. She might have come to see the boys.

Thinking about the boys gave his conscience a twist. He'd left the boys alone the whole of the day before. Well, not exactly alone. Carmen had been in the house but, though she'd said she'd be happy to watch them, she didn't really pay much attention to them. He should have realized she'd be little help with the boys. They needed constant supervision.

Jessie entered the yard at a gallop and yanked the reins to stop Henry in front of James. Jumping from the saddle in one movement, she stomped up to face him. "Just tell me why you did it!" she demanded. "I can't believe you'd be so petty."

James stared down at her angry face. "What?" he asked.

Jessie planted her left hand firmly on her hip. "Don't you dare try to play innocent with me. I already know you did it. Just be man enough to admit it and tell me why."

James shook his head. "I really don't know what you're talking about. If you calm down a minute and tell me why you're so upset, maybe I could answer you."

Jessie glared up at him. So he wanted to play games, did he? "Fine, some of my cattle were rustled last night. I know you did it. I just want to know why. I can't believe you'd steal my cattle just because I wouldn't talk to you after we—after we—well, after," she finished in a huff.

James stared down at her incredulously. "Some of your cattle were rustled and you think I did it?" he finally asked.

"I know you did it. Their tracks lead smack onto Triple X land."

James was frowning now. Rustling was a serious offense and accusing someone of such a crime was equally serious. "Did you see the cattle on my land?" he asked.

"No, Johnny tracked them here."

"So it's possible whoever stole them could have simply been crossing Triple X land."

Jessie hadn't thought of that. She'd been so sure James had done it out of spite that she'd thought of no other possibilities. "I suppose," she said, some of her steam evaporating.

"Don't you think you should be sure of your facts before you accuse someone of such a crime?" he asked.

Jessie lowered her eyes. What if he is innocent? she thought. But no, it was too much of a coincidence that her cattle would disappear onto Triple X land the same night she angered James. Raising her chin in a confident manner, she met his gaze. "I'm going to follow their tracks. When I find them on your land you'll owe me an explanation."

"If we find them on my land I'll start an investigation."

"We?"

"Yes. I'm going with you. Wait while I saddle a horse."

A short while later, Jessie rode beside James as they neared the place where her cattle had crossed onto the Triple X. Turning to follow the tracks, she kept her eyes straight ahead, not letting herself look at him. Being this close to him was reminding her of the night before, and of the other times she'd been in his arms, and it was nearly impossible to keep her mind on the trouble at hand.

She forced her mind back to the cattle and thought about how she'd let him have it with both barrels when they found them. She'd convinced herself his innocent act had been just that, an act, followed by an act of interested concern. Any minute now she expected to round a bend or descend into a gully and find her cattle munching on scrub grass. He'd act surprised and apologetic, and try to convince her they'd wandered over on their own. Oh, how she'd jeer at him. She'd let him know how foolish he was to play such games with her.

James watched the play of emotions on Jessie's face and wondered what she was thinking. One minute she would look angry, the next she'd be almost smiling, her eyes narrowed evilly. She couldn't really believe he had anything to do with her missing cattle, could she?

Looking back to the ground, he studied the tracks. It looked as if only one rider had led the cattle this way, which was unusual. Rustlers usually traveled in groups. Frowning, he worried that whoever the thief was, he might not be through rustling yet, and depending on how desperate he was, the night watches could be in danger. Jessie's cattle weren't the only cows on the range. He had his own herd and men to worry about.

A sight in the distance caused the hair on the back of his neck to raise. Pulling back on the reins, he stopped. "Jessie, maybe you'd better wait here," he said.

Jessie tugged Henry to a halt and turned to look at him. He was staring intently at the sky ahead. "Why? What do you see?"

"It may be nothing, but I'd feel better if you'd wait here for me. I'll come back for you if it's your cattle," he told her.

Jessie snorted. "Not likely. You could ride up ahead for a while, then come back and tell me you'd found nothing. Those are my cattle and I'm coming with you to find them."

"Will you stop being so damned stubborn," he snapped. "Look at the sky, Jessie. Have you forgotten what a sky full of vultures can mean?"

Jessie blinked at his words. She hadn't even noticed the vultures. Swiveling in the saddle, she gazed at the sky ahead of them. There were at least a dozen of the horrid birds circling in an ever narrowing spin. She saw one of them drop and rise again and shuddered. "I've always hated vultures," she said in a whisper.

"Will you wait here?" James asked her again.

"No. If one of my cows is down I have a right to know it. I've seen dead cows before, James. You don't have to protect me from it."

James studied her for a moment. "All right," he said. She had been born and raised the first fourteen years of her life on this land. Perhaps she could stand the sight of a dead animal. Nudging his mount forward, he nodded in the direction of the vultures. "Let's go."

Jessie followed him silently. If an innocent animal had died because of James's prank she was going to be furious.

❊ 13 ❊

James noticed a certain skittishness in his mount as they neared the area below the circling vultures. "We're getting closer," he said.

Jessie had seen a change in Henry, too. He kept putting his ears back and rolling his eyes wide, sidestepping now and then. "They smell something," she observed.

"We will, too, before too long, I'm afraid," James said.

Jessie remembered when, sometimes as a child, she'd come across dead cows, bloated and maggot covered. It hadn't happened often, but it was a sight one didn't soon forget. She tried to steel herself to see it again. As she followed James around a bend in the large wash they'd been traveling through, she was unprepared for what they found. "Oh my God," she breathed, shock and disgust turning her stomach.

Just ahead of them, in a wild mass of bloody, swollen flesh, were the tangled remains of her cattle. Vultures had begun to land and tear chunks of flesh from the carcasses, while flies swarmed like a black cloud around them.

Jessie's hands clenched into angry fists as rage began to build inside her. Pain shot up her arm from her right hand, but she couldn't relax her fingers. It was all she could do to keep from vomiting as she viewed the sight through tear-blurred eyes. After several seconds, she spoke. "All of them," she murmured. "Why did you kill all of them?"

James was just as stunned as Jessie by what they'd found, but his first concern was why someone would bother to steal this many cows just to run them into a wash and kill them. It had been done deliberately, with malice, and he was suddenly filled with fear for Jessie's safety. If the person who did this had a grudge against her, would they stop at just killing her cows? And was it just a coincidence the cattle had been killed on his land? When he heard Jessie's words, shock registered through his system. "I didn't do this, Jessie. I can't believe you'd think I could."

Jessie turned her tear-streaked face toward James. All the evidence pointed to him. She'd been certain the rustling of her cows was a prank to get even with her for last night. He'd been at her place. He'd been angry with her. And the cattle had been run onto his land. She was just amazed his anger had taken him this far.

James saw the disbelief in her eyes. "I didn't do this, Jessie!" he practically yelled at her. "I couldn't do this! Don't you see that this was done deliberately?"

"Oh yes, I see that," she retorted.

"I didn't mean me. Think about it. Someone rustled your cattle and killed them on my land. Doesn't that make you wonder about their motives?"

Jessie raised her chin and stared at him down her nose. She already knew his motives. He didn't want her here except to satisfy his occasional lust, and he'd predicted she'd fail in her attempt at ranching. This was just one way to make his prediction come true. "I'm going home, James," she said stiffly. She pulled the reins to the side and turned Henry back toward her ranch. Before spurring him from the horrible scene of death and decay, she glanced back over her shoulder. "You won't win, James. The next time you come around my place in the middle of the night be sure you're ready to meet your maker, because I'll be waiting with my guns loaded." She turned her back on him and nudged Henry forward.

"Jessie, damn it, I didn't do this!" he called after her. "Why won't you listen to me? For Christ's sake, listen to me! You could be in danger!" He could see it was no use. She'd set her mind against him. He narrowed his eyes as he watched her disappear around the bend. Why was she being so stubborn?

Jessie cried all the way back home. As she dismounted, Tinker and Johnny ran up to meet her, followed by Smokey who jumped and yapped at her knees.

"What's happened?" demanded Johnny when he saw her tear-streaked face.

"The cattle are dead," she sobbed.

"Dead? All of them?" asked Tinker.

Jessie nodded. "I saw them. Someone led them onto Triple X land and shot them," she said, bending to absentmindedly scratch behind Smokey's ears.

Tinker rubbed his whiskers as he pondered the news.

"What are we going to do about it?" asked Johnny.

Jessie looked up at him. "Do about it?" The sight of the dead cattle had pushed any thoughts of what to do next from her mind.

"Yes. Are you going to the sheriff?"

Jessie looked out across the range in the direction of the Triple X. "I don't know. What good would it do?"

"The sheriff might be able to catch who did it," said Johnny.

Jessie felt her heart sink with the realization that she already knew who did it. "It doesn't matter. It won't bring the cattle back."

"But, Miss Jessie." Johnny tried again.

"What did Mr. Bonner say about all this?" asked Tinker.

Jessie turned her gaze toward him. "He said he didn't do it," she told him.

Tinker tilted his head in surprise at her words. "O'

course he didn't do it. Any fool knows James Bonner would never do nothin' like this. Where'd he ever get the notion somebody'd think he did it? I mean, did he have any theories about who might 'a' done it?"

Jessie looked at Tinker sadly. The old man believed in James completely. She didn't have the heart to tell him what she knew about him. "He said something about the motives of the person who did it," she said.

"Anything else?"

"I don't know. I think he said something about me being in danger," she relayed.

Johnny took a protective step toward her after she spoke.

Tinker once again scratched his whiskers and pondered her words. "I wonder," he mumbled.

"Yes, Tinker?" Jessie asked.

"I don't want to upset you no more than you already are," he said.

Jessie frowned. "What is it?"

Tinker paused for a second. "Well, what about the fire?"

Jessie stood still as his words sank in. "You think the same person who stole and killed my cattle might also have started the pigpen fire?" Her heart raced nervously with this new thought.

"It's a possibility," he said.

Jessie breathed out heavily. This was something that hadn't occurred to her. "Maybe I will go talk to the sheriff," she said after a moment.

Riding Henry up to the sheriff's office a while later, she jumped from the saddle and stepped up on the wooden sidewalk. Opening the door, she was surprised to see James sitting across from the sheriff.

"Hello, Jessie," he addressed her.

Every nerve in her body responded to the timbre of his voice. "Hello, James," she responded coolly. "Sheriff Hawthorne," she acknowledged, closing the door behind her.

The sheriff nodded in her direction "Hello, Jessie. I'm

glad you stopped by. James has been telling me what happened out your way."

"I'm sure he has," she said. How clever of him to come straight to the sheriff, she thought. This makes him look innocent.

"I was telling the sheriff he should come out and see for himself what's been done," said James.

Jessie nodded. "Maybe he should look at my pigpen, too," she said.

"Your pigpen?" James questioned.

"We've cleaned up the mess and built a new pen. The fire completely destroyed the old one," she explained, watching his face for any signs of deceit.

"You had a fire at your place? Why didn't you tell me?" he demanded. "When did this happen?"

"Calm down, James," the sheriff told him. "I'll get the facts and look into it." He then looked Jessie's way. "I'm planning on going out to the Triple X and your place in the morning. Will you be around to show me where the cattle were and to let me look at your pigpen?"

Jessie nodded. "I should be home all day tomorrow," she said.

"Good, I'll see you then."

"Thank you, Sheriff, and good-bye." She turned away from the men and reached for the doorknob. James stopped her by putting his hand over hers. She hadn't heard him stand up so his movement startled her. Looking up into his eyes, she was weakened by the strong emotions reflected in them. "I have to go home, James," she said quietly.

"I didn't do it, Jessie," he told her equally quietly.

Jessie lowered her eyes to where his hand was touching hers, the heat from the contact searing her flesh. "I have to go," she repeated firmly.

James sighed and released her hand. She wouldn't believe him and there was no way to prove himself innocent. At least not until the real rustlers were caught.

Jessie's hand felt icy cold now that James had stopped touching her. Turning the doorknob, she pulled the door open and stepped outside. Just before the door closed behind her she heard the sheriff ask James what was going on between them. She stepped angrily off the sidewalk. "I'd like to hear him explain that one," she fumed as she approached Henry.

Early the next morning, Sheriff Hawthorne rode into Jessie's front yard. "Good morning, Sheriff," she called from the porch as she sipped her morning coffee. Holding up her mug, she asked him, "Would you like a cup?"

"No thanks, Jessie. I want to get over to see those dead cows before it gets too hot."

Jessie knew why. The heat made the smell unbearable. "Just let me put my cup in the sink and I'll be ready to show you the pigpen," she said. Just then Smokey came charging from around the barn, teeth bared and a steady stream of threatening barks coming from his little body. "Smokey, that's enough," Jessie scolded. "This is the sheriff."

Sheriff Hawthorne laughed from atop his horse. "Don't yell at him, Jessie. He's going to be a great watchdog."

"Believe it or not, he already nearly is. He's turned into a great alarm. He just needs to grow some so he's got something to back up his bark." She grinned affectionately at her puppy. "Come here, you," she said to him, setting her coffee mug on the porch railing.

Smokey seemed to smile with pleasure when he heard Jessie call. Forgetting about the stranger in his yard for the moment, he ran and jumped on Jessie's legs, licking her and wagging his tail energetically.

Jessie bent over and scooped up her pet, lifting him to her chest. "You're sure getting heavy," she complained lightheartedly, giggling when his little pink tongue found the underside of her jaw. "Isn't he wonderful?" she said to the sheriff.

"He looks like one of the Webber's pups," he commented.

"He is."

"So he's one of Lady's?"

Jessie nodded, burying her face for a second in Smokey's soft fur.

"Then he'll probably end up being one of the best watchdogs around. Lady whelps some good puppies."

"I know, and I love him," Jessie answered. Putting the puppy down, she picked up her mug once again. "Just a second," she said, turning to enter the house. When she returned a moment later, she had a beef bone in her hand. Letting Smokey smell it first, she tossed it out into the yard, laughing as he attacked it, barking.

The sheriff grinned at the scene, then dismounted. "That should keep him busy for a while," he said. Tethering his horse to the hitching rail, he glanced around the place. "How far away were the cattle the night they were taken?"

"Not too far," Jessie said. "Smokey barked up a storm that night, but I just thought he had to go outside. I'll never make that mistake again."

Sheriff Hawthorne continued his perusal of the surroundings. "Show me the pigpen," he said.

Jessie led the way to the pen. "There's not much to see. Like I said in your office, we cleaned up the mess and built this new building." She gestured toward the new structure.

"This is real close to the house," he commented.

"Yes?"

"It just seems strange that someone would take the chance of being seen just to burn an old pigpen," he said.

"I tried to tell Tinker that I thought the fire might have started some other way, but he was certain someone started it."

"Tinker's right. Buildings don't just burst into flames for no reason," he told her. "Let's go see where your cattle were."

Jessie followed the sheriff back toward the house. They mounted, and headed for the range, Jessie leading the way. A short while later, they reached what was left of her small herd. "We've moved them in even closer," she commented. "They were a little farther out when the others were taken." She continued leading. Taking a deep breath, she glanced around her. The air felt different this morning. Maybe the weather was going to change.

The site where the cattle had been held no new clues for the sheriff. "James said there was only one rider," he murmured.

"What's that?"

The sheriff looked up at her. "There was only one rustler," he said louder.

Jessie set her jaw. She could have told him that.

The sheriff continued looking around, staring at the ground, riding in a circle around the tracks, following them a short distance, then doubling back. "These tracks lead straight to the Triple X?"

Jessie just nodded.

"You're wrong about James," Sheriff Hawthorne suddenly said.

Jessie's eyes opened wide in surprise. "I beg your pardon?"

"James told me you accused him of doing this."

"So?" Jessie raised her jaw defiantly.

"So, you're wrong. Anyone around here would be happy to tell you James Bonner couldn't do a thing like this."

"I may know a side of him you don't," she responded.

"Well, I'll never know him the way a woman can, but I know what kind of a man he is. He's hardworking, honest, and above all, fair."

Jessie snorted at this last. "You don't know everything that's involved here, Sheriff."

"I know he won't sell you the Triple X," he said.

Jessie suddenly wondered what else the man knew. James wouldn't have told him they'd slept together, would he? "Is there anything else you need to see here?" she asked uncomfortably.

"Nope, this should just about do it. I'm going to follow the tracks to the Triple X and the sight of the killings. Do you want to go along?"

Jessie shook her head. "No. I saw it yesterday. That was enough for me."

The sheriff shrugged. "All right, then I'll see you later, Jessie. I'll let you know if I find the rustler."

"Thank you, Sheriff." She turned Henry around and started back to the house, leaving the sheriff to his work.

James poured syrup on the boys' pancakes and smiled at their shiny faces. He knew they wouldn't stay clean long once they'd eaten their breakfasts, but it was nice to start them out in the morning washed and combed.

"Where's the butter?" asked Jamie.

James had wondered that, too, but hadn't been able to find any in the icebox. He let his eyes scan the kitchen. Carmen was a less than efficient housekeeper. There were dirty dishes still in the sink from the night before, along with the huge pile from the crew's breakfast. He could actually see small chunks of dirt and food on the floor under the edge of the cabinets. Scowling, he wondered why she thought he should keep her on in a position she was so obviously unable to fill correctly.

"Uncle James, me and Jamie think there's a cougar living in the rocks by the purple mountain," said Jeremy, sticking his finger in the syrup on his plate.

James looked at him in a distracted fashion. "A cougar?" Rising from the table, he crossed to the icebox and opened it, beginning a search for butter once more.

"The cat in the barn told us about him," said Jamie.

James looked back at the twins. "The barn?"

"Yes," said Jeremy, blinking up at his uncle.

"You boys be careful when you play in the barn," James warned.

"We are careful. We just talk to the cat," responded Jamie.

"That's good. Cats are harmless enough," said James.

"We thought we might go visit him today," said Jeremy. "We were going to ask Aunt Jessie about it, but she's not here."

James was once more staring into the icebox, digging

through items wrapped in butcher paper and jars of leftover food no one would eat. His anger grew as he searched for the butter.

"What do you think, Uncle James? Can we go visit him?" asked Jeremy.

James glanced over his shoulder at the boys. "Yes, go ahead. I'm sure he'd like that."

The twins exchanged surprised, happy looks. "Thanks, Uncle James," they said in unison.

"You're welcome," he answered, glad it took so little to keep them happy. He turned and looked at the closed door to Carmen's room. She'd disappeared into her room right after breakfast complaining of not feeling well and hadn't come out since. Scowling at the door, he berated himself mentally for feeling sorry for her. He should have stuck to his guns and fired her when he had the chance.

Determination strengthening his resolve, he crossed the kitchen and rapped loudly on her door. "Carmen, there's a lot of work to do out here," he called.

"Come in, James," Carmen called weakly.

James frowned at the sound of her voice. Turning the knob, he pushed the door open slightly and peered in. Carmen lay on her bed with a washcloth over her eyes. Her hair was damp around her face and she looked a bit flushed. Perhaps she was truly ill. "What's wrong, Carmen?" he asked, stepping farther into the room.

Carmen lifted the cloth from her eyes and looked up at him. "I don't know. I felt fine when I got up this morning, but now I feel horrible," she whimpered.

"Do you have a fever?" he asked, worried she might have something contagious, something the twins could come down with.

"I don't think so," she answered. "I haven't been feeling well for a few mornings. It passes."

James studied her face, concerned there was sickness in the house. "You stay in bed today. I don't want you getting any worse, and I don't want the boys getting sick," he told her.

Carmen struggled to sit up. "I'm fine, James. Really," she insisted, weakly.

James rubbed his jaw. "I think I'll send for the doctor," he said.

Carmen shook her head. "That isn't necessary."

"I'd rather be safe than sorry. It won't hurt to have him look at you. I'll let your father know you're not feeling well. I'm sure he'd want to know."

"James, all this isn't necessary. I'm fine," she protested.

"Uncle James, we want more pancakes," called Jamie from the table.

James glanced back at the boys and wondered fleetingly what he was going to do with them all day now that Carmen was ill. Turning his attention back to her, he raised a finger at her. "You stay in bed. I have to go take care of the boys." He closed the door behind him as he left her room.

Sighing, he headed for the stove and the bowl of pancake batter.

"I want three more!" squealed Jeremy. "I'm so hungry this morning."

Jamie giggled and bobbed his head. "Me, too!" he added.

James grinned at his nephews, but his insides twisted with concern. What would he do if they became ill? And what was he going to do with them all day? He had work to do, work they couldn't help him with. "Boys, I need to ask you a big favor," he began, watching their tiny faces for understanding. "I have to work today, and Carmen is too ill to watch over you. Can I trust you to keep out of mischief?" he asked.

Jamie and Jeremy exchanged glances. "We told you what the cat in the barn said," began Jamie.

"Yes, yes, that should keep you busy," responded James, pouring batter into the hot skillet. If they were occupied in the barn they couldn't get into too much trouble. "You just be careful," he told them.

"We will," they answered in unison.

Minutes later, James filled their plates with a fresh batch of hot pancakes. "Can you boys finish up by yourselves?" he asked. "I should be getting to work."

"Sure," they answered together, digging into the pancakes.

James grinned at them, heading toward the door. They were just so darned cute. "I'll see you boys at dinnertime, then. Put your dishes on the counter when you're through, and have fun today. Just stay out of trouble."

"We will," they answered together.

Leaving the kitchen, he headed out to saddle his horse. Noticing the air felt heavier than it had in days, he scanned the sky. A dark band of clouds was sitting on the horizon. He studied them hopefully for a few seconds. Clouds on the horizon didn't necessarily mean rain. He'd seen times when clouds would hang in a far-off sky for days, then just disappear.

A short while later, he'd saddled and mounted his horse and was headed out to the range. With a herd his size it was nearly impossible to tell if a few were missing, but he wanted to check on them anyway. Looking back over his shoulder, he saw the twins running for the barn. Smiling, he turned back around, satisfied they were occupied for the time being.

Jessie watched the sky most of the day. The dark clouds didn't seem to move in any direction, and she began to wish that they'd swing her way. "It sure has been hot lately," she grumbled to Tinker as she held a wood pole in place while he wired it to the new gate they were building.

"Yup," he agreed, sweat pouring down his face and dripping off his nose.

"Do you think those clouds will come this way?"

"Don't know," he answered. "Hold it a little higher," he directed her.

Lifting the pole another inch, she frowned at the clouds again. "Do you think we could dig out a spot along the creek to make a swimming hole?" she asked.

Tinker stopped wrapping the wire and straightened to look at her. "I suppose. It'd be a big job, but we could do it. Is it something you want done right away?"

Jessie realized how foolish she sounded when they had so many more important tasks yet to complete. "No. I was just thinking someday," she answered.

"Good. 'Coz I don't think we'll get to it this summer," Tinker responded, once again bending to the wiring. "Have you thought of a name yet?" he asked.

"A name?"

"For the ranch," he clarified.

"No," she murmured her answer. She hadn't really thought about it since the day the sale was finalized. "Do you have any ideas?"

Tinker took one hand from the wire and rubbed his chin. "How about, Tinker's?" he teased.

Jessie laughed. "That sounds pretty good, but I don't think it's perfect. Got any other suggestions?"

"Maybe the H S H?"

Jessie stared at him for a moment. "The H S H? What's that?"

"The Home Sweet Home," he replied.

Jessie thought about it and a lump grew in her throat. The Triple X would never be her home again. She was working hard, putting everything she had into this ranch. She might as well acknowledge it as home. "I think that's a wonderful name," she said, her voice cracking slightly.

Tinker looked back at the wiring, not wanting to embarrass her by seeing her tears. "Good," he said gruffly. "It'll be easy to carve that in the sign."

Jessie laughed at his words. "I love you, Tinker," she said on impulse, and knew it was true.

It was Tinker's turn to get teary. "Gosh, Miss Jessie. I care about you, too. Both me and Johnny do."

Jessie smiled, then began to laugh. "We're not going to get this fence done by standing here talking," she said, sniffing.

"Nope. At this rate we'll never get that swimmin' hole dug. And you know, jumpin' in cold water would feel real good right about now."

"Gee, Tinker, I'd be happy to dump a bucket of cold water on your head anytime you like," Jessie said, teasing, an innocent smile on her face.

"I'll just bet you would," said Tinker. "And I'd be happy to do the same for you."

Jessie giggled at their silliness.

❋ 14 ❋

By the time James returned to the house that evening every muscle in his body ached. He'd spent most of the morning checking on his cattle, then, after he saw the sheriff and was sure he could proceed, he burned the carcasses of Jessie's dead cattle. He was exhausted, famished, and needed a bath.

Entering the kitchen, he grimaced at the sight of the dirty dishes still piled in the sink, breakfast's remains hardened and dry. Looking around him, he could see Carmen had taken his advice and stayed in bed all day. He suddenly wondered what the boys had eaten for lunch. There were no sandwich crusts or dirty milk glasses to be seen.

"Boys," he called as he left the kitchen. "Boys, come down here," he directed up the stairs. The silence of the upper floor was perplexing. "Jamie, Jeremy, are you up there?" he yelled a little louder. Frowning, he wondered what they were up to. They were always busy, but so far they'd never failed to appear when he called them. Calling to them one more time with no response, he finally took the stairs two at a time. The sight of their empty bedroom sent a cold chill of dread down his spine.

Running back down the stairs, he went once more into the kitchen. Crossing to Carmen's door, he hesitated only a second before walking in. She was asleep. "Carmen," he said, crossing the room to shake her awake.

"James? What's wrong?" she asked groggily.

"Do you know where the boys are?" he asked.

Carmen pushed herself up against the stack of pillows on her bed. "No. I haven't seen them." she answered.

Worry escalated through his system. "Did you hear them at all?"

She shook her head. "No. They must have played outside all day. I never heard them once."

"Damn," he muttered, leaving her bedside.

James gritted his teeth as he charged through the house and outside. Running toward the barn, he prayed they were playing there safely. Those two little boys were his responsibility. With Carmen ill, he shouldn't have let them out of his sight without securing some kind of supervision for them.

Except for a few soft noises from the animals in their stalls, the barn was silent, and the silence was oppressive. "Where are you?" James said into the hollow emptiness.

Leaving the barn, he walked around back of it. He could see a few hands working around the place, but there was no sign of the twins. His heart had begun to race with worry. Running to the first man he saw, he stopped. "Have you seen the twins, today?" he asked.

The man shook his head. "Sorry, Mr. Bonner. I just got in from the range."

James felt the worry increase. Running to the next man, he inquired, "Did you see the twins today?"

"No, sir," was the response.

James asked every other man in sight, and all had the same answer. No one had seen the boys all day. Turning back toward the barn, his mind raced wildly. Where could they have gone? he wondered. An iron vise of fear gripped his heart. Leaver Creek! The swimming hole! Running as fast as he could, he resaddled and mounted his horse, then spurring the animal hard, he started him on a pounding course to the water.

Galloping through the trees, he jerked hard on the reins, stopping the horse at the water's edge. Jumping down, he looked frantically in the water and along the bank. Were they here? Had they been here? Closing his eyes, he said a prayer for them, "Please let them be all right, Lord."

Wading out into the creek, he searched the banks where tall grass might have hidden tiny bodies. When his search turned up nothing he was relieved beyond words, but he was still sick with worry. Sloshing out of the creek, he slipped and fell in the mud at the water's edge. Landing in the grass, he lay there for a second, trying to catch his breath.

Unbidden, thoughts of Jessie entered his mind. This is where he'd first made love to her. Then, like a flash of lightning it hit him. Jessie! The twins might have gone to visit Jessie! Scrambling to his feet, he jumped into the saddle and tugged on the reins, turning the animal in the direction of Jessie's ranch. He urged the horse on, and soon they were traveling swiftly over the range in a direct route to Jessie's house.

Jessie sat at the table with Tinker and Johnny. They'd just finished dinner and were sipping their coffee, enjoying this quiet time of the day. "The Home Sweet Home," she said, smiling. "I love it."

"Here's to the Home Sweet Home," said Johnny, raising his coffee mug.

They all raised their mugs together. It was then Smokey began to raise a ruckus outside. Before any of them could get up to see what the problem was, the door burst open and James, wet from the waist down and covered in mud, exploded into the room.

"James?" Jessie said, pushing herself from the table.

Johnny and Tinker stood also, concern evident on their faces.

"Are the boys here?" he said. "Please tell me they're here."

Jessie's eyes widened with fear. "They're not here, James," she said slowly. "Where are they?" she asked, afraid of the answer.

James stared at her with wild panic in his eyes. "I don't know. I can't find them. They're not at the ranch. I was praying they'd be here," he said haltingly.

Jessie grasped him by the arm. "They've got to be somewhere. Where did you look?"

"I've looked everywhere. The house. The barn. The creek. I've asked everyone I could find if they'd seen them and no one has. Where could they be, Jessie?" he pleaded.

Jessie's breaths were coming faster. Gazing downward, she tried to think the way the boys did. "When was the last time you saw them? she asked.

"This morning."

"What were they talking about? What did they say to you?"

James tried to remember their conversation. He mostly remembered being irritated with Carmen because the kitchen was so filthy and then discovering her illness. "I don't know," he sighed.

"Think!" Jessie demanded.

James stared hard at her. "They said something about a cat."

"A cat? What about a cat?"

"The cat in the barn," he suddenly remembered. "They'd been talking to the cat in the barn. But I checked the barn, Jessie. They weren't there."

Jessie thought for a moment, biting on the inside of her lower lip. "If they think the cat in the barn told them to do something, that's what they're doing."

"They asked my permission to visit it," James said.

"The cat in the barn? Why would they ask permission to visit a cat they'd already been talking to?" Jessie wondered out loud. Cold fear crept through her. "What else did they say, James. Did they tell you what the cat told them?"

James racked his brain trying to remember. He remembered pouring syrup over their pancakes. He remembered they'd asked for butter. He remembered them talking about the cat in the barn. Then he remembered. "The cougar," he whispered.

Jessie's mouth dropped open for a moment.

"The cougar?" Johnny asked. "What cougar?"

"There isn't any cougar, at least none that I know of, but the boys think the cat told them about one. They said it was in the rocks by the purple mountain."

"That's where they are," Jessie said, fearfully.

"There ain't no purple mountains 'round here," said Tinker.

"There are if you're five years old. Come on," Jessie said, heading out the door. Running to the center of her yard, she began looking toward the horizon in a slow circle.

The men followed her outside and watched from the porch.

After a few minutes, Jessie yelled, "There!" and pointed with her left hand.

James jumped from the porch and ran next to her. Looking in the direction she was pointing, he saw it. The dark purple mass of the nearest mountain. "I'll be damned," he breathed. "I've lived here for years and I've never thought of that mountain as purple before."

"You've never looked at it through the eyes of a child before," Jessie told him. "Now let's get going. I'll grab some canteens of water, some rope, some food, and some blankets. You saddle Henry for me," she directed as she headed back toward the house. "Tinker, you go to the Triple X. Wait there in case they find their way back. Johnny you wait here. They still might come here. If they show up either place, ride out after us. Fire two rounds at a time as a signal until you hear us respond the same way. Then we'll know they're safe and head back."

James watched her in amazement as she organized herself for the search. Turning away, he went to saddle Henry.

Two hours later, they rode side by side in silence one

minute, listening for any sound that might lead them to the twins, then shouting their names the next, in hopes of being heard themselves. As they guided the horses down into a ravine, Jessie noticed the terrain was getting more rocky and more difficult to traverse. "Do you think there are any cougars near here?" she asked quietly.

James shrugged. "Probably, though I've never seen any," he answered.

"Do you think the boys are all right?" she asked, needing to be reassured.

"Yes. They're fine, just lost, but we're going to find them," he said with conviction.

Jessie sighed, temporarily relieved. She looked ahead, searching the terrain for the boys, but she could see James out of the corner of her eye. He sat straight in the saddle, shoulders squared, hips rocking with the movement of the horse between his legs. Narrowing her eyes, she cursed his good looks. Even now, while they were searching for their nephews, she couldn't help feeling her body temperature rise just looking at him. Even though she still believed him to be the one and only suspect in the crime of rustling her cattle, she couldn't stop the heavy pulse of blood through her body as she watched him. It just isn't fair, she thought.

James watched Jessie as they rode. He was still amazed by how she'd calmly taken charge of the situation back at her house. He wondered how she knew so much about the way little boys thought. "How do you do it?" he asked.

"Do what?"

"Know what the boys are thinking."

"Oh, that," she said, a wry grin turning up one side of her mouth. "I grew up here, remember?"

"Yes?"

"The animals used to talk to me, too."

James looked at her incredulously. "What animals?"

"All animals. The birds, the horses, the insects, the cats and dogs, even the fish in the creek," she answered.

"So, do you think the animals talk only in this part of

the world, or do animals everywhere carry on conversations?" he tried to tease her.

Jessie smiled at his attempt to take her mind off their worry. "I don't think it's the animals. I think it's the boys. It runs in the family. Remember, the boys are related to me, too."

"Do animals talk to everyone in your family?" he asked.

"I don't know about anyone else, though I suspect they did to my mother."

"Why your mother?"

"Because she talks to them even today. I do, too. Don't you ever talk to your horse?"

James thought for a moment. "I don't think so," he answered.

"That's why you can't think like the boys," she said.

James chuckled to himself, then felt his mood sink again. "Jeremy! Jamie!" he yelled as loudly as he could.

Jessie yelled, too. She could hear their voices echoing back at them, but she couldn't hear the boys. Glancing around her, she hated to see the sky darkening. It would be night soon, and the thought of the boys being alone out here in the dark sent chills up her spine. They had to find them before then.

Jeremy sat very still and held Jamie's hand. "It'll be all right, Jamie. Somebody will find us," he said, tears rolling silently down his dirty face.

Jamie stared up at the stars that had begun to dot the pale sky. His leg hurt something fierce, but he didn't want to worry Jeremy. "I'm okay," he breathed. He just wished he wasn't so cold.

"Do you think the cougar will find us?" Jeremy asked, his voice quavering slightly.

"I don't think there is a cougar. I think the cat lied to us. We should have asked Aunt Jessie before we came to visit him," Jamie answered weakly.

"We asked Uncle James," said Jeremy, swiping at his tears.

"Uncle James doesn't hear the animals," said Jamie. He began shivering.

"Are you cold?" asked Jeremy.

"A little," Jamie replied.

"Should I lie down next to you?" Jeremy asked.

"I don't think there's room," Jamie answered.

"Probably not," agreed Jeremy, looking down from the tiny ledge where they'd fallen. They were high enough up that they'd die for sure if they fell from here. More tears ran from his eyes. He was getting really scared. He wished someone would come looking for them.

"Do you think we should yell for help again?" asked Jamie.

"Okay," agreed Jeremy. "Help!" he yelled at the top of his lungs. "Help, we're down here!"

Jamie opened his mouth to scream, but only managed a tired sound.

"You rest, Jamie. I'll yell for both of us," said Jeremy. Tilting his head up, he screamed all the louder. He was screaming for two now.

Jessie and James rode until it was nearly too dark to see anything. "Damn it. I won't give up," said Jessie, knowing they'd have no choice but to quit in a very short while.

James felt as though he'd swallowed a hot poker. His stomach ached with worry and his chest burned from the sense of responsibility he felt for the boys being missing. "If anything has happened to those boys I'll never forgive myself," he swore through clenched teeth. "Damn it, why didn't I stay home with them?" he berated himself.

"There is no guarantee they wouldn't have taken off with you sitting in the kitchen," Jessie said trying to soothe him.

"But they wouldn't have gotten so far," he said.

Jessie sighed. She was feeling her own guilt. She was their aunt, for heaven's sake. She knew everything at the

Triple X wasn't perfect. She sensed Carmen was less than a good caregiver, but she'd been so wrapped up in her own pain concerning the Triple X that she'd stayed away when she should have been there for the boys. That brought another thought to her mind. "Where was Carmen today?"

"She was ill this morning. I told her to stay in bed," James answered.

"Oh. I hope it's nothing too serious," Jessie commented.

James shrugged his shoulders. "I don't know. She told me she hasn't been feeling well for a few days."

Jessie listened to his words but was more concerned about the twins than about Carmen's illness. She had another thought. "You should have let me know Carmen was ill. I would have helped with the boys."

"Things between you and me aren't good, Jessie. It honestly didn't occur to me," he responded.

James's words made her feel even worse. "Jamie, Jeremy!" she shouted. She had to find those boys.

Jamie shivered more violently.

"Jamie? Stop it, you're scaring me," cried Jeremy. "Somebody, please find us!" he screamed. "Jamie's hurt!" he cried. "HEELLLP!" he screamed, fear making him louder.

Jessie pulled Henry to a sudden stop. "Did you hear that?" she whispered.

James listened. "No, what did you hear?"

"Sshhhh." She listened again. "There. Did you hear it that time?" James was already spurring his mount in the direction of the sound. "Come on, Henry. We've found them!" she said.

"Jeremy! Jamie!" yelled James. "Where are you?"

"Jaammiiee!" shouted Jessie. "Please answer us!"

Jeremy sobbed over his brother. Jamie had gone to sleep, and no matter what he did, he couldn't get him to wake up again. Then he heard someone call his name. "Help!" he yelled. "We're down here! Help!"

Jessie pulled Henry to a stop. James was at her side. "Jamie! Jeremy!" she yelled again. "They sound close," she said to James.

"They should," he replied, his voice full of horror as he stared out across a vast ravine.

Jessie followed his gaze with her eyes. "Oh my God," she breathed. Through the rapidly enclosing darkness she could barely see them. On the other side of the ravine, the boys were perched on a tiny ledge of rock approximately twenty feet from the top and over one hundred fifty feet from the bottom. "What are we going to do?" she whispered fearfully.

"We're going to get them off that ledge," James said firmly.

Rounding the top of the ravine, Jessie kept her eyes on the boys whenever she could. She'd yelled to them to be still, that she and James would be there soon, but she was terrified they'd try to climb up and fall into the ravine.

Finally, she and James reached the area directly above the boys. Dismounting, they walked to the edge and looked over. The boys looked so tiny that Jessie had to swallow hard to keep her tears in check. "What do we do first?" she asked James.

James had been sizing up the situation. "Get me the rope," he directed.

Jessie ran for it and returned immediately.

"Boys, we're going to throw a rope down to you. Tie it around your waists and we'll pull you up," he called over the cliff to them.

Jeremy gazed up at his uncle and aunt. "We can't," he yelled back up.

"You have to. There's nothing to be afraid of. We'll pull you up slow and gentle," urged James.

Jeremy began to sob again. "We can't Uncle James. Jamie is asleep and I can't wake him up."

"Oh dear God," breathed Jessie, thinking the worst. The tears she'd been fighting filled her eyes.

James gripped her by the arm. "He's all right," he

stated angrily. "Get a hold of yourself. I need you right now."

Jessie held her teeth together tightly, willing her tears to stop. James was right. She couldn't fall apart now. "I'm okay," she said.

"Good. I'm going to have to go down there. I'll tie one end of the rope to me and the other end to your saddle. When I get down to them, you'll have to pull them up one at a time, then me. Can you do it?"

Jessie looked down at the boys once more. There was only one flaw in James's plan. "I'll have to go down," she said.

James frowned at her. "Don't be difficult, Jessie. If you can't pull us up just say so. I'll think of somethi—"

"I'm not being difficult, James," she interrupted. "Look at the size of that ledge. There's barely room for them, let alone you. You're huge," she said.

James blinked at her description of him. He was hardly huge, but she was right. The ledge was tiny, and compared to two five-year-olds and to her, he was huge. "Do you know what you're saying?" he asked.

"Yes. I know exactly what I'm saying. I have to go down there."

"But what about your arm?"

Jessie glanced at her bandaged right arm. "I won't let it matter," she said.

James knew she meant it. "All right," he said. "Tie one end of the rope around your waist. I'll tie the other end to my saddle. Then I'll lower you over the side. Let the horse do the work. You just guide yourself down with your feet. Once you get to the ledge you can check on Jamie, then I'll tell you what to do."

She nodded. There was nothing further to say. Picking up the rope, she wrapped it around her waist and tied it securely. Crossing to the edge of the cliff, she turned to face James. "See you later," she offered.

"Later," he responded, and mounted his horse.

The climb down was rough. There wasn't much to

hang on to, and when she did find something it was usually with her right hand. Grabbing for a hold on a root that protruded from the rock face, she felt a jagged snap in her wrist and winced as excruciating pains shot up her arm. By the time she reached the ledge, her hand, wrist and arm were throbbing violently.

"Aunt Jessie," wailed Jeremy as his aunt landed on the ledge beside him. He tried to reach up to her.

"No, Jeremy. Sit still. I'll hug you in a little while. I have to check on Jamie now, all right?"

Jeremy nodded, sniffing.

Jessie squatted and reached to feel Jamie's throat. She was terrified he was dead. When her fingers felt the soft, warm flesh of her little nephew and the pulse beating beneath her fingers, she nearly began to cry again. This time from relief and joy.

"Jessie, how is he?" James yelled down to her.

"He's unconscious, but alive. I'm going to have to lift him out. I'm sending Jeremy up first."

Jessie took the rope from her waist and tied it around Jeremy's. "You hang on tight and let Uncle James pull you up. Use your legs to keep yourself from banging against the rocks, okay?"

"Okay," he answered, fear in his voice.

Jessie gave him a quick hug, then yelled up at James, "He's ready."

The rope grew taut as James began to pull up his tiny cargo. He'd have to use the horse to pull up Jessie and Jamie together, but he brought Jeremy up by hand. When the small boy appeared over the top of the cliff, James felt his heart swell with relief and love. "Come on, just a little farther," he said, then he grabbed him, pulling him into his arms, hugging him with all his strength.

"Uncle James, you're squeezing me," Jeremy croaked.

James laughed and released him. "You go sit under that tree," he directed as he untied him. "I've got to get Jessie and Jamie up here now."

"Yes, Uncle James," Jeremy replied weakly.

James heard the tone in his voice and looked at him puzzled. "What's the matter? Everything will be all right."

"Are we in trouble, Uncle James? Will we be punished?"

James fought the urge to laugh out loud. "I think sitting on a ledge all day is enough punishment, don't you?"

Jeremy nodded his head rapidly.

"I don't think you'll be taking off on any more visits, do you?"

Jeremy shook his head violently.

"Then, as soon as I get Jessie and Jamie up here the issue will be closed. Deal?"

"Deal." Jeremy ran to sit under the tree his uncle had pointed to, a smile lighting his dirty face.

James turned his attention back to Jessie. Tossing the end of the rope over the cliff, he called down to her, "Let me know when you're tied securely."

"All right," she called back, catching the rope with her left hand. Tying it around her waist wasn't so easy this time. Her right hand didn't want to work properly so she had to use her teeth to tighten the rope. She prayed it was tight enough. Bending over as far as she dared, she lifted Jamie with her left hand. Realizing she was going to have to use her right hand to get him up on her shoulder, she set her teeth, took a deep breath, and reached for him. The responding pain in her wrist caused her to break out in a cold sweat. Bile rose in her throat, and she had to fight to keep from crying out. After a few seconds of breathing deeply and slowly, she was able to maneuver him up to rest over her left shoulder. "I'm ready!" she called to James.

James heard Jessie and began to back his horse slowly. He had to be very careful not to pull too fast.

Jessie felt the rope tighten as James started to pull her up. Holding Jamie on her shoulder with her left hand, she tried to grasp the rope with her right. Her fingers were almost useless, and she ended up just balancing herself against the tension of the rope with her feet and legs. She practically walked up the side of the rock face.

As the edge of the cliff came into view, she sighed in relief. "We're almost there," she said, though she knew Jamie couldn't hear her. It was then the rope slipped.

Surprise and fear jolted through her as she felt the knot giving way around her waist. If it let go altogether, she and Jamie would fall to their deaths. "James!" she screamed. "The rope is letting go!"

James heard Jessie's terrified scream and felt his heart lurch in sympathy. "Hang on, Jessie! I've almost got you!" He nudged his horse farther back.

Jessie could almost reach the edge of the cliff, but her free hand, her right hand, wouldn't be able to support the weight of a flea at the moment. "James, I can't hold on! My arm!" she screamed.

James realized she was in real danger, and jumped from his horse. "Jeremy, come here quickly," he called to the child.

Jeremy ran to his uncle's side. "Yes, Uncle James?"

"You have to stand here and hold my horse. You can't let him move even one step. Can you do it?" he said quickly.

Jeremy looked wide eyed up at the huge animal. "Yes, Uncle James. I can do it."

"Good boy," James said, then raced to the edge of the cliff.

James could see Jessie and Jamie dangling just below him. "Hold on, Jessie. I'm going to reach down for you."

Jessie felt the rope slip again and gasped. "James, please hurry," she begged.

Lying on his stomach, he stretched over the edge and felt for them. They were just out of his reach. "Jessie, you're going to have to help me. Reach up to me," he said.

Jessie raised her right arm to him.

James saw her bandaged hand reaching up to him. He knew he was going to hurt her by pulling on that arm, but it couldn't be helped. It was the only way to get them up to safety. Reaching as far past her wrist as he could, he began to pull.

Jessie was blinded by the pain in her arm. Biting down on her lip to keep from screaming, she barely knew it when James pulled her and Jamie up into his arms.

James lifted Jamie from Jessie's shoulder and laid the boy out flat on the ground. He let Jessie slump to the grass to rest while he examined the boy. He'd check her out in a minute.

Jessie lay in the dirt next to James. The pain in her arm was agony, but she was more concerned about Jamie. "Is he all right?" she panted.

"I think so. His leg is broken and he's unconscious. I don't know whether or not he has internal injuries. But at least he's alive. We've got to get him back to the ranch."

"Yes," she breathed. "I'll help you." She tried to sit up, but felt a wave of nausea wash over her. Rolling to her side, she vomited into the dirt, her body heaving with the spasms.

James turned to her, raising her hair away from her face, supporting her while she was sick. "Are you all right now?" he asked as the spasms subsided.

Jessie turned back over and looked up at James. "Yes, I'm sorry I got sick. Thank you," she said.

James was amazed by her. He was certain if he'd been through what she had, he'd have done more than vomit. He glanced toward her right arm. "Let me have a look at that," he said.

Jessie tried to raise the arm, but couldn't. "Sorry," she said again.

James reached across her and gently picked up the arm. "My God, Jessie." he exclaimed. "The bandage is soaked with blood. What happened to it?"

Jessie just shrugged. She didn't have the strength to explain.

James untied the knot holding the bandage in place

and began to unwind it. When it fell free, he looked at her arm in shock. One of the broken bones was protruding through a jagged tear in her flesh. "I pulled you up by this arm," he moaned. "Jessie, I'm so sorry," he said, realizing how badly he must have hurt her.

"It's all right," she said weakly. "You saved my life."

❋ 15 ❋

James studied Jessie's arm. "I'm going to have to try and stabilize this, Jessie," he said softly.

"I know," she answered.

"It's going to hurt."

"It already does. A little more won't matter. Do what you have to do," she said.

"You're bleeding quite a bit. I'm afraid the break might have nicked the vein, so I can't try to set it. I'm just going to tighten the splints over it. I hope that will hold it until we can get you to the doctor."

Jessie nodded in response.

"Is Aunt Jessie all right?" Jeremy called from where he still held James's horse.

"She's fine, Jeremy. Just wait there a few more minutes, then I'll come get my horse."

"Okay, Uncle James," Jeremy called back.

James picked up the splints that had already been on Jessie's arm. Placing them firmly over the break, he began to wrap the bloody bandage around it as tightly as he dared. He could see Jessie flinching as he worked, and his heart pulsed in sympathy for her.

Jessie clenched her jaw as James wrapped her arm. Several times while he was working on her she felt the dark edge of unconsciousness tugging at her, but she fought it. She had to remain alert until they got the boys back to town.

"There, that's the best I can do, Jessie," James told her quietly.

"It's fine," she said. "Now let's get these boys to town." Pushing with her left hand, she tried to sit up. "This is silly," she said when she could barely raise herself.

James lifted her to a sitting position. "I think you're a little shocky, but I'm sure you'll be fine. Just sit here for a minute while I see about securing Jamie's leg."

James found a young sapling nearby and used his bowie knife to cut it at the base. Then he cut it in two, bringing the pieces back to where Jamie was lying. Setting the pieces of wood alongside the boy, he measured them against his short legs. He cut the wood down to the right length and threw the excess aside, then he reached for the end of the rope lying on the ground next to them. After cutting short, equal lengths from it, he tied the wooden splints he'd made to Jeremy's broken leg. "I'm almost glad he's unconscious," he murmured.

Jessie nodded. "Me too. The little guy sure doesn't need to feel any more pain than he already has."

"Are you ready to head back?" James asked.

"As I'll ever be," she responded. That wasn't entirely true, but hers and Jamie's injuries didn't leave them with the option of sitting there much longer. "I'll let Jeremy sit behind me. Can you handle Jamie?" she asked.

"I'll hold him across my lap," he responded.

Several minutes later, they were ready to start the long ride to town and the doctor.

As night settled in around them, Jessie was grateful for the partial moon overhead. The glimmering rays illuminated their path and made it possible for them to travel without much danger. The way was still rough though, so their progress was slow. They couldn't take the chance of jostling Jamie too much.

Nearly two hours later, James thought he heard riders approaching them. "Who's there!" he called.

"It's Juan, James," Juan returned.

James was relieved to hear a familiar voice. He was still concerned about who stole and killed Jessie's cattle. As Juan and some other men rode closer, he reined in.

"Boy, are we glad to have found you. I see you've got the boys," Juan said.

"Yes, they'd fallen over a cliff onto a ledge. Jamie's hurt. We're bringing them into town to the doctor," James explained.

"The doctor is at the Triple X. When Tinker told us what was going on, and after you didn't come back for so long, I sent for him. I was afraid his services might be needed."

"Good man," said James.

Jessie listened to this exchange, but didn't have the strength to add anything.

"Let's go," James directed. "The Triple X isn't far now."

Jessie lay on the soft mattress of the bed she'd used before at the Triple X. The doctor had left after setting her arm once more, and the laudanum he'd given her was just beginning to take effect. A cool breeze blew through the open window, lifting the lace curtain hanging there. Jessie mused that it looked like a ghost, just before she fell into a deep, deep sleep.

James leaned against the frame of the open door to Jessie's room, crossed his arms over his chest, and watched her close her eyes. Moonlight danced over her beautiful features, enhancing them, making her look like an angel. He was glad she was finally asleep. She'd been through so much today, and she'd proved to be tougher than any man he'd ever known. Even when he'd pulled her and Jamie up over the edge of the cliff by her broken arm, she hadn't so much as cried out.

Jeremy and Jamie were asleep too. The doctor had set

Jamie's leg and determined he'd suffered no internal injuries. All things considered, he and Jeremy had been very lucky.

Straightening, James uncrossed his arms and turned from Jessie's room, heading downstairs.

As he entered the kitchen he saw the mountain of dishes still waiting in the sink. Shaking his head, he remembered he hadn't eaten all day. Opening the bread box, he found the heel of a loaf. Searching the icebox, he found a chunk of cheese and some milk. Taking these items to the table, he began to eat. Using his bowie knife, he cut slabs of cheese and bread and pushed them together. When he shoved the combination into his mouth he was certain he'd never tasted anything better. He washed it down with the milk.

Hearing Carmen moving around in her room, he wondered whether or not she was feeling any better. If the filth in the kitchen was any indication, she'd been too ill to do anything all day or this evening. He realized he still wanted her out of the house. He had only let her stay because he'd felt some pity for her, but it wasn't working out. He needed someone competent in the house, especially while the boys were visiting.

Rubbing his hand over his eyes, James admitted to himself it wasn't Carmen's fault the boys had taken off and Jamie was injured. He accepted that it was his fault for not seeing to it they were supervised in his absence. But the mess in the house and the fact that there was almost no food was making the situation more difficult. He had to tell her to go.

He was just so tired. Stuffing more of the bread and cheese into his mouth, he chewed slowly, not looking forward to the scene he was sure she'd make when he told her she was fired.

Waiting was doing him no good, he decided after a few moments. Pushing himself up from the table, he walked to the door to her room and knocked.

"Yes?" Carmen inquired.

"It's me, James. May I talk to you for a moment?"

Carmen lowered her lids as she stared at the door. It was late. What could he want now? she wondered. Arranging herself on the bed in a provocative pose, she tilted her chin downward. "Yes, James. Come in," she called.

James turned the knob and pushed open the door. His gaze swept the room quickly, then focused on Carmen seated on her bed. She was wearing a thin, white cotton gown, and one shoulder was bare as the garment fell loosely, exposing the high, rounded mound of one breast. Her hair was a silken black shawl around her back, and her lips were parted in a soft smile.

"What is it, James? What can I do for you at this hour?" Carmen asked huskily as she felt his gaze on her flesh.

James gritted his teeth for a moment before answering. "You look like you're feeling better," he commented.

"Much. I told you it passes."

"Good, because I wouldn't want to—" He watched her lean toward him as though listening intently, the gown falling farther, the deep plum color of one nipple peeking above the edge of the fabric.

"Yes, James?" she purred.

Taking a deep breath, he stared hard into her eyes. "Carmen, this arrangement isn't working. I gave you another chance, but I'm not satisfied with the way you're keeping the house. And after what happened with the twins today—"

"That wasn't my fault," she said defensively, straightening her posture.

"No, of course not. I didn't mean to imply that it was. But when a crisis happens it seems to bring other things into focus. I have certain standards I want to live by, especially with the boys here. So, I'm afraid I'm going to have to let you go," he finished.

"You can't do that," Carmen protested, pulling herself up even straighter.

James nodded in her direction. "I'm afraid I can. I'd like you to move out first thing in the morning."

Carmen narrowed her eyes in anger. "I know why you're doing this," she hissed. "It's because you want that slut, Jessie Braddock, taking my place."

James's own eyes slimmed dangerously. "I won't let you talk that way about her," he warned, remembering Jessie's valiant behavior during the twins' rescue.

Carmen rose from the bed and paced toward him. "And what are you going to do about it? Will you strike me? I doubt it. I just can't believe you've let yourself become so blinded by her. I told you what she said about you. She only wants the Triple X, not you. She thinks you're a fool, but she's willing to do anything to become owner of the ranch once more." Her voice then dropped in tone, becoming softer, more vulnerable. "All I want to do is love you, James," she nearly whispered.

James felt himself flinch inwardly. "I'm sorry, Carmen. I don't feel the same," he told her. "And I want you to leave the house in the morning."

Carmen's chin came up defiantly. "Why should I wait until morning? I'll go now," she announced.

"You don't need to do that. It's late. You'll wake your father."

"I need to wake my father. There are things I need to tell him," she said. She whirled away from him, pulling open drawers in the bureau and grabbing the clothing within, tossing it wildly on the bed.

James clenched his jaw and steeled himself against her dramatics. Backing out of the room, he pulled the door closed behind him.

Going back to the table, he sat down once more, deciding to wait until Carmen had gone before going to bed. Yawning, he stretched and cleared the leftover food away from a spot on the table. Leaning over, he let his head rest on his forearms. Maybe he'd close his eyes for just a minute, he thought. In seconds he was asleep. He didn't see Carmen leave a half hour later.

* * *

Jessie carefully made her way through the house. The sky was a pale gray, though the sun hadn't yet shown its face above the distant mountain peaks. It wouldn't be long before the temperature began to rise, but for now the house felt cool.

She didn't know what had awakened her, maybe concern for the boys, but after she'd looked in on them, she hadn't wanted to go back to sleep. Instead, she'd decided to go downstairs. She was thirsty and a little hungry and though she doubted Carmen would be up and cooking breakfast yet, she was certain she'd be able to find something to eat.

When she entered the kitchen she gasped at the mess she saw. Dirty dishes filled the sink and covered every counter top. Smelly, greasy pans were sitting on a cold stove, and food, left uncovered, was swarming with flies. She noticed James slumped over the table. "James?" she called in alarm, crossing to his side. "Are you all right?" she asked, touching him gently on the shoulder.

James awakened slowly. He felt as though he was stuck in some dark tunnel, and struggled to reach the end of it.

"James?" Jessie tried again.

James opened his eyes and saw his own kitchen. Looking around him, he saw someone standing before him. As he raised his head to see who it was, he winced from the kink in his neck. "Jessie?" he questioned, turning his head from side to side. "What time is it?"

"About five thirty, I think. What are you doing down here? Did you sleep here?" she asked.

James continued flexing his neck and shoulders. "Yeah, I guess so. But what are you doing down here?" he asked, suddenly concerned for her.

"I guess I got hungry," she answered, then looked around the kitchen. "But it doesn't look like there's much chance of getting anything to eat."

James let his eyes follow the same path as Jessie's. "It does look pretty bad, doesn't it?"

Jessie nodded. She remembered he'd said Carmen was ill the day before, but this mess looked like more than a day's worth of accumulated dirt. "What time will Carmen be awake? Maybe she'll feel better today and clean this."

"Carmen won't be cleaning this," James replied with a sigh.

"Is she so ill, then? I'll help her with the mess," she offered.

"You're not doing anything," James told her, surprised she'd even think such a thing.

"I wouldn't mind, really. I don't feel too bad. Just a little stiff and sore. And a little groggy from the laudanum," she told him. It was true. Now that her arm had been set again, it didn't feel too bad, just a dull ache running up her arm.

"You aren't going to lift a finger to help clean this mess," James said firmly.

"But if Carmen—" She began to argue.

"Carmen isn't here any more," James said. "I told her to leave last night."

Jessie looked at James in surprise. Had something happened between Carmen and him that she didn't know about? A lovers' quarrel, perhaps? Whatever the reason, she was glad the woman was no longer under the same roof with her nephews. "I see," she responded, not sure what other remark to make. His and Carmen's relationship was really none of her business. And this might only be a temporary situation. If they'd had an argument they could very easily make up in the afternoon, and Carmen could be back in the house by that evening.

"So, I'll clean the kitchen before I go to work," James said, glancing around the filthy room.

Jessie looked around too. "What are you going to feed the crew?" she asked.

"Damn," James sighed. "I hadn't thought of that."

"Looks like you need my help whether you want it or not," Jessie told him.

"You're in no condition to do anything," he said.

Jessie looked down at herself. Her clothes were rumpled from sleeping in them, and they were dirty. Her right arm was bandaged from her fingertips to her elbow, and as her gazed dropped even lower she noticed a hole in the toe of her left sock. "I beg to differ," she said lightly, a smile on her face. "I'm in no condition for anything but manual labor, preferably cleaning something. Maybe a little of the clean will rub off on me."

James smiled at her. "Nice try, but you're not cleaning my house."

Jessie felt a stab of sadness at his choice of words. She knew he didn't do it on purpose, but he'd reminded her this was no longer her home. "I suppose you're right," she said softly, her eyes dropping.

James didn't know what caused the sudden change in Jessie's mood, but he was sorry to see the difference. "Well, maybe you can help with breakfast?" he suggested.

"I can do that," she answered, attempting to regain a little of her earlier mood. "I don't think there's a fire. Would you start one?"

"It's the first thing I'll do," he answered, smiling down at her.

Less than an hour later, Jessie was turning bacon in one pan and lifting flapjacks from another. The stack was getting high and she wondered when the men would begin to arrive.

"I could use another cup of coffee," said James from where he stood in front of the sink, his arms immersed nearly up to his elbows in sudsy water.

"You've got it," she replied, smiling. Retrieving his cup from the counter beside him, she brought it to the stove and filled it from the huge pot. Returning it to his side, she grinned at him. "This is fun," she said, surprising herself. Spending time with James this way was fun. If she didn't allow herself to dwell on their troubles she found she truly enjoyed his company.

James looked at the grimy apron Jessie had donned and shook his head in mirth. "Only you would think this is fun," he replied, chuckling.

Jessie heard the outside door open and turned to see who their first arrival was. The look on Juan de Silva's face told her something was wrong.

"James, may I have a word with you?" Juan asked, turning his hat nervously in his hands.

James frowned. He had been afraid this was coming. Juan was going to quit because he'd kicked Carmen out. Sighing, he removed his arms from the dish water, and reached for a towel. "Sure, Juan. Have a seat." He gestured toward the table.

Juan glanced toward the table, then at Jessie. "I think we should talk in private," he said.

"I'd be willing to leave so you two can talk," offered Jessie.

"No, you're still watching the breakfast. Juan and I can go into the dining room. Will that be all right, Juan?" James said.

Juan nodded and waited to follow James.

As he held the door for Juan, James looked back toward Jessie. "Will you bring in some coffee for Juan, please?" he asked.

"Certainly," she replied. When James disappeared into the dining room, she couldn't help wondering what Juan wanted to discuss with him. She was certain it had something to do with Carmen and probably concerned the fact that James had asked her to leave last night. "Oh, well," she sighed, looking for a clean cup for Juan. "It's none of my business."

James sat down at the head of the table and gestured for Juan to take the seat next to him. "What can I do for you, Juan?" he asked, getting the ball rolling.

Juan sat down slowly. He placed his hat on the table in front of him and worried the brim with his fingers. "There's something I have to tell you, James, and it is difficult for me to say it."

James sighed inwardly. He didn't want to lose Juan. The man had become more than an employee, he'd become a friend. "It's all right, Juan. I'm sure I'll understand anything you have to say," he offered, trying to make a difficult situation easier on his friend.

Juan glanced downward at his own fingers. He was sorry for what he had to tell James. He didn't want to cause him hardship, but Carmen had left him no choice. "You see, James, it's Carmen," he paused, not knowing exactly how to continue.

"I know. She's angry with me," said James. "But she didn't have to leave in the middle of the night. She could have waited until this morning. I'd hate to see you leave over this," he said.

Juan looked perplexed. "I am not leaving," he said.

James paused for a second. "Good, I was afraid you'd come to me to quit your job," he said, smiling.

"No, James. I came to tell you Carmen's pregnant with your child."

Jessie heard the words as she carried Juan's coffee through the door, and froze in her tracks. Her heart began a thunderous pounding, and she felt suddenly cold all over. "I—I'm just going to—." she choked. Backing out of the room as quickly as she could, she set the coffee cup on the counter and raced out of the kitchen by the back door.

James looked up in horror as Juan's words registered. He was stunned to see Jessie in the doorway. He felt as though he'd been kicked by a horse when he saw the look on her face. "Jessie!" he yelled after her. Standing up, he took two steps after her, then stopped. Turning toward Juan, he felt his world coming to an end. "When did she tell you this?" he asked.

"Last night," answered Juan. "She's been crying since she came home. It was all I could do to get her to calm down enough to drink a cup of coffee."

"Is that all she said?" James asked, as if it weren't enough.

"No. She tells me she loves you and that she thought you loved her, too. She says you turned against her when Miss Braddock arrived."

James sank back down to his chair. Leaning forward, he put his elbows on the table and rested his forehead in his palms. "I didn't turn against her, Juan. I never loved her to begin with," he said.

"But, the baby?" Juan questioned.

James closed his eyes. How could he tell Juan his daughter was a slut? That she'd crawled into his bed nude one night when he was drunk? "It was a mistake," he simply said.

Juan sat very still. He was going to be a grandfather and this man was the father. His daughter was crying her heart out in her room and his son was ready to fight over the situation. He studied the man before him. He liked him and respected him. Sighing, he stood up. "Carmen is sometimes difficult. She has been since her mother died. She is sometimes willful and disobedient. But she is a good girl, and I know you will do the right thing by her," he said slowly.

James raised his eyes to meet his friend's gaze. The man expected him to marry his daughter. Any man would expect the same, but did Juan really want to condemn his daughter to a loveless marriage? "I don't love her," he said.

"You will learn to love her," Juan told him. He then turned away. "I have work to do now. We will talk again later."

James watched Juan walk from the room. His head was bowed and his back was bent slightly. He was a man with a burden, and James felt pity for him.

Letting his gaze drop back to the smooth surface of the table he wondered why life had dealt him such a hand. "What am I going to do?" he wondered out loud. He couldn't even imagine being married to Carmen. It was then he noticed the smell of burning bacon. "Oh hell," he shouted as he ran to stop breakfast from going up in flames.

Jessie had raced away from the house as fast as she could. When she finally stopped running, she was far from the buildings and walking toward a stand of trees that guarded her family's cemetery. Her mother's parents were buried there. She'd never met either one of them, but the stories her mother had told her about them made her feel comforted as she neared the tiny plot of land.

Out of breath, she lowered herself to sit at the foot of the graves. Her right arm was throbbing from the exertion of running so she held it upright, relieving some of the pounding. Closing her eyes, she remembered the look in James's eyes when Juan told him about Carmen's pregnancy. He'd been surprised. He'd been angry. But he hadn't immediately denied it was possible. "Why should I even be surprised," she railed. "I knew they were lovers," she told herself.

Lying back on the cool grass, she looked up through the trees. The leaves created a canopy over her head, shielding this spot from the heat of the sun. "Why do I even care?" she said. Closing her eyes again, she forced herself to remember everything Carmen had ever said to her. It was no wonder the woman had resented her so. She probably knew she was pregnant but was afraid to tell James. Her pregnancy was probably the reason she'd been ill. "Damn," she whispered.

After thinking about the situation from every angle, she sat up again. Her heart beat shallowly beneath her breasts, and she felt cold inside, a cold she didn't think would go away anytime soon. James had made her the other woman. He'd used her. It didn't matter that her body came to life beneath his touch. It didn't matter that his kisses brought her to the brink of sensual insanity. He belonged to Carmen, and he always would. Together, they would live on the Triple X forever.

Sighing, she stood up. She'd left breakfast cooking on the stove. It was probably ruined by now. She'd just have to clean the mess and start over. "In more ways than one," she scoffed at herself.

James dropped a strip of bacon in the pan and watched it begin to sizzle with the others already browning in the grease. When he heard the door open, he was sure it would be a few more stragglers coming in for breakfast. The table was nearly full. The men were stuffing themselves with flapjacks and bacon. Turning around, he was surprised to see Jessie. His heart began a rapid beat. "Jessie, I need to talk to you," he said quietly as she neared.

"No you don't, James," she answered calmly. "We really have nothing left to talk about."

"But Jessie, I want to explain."

Jessie stared directly into his dark eyes, her senses reeling. Fighting to stay collected, she said, "You don't owe me any explanations, James. Now hadn't we better finish this breakfast?" Turning her back on him, she stepped up to the stove. Picking up the fork, she maneuvered the bacon around in the pan, then set the fork back down.

James felt as though the floor was falling out from under him. "Jessie, please listen to me," he tried again.

Jessie could take no more. "No!" she blurted, then lowered her voice when she noticed the murmurs and stares from the table. She wasn't going to cause a scene in front of these men. "I won't listen to you, James. There's nothing you could say that would change anything. You're going to be a father. Carmen is going to be a mother. I hope you'll be very happy together," she whispered.

James could see the curious stares from some of his men. "Come with me," he said, taking her by the hand and leading her into the dining room.

Jessie let herself be led rather than embarrass herself by fighting with him. "What?" she said when the door was safely closed behind them.

"Carmen and I are not going to be happy together," he said.

"That's too bad, though it's really none of my business. May I go finish cooking breakfast now?" she asked.

"No. I'm not going to marry Carmen. I'm not in love with her," he said.

"That's unfortunate, but whether you want to marry

her or not is a moot point now, don't you think? The woman is pregnant with your child."

James clenched his jaw in anger. "So she claims," he fumed venomously.

Jessie's arched brows rose. "Do you doubt her? Isn't it possible?"

James felt defeated. "Yes, it's possible."

Jessie's heart hardened. "Then I'm sure you'll do the right thing," she said.

"That's the same thing Juan said," he murmured.

"Because it's true," she offered.

James stared into her emerald eyes. There was something between them, something more than the spark that exploded into an inferno every time he touched her, something he suspected would have eventually brought them together despite the Triple X. Now that something would never get the chance to flourish. She'd closed her heart to him. He could see it in her eyes. "I'm sorry, Jessie," he murmured.

"You don't owe me an apology, James. I'm nothing to you and you're nothing to me. I truly hope you have a happy life with Carmen." She turned and went back through the door into the kitchen.

James sank into a chair at the table, tears burning his eyes. "Damn it," he whispered, reaching up to wipe the moisture from his eyelashes.

❋ 16 ❋

Jessie spent most of that day nursing Jamie. Her heart went out to the little boy. She could tell he was in a great deal of pain, but he refused to cry or complain about it.

"Aunt Jessie, will you stay with me for a while?," he asked while they were eating lunch together on his bed.

"Yeah, will you?" chimed in Jeremy.

"I'll be here all day," Jessie answered.

Jamie's expression saddened. "Oh," he murmured.

"What's wrong?" asked Jessie.

"I want you to stay with me for lots of days," he said.

Jessie felt a stab of guilt as she looked into his sad eyes. She still thought what happened to the boys was partly her fault. If she'd been here more often to see them they might not have taken off on their adventure.

Dropping her gaze for a moment, she thought of James and Carmen. She didn't want to spend even one minute around them that wasn't absolutely necessary, but looking back up at her nephew, so small in his bed, she couldn't put her own feelings ahead of his needs. "I'll stay for a while," she promised.

"How long?" asked Jeremy, a huge grin on his face.

"That will depend on how Jamie does with his recovery. The doctor said he can start getting out of bed in a few days if he feels up to it. He's going to bring a wheelchair and some crutches for him the next time he visits," Jessie explained.

"All right," they answered together, identical smiles now on their faces.

Jessie watched the contentment of the small boys as they resumed eating their lunches. Her own appetite hadn't been very good when she sat down to eat. At the thought of remaining under the same roof with James for a while longer it disappeared completely. "I'm going to take my plate downstairs. You two finish eating and when I return I'll read you a story. Then Jamie has to take a nap," she said.

"A nap?" Jamie asked, a slight whine in his voice.

"Doctor's orders," she replied.

"Doctor's orders," repeated Jeremy.

Jamie grimaced but gave up the fight. "All right," he agreed.

Jessie stood up and, taking her plate with her, left the room. Once downstairs, she listened before entering the kitchen. She'd been trying to avoid James since this morning and so far she'd been successful.

The kitchen sounded quiet so she entered and was relieved to find it empty. Dumping what was left of her sandwich into the garbage pail, she set her plate in the sink to be washed later. Sighing tiredly, she crossed to the table and sank into one of the chairs. Resting her forehead on her left hand, she closed her eyes and tried to keep from thinking about James and Carmen.

At the sound of the back door opening, she looked up, afraid it might be James. It wasn't. It was Carmen, and the expression on her face was one of smug satisfaction. Jessie pushed herself away from the table and stood up. "You can have the kitchen to yourself, I was just leaving," she said.

"No, I want you to stay," said Carmen. "I want to talk to you."

Jessie raised her chin and looked from under her thick lashes at the woman. "We have nothing to say to each other," she said.

"You're wrong. I have something to say to you," Carmen nearly purred, running one fingertip along the table as she slowly advanced. "I wanted to tell you to your face that I won," she said.

Jessie could feel her muscles tighten, but she refused to let Carmen see her words had any affect on her. "I don't know what you think you've won. We weren't in a competition."

"I knew you would say that, but we both know you're lying. You want this ranch, and you wanted James. Now I have both." She smiled evilly, her red lips stretching across her face.

"It's true, I wanted this ranch, and I'd be lying if I said I didn't any more, but I've come to terms with the fact that James is the legal owner, if not the rightful one. As for me wanting him," she paused momentarily, "I'm afraid your information is incorrect. I never wanted James and I still don't."

"That's a lie." Carmen threw back at her. "I know you had sex with him. He told me all about it. Are you trying to tell me you had sex with a man you don't want? What does that make you?" she challenged.

That makes me stupid, Jessie told herself, clenching her left fist. "I don't care what James told you. I don't want him and I never did," she said.

Carmen laughed out loud. "Your lies are pathetic. I've seen the way you look at him and I've seen the way he looks at you, but it doesn't matter. I'm pregnant with James's child, and I'm going to marry him. Then I'll be mistress of the Triple X. And when I do, you will no longer be welcome here."

James scowled from the door. "Carmen, Jessie will be welcome to visit here any time she chooses," he informed her stiffly.

Jessie looked at him in surprise. She hadn't heard him come in and she guessed from the startled look on Carmen's face that she hadn't either. "It doesn't matter, James. I won't be coming back," Jessie told him. "Now, if you'll both excuse me, I'm going upstairs to be with the boys," she said as she crossed the room.

James watched Jessie leave, his eyes narrowed in anger. "I heard what you told her," he said, his voice barely above a whisper.

Carmen whirled to face him. "James, let me explain," she pleaded, her eyes filling with tears.

"There's nothing to explain, Carmen."

"But there is. I told her she wouldn't be welcome here because I know you care for her. I couldn't bear to have her here while I'm growing fat with your child. It would break my heart," she sobbed.

James stood staring down at her. Her physical beauty was obvious, but her soul was so blackened he found her repulsive. "Carmen, I'm not sure I'm going to marry you," he stated.

Carmen's eyes widened with fear. "You have to. I'm pregnant with your child!"

James lowered his gaze to take in the smooth surface of her stomach. "So you say," he said.

"You think I would lie about such a thing!" she exclaimed.

"Time will tell," he answered.

"And when you see I am telling the truth?"

James sighed heavily. "I'll decide then."

"But you can't make me wait until the pregnancy is showing. People will talk. I'll be a laughingstock," she wailed.

"We'll wait," he responded firmly.

Carmen ground her teeth together. "You're only doing this because of her," she spat, pointing in the direction Jessie had gone. "You want that slut, and you think if you keep me waiting long enough I'll give up on you. Well, I won't! You belong to me, and this baby will prove it." She walked haughtily past him toward the door. "And we'll see how long you wait to wed me when I tell my father and brother how cruel you're being," she threatened.

James had had enough. Reaching out and grasping her arm, he pulled her closer. Staring down into her face, he spoke to her between clenched teeth. "Don't threaten me with your family, Carmen. I won't be forced to do anything I don't want to do. If it turns out you are telling the truth about the baby, then I'll marry you, but it will be a marriage in name only. Do you understand me? In name only!"

Carmen flinched as James's grip on her arm became tighter. "Let go of me. You're hurting me!" she complained, jerking her arm free. "Let me tell you something, James. You may think the marriage will be in name only, but I will make you want me again. Wait and see."

James shook his head. "It'll never happen," he said calmly, convincingly.

Carmen's mind raced angrily. She couldn't bear the thought of never making love to James again. "It's all her fault," she snarled. "If Jessie hadn't arrived you'd still be happy with me."

"You know that's not true," James argued.

"It is true. I wish she'd never come here!" she screeched, her hands curled into claws. Turning on her heel, she went for the door, kicking it open violently and letting it crash against the side of the house as she exited.

James stepped to the door, catching it when it swung slowly back toward him. Watching Carmen stomp her way across the yard, he saw her intercept her brother Marco and observed her gesturing angrily as she talked to him. Marco's reaction was to put his arm around his sister's shoulders in sympathy. Grimacing, James wondered how long it would be before he got a visit from an outraged Marco. It didn't matter. He wouldn't marry Carmen until he was certain she was pregnant.

Jessie heard Carmen and James arguing downstairs for a while, but she couldn't make out their words. She was relieved she couldn't hear what they were saying. She already knew they were arguing about her and that was bad enough.

"Is Uncle James mad at Carmen?" asked Jeremy.

Jessie glanced down at the youngster. "They're having a disagreement," she conceded.

Three nights later, Jessie slept fitfully. Tossing and turning, she awoke many times. Finally, she gave up trying to sleep and sat up, propping her pillows against the headboard. She was going home in the morning. Jamie's leg was hurting him less and the doctor had brought him the wheelchair. He'd ridden it through the house all afternoon, sometimes letting Jeremy push him.

Sighing, she moved her legs restlessly under the blankets. "Maybe I should just get up and go home now," she murmured, then thought better of it. She had to say good-bye to the boys.

During the past three days, she'd managed to avoid James except at meals. Twice he'd tried to convince her to meet him somewhere to talk, but both times she'd let him know with certainty that they had nothing to discuss. The hurt look in his eyes had nearly persuaded her to give in, but she'd managed to stick to her resolve. She wasn't going to be the further cause of problems between him and Carmen if she could help it. He'd gotten the girl pregnant, now he had to accept his responsibilities.

Staring blankly, she rested against the headboard. Her right arm had begun to itch so she raised it to peer at the bandage. The itching was under one of the splints and not easy to get to. Turning her arm over, she tried to see a way of scratching the irritating spot. It was then she realized there was an unusual amount of light in the room for the middle of the night. She also noticed a glowing orange tint to the light. "What's going on?" she mouthed. She heard some shouting outside.

Jumping out of bed, she pulled back the lace curtain and peered out the window. What she saw there filled her heart with terror. "Brush fire!" she yelled. A wall of flame several miles wide was driving toward them straight from hell.

James opened Jessie's door with a crash. Standing in the opening, his eyes burned with fear and anger. "Get the boys and go to the creek!" he shouted. "I'm going with the men to try and stop it."

Jessie turned toward him, fear gripping her throat. "But it's huge," she said.

"We've got to try. It's heading this way."

Jessie nodded. "I'll get the boys." She saw him turn and run from her doorway. She heard him moving through the house and outside. Turning back to the window, she could see him in the yard, giving orders to his men. Moments later, he was riding away on horseback toward the fire. A cold hand of terror closed over her heart. What if he never came back? Pushing such morbid thoughts from her mind, she hurriedly pulled off her nightgown and got dressed.

James rode hard toward the fire. He and his men carried shovels and picks across their saddles. They had to build a firebreak, and they had to do it fast. That fire was eating up the dried grasses of the range with the speed of a locomotive.

Yet, as he rode he didn't think about the fire. He thought about Jessie. He pictured her the way she looked when he'd burst into her room only minutes earlier. She'd been standing in front of the window, silhouetted against the orange glow of the fire. When she'd turned to face him, she'd been illuminated by the fire, the long curls of her hair glimmering warmly in the light, the soft curves of her face emphasized by the red-orange glow. He'd also seen the outline of her body beneath the fabric of her thin cotton gown. He'd seen the upward thrust of her breasts and the smooth plane of her stomach. The sight of her had nearly chased the importance of what he was doing from his mind. He could very easily have laid her down on the bed and buried himself within her. Frowning at the futility of these thoughts, he spurred his mount to a faster speed. "Damn," he shouted, the sound being lost in the roar of the oncoming monster of flames.

"Come on boys, wake up," Jessie urged them. "We're in a hurry so you have to get dressed quickly. Jeremy you dress yourself while I help Jamie. Please hurry," she asked them.

Jeremy and Jamie awakened groggily. "Where are we going, Aunt Jessie?" asked Jeremy.

"We're going to the swimming hole," she answered.

"At night?" Jamie questioned incredulously.

"Yes, just this once," she answered.

"But what about my leg?" he asked.

Jessie stared hard at the bandaged leg. "It will be fine," she told him.

"Why are we going now?" asked Jeremy. "I'm tired now. Can't we go tomorrow?"

Jessie grabbed his hands and pulled him to an upright position. "No, we can't wait until tomorrow. I don't want you boys to be frightened, but there's a fire out on the range. It's probably not going to get anywhere near here, but as a precaution we're going to go to the creek. If the fire does get a little close we'll be safe in the water," she told them in a calm voice.

"A fire? Can we see it?" Jeremy asked, suddenly perking up.

"I'm sure you'll see it once we're outside. So, let's hurry," she said.

Jeremy leaped from the bed and pulled open his bureau drawers. Jessie smiled gratefully that he was cooperating. She proceeded to dress Jamie.

A short while later, Jessie carried Jamie out of the house with Jeremy right beside her. Looking around her, she spied a wagon, hitched and ready to go. "Thank you, James," she whispered, knowing he'd left it for them.

"Look at the fire, Aunt Jessie. It's so big," exclaimed Jamie.

"Yes it is," she agreed, her heart filled with a renewed sense of fear. The fire was much closer now. She realized that if it continued on its course it would take out her ranch long before it ever reached the Triple X. She said a prayer that Tinker and Johnny would be all right and that they'd think to save Smokey and the other animals if they could.

Jessie settled Jamie in the back of the wagon then lifted Jeremy to the seat. "Hang on boys, I'm going to go a little fast."

Both boys cheered as she slapped the reins hard against the horse's rump and they felt the wagon lurch forward. "Here we go!" they shouted, happily unaware of the potential danger around them.

Jessie guided the horse and wagon to the swimming hole as fast as she could. She could see the flames of the fire licking the sky and consuming everything in its path as it bore down on them. As she pulled the wagon beneath the willows by the creek, she looked back over her shoulder and wondered where James was in that inferno. Saying a prayer for his safety, she plunged through the overhanging branches into the dim light by the creek.

James felt as though his lungs were going to burst from the heat as he dug side by side with his crew. Every muscle in his back and shoulders ached with exhaustion, and he felt as though his skin were on fire. Glancing to either side of him, he surveyed his crew. Each man swung a pick or stomped a shovel blade into the sod, turning it as quickly as he could. The firebreak they'd been working on was nearly twenty feet wide and approximately a quarter of a mile long. He hoped it would be enough to keep the fire from destroying the Triple X. The sweat ran in rivulets down his face and his eyes burned as he dug and prayed at the same time.

"It's almost here!" shouted someone down the line.

James looked up at the blaze. It was, indeed, bearing down on them. "Come on, men. We've got to get away from here in case the fire jumps the break!" Running toward his horse, he grabbed the reins and jerked them free of the bush they'd been tied to. Mounting in one leap, he controlled the frightened animal and waited until he saw all his men were safely on horseback and riding out of danger's way. He spurred his horse away from the fire.

The men scattered in several directions, then stopped to watch the fire. James could see several of them in the reflected glow of the flames. He continued to pray.

The fire raged toward the break. Reaching it, the blaze seemed to slow, and James waited, watching expectantly. Gripping the reins tightly, he stared into the flames, willing them to stop. Suddenly, a patch of fire appeared on the other side of the break. "Damn it!" he cursed, jerking the reins to the side. They'd failed. The fire now raged out of control.

Turning in the saddle, he looked away from the fire, following its probable path with his eyes. The tall stand of willows at the swimming hole would fall victim to the flames in a matter of minutes. "Jeessiiee!" he shouted, spurring his mount to a gallop. He had to get to Jessie and the boys. He had to make sure they were in the water. Frantic with fear for their safety, he rode like a wild man, sweat pouring down his body, muscles straining as the terrified horse tried to bolt.

Jessie could see the glow of the fire getting brighter. "The firebreak didn't stop it," she murmured, her heart slamming against her chest in terror. Looking at the two tiny people entrusted to her care, she knew what she had to do. "Come on, boys. We're getting in the creek," she told them. Running around the side of the wagon, she reached in and pulled Jamie into her arms. "Jeremy, follow me," she ordered.

"I'm scared, Aunt Jessie," Jamie said into her ear.

"We're going to be fine," she told him.

Stepping into the water, Jessie was surprised by how cold it felt. It had to be because the heat of the fire was already making the air around them feel like an oven. "Jeremy, follow me in, and hang on to my belt with both hands," she said.

"It's cold," he whined.

"I know it is, baby, but we have to stay in the creek until the fire passes." She realized she had to shout to be heard over the roar of the inferno.

The water lapped around her hips as she walked farther into the creek. "Jeremy, Jamie, I'm going to sit down now. I'll hang on to both of you and you can hold on to my neck, all right?"

Both boys nodded, their eyes full of fear.

Jessie lowered herself slowly. The water was like ice and she could feel the boys shivering with her. "Hang on tight," she instructed. Putting her arms around her tiny nephews, she hugged them to her, praying they'd live to see a new day.

James burst through the branches of the willows, the fire only a hundred feet behind him. "Jessie!" he shouted. "Where are you!"

Jessie saw James on horseback, looking like the devil himself in the glow of the fire. "James, we're in the water!" she yelled back.

James squinted toward the creek. He could barely make out three heads bobbing in the water. "Thank God," he murmured. Jumping from his horse, he struck the animal on the rump, setting him free to escape the fire. He noticed the horse still hitched to the wagon, and pulled his knife. Cutting the leads as quickly as he could, he sent the animal running for his life. He ran for the creek just as the treetops overhead burst into flames. He splashed into the water and fell beside Jessie and the twins. Wrapping his arms around them, he held on tight.

Jessie saw the explosions of fire in the trees. "What do we do?" she shouted.

"We'll have to go under for a second to get our hair wet," James instructed.

Helping the boys, they dunked their heads in the cold water.

"I'm ssoo—ccccold, Uncle—JJJames," said Jeremy.

Jamie nodded. "MMMe tooo," he agreed.

"I know it, boys, but we've got to stay here until the fire is gone."

Jessie's eyes met James's over the boys' heads. She couldn't keep the fear from showing there. "How long will it take?" she asked, beginning to choke on the smoke.

"I don't know," James answered. He, too, felt the smoke in his lungs. "We've got to do something about this," he said. Releasing his hold on Jessie and boys for a moment, he tore off his shirt. Then, making a tent with the wet garment over their heads, he wrapped his arms around them once more.

Jessie could hear the fire destroying the world around them. The trees screamed their agony as the flames ate away their flesh, ripping the bark from trunks, devouring thousands of leaves in mere seconds. She could see the red-orange glow of the flames reaching out to them through the fabric of James's shirt, and she clung to him and the boys in terror.

The fire burned for what seemed like hours. Flames shot out overhead and all around them. Twice James had to wet his shirt and hang it back over their heads. The first time he did, Jessie looked around at the devastation going on overhead. She was so horrified by what she saw that when he wet the shirt again she just closed her eyes and prayed they'd see morning.

Finally, when Jessie was certain the fire would burn forever, James lifted the edge of the shirt and peered out. "James?" she whispered hoarsely.

"It seems to have passed," he said, lifting the shirt a little more.

Jessie looked out from under the shirt. The gray glow of dawn had begun to illuminate the sky, though the smoke from the fire remained to keep them in darkness. Everywhere she looked were the blackened remains of casualties of the fire. Tall, charred pillars of wood, crippled and twisted from the fire, were all that was left of the beautiful willows that had grown in this spot for a hundred years. The plush grass that once cooled the earth now lay like black dust over the barren wasteland left in the wake of the blaze.

"Aunt JJJesssie?" said Jamie. "Is ittt—over yyyet?"

"I think so," she answered him.

James pulled the shirt completely from their heads. The air was still thick with smoke, and small patches of fire clung to life nearby, but the main fire had passed. "We made it," he said gratefully. Standing up, he lifted Jeremy with him and watched as Jessie emerged from the water with Jamie in her arms. "We made it," he repeated reverently.

Jessie nodded as tears of gratitude filled her eyes. They were alive. She smiled through her tears as she felt Jamie shivering in her arms. He was alive to shiver, to feel the cold, and to cough on the smoke that filled the air. "Let's get out of here," she said.

James led the way out of the creek. "I suppose we'd better go see if there's anything left," he said once they were standing on dry ground again.

"Do you think . . . ?" Jessie began, thinking about the house.

"I don't know," James answered solemnly. Putting Jeremy down, he reached to take Jamie from Jessie's arms. "How's your wrist?"

Jessie lifted the arm and looked at it. "It seems all right. To tell you the truth I'd forgotten about it," she answered.

"Let's go, then," said James.

The walk back to the house was slow going. The ground was hot and small fires still burned everywhere, frightening the children. After they'd been walking for quite a while, Jessie squinted ahead, not believing what she was seeing. She felt her heart break as she realized the truth. "Oh, James, it's gone," she breathed, tears blurring her vision. "It's all gone."

James stopped walking and stared at the mass of burned rubble that had been his home. One section of one wall, the foundation, and a partial chimney were the only things left to show where the house had once stood. Smoke drifted up from several areas inside the foundation, and he could see a small fire still burning along a beam that leaned against the partial wall. Turning slowly, he surveyed the rest of the ranch. The barn was gone, as were the corrals, the pigpen, the chicken coop, and everything else that had made up the Triple X. He only hoped the people who worked for him had made it to safety.

Jessie stared at the pile of charred remains and didn't try to stop her tears. This had been her home, her dream. All her childhood memories began with this house. Every Christmas, every birthday. Nearly every important event that had occurred in her life had happened here. She realized that she hadn't given up the hope that someday it would be hers again.

Walking forward, she stepped carefully over the barrier of the foundation. Charcoal crackled under her boots as she walked through the rubble. She identified each room as she passed through it, finding tiny pieces of the furnishings unburned. In the dining room she found the brass-capped foot of one of the table legs, also the top to a glass brandy decanter. In the kitchen, the sink lay on its side where it had fallen when the wood around it disintegrated. Silverware, blackened but still intact, lay in a heap on a pile of smoldering wood. Pots and pans, pieces of broken dishes, and the handle from the icebox were lying along what had been one of the walls. In the office she saw the safe lying on its side, and all that was left of James's pool table was the slate top, blackened and cracked.

Turning back to face James, she couldn't even speak.

"Jessie, are you all right?" James asked her, the look on her face frightening him.

Jessie nodded, afraid if she opened her mouth she'd scream.

James sat Jamie carefully on the ground and told Jeremy to stay with him. Walking toward Jessie, he stepped over the foundation and crossed to where she stood, staring at him with hollow, tear-filled eyes. "There's nothing we could have done," he said.

Jessie knew he was right. The fire had burned out of

control. It was just bad luck that it burned the ranch. She knew she'd probably find the same destruction at her ranch.

She could finally trust herself to speak. "I'm all right, James. This was just such a shock."

James breathed easier when he saw her returning to herself. "I know it was. It was to me, too. But we survived, and that's what's really important."

She glanced back at the boys sitting in the dirt. "You're right, of course."

"Uncle James, I'm hungry," whined Jamie. "Can I have a sandwich?"

Jeremy looked at his brother and frowned. "How can you have a sandwich? The kitchen burned up," he answered in a tone that suggested sarcasm.

James felt his heart lift a little at Jeremy's words. "We might not have a kitchen, but we'll get something to eat," he said. "Even if we have to walk to town."

"James!" shouted Juan from a distance. "James, you are alive! We thought you were caught in the fire. Thank God you are all right!"

❋ 17 ❋

"Juan, it's good to see you!," called James, walking toward the wagon the man was driving. Several people were riding in the wagon with him, and James felt a sense of relief to see familiar faces. As he met the wagon, he looked into Juan's eyes. "Did everyone get away safely?" he asked.

Juan raised his shoulders. "I don't know. I found these men on foot at the end of the firebreak. Their horses had bolted. We barely made it away in time."

James's eyes lowered in concern for his crew. He employed over thirty people on the Triple X. The men in the wagon were only a handful of them. He sighed heavily as he said a silent prayer for the others still missing.

"Have you seen Carmen and Marco?" asked Juan, his voice full of fear.

James looked back up into his friend's eyes. "No, I haven't," he said quietly. He realized he hadn't even thought about Carmen or Marco. "I'm sure they're fine," he said, not sure at all. Where had they been during the fire? he wondered.

"James?" Jessie called. "Look." She pointed toward town.

James turned in the direction she indicated. At least

twenty riders were coming toward them. In seconds, he recognized several as his employees. The others were townspeople, all riding hard toward the ranch.

As the group neared them, James went forward to greet them. "Hello," he said, smiling.

"Mr. Bonner, we're sure glad to see you," one of the cowboys said.

"I'm glad to see you, too, Tom. Do you know if any of the others got away?" James asked quickly.

"Heck, yeah," answered Tom. "Everybody's fine. Me and a few of the boys here decided to come back with these folks from town to see if there was anything left." He quickly scanned the burned area. "Ain't much, is there," he observed.

"Not much," replied James.

"Mr. Bonner," began Mr. Medley, the store owner, "we're certainly glad to see you survived. The orange glow of that fire lit up the night sky like the Fourth of July. We were afraid you'd all been caught in the blaze. Thank the Lord you were spared."

"My thoughts exactly," said James. "But as you can see, we were the only things spared." He gestured toward the burned-out ruins of the house and barn.

Mr. Medley nodded. "Well, my missus and quite a few of the other ladies are loading up the wagons back in town."

"Wagons?"

"Yes, sir. We rode on ahead to make sure there was a reason to come out. As soon as one of us gets back to let them know it's all right to come out, the ladies are bringing food and clothing and some tents I dug up from the storeroom."

James was gratified by his neighbors' generosity. "I don't know what to say, Mr. Medley," he said.

"There's nothing to say," responded the store owner. "I'll go tell the missus to get the ladies started this way." He nodded at James and Jessie, then turned his mount back toward town.

"Mr. Medley, did anyone see Carmen and Marco?" asked Juan before the man left.

"Yes, Mr. de Silva. They both rode into town last night. They're fine. They'll be riding out with the wagons."

"Thank God," sighed Juan.

"What about Tinker and Johnny?" Jessie inquired.

"Yes, they made it, too. And that dog of yours made such a ruckus barking that I finally gave him a bone to shut him up."

Jessie smiled. "He does love bones," she said.

"And he'll be busy a long time with the one I gave him."

Jessie raised her brows in curiosity.

"It's as big as he is," the store owner clarified, grinning.

"Does anyone know how the fire started?" asked Tom, surveying the damage.

James turned his gaze toward Tom. "I'd guess lightning. We've had those clouds on the horizon for a few days," he said.

"Yeah, probably," agreed Tom.

"I'm going back to town now. I'll see you a little later," said the store owner, nudging his horse forward.

"See you later, and thanks again," said James.

After Mr. Medley left, the other men dismounted. Some of them began to discuss with James where the tents should be set up. Others started to clear the ground of burned debris. Still others began to look for scattered livestock.

Jessie watched the bustle around her and decided she and the boys needed to clean up a little. Helping them to the pump, she wiped the blackened handle as well as she could, then began to pump water over their hands. "You wash your faces, too," she told them.

Jeremy dove into the washing process, splashing water everywhere. Jessie had to help Jamie, but soon they were all a bit cleaner than they'd been. "I guess that will have to do until the tents get here and we can have more privacy," she commented.

A little over an hour later, the wagons rolled in full of supplies.

The following two weeks passed in a blur for Jessie. She'd found her ranch in the same state as the Triple X, and every day was spent cleaning, clearing, and rebuilding. On her first trip to town for supplies, she'd wired her parents the news about the fire and let them know she was all right. After that, the only thing that interrupted the continuous flow of work were her visits to the twins. She'd vowed to never again let her personal feelings about James and Carmen interfere with her responsibility to her nephews. They would only be guests on the Triple X for another month or so, and she was determined to make that time as safe and enjoyable for them as she could.

Carmen had returned to the ranch looking none the worse for the fire. She claimed that Marco had saved her life, and bragged to anyone who'd listen how brave her brother was. Marco, on the other hand, looked haggard, and seemed to resent the attention his sister brought him. "Leave it alone, Carmen," he told her rudely one afternoon within earshot of Jessie and the boys.

"Why is Marco angry with Carmen?" asked Jamie from his new wheelchair.

Jessie raised her shoulders. "I don't know," she answered. She'd been careful to avoid Carmen whenever possible. The woman was surly and short with her when they did have to speak, and Jessie could see her hatred in every passing glance.

"Look, Aunt Jessie, someone's coming," said Jeremy, pointing toward a wagon just coming into view.

Jessie glanced at the wagon for just a moment. "It's probably someone with more supplies," she commented.

"Do you think they're bringing candy?" Jamie asked.

Jessie laughed at her small nephew. "I don't think so," she answered him. She and the children were playing a game of cards at a small, rough wood table James had built in front of one of the tents. It was Jamie's turn to deal, but she had to shuffle for him, so she reached across the table to scrape the cards toward her. As she glanced at the wagon again, she felt as though she should take an interest in the approaching vehicle.

After a few minutes of watching, she could see a woman driving the team of horses that pulled the wagon. Something looked familiar about her, the way she sat straight in the seat, her grip on the reins. "Mother?" Jessie said a second later. "It's Mother!" she squealed. Jumping up from the table, she dropped the cards and began to run toward the wagon. "You boys wait here," she yelled over her shoulder.

Rachel could see her daughter running toward her and felt her heart swell with love. "Jessie!" she called, slapping the reins over the rumps of the team she was driving. Ever since she'd received Jessie's telegram about the fire, she'd been insane with worry. She'd jumped on the first train and headed West.

Jessie met her mother's wagon at a dead run and jumped up onto the passenger's side. Throwing her arms around Rachel's shoulders, she began to cry. "Oh, Mother, I'm so happy to see you. I'm so glad you came," she sobbed into her mother's neck.

Rachel dropped the reins and held her daughter. It was obvious her little girl had been through a lot and she was glad she'd made the journey. "Here, now, Jessie. Let me look at you," she said gently, lifting Jessie's chin so she could see her face. Looking her up and down, she saw the bandaged arm. "What happened to your arm?" she asked.

"I broke it," she sniffed.

"That's obvious. How?"

Jessie grimaced. "I fell off my horse. I'll tell you about it later. Right now I'm just glad you're here," she said, staring into her mother's eyes. Jessie gazed at her mother's beautiful face and felt her eyes fill with tears once more.

Rachel saw things in Jessie's eyes that wrung her heart. She saw a deep sadness in the green so like her own. She knew Jessie was hurt because she couldn't own the Triple X, but there was more. There was something she hadn't written in her letter nor mentioned in the brief telegram. She looked tired, and she was thinner and there were dark circles under her eyes. Had the stress from the fire caused this?

The fire. Her mind said the words and her heart felt the pain. As she'd ridden within sight of the Triple X, she'd seen the devastation. The fire had swept through and destroyed everything in its path. "It's pretty bad," she whispered, moving her attention from her daughter to the ranch.

Jessie nodded. "It took out everything. My place is the same." A slight tone of disappointment colored her words. For just a moment while her mother had looked at her, she'd felt a closeness, a bonding she'd longed for. Rachel had always been a loving, responsible mother, but since she'd sent Jessie to Charleston things had been different between them. Rachel was still loving and affectionate, but it seemed as though she didn't understand her daughter, and Jessie felt it like a wedge between them.

Rachel heard the sadness in Jessie's voice. "You can rebuild, Jessie," she said.

Jessie sighed. "Yes, I will," she replied.

Rachel picked up the reins once more. A quick slap on the horses' rumps had them moving toward what was left of the house. "My God," Rachel breathed minutes later as she pulled the horses to a stop. "It's completely gone," she said.

"James has hauled a lot of the mess away already. Anything that was found in the rubble was put off to the side," Jessie said, pointing toward an odd array of burned and charred pieces of furniture and bric-a-brac.

Rachel stepped down out of the wagon and stood before the foundation of what had been her home. She'd been born here, raised here, lost her parents here, been married and borne her children here, and now it was gone. Her chest filled with a sadness so great she wasn't sure she could contain it. Memories flooded her in a swirling whirlpool. Pictures of her life floated before her. "It's really gone," she murmured, her words thick with emotion. She was going to have to come to terms with this. She just didn't think she could deal with it now. Not with Jessie waiting behind her.

"Aunt Jessie? Who is this?" asked Jeremy, tugging on Jessie's arm.

Jessie had climbed down from the wagon and was standing near her mother. At the touch of her nephew she looked down at him. "This is your grandmother," she said softly.

Rachel heard the words behind her and quickly wiped away the tears that wet her eyes and cheeks. Turning around, she gazed down at the adorable face of one of her grandsons. "Which one are you?" she asked, smiling.

"I'm Jeremy. Jamie's over there in his wheelchair," he said, pointing behind him. "Are you really my grandmother?"

"Wheelchair?" Rachel asked, concern filling her voice.

"Yes, he broke his leg. I'll tell you all about that later, too," Jessie said.

Rachel wasn't satisfied, but knew she'd have to wait for explanations. Looking down at Jeremy once more, she said, "Yes, I'm your grandmother. But I haven't seen you since you were two years old."

Jeremy's face lit up when the beautiful lady confirmed she was his grandmother. He took her by the hand. "Come say hello to Jamie," he instructed, pulling on her hand.

Rachel grinned at Jeremy, then at Jessie. She allowed herself to be led to Jamie's side. "So, you're Jamie," she said.

"Yes, ma'am," answered Jamie.

"This is our grandmother," announced Jeremy as though he'd discovered a treasure.

"Really?" murmured Jamie.

Jeremy nodded rapidly.

"Yes, I'm your grandmother," said Rachel. "And do you know what a grandmother's job is?" she asked in a mysterious tone.

Both boys shook their heads in wide-eyed wonder.

"It's to spoil her grandsons," Rachel answered matter-of-factly.

Two identical grins beamed up at Rachel. "Does that mean you give us candy?" asked Jamie.

"Jamie," warned Jessie in a falsely stern tone.

"Yes it does," answered Rachel as though Jessie hadn't spoken. "As a matter of fact, I happen to have some candy in my valise. Should I get it?" she asked.

"Yes! Yes!" came the united answer.

Rachel smiled and walked back to the wagon. It took her a few seconds to locate the peppermint sticks in her valise, but she was soon handing them over to the twins. "How am I doing so far?" she asked.

"Wonderful. Mmmmmmm," said Jamie, the peppermint stick in his mouth. Jeremy was too busy chewing a chunk he'd bitten off to answer.

"That should spoil their dinners very nicely," teased Jessie.

"Someday I'll spoil your children the same way," said Rachel.

A cloud of emotion covered Jessie's face. "Yes. Someday," she said. "If I ever have children."

Rachel frowned slightly. There was something wrong with Jessie and she meant to get to the bottom of what it was. "You don't think you'll have children?" she asked innocently.

Jessie shrugged. "Who knows?" she responded, looking away from her mother.

"Rachel?" called James as he exited the barn. "I thought it was you, but I couldn't believe my eyes," he said coming nearer.

"Jamie, it's so good to see you again," Rachel responded, her hand outstretched in greeting.

"He's not called Jamie anymore, Mother," said Jessie, stiffly.

"What?" Rachel asked as James took her hand. "Then what do I call you?"

"Just James now, Rachel," he replied, glancing toward Jessie. Since the fire, Jessie had become distant again. She visited with the boys nearly every day but always managed to avoid spending time with him. He often felt her looking in his direction, but she would never meet his gaze when he looked at her. He narrowed his dark eyes in concern as he studied her. She looks tired, he thought.

"James it is," said Rachel graciously. She watched the interaction, or lack of it, between James and Jessie, and sensed the tension between them. Were they still fighting over the Triple X? she wondered.

Jessie felt James's eyes on her and refused to look in his direction. Instead, she gazed at the boys or her mother. She wouldn't let herself be affected by James Bonner again. The sight of his handsome face and devastating body made her weak and left her wanting him physically, but he belonged to Carmen and would soon share a child with the woman.

"I think we should all have dinner together tonight in town," said Rachel. "It'll be my treat," she added.

"That's very generous of you, Rachel, but—" started James.

"I'm sure James is busy, Mother, and—" Jessie began.

Rachel raised her hand to stop their protests. "I won't take no for an answer from either one of you," she informed them firmly.

"No for what?" asked Carmen sweetly as she emerged from one of the tents.

Rachel raised one brow in the woman's direction. Whoever she was, she was beautiful.

James glanced quickly in Jessie's direction and saw her staring directly at the ground. It would fall to him to introduce Carmen. "Rachel Braddock, this is Carmen de Silva," he offered.

Rachel turned toward the woman, her hand extended.

Carmen tried to hide her surprise but didn't succeed. "You are Jessie's mother?" she asked.

"Yes."

"But you are so young," said Carmen.

Rachel laughed. "Thank you, but I'm nearly forty-seven. The twins are my grandchildren," she said, gesturing toward the boys. "It's nice to meet you, Miss de Silva," she added.

"It's nice to meet you, too, Mrs. Braddock," responded Carmen. She wondered what the older woman was doing here. Was she just here for a visit, or had Jessie summoned her mother for help in getting James to sell the Triple X.

"And what is your position here on the Triple X?" asked Rachel, expecting to hear she was one of the cowboys' wives.

Carmen stepped closer to James and placed her hand under his arm, linking it with her own. "James and I are to be married," she answered coyly.

James's brows drew together and his eyes filled with black storm clouds as fury charged through his system. Carmen knew he wouldn't cause a scene in front of Rachel and had taken advantage of the situation.

Jessie turned on her heel and went back to the table and began to pick up the cards she'd dropped earlier. She couldn't stand the sight of James and Carmen together. It reminded her of how he'd made love to her while sleeping with Carmen, of how the woman now carried his child.

Rachel was surprised to hear the news of James's impending wedding, but she was more surprised by the reactions of James and Jessie. James looked as though he would like to kill someone with his bare hands, and Jessie immediately left them to perform the unimportant task of picking up cards. "Congratulations," she offered. "When did this happen?"

"Not long ago," answered Carmen before James could speak.

"And when is the wedding to take place?" she asked.

"We haven't set a date," said James, stepping away from Carmen as gracefully as he could.

"Soon, though," answered Carmen.

Rachel glanced briefly behind her to where Jessie was taking an inordinately long time to gather a few cards into a pile. "Then I insist you join us for dinner tonight, Carmen," she said. She saw Jessie freeze for a moment.

"Is that what you were talking about when I came out of the tent? I'd love to join you," Carmen gushed. This was what she'd been waiting for, acknowledgment as James's intended bride. It was ironic that it was coming from Jessie's own mother. "You have no idea how much this means to me," she said. "Perhaps we could consider this our engagement dinner? The fire has disrupted our lives so much that we haven't done the usual things couples do during their engagement," she explained.

Rachel looked from Jessie's stiff form to James's angry one and then to the smiling Carmen. "I think an engagement dinner is a lovely idea," she said.

"How was I to know you hated her?" asked Rachel two hours later as she rode with Jessie on their way to town.

"I didn't say I hated her," said Jessie.

"Your sullen attitude makes it pretty obvious," Rachel said pointedly.

Jessie sighed. She'd tried to explain how she felt about Carmen when her mother had questioned her, but she hadn't felt it was her place to inform her about Carmen's pregnancy. And she certainly couldn't tell Rachel that she'd slept with James while he'd been involved with Carmen. "Can't you leave it alone, Mother?" she asked.

"No, I can't," Rachel answered. She'd been needling Jessie since they'd left the Triple X. "There are only a few things that will cause women to dislike each other. Since you won't tell me what your reason is, well, I'll just have to assume the worst."

"The worst?" said Jessie.

"From my experience, women only get their backs up over two things, their children and their men. Since you have no children I can only assume your problems with Carmen have something to do with James."

Jessie clenched her jaw. Tugging the reins, she stopped the wagon and turned to face Rachel. "Mother, please respect my feelings in this and drop it," she said firmly.

Rachel tightened her own jaw in frustration. "I suppose, if I must," she said.

"Thank you," Jessie responded, her tone indicating the subject was officially closed. Snapping the reins, she started them on their way to town once more. To town and the dinner that was sure to be pure hell from beginning to end.

Rachel studied her daughter's profile as she drove the team. Jessie was an unusual girl. She always had been. Her other daughter, Tish, Jessie's older sister, had always been open and easy to read. Tish had never been able to keep anything from Rachel, making it unnecessary for her to nag or prod her for information. Taking in the stubborn tilt to Jessie's jaw, she knew she'd have to take a different tack to find out what she needed to know. "It's a lovely night," she commented.

Jessie just nodded.

Dinner was everything Jessie had feared it would be. Carmen acted the role of the blushing bride-to-be, and James sat quietly by her side, a storm of emotion brewing in his dark eyes. Once, when he'd managed to capture Jessie's attention, the heat that flashed between them practically took her breath away. Keeping busy helping the twins was the only way she'd been able to get through the long meal.

"Take me to the Triple X," said Rachel some time later.

Jessie glanced at her mother. "I thought you'd be staying with me," Jessie answered. They were on their way home from dinner. The night sky was full of stars and the moon glistened overhead.

"I am staying with you," answered Rachel. "There's just something I need to do before I go to your house."

"Then I'll wait for you," Jessie stated.

"No. I don't know how long I'll be," Rachel told her.

"But Mother, it's getting late. You won't have a way to get home."

"Jessie, I'll be fine. I'm sure I can borrow a horse from James."

"All right," Jessie gave in, wondering what it was her mother needed to do at this hour. She guided the team past the turnoff to her ranch and headed for the Triple X.

As they crested the small hill that gave them their first view of the Triple X, Rachel put her hand over Jessie's. "Stop for a minute," she said quietly.

Jessie pulled back on the reins. "What?"

"Just look at it," Rachel said, barely above a whisper.

Jessie let her gaze follow her mother's. In front of them was the Triple X—at least, what was left of it. The land was there, it always would be, but the buildings, the home they'd both known, was gone. "Mother?" Jessie whispered.

"I'm going to walk from here," Rachel said.

"But we're more than a mile away, yet."

"I know it," said Rachel, climbing down from the wagon. She started walking toward the Triple X. "I'll see you later," she called over her shoulder.

Jessie sat there for a few minutes and watched her mother. She didn't understand what Rachel was doing, but she had no doubt she'd be fine. There was no one more capable than Rachel Braddock. She turned the wagon and headed for home.

Rachel heard the creaking of the wooden wagon wheels moving away from her and was grateful to be alone. She'd needed this since this afternoon. All the hustle and bustle since her arrival had been interesting, but she had also been pushing her emotions to the side.

She needed to feel those emotions, to deal with them and get past them.

Scanning the Triple X, seeing the lonely foundation, blackened by the fire, she felt the swell of sadness beneath her breasts. Walking slowly, she approached the ranch. Letting her gaze swing in one direction and then another, she was met by sight after sight of ruin. Off to her right were the burned trunks of the trees that had stood beside the swimming hole for as long as she could remember. The moonlight illuminating the ground behind them made them look like frightening creatures clawing the sky with stark, bony fingers, instead of the large, graceful givers of shade they had once been. Her mind was filled with the memories of afternoons spent cooling off after working hard to keep the Triple X successful enough to support her and her family and employees.

Continuing her walk, she neared the remains of the house. Passing the foundation, she moved toward the pile of rubble James had saved. The moonlight overhead lit the area well and she was able to distinguish the items without much trouble: a table leg, pots, pans, part of a chair, bits of broken vases, and silver picture frames. Her heart felt the loss of the pictures those frames had held. Why hadn't she come back sooner to collect these things from the house. Had she forgotten what they meant to her?

Moving down the line of debris, she stopped when she came to what was left of a large leather chair. She clenched her jaw against the urge to cry out loud when she realized it was her father's office chair. She doubled her fists in anger. She'd sat in his lap in that chair too many times to count, and now it was charred, useless, and discarded.

Then her eyes spied something under the chair. Lifting the edge of the chair with her toe, she felt her heart break completely when she recognized the fabric of her father's old coat. She bent over and picked up the burned and torn piece of fabric. The long duster had hung in the office for as long as she could remember. Apparently James hadn't removed the garment either. Now all that was left of it was a section containing one of the pockets. Reaching inside it, she was disappointed to find it empty. She remembered when, years ago, she'd found papers in this pocket that had changed the course of her life. Now, of course, all she felt was ashes. "Why?" she cried. "Why didn't I make some attempt to save these things?" she asked herself.

Still holding the piece of fabric, she looked to her left. Her gaze followed the rugged terrain until she spotted more tree trunks, these marking the spot where her father and mother were buried. This was the direction she headed.

As Rachel neared the tiny cemetery, she began to cry. Her parents' headstones were blackened and the ground was covered with burned branches and debris. The trees overhead were reflections of the trees over the swimming hole, stark reminders of the horrible destruction of the fire. Standing at the foot of her father's grave, she sank down to her knees. "Oh, Papa. How many times did I sit here and ask your advice?" she whispered, tears coursing down her face. "I think I need your advice now."

❦ 18 ❦

Rachel sat at her parents' graves for a long while. She let her mind wander back over the years, exploring memories she'd long ago let herself forget. When she was through, her face and neck were wet with tears. "Papa, how could I have forgotten what it was like to ride free across the range, feeling the power of life flowing through me? How could I have let myself forget what it meant to know this land, the land you and I both worked so hard to keep? It was ours, our heritage," she sobbed. Looking at her father's headstone, she could barely make out the name engraved there, Hyram Walker. "Jessie remembered, didn't she, Papa?" she asked. "Jessie remembered what this land means."

Rachel let her head fall forward again. "And now it's too late to do anything about it. The Triple X belongs to James and he'll never let it go."

She thought about Jessie again. "Why did Jessie remember when I forgot?" she asked. "Why does Jessie care in a way Tish never did?" She searched for an answer, but could find none.

After a while, she pushed herself to her feet. "What have I done?" she sighed, sadly. "I've sold my home, Jessie's home." She shook her head. "And there's no undoing it."

Turning from the graves, she began a slow walk back to the old house's foundation. Stopping once more at the pile of debris, she dropped the piece of her father's coat. It was too charred to keep.

"Rachel?" James said as he stepped out of the darkness. "What are you doing out here?"

Rachel turned toward the sound of his voice. "I had some things to settle," she answered. Wiping her eyes with the back of her sleeve, she gazed at the handsome young man. He resembled his brother, Luke, who'd married Tish, and she felt a closeness to him. "Can I talk to you for a few minutes?" she asked.

James studied her for a moment. She'd been crying. He could understand her sadness. "Let's go sit in my tent," he offered.

Rachel glanced up at the sky. "Can we sit out here?" she asked.

James nodded. Leaving her for a few minutes, he returned with two chairs. "Will this do?" he asked, positioning them so they faced the giant white face of the moon.

"Perfect," she sighed, sitting down in the closest chair.

James lowered himself to sit beside her and waited for her to speak.

"What's going on between you and Jessie?" Rachel asked bluntly.

"Whew, you don't pull any punches, do you?" James asked.

"I've never been known to," she answered, "though I think I've been out of character for a few years," she added. "So, answer my question."

"At the risk of being rude, I have to ask you whether it's any of your business," he responded.

"Jessie is my daughter, so it's my business."

"Jessie is a grown woman."

"So I've noticed," said Rachel, her green eyes narrowing. "She wasn't when she left Charleston. That makes me wonder what's happened here to make her mature so quickly. Does it have anything to do with you?"

James shrugged. "I don't know," he answered.

"I think you know very well. I think you're just too much of a gentleman to say. Either that or you're afraid I'll shoot you if I find out you've been sleeping with my daughter."

"Wait a minute. I never said—" sputtered James, quickly getting to his feet.

"Relax, James. Sit back down. I know you didn't say it, but I can see there's something going on. The tension is so thick between you two you could cut it with that bowie you've got strapped to your side," she said. "Come on, sit down."

James slowly sat down once more. "I really don't think I should be discussing this with you," he said after a moment.

"One thing you need to learn, I'm not your enemy. If you need to talk to someone, you can talk to me," Rachel told him.

James just sat there waiting, not knowing what to say.

"Here's where it stands as I see it. Whether you admit sleeping with Jessie or not is irrelevant, there's something between you. Something I doubt is going to go away just because you marry Carmen. Which brings me to Carmen. Do you love her?"

"My God, you're blunt," James breathed. Leaning forward, he rested his head in his hands. Maybe he should confide in someone, he thought. It would feel good to spill his guts for a while. He just questioned the wisdom of using Rachel for that purpose. "No, I don't love Carmen," he finally admitted.

"I didn't think so," said Rachel. "The anger I felt from you around her wasn't the emotion I'd expect from a soon-to-be groom. Is she pregnant?"

James still wasn't used to this kind of straightforwardness, but he managed not to comment on it this time. "She claims to be," he answered.

"Do you doubt it?"

He raised his shoulders. "I was only with her once. It

is possible. I suppose it's probable," he said. "She wouldn't say such a thing unless it were true," he added with a resigned sadness.

Rachel raised her brows. Oh wouldn't she, she thought to herself. "This one time you were with Carmen, was it after you'd been with Jessie?"

"No!" James said adamantly.

"How do you feel about Jessie?"

James had to stop and think about it. "I'm not sure," he said. He couldn't very well tell Rachel that he got hot every time Jessie was nearby.

"Does she make you feel crazy?" Rachel helped.

James nodded. "Yes. Half the time I don't know whether to kill her or ki—"

"Kiss her? Sounds familiar," she said, thinking about her own relationship with her husband, Sin. "How does Jessie feel about you?" she asked.

"Most of the time I think she hates me. She resents the fact that I won't sell the Triple X to her. And I won't," he added for emphasis. "But sometimes," he went on more quietly, "sometimes I feel like she cares about me." His lids lowered as he remembered the way she melted in his arms.

Rachel noticed the look in his eyes. "Seems like we've got one complicated situation here," she commented thoughtfully.

"A losing situation," James responded.

Rachel sat very still for a while. She didn't know how to help her daughter or James. They'd gotten caught up in a sad situation, and she couldn't help feeling partly responsible for it. If she hadn't sold the Triple X to James, Jessie might not have returned to the ranch for some time yet. Then James and Carmen could have worked through their relationship without the added complication of Jessie's arrival.

Placing her hands flat on her thighs, Rachel stood up. "I guess I'd better be getting back to Jessie's place," she said.

James looked up at her. The moonlight shimmered on her dark red hair and caught the fiery glow of her emerald eyes. Standing, he looked down on her. "You and Jessie are so much alike," he observed.

"We do look a lot alike, except for hair color, of course," Rachel responded, used to people making the comparison.

"It's not only that you look alike. There's more to it than that. You have the same mannerisms. You're both direct and honest. And I'd guess you think and feel the same about things." He smiled. "Yes, I'd say she grew up to be just like you, but I suppose that's not surprising. Most women probably grow up wanting to be just like their mothers," he commented.

Rachel stared hard at him. A conversation from years earlier came back to haunt her, from the night she and Sin had decided to send Jessie to Charleston. It had been Jessie's outburst that she wanted to be just like her mother that had caused Rachel to agree with Sin to send her away.

A huge, swirling puzzle began to fall into place in Rachel's mind. Everything Jessie had said and done suddenly made sense to her. The reason behind it had been so obvious that she hadn't seen it until James's innocent comments had forced her to look at it. Despite the efforts made by the finishing school, despite the efforts of Rachel and Sin themselves, despite Jessie's own attempts to conform, she'd grown up to be just like Rachel. She was willful, independent, stubborn, and determined. She loved open spaces and freedom, and she had a wild streak in her a mile wide.

Rachel had to sit back down.

"Rachel, are you all right?" James asked, concerned.

Rachel looked up at him as though in a daze. "I'm fine," she said. "Just stupid." Standing back up, she glanced around her. "Do you have a horse I could borrow until tomorrow?" she asked. "I have to talk to Jessie," she said hurriedly.

"Of course, but are you sure you should be riding in

this state?" he inquired, confused by her sudden urgency.

"I'm sure, James. I'm fine. I just need to talk to Jessie."

"All right," he answered. "I'll saddle one of the horses for you."

Ten minutes later, Rachel was racing across the open range. She had to get to Jessie as fast as she could.

Smokey loudly announced the arrival of a rider entering the yard. "Smokey, hush," Jessie told him. "It's Mother." Jessie peered out of the tent flap, then pulled it aside when Rachel jumped from her horse and practically ran toward her. "What's wrong?" she asked.

Rachel stopped in front of her daughter. "I have to talk to you," she said a little out of breath.

"Come in and sit down," urged Jessie.

Rachel entered the tent and sat on the cot that Jessie had given her to sleep on. Patting the cot, she gestured to Jessie to sit beside her.

"What is it, Mother?" Jessie asked, lowering herself to the cot.

Rachel looked into Jessie's eyes, eyes so like her own. "Oh, Jessie," she began. "I'm so sorry."

Jessie frowned in curiosity. "Sorry?" she asked. "For what?"

"For selling the ranch, for sending you to Charleston, for not understanding, for everything," said Rachel in a gush.

Jessie was stunned by her mother's words. "But Mother, I don't understand."

Rachel took Jessie's hands in hers. "You may not understand me now, but I finally understand you."

Jessie just shook her head, still confused.

"I went to talk to Papa," Rachel began. "I cried and asked him for answers. Of course, there were none. I realized what a mistake I'd made when your father and I sold the Triple X, and I wanted to know why you remembered the things I'd forgotten. It wasn't until I talked to James that it all made sense."

"You talked to James?" Jessie asked, her heart suddenly hammering against her chest.

"Yes, and I believe he's in love with you," she said. "But that's not what I need to tell you now."

Jessie blinked at her mother's words. James, in love with her? Why would Rachel think that? The man had used her. He'd humiliated her.

"I finally understand, Jessie. As hard as we all fought against it, you grew up just like me," Rachel said, still gripping her hands.

Jessie looked into her mother's eyes. Something there touched her. She saw the one thing she'd always longed to see. Complete acceptance. "Mother?" she whispered.

"You feel it, don't you?" Rachel asked. Leaning forward, she wrapped her arms around her daughter.

Jessie let herself fall into the safe cocoon of her mother's arms. "Why now?" she asked.

Rachel shrugged. "It feels like a horrible trick of fate, doesn't it? It took me selling the Triple X to bring us together, and in that togetherness we believe the ranch should never have been sold."

"James will never sell it back to us," said Jessie leaning away to look at her mother.

"I know it. I don't blame him. He's worked hard on the ranch. It's his home now," responded Rachel.

"So, I guess I just build a new life here," Jessie said with resignation, her hand gesturing to take in her ranch.

Rachel nodded. "You'll make this a wonderful home, Jessie."

"I already had a good start on it before the fire," she sighed. She looked into the sympathetic eyes of her mother. "Oh, Mama," she said, tears filling her eyes. Leaning forward again, she wrapped her arms around her mother. "I love you so much."

"I love you, too, baby," said Rachel, her own tears falling freely.

Jessie held onto her mother for several minutes. It felt so good to finally feel close to her mother again. If only

Under a Texas Moon

other aspects of her life could work out so well. "Mama?"

"Yes?"

"What did you discuss with James?"

Rachel had been expecting this. "We talked about you, and about Carmen," she said.

Jessie looked up at her mother, her face revealing the nervousness in her stomach. "What about me?" she asked.

"I'm sure he's in love with you, though I don't think even he realizes it yet."

Jessie snorted her disbelief. "He's going to marry Carmen," she said.

"He's not in love with Carmen," Rachel responded. "He's only marrying her because she says she's pregnant."

"James told you this?"

Rachel nodded.

"Well, it doesn't matter whether he loves her or not. She's carrying his child. That sort of settles things," she said, bitterness in her voice.

"But how do you feel about James?" Rachel asked.

Jessie let her gaze drop. How did she feel? She felt used and hurt. She felt angry, and she felt like a traitor to herself every time she remembered the way his touch brought her to life. These were things she couldn't confide in her mother, even with their new-found closeness. "I'm angry he won't sell me the Triple X," she answered.

Rachel could see there were a thousand other things Jessie wanted to say but wasn't able to. She understood the girl's pride. She knew what pride felt like. "You'll have to get over it," she said. "James is your neighbor, and he's part of your sister's family. Your lives are bound to touch many times in the future."

"I know it, but after the boys leave I won't have to see him often," she said.

Rachel studied her daughter sadly. If only there were

271

something I could do to help her, she thought. But there wasn't.

Jessie awakened the following morning with a splitting headache and nausea roiling deeply within her. I don't need this now, she thought. I've got too much to do to be sick. After lying perfectly still for nearly half an hour, she was finally able to sit up.

"Jessie, what's wrong, dear? You don't look well," commented Rachel as she observed her daughter sitting up in bed.

"I think I'm coming down with something. I haven't been feeling myself lately. I'm not surprised, what with everything that's been going on," Jessie answered.

"I'm surprised you're holding up as well as you are," said Rachel. "Is there anything I can get for you? Coffee? A biscuit?"

Jessie shook her head. "Nothing sounds very appetizing," she answered. "Maybe later. But thank you anyway."

"You're welcome," Rachel replied.

"What are you doing today, Mother?" Jessie asked as she swung her legs over the edge of the cot.

"I thought I'd go visit with the boys, unless you need my help here."

Jessie shook her head. "I'm glad you have plans. I'm going to be out on the range assessing the damage to the grass most of the day. I have to see whether or not there'll be enough food for winter. I already doubt it, but I've got to make sure," she said.

"Of course, dear. You go on and do what you have to. I'm perfectly capable of entertaining myself. I figured James could use a hand with the boys while he works on the new house. I'm sure those two are a handful,"

"Oh, Mother, you have no idea," exclaimed Jessie.

"Don't I? I raised you, remember?"

Jessie giggled. "I guess you did, but I was a perfect angel, wasn't I?" she teased.

"In every way," Rachel agreed, grinning at her daughter.

They'd talked well into the night and ended up, sometime near morning, laughing together like best friends. The new rapport between them was comfortable and pleasant.

After breakfast, Rachel rode off to the Triple X, and Jessie mounted Henry for her ride over her property. She had, of course, already ridden across the land to see how much of her ranch had been affected by the fire, and she had discovered that virtually all of it had been burned. She now had to see just how long lasting the damage would prove to be. It would depend on whether or not the roots of the grass had been killed by the heat from the fire. She would see that today. If there were new shoots pushing their tiny green heads above the blackened soil, she might be able to get by with buying a minimal amount of hay for winter. If not, she'd have to purchase a great quantity and would end up strapped for cash.

"Come on, Henry," she said, nudging the horse with her heels.

The ride was depressing. Acre after acre of grass and sage were charred black. Tumbleweed, looking like flying spider webs of burned silk, rolled across the open range with nothing in its path to slow it down.

After a while, Jessie tugged the reins, stopping Henry. Sighing, she stood in the saddle and twisted out the kinks of her ride. Her nausea had passed, but her head still ached, and so far she'd seen no signs of new growth underfoot. "Damn it, Henry. It looks like we're in for a hard winter," she murmured. "I hope we make it." Sitting back down, she stared off into the distance. She'd reached one edge of the burn and wondered how far it extended. "Might as well go have a look," she said.

Traveling along the rim of the burn was strange. On one side of her, the world was unspoiled and ruggedly beautiful, green with grass, sage, and pinion. On her other side was a black, dead, almost eerie world of fallen, twisted tree trunks and ashes. Shaking her head, she grimaced. "Nature has a strange way of doing things," she commented quietly.

Crossing a ridge, she realized she'd left her land minutes earlier, but she kept on her course. It looked as if the burn was about to end. Turning with the contoured edge of the blackened earth, she felt a sense of surprise that the fire had started so close to the ranch. She'd assumed it had started much farther away, near the mountains and the thunderheads they'd all seen for days before the fire. Backtracking over the fire's path, she was soon within sight of a spot that seemed to stick out like a point of origin. It looked as though the fire had spread from this site.

Dismounting, Jessie walked around the area. She studied the ground and began to feel suspicion running through her. She'd seen lightning strikes before. There was usually a burned depression in the earth, a definite mark left by the force of the strike. Here, there was no sign lightning had struck. The area was burned evenly from a single starting point. Narrowing her eyes, she walked back and forth over the ground. Had the fire started some other way? she wondered.

Circling the area once more, she stopped, then turned to study it from another angle. When she did, she noticed something. Kneeling down, she found several tiny bits of wood. The leftover ends of wooden matches! The fire had been started deliberately! As she stood up, she felt and heard something under her boot heel. "What's this?" she said, picking up a small metal object. A split second later her blood ran cold as she recognized Carmen's ankle bracelet. Gripping it tightly in her fist, she mounted Henry with one jump and spurred him to a gallop toward the Triple X.

James was working on a section of the frame on his new house when he saw a rider galloping full speed across the range in his direction. It took him only seconds to realize it was Jessie. "What's gotten into her now?" he murmured, dropping the nails and hammer he'd been holding into a large metal can. Wiping his hands on his trousers, he watched her come.

Jessie could see James standing in the middle of the yard as she rode in. He was watching her intently, and she was instantly aware of his masculinity, the broad expanse of his shoulders, the strength of his forearms visible beneath the rolled up sleeves of his shirt. She felt her pulse take a leap upward in tempo, and frowned at her own body's traitorous response to him. "Damn it," she cursed. She didn't need to feel this way now when she had to tell him about Carmen.

James could see the angry expression on Jessie's beautiful face and wondered what had set her off this time. "What can I do for you, Jessie?" he called as she rode in.

Jessie pulled back on the reins and brought Henry to a stop in front of him. "You can tell me where Carmen is," she answered.

James raised his eyebrows in surprise. He never thought he'd ever hear Jessie asking to see Carmen, but from her expression and tone he knew this was no social visit. "What business do you have with Carmen?" he asked, wanting to avoid more trouble if he could.

Jessie jumped from the back of her horse and stomped her way to within a foot of James. Staring hard up into his eyes, she raised the anklet with her left hand and let it dangle from her fingers. "I want to speak to her about this," she answered.

"A piece of chain?" he asked perplexed.

"Don't you recognize it?" she demanded. "Or are you just trying to protect her?"

James took a defensive stance, his hands on his hips. "I'm not trying to protect her. At least not until I know what it is she's being accused of," he responded.

Rachel emerged from one of the tents, the boys right behind her. "Jessie, what's going on?" she asked.

"Just a minute, Mother, and you'll find out," Jessie

answered her. She turned her attention back to James. "This just happens to be Carmen's ankle bracelet, and do you know where I found it?" she asked. "Well, do you?"

James shook his head. "No," he answered.

"I found it at the far side of the burn, at what looks like the point of origin, to be exact," she stated bluntly.

James frowned at her accusation. Carmen was a lot of things, but he had a hard time believing she'd have started the fire that destroyed the Triple X. "Don't be ridiculous, Jessie," he said. "Carmen wouldn't have wanted to burn the Triple X. It's her home, too. She—"

"Don't you dare defend her to me!" shouted Jessie. "She wasn't trying to burn the Triple X, you big idiot. She was only trying to burn me out, but the fire got out of control. Now, where is she?" she demanded.

"Here I am," came Carmen's defiant voice from another of the tents.

Jessie turned slowly to face her. Holding up the chain, she looked at Carmen with pure hatred sparking in her green eyes. "Did you lose something?" she asked

Carmen raised her chin, then lifted the hem of her skirt ever so slightly. "No," she responded smugly.

Jessie looked down at Carmen's ankle. There, shining against her skin, was a chain identical to the one she held in her fingers. "I don't understand," she murmured. It had all made such perfect sense to her. Carmen had tried to burn her out to get rid of her. She was sure of it. But Carmen still wore her anklet. The piece of chain she'd found had to belong to someone else. But who?

Carmen walked forward, crossing the yard to stand next to James. Linking her arm with his, she smiled at Jessie. "It seems you are wrong, Miss Braddock. And I am offended you could think such a horrible thing about me."

Jessie turned to look at James and Carmen standing together. Behind them was the foundation of her old home and the new section of frame going up. It all looked so permanent, so final. She couldn't say another word. Turning away from them, she walked back to where Henry stood waiting for her.

"James, can you believe Miss Braddock could accuse me of such a horrid thing?" asked Carmen loudly.

Jessie flinched at the sound of her words. She had believed Carmen started the fire. The chain had been her proof. As she climbed into the saddle, she dropped the chain in the dirt at Henry's feet.

James saw the defeated bow to Jessie's back, the dejected expression on her face. He wouldn't answer Carmen, but he did find it hard to believe Jessie had accused her of starting the fire. A person would have to be without conscience to start a brush fire. There was no way of knowing where the fire would spread, no way of knowing that people wouldn't die.

Rachel took several steps forward. She'd just witnessed Jessie's defeat and it broke her heart. She knew how the women felt about each other, but Jessie's accusation had come as a shock to her. "Jessie?" she called.

Jessie heard her mother's voice. "I'm going home, Mama," she stated simply. Tugging the reins sideways, she turned Henry toward her ranch. Just before spurring him forward, she raised her chin and squared her shoulders.

James noticed the proud, almost defiant way Jessie sat her horse and was suddenly filled with a surge of admiration for her. Her accusation had been false but understandable, and she wouldn't ride away with her tail between her legs.

"Can you believe what she accused me of, James?" Carmen tried again.

"Shut up, Carmen," James said sternly.

❊ 19 ❊

Jessie slept little that night. She tossed and turned and relived the scene with Carmen and James again and again. When she finally awoke after sleeping only a few hours, she suffered another pounding headache and severe nausea. Lying as still as she could on her cot, she swallowed several times to keep from vomiting. After a while she could no longer fight it. Leaping from her bed, she raced outside to the new outhouse.

When she returned to the tent fifteen minutes later, weak and trembling, she was met by Rachel's stern expression.

"How long before you admit what's wrong with you?" Rachel asked.

Jessie lowered the tent flap behind her and crossed to sit on her cot. "I don't know what you mean. I'm just coming down with a bug of some kind," she responded, wiping cold sweat from her forehead.

Rachel scoffed. "Really?" she said sarcastically. "Jessie, honey, I think it's time you and I had a talk about the birds and the bees."

Jessie looked up at her mother in horror. "You don't think . . ." she said. "I mean . . ." Her mind raced, trying to remember when she'd had her last time of the month. It had been too long. "No," she said. "It can't be.

I'm just coming down with something," she tried to convince herself.

"I don't think so, Jessie. You've been looking thinner and more tired every day. I think you're pregnant," Rachel said.

Jessie's head fell to her hands. She hadn't thought things could get any worse than they already were, but she'd been wrong. "What am I going to do?" she murmured.

"You're going to have a baby," said Rachel.

Jessie looked back up at her mother. "That's not what I meant," she said in an exasperated tone.

"I know it, but you needed to get a little angry in order to deal with this. Now you tell me. What are you going to do about this?"

Jessie let her gaze fall to the floor of the tent. "I'm going to have a baby," she whispered. James's baby, she thought. Raising her head once more, she speared her mother with a pointed gaze. "James can never know," she said.

Rachel frowned. "I don't know if that's a good idea," she said.

"I don't care whether it's a good idea or not. I don't want him to know, and if you ever tell him I'll never forgive you," Jessie vowed.

Rachel sat looking at her daughter. "What do you want me to do?" she finally asked.

Jessie stared blankly for a while, deciding what course to take. "Help me pack. It won't take long. I don't have much left," she said.

An hour later, Jessie stood in her front yard with Smokey in her arms. "You have to promise me you won't deliver him to the boys for at least a week, and when you do, remember what I told you," she said to Tinker. "No one is to know I've left town until then. Do you understand?" she asked.

Tinker shook his head. "Not really."

Jessie sighed. "You and Johnny will be paid through the end of the month. You're welcome to stay on until then. I'm having the banker put the place up for sale again, though I doubt it will sell very quickly." She glanced around her. She'd only just begun to build the frame to the house, but it would have been her home. Now it would be someone else's. Fighting back the tears that threatened to spill over her lashes, she squeezed the puppy once, then handed him to Tinker.

"We'll take care of things," said Johnny. "Are you sure you want to give up?" he asked her timidly.

Jessie hadn't told them the real reason she was leaving. She couldn't. She'd let them think she'd been beaten. "I'm sure I'm doing the right thing," she answered him. "You'll deliver the note to James this afternoon?"

"Yes," he replied, then lowered his eyes. "We're gonna miss you," he said.

"I'll miss you both, too," she said, her voice cracking with emotion.

"Let's go Jessie. We have a lot to do in town before the stage arrives," said Rachel, seeing the difficulty Jessie was having saying good-bye.

Jessie turned toward her mother. "Yes," she sniffed. "You're right. I'm ready." Climbing into the wagon next to Rachel, she grasped the reins and started them on their way to town. As they rode out of the yard, huge, hot tears rolled down her cheeks.

"Are you sure, Jessie?" Rachel asked.

"Yes. James can never know," she insisted.

James was on top of the roof of his new house. Sweat dripped down his bare chest as he pounded nails into the wood under the hot sun. He could hear the twins playing in the yard below, and he knew Carmen was in her tent resting, the one thing she managed to do most of the time.

Glancing down at the boys, he could see Jeremy pushing Jamie across the yard in the wheelchair. Jamie had started getting around very well on his own, but the wheelchair was fun to play with. He grinned down at the two. They'd calmed their antics some since the cougar incident.

Remembering that frightening night, he was reminded of Jessie. It had been a week since she'd accused Carmen of starting the fire. He frowned as he remembered the note she'd sent to him the next day. It had said she would be busy with building her house and would he please explain to the boys why she wouldn't be able to visit them for a while. The note had also informed him that Rachel had been called back to Charleston on business.

"Uncle James, someone's coming," called Jeremy from the yard.

James looked in the direction of the road. He could see a rider coming slowly toward the house, and began the climb down from the roof.

It took James several minutes to recognize the person coming to visit. When he did, he was surprised to see Tinker with Jessie's puppy lying across his saddle. "Hello, Tinker," he said as he approached the man. "Is there a problem?" he asked.

Tinker shook his head. "Not a problem, Mr. Bonner. I just came to give the puppy to the twins."

James frowned in curiosity. "Does Jessie know you're doing this?" he asked.

"Yes, sir. She's the one who told me to do it."

"Why does Jessie want you to give her puppy to the boys?" James asked, still frowning.

"Because she went back to Charleston. She couldn't take the little fella with her, so she wanted the boys to have him," Tinker explained.

James heard only the first part of what the old man said. His heart had started to beat wildly within his chest. "Jessie went back to Charleston? When? Did she leave today? Has the stage left yet?" he poured questions at Tinker.

The old man blinked at the rapid-fire questions. "Jessie left a week ago," he answered after a moment.

"Why?"

Tinker shrugged. "Guess she couldn't make it ranching," he answered. "I know the fire took a lot out of her."

James felt deflated. The world had suddenly grown a little darker, as though a cloud had drifted across the sun. "A week ago? Why didn't she say good-bye?" he asked, then realized he already knew the answer. The note she'd sent had been a decoy meant to keep him from knowing she'd gone. She hadn't wanted to see him again.

Sighing heavily, he reached up for the puppy. "Hello, little fella," he said, sadly.

"Uncle James, that's Smokey!" the boys squealed in unison.

"Yes it is. He's yours now. A gift from your Aunt Jessie," he said, handing Smokey to Jamie.

"Ours?" they asked, their eyes wide with wonder.

"Yep," James answered.

"Your aunt wanted me to give you a message from her about the puppy," said Tinker.

"Yes?" asked Jamie.

"Jessie said to be sure to let you know that this puppy won't tell you any lies." He turned to James. "I don't know why she wanted me to say that, but she insisted."

James knew why, and it made his heart ache to remember Jessie and her rapport with the boys.

"We know, Mr. Tinker," said Jeremy. "Come on, Jamie, put him down," he directed at his brother. The two took off after the puppy as soon as his feet hit the ground.

"I guess I'd better be going," said Tinker.

James watched the old man turn his horse to leave. "Ah, do you have another job yet?" he asked.

"No. Me and Johnny have been lookin', but there's not a lot of jobs around here."

"Would you like to come work for me?" James offered.

Tinker's face lit up. "That's real nice of you to offer, Mr. Bonner. Me and Johnny would really appreciate steady work."

"Good. I don't have a new bunkhouse built yet, but

we'll find room for you in one of the tents if you want to move over."

"I'll tell Johnny as soon as I get back to the Home Sweet Home," he answered, grinning.

"The Home Sweet Home?" James inquired.

"Yeah, that's what Jessie named the ranch," he explained. "Thanks again, Mr. Bonner. Me and Johnny will be back early tonight." He prodded his mount away from the ranch.

James lowered his gaze to stare at the ground. Jessie had called her ranch the Home Sweet Home. Not a name a person would give to a place she thought she might have to leave.

"James, what did that old man want?" Carmen asked as she stepped from her tent.

"He came to give a puppy to the boys," James answered absentmindedly.

"Why?"

"Jessie wanted them to have it. She's gone back to Charleston," he answered.

Carmen's eyes lit up. Her plan was working. Placing her hand over her abdomen, she smiled. "I'm glad she's gone. She was upsetting to me."

James leveled his gaze on her, his suspicions about her pregnancy were increasing daily. "I'm not happy she's gone," he told her.

Carmen frowned. "You only say that to hurt me because you made me pregnant. James, when are we getting married? Papa and Marco are worried you won't do the right thing by me," she whined.

James narrowed his gaze to her stomach. "Let your father and brother worry," he said, and stormed away from her.

James didn't know where he was going. He only knew he had to put some distance between himself and Carmen. Walking hard and fast, he reached the swimming hole without even realizing it was where he was headed. Sinking to the ground, he pulled his knees up and let his arms hang loosely across them.

Looking around him, he was saddened by what he saw. He hadn't returned here since the night of the fire when he and Jessie and the boys had waited for the blaze to pass. The trees that had shaded this spot for so long were charred skeletons of their former grandeur. Lowering his gaze to the ground, he remembered the way he'd made love to Jessie that first time. She'd given him her virginity with such passion that he'd been shocked when he'd felt her maidenhead. He also remembered how he'd accused her of using sex as a way of convincing him to sell her the Triple X. Sighing, he began to wonder if he'd been wrong about her.

The news about Jessie's departure was common knowledge in town, as James discovered when he went in for supplies the next day. The ranch had been put up for sale again, and she'd sold the cattle she had left to another rancher.

"It was a shame to see her go," said Mr. Stilwell, the banker, when he ran into James in the street. "She was quite a woman," he observed.

"Yes, she was," James agreed. "I have to be going. It was nice talking to you," he said to the banker.

Moments later he was confronted by Jessie's friend Val. "Did she tell you she was leaving?" Val asked, still hurt Jessie hadn't said good-bye to her in person but had only left a note for her at the general store.

"Sorry," James responded.

"But she spent so much time out at your place, I just assumed . . ." she said.

"She visited the twins quite often, but she and I didn't speak much," explained James.

"I suppose I'll just have to write to her," Val sighed.

"That would be a good idea," answered James. "I'm sorry, but I have to be going," he said, tipping his hat to her.

A few minutes later he entered the general store, relieved to find it empty. He didn't want to fend off more questions about Jessie's departure.

"I was sorry to hear Jessie moved back to Charleston," said Mrs. Medley as James approached the counter.

"Yes, well, I suppose she did what she had to do," he answered.

"Yes, I suppose. What can I get for you, Mr. Bonner?" Mrs. Medley asked.

James pulled a list from his pocket. "Flour, sugar, coffee, yeast, salt, pickles, a new broom and dust pan, and some lamp oil," he read.

"It'll just take me a minute to gather those things together. You go ahead and look around the store while you wait. You might see something else you need," Mrs. Medley told him.

James wandered around the store until Mrs. Medley began placing sacks of supplies on the counter. He loaded them in the back of his wagon. When the process was complete, she handed him the bill.

"Did Carmen get the clasp fixed on that ankle bracelet?" Mrs. Medley asked as she watched James counting his money.

James raised his eyes. "What ankle bracelet?" he asked.

"The one she was so desperate to buy. Didn't she mention it to you?"

"No," James replied, lowering one dark brow.

"That's strange. She was so adamant about buying that particular anklet, even though the clasp was broken, I was sure it meant something important to her."

"When did she buy it?" he asked.

"Let me see." Mrs. Medley put her finger to her lips as she thought about it. "You know, I think it was just after the fire. She came in here in a regular state. Looked at all the ankle bracelets I had to sell, then insisted I sell her the one with the broken clasp. I told her it wasn't for sale. I was going to send it back to the manufacturer because it had come broken in the shipment. But she wouldn't have another. She said it didn't matter that it was broken, that she'd wire it together if she had to."

James felt as though he'd been kicked by a mule. Had

Jessie been right? Had Carmen started the fire? Was the anklet Jessie had found the proof? Laying a pile of money on the counter he walked out of the store. He could hear Mrs. Medley calling him back because he'd left her too much. It didn't matter. All that mattered was getting back to the ranch and confronting Carmen.

The ride home seemed endless. He could only go so fast with a loaded wagon, but eventually he saw the new house and the tents in the distance. Slapping the reins over the horses' rumps, he urged them to go a little faster.

As he guided the team and wagon into the yard, he looked around for Carmen. His eyes narrowed dangerously as he spied her tent. She was probably inside, feigning tiredness because of her pregnancy. She's probably not even pregnant, he thought. He was going to find out once and for all.

Jumping from the wagon, he crossed the yard in several swift strides and pulled open the flap to Carmen's tent. "I have to talk to you," he growled when he saw her lying on her cot.

Carmen jumped up. She didn't like the tone of his voice. Something was wrong. "Is it important, James? I have a headache," she pouted, putting one hand on her forehead and the other on her abdomen.

James watched her dramatics and scowled. "It's important, Carmen. I want you to tell me about your ankle bracelet."

Carmen felt the cold hand of fear close over her heart. "What about my ankle bracelet? It's just a chain," she said.

"I want to know why you had to purchase a new one," he said.

"I don't know what you're talking about."

"Don't you? Mrs. Medley wanted to know if you'd had the clasp repaired yet. Did you? Or did you wire it together like you told her you would?" he asked quietly.

"Mrs. Medley's crazy," Carmen said.

"I don't think so. She was just concerned because you

bought defective merchandise," he said. "Why did you, Carmen? Why did you insist on buying a broken ankle bracelet?" He wanted to hear the reason from her own lips. He wanted her to admit she'd lost her other one while starting the fire that destroyed his home and nearly killed the people he loved.

Carmen began to move sideways inside the tent. She could see the rage in James's dark eyes and feared she might need to escape through the flap. "I deny it, James," she said. "Mrs. Medley must have me confused with someone else."

"Really? Then let me see your ankle bracelet. Let me see that the clasp isn't broken."

Carmen sidestepped even farther. "I don't have to prove myself to you, James. I'm insulted you'd imply I might be lying," she said.

"Just show me the ankle bracelet, Carmen. If I'm wrong I'll apologize."

Carmen bolted for the tent flap but she wasn't fast enough. She saw James dive for her and felt his hands close around her legs. "Nooo!" she screamed as she fell, kicking to get away from his grasp.

James held on tight to Carmen's legs. Her kicking was only making this job a little more difficult. In seconds he'd maneuvered himself so he could see the ankle bracelet. A tiny piece of wire was holding the two ends together. He clenched his jaw and tried to control the blind rage he felt coming over him.

"James, let me go!" Carmen screamed.

"Uncle James, what's happening?" yelled the boys as they ran toward the tent.

"Go back to your own tent," James ordered them. "We'll talk later."

The twins looked at their uncle in surprised wonder. They'd never heard him use such a frightening tone of voice before. "Yes, Uncle," they agreed, and obediently ran for their tent.

"Papa!" screamed Carmen. "Marco!"

James held on tightly to her, moving his grip up until

he could grasp her hands. Pulling her to her feet, he stared down into her face. "Why, Carmen?" he demanded, his grip on her arms tightening as he thought about his tiny nephews. "You could have killed everyone! Didn't you think of that? How could you be so stupid and evil?" he shouted, his voice getting louder with each word.

Carmen struggled to free herself. She flinched as James's hands tightened painfully over her wrists. "James, I didn't do it. I swear I didn't do it."

"You're a lying bitch, Carmen, and you make me sick. If you were a man I'd kill you with my bare hands. Because you're a woman I'll only turn you over to the sheriff. He can deal with you!"

"No, James. I didn't do it," Carmen cried. "I love you. I would never do anything to hurt you. Don't you believe me?" She saw Marco running toward her. "He did it," she said. "Marco did it. He wanted me to marry you so we could have the ranch, but you were falling in love with Jessie. He wanted to get rid of her so you'd be mine again."

James turned as Marco lunged at him. Releasing Carmen's arms, he caught the attack head on, rolling over and over in the dirt with Marco. When they came to a halt, James felt Marco trying to shift his weight to gain the advantage. He easily flipped the younger man over onto his back, bringing his fist down to crash into his face, and splitting the skin under his eye.

"Noooo!" screamed Carmen. "Papaaaa!" she shouted. "Where are youuu!" She watched as James fought Marco with the unfair advantage of age and size on his side.

Marco tried to get up, but each time he did, James struck him back down again. "Why, Marco? Didn't you think about the twins? They could have died!" he screamed as he pounded the younger man with his fists. "Jessie could have died, though that was your plan all along, wasn't it! Was getting a piece of this damned ranch really worth murdering innocent people?" he demanded. The rage burned anew in his soul and he lifted Marco with one hand to punch him with the other. It was that moment when he saw the young man could no longer defend himself. Dropping him in the dirt, he turned toward Carmen once more.

Carmen had watched in horror as James beat her brother to a pulp. Now he was advancing on her with the same cold look in his eyes. "No, James. I didn't mean it," she cried with terror in her heart. "I only wanted Jessie out of the way. I didn't know the fire would spread the way it did. I just wanted to burn her out, not destroy the Triple X. You have to believe me," she pleaded.

James reached Carmen's side and grabbed her wrist once more. Dragging her along behind him, he walked to the wagon. "Get in," he ordered her.

"But James, you have to believe me. I love you. I only wanted you to love me too. Don't you see? Don't you understand?"

The pounding of horses' hooves took James's attention for a moment. It was Juan riding into the yard. James looked around and noticed that quite a few of his hands had witnessed what had happened, was still happening. One of them must have alerted Juan.

Juan jumped from his horse and ran to his son. "What has happened?" he cried at the sight of Marco's bloody face.

"Papa!" wailed Carmen from James's side.

Juan hurried to face James. "What is going on here?" he demanded.

James felt sorry for his friend. "Carmen and Marco started the brush fire. They were trying to burn Jessie's ranch, to kill her, but the fire got out of control," he explained. "I'm taking Carmen to the sheriff."

Juan looked at his daughter. "Is this true?" he asked in a whisper.

"I didn't mean for it to happen, Papa. I only wanted to get Jessie out of the way. If she was gone I knew I could make James love me again," she cried.

"I never loved you, Carmen. You knew that. I don't even remember being with you that night. You crawled into bed with me after I'd been drinking."

Juan studied his daughter sadly. "Are you with child?" he asked her quietly.

Carmen tried to pull her wrist from James's grasp. "Papa," she cried. "Don't—"

"I asked you a question, girl," said Juan more firmly.

"I had to tell you I was pregnant so you'd make James marry me," she sobbed.

James looked at her in surprise as a flood of relief washed over him. She wasn't pregnant. She never had been. Glancing back toward Juan, he noticed the small faces of his nephews peering out from behind the flap of their tent. Moving his arm, he placed Carmen's wrist in her father's hand. "She's your problem, Juan. So is Marco. I want them off my property in ten minutes. I don't ever want to see either of them again, and if I do I'll turn them over to the authorities." He began to walk toward his nephews, then stopped. Turning back toward Juan, he spoke again. "And if there are any more fires around here in the near future I'll know who to blame."

Juan hung on tight to Carmen's wrist and tried to pull her toward his horse. His heart was filled with a greater sadness even than when his lovely wife died. He understood the favor James was bestowing on him. "Come help me get Marco on his horse," he said to Carmen.

"No! He can't do this to us," she wailed.

"You are lucky he's not taking you to the sheriff," Juan told her.

Carmen watched James's back with a new emotion. Hatred burned within her. How dare he discard her this way? Jerking her arm from her father's grasp, she grabbed the handle of his gun and drew it from its holster. Jumping from his reach, she aimed the gun at James. "Turn around, you bastard. I want to see your face when I kill you," she said.

James heard Carmen's words and turned slowly. "I see how much you love me," he mocked her.

"I did love you. I loved you enough to kill for you, but now I'll just have to kill you. You don't appreciate me or what I've done for you," she said as she began to squeeze the trigger.

An explosion of gunfire from behind him sent James sprawling to the ground. When he looked up, he saw Carmen holding her wrist, blood dripping from her fingers. Glancing frantically around, he saw Marco leaning on his elbow and holding his pistol, smoke rising from the weapon. "Marco?" James breathed in surprise, rising to his feet once more.

"You're not pregnant?" Marco said to Carmen. "You made me rustle and kill Jessie's cattle and help you start fires that could have killed people and you weren't even pregnant?"

Carmen held her wrist tightly and stared in horror at the blood dripping from between her fingers. When Marco spoke to her, she shifted her gaze to him. "I had to tell you that, Marco. It was the only way to get you to do what I wanted."

Marco raised the pistol again, this time centering his aim over his sister's heart.

"No!" shouted Juan, stepping in front of his daughter. "We will go away from here," he said. "We will start over."

Marco pushed himself up to his knees, grunting at the pain in his side where James had punched him. "I'll go nowhere with her, Papa. Look what she's turned me into," he said. Standing up, he staggered toward his horse. After he pulled himself into the saddle, he looked back at James. "I'm sorry, Mr. Bonner," he rasped. "Maybe saving your life just now made up for what I did just a little. Good-bye." He pulled the reins to the side and nudged his horse toward the road.

James almost felt sorry for Marco as he watched him ride away. He then looked back at Juan and Carmen. "Get her out of my sight, Juan," he said.

Juan once again pulled Carmen in the direction of his horse. He stopped only to pick up the gun she'd dropped when Marco shot her, and this time she didn't fight him. Moments later he held her in front of him as he rode away from the Triple X forever.

James turned back toward the twins. Their little faces were wet with tears and his heart went out to them, wishing they hadn't seen something so frightening. "Are you two all right?" he asked as he neared the tent.

Both boys burst from the tent, Jeremy at a run, Jamie hobbling along behind him as fast as he was able. "Uncle James!" they cried, falling into his arms.

James wrapped his arms around them tightly, lifting them from the ground. Turning slowly as he held them, he thanked God for them, grateful beyond measure that Carmen's insanity and Marco's complicity hadn't caused their deaths. "I love you both so much," he told them.

"We love you, too, Uncle James," they said together.

❦ 20 ❦

In the days that followed the scene with Carmen and Marco, James tried to get his mind back on the rebuilding of the Triple X, but everywhere he looked, he saw Jessie. Everything he did reminded him of her, even his nights were full of dreams about her. He was becoming tired and irritable, and everyone on the ranch was beginning to feel it.

"James. James would you please hand me some more nails?" asked Tom, one of the hands helping with the house. "James," he said more loudly.

James looked up, surprised at Tom's tone. "You don't have to yell," he said.

"Apparently I do. I've been trying to get your attention for a few minutes. Where were you, anyway?" he asked.

James took a deep breath. "Nowhere. What did you need?"

"More nails," he responded.

James handed Tom the nail can, then turned back to the section of roof he'd been working on. Looking at his lack of progress, he realized Tom was right. He hadn't been here. His mind had once again gone in search of Jessie. "Damn it," he muttered.

"What's that?" Tom asked.

"Nothing," replied James. "But I think I'm done for the day." He set his hammer in the tool box beside him, then crawled along the roof rafter to the edge of the structure. Climbing down the ladder took only seconds and he was soon standing on the ground.

Glancing around him, he saw the boys playing with his new housekeeper, Mrs. Hanks. He doubted he'd have any romantic problems with the nearly sixty-year-old woman.

Placing his hands on his hips, he tried to decide what exactly it was he wanted to do next. He wasn't accomplishing much work, but he didn't know what to do with himself. "I might as well go for a ride," he finally said to himself.

Saddling his horse took only a few minutes and he was soon mounted and riding away from the tents and work.

An hour later, James sat on a ridge looking down on what had been Jessie's ranch. One section of framing had been put into place before she'd stopped construction on the house and gone back to Charleston. Tinker and Johnny had both informed him that she'd given up on ranching, that she'd felt beaten by the fire, but he had a hard time believing that. Jessie was a fighter.

He remembered the way she'd looked the day she'd accused Carmen of starting the fire, the day before she left. She had looked defeated for a moment, but as she'd ridden away he's seen her pull herself up strongly. Had it been an act? Had she truly felt beaten? His heart ached at the thought.

Curling his fingers into a fist, he punched himself on the thigh in frustration. He couldn't get her out of his mind, and he was realizing it went much deeper than that. There was more between them than just physical attraction. Something had started between them. It may have started for the wrong reasons, but it had started just the same, and it wasn't going to go away simply because she'd gone back to Charleston. "We're not through, yet, Jessie," he said out loud.

* * *

Jessie sat at her vanity and stared at her reflection in the mirror. She'd been home for nearly two weeks now, but she couldn't get used to the unproductive life-style. It seemed everything in Charleston revolved around the next social event on the calendar, and in her condition, she hardly felt like socializing.

She grimaced at herself in the mirror. She'd made her mother promise not to tell her father she was pregnant, but she knew it would be only a short time before he would be able to see for himself why she'd been behaving so irritably since her return. When he did find out, he'd be so disappointed, the whole family would, and she felt sorry for that, but there wasn't really anything she could do about it. The tiny life growing inside her certainly couldn't go away to suit someone's delicate sensibilities, and she'd discovered that she didn't want it to. There was something very wonderful about knowing she was carrying James Bonner's baby. With James so far away, and probably married to Carmen by now, it was a safe way for her to enjoy a part of him.

"Jessie, there's someone here to see you," Rachel called through the door as she knocked.

"You know I don't want to see anyone, Mother," Jessie called back.

Rachel opened the door slowly and stuck her head in. "Are you sure? You might want to reconsider," she said.

Jessie looked suspiciously at her mother. "Why?"

Rachel entered the room and crossed to sit at the foot of the bed facing her daughter. "Because it's Frederick—"

"Mother," Jessie interrupted exasperatedly.

"Don't interrupt me. You need to get on with your life. Start seeing your old friends again."

"Have you forgotten my condition?" Jessie asked.

"It's hardly something I can forget," replied Rachel. "But it shouldn't turn you into a hermit."

"I think Father would disagree with you if he knew."

"Perhaps, but I'm not your father. Now, pinch your cheeks, put on a smile, and come downstairs," instructed Rachel. "Besides, I think Frederick is quite in love with you. He seems thrilled you've come home."

Jessie rolled her eyes at her mother. "Love is something I don't need right now," she said.

Rachel raised one brow at her daughter. "Oh really?" She knew love was exactly what Jessie needed. Unfortunately, she needed the love of a tough Texan who belonged to another woman. But maybe, just maybe, love from someone else would help to heal her wounded heart. "Frederick would make a wonderful husband," she offered.

"Husband?" Jessie said incredulously, nearly choking on the word. "I'm pregnant, Mother."

"I'm perfectly aware of your condition. If you remember correctly, I knew it before you did."

"And you think I should trick Frederick into marrying me just so I don't have this baby out of wedlock?"

"I never said any such thing. All I want is for you to go downstairs and visit with an old friend. Is that so much to ask?"

"You also said Frederick would make a wonderful husband," accused Jessie.

"Well, he would."

Jessie glowered at her mother for a moment. "I'm not looking for a husband," she finally said. "Not now. Not ever."

Rachel sighed. "Don't say that, Jessie. You'll want to marry someday."

An image of James's handsome face flashed into Jessie's mind. "I don't think so, Mother," she said quietly.

Rachel's eyes stung with tears.

Jessie saw her mother's sad expression and regretted the moment. "But I'll go down and visit with Frederick," she said, her voice full of false brightness.

Rachel nodded, proud of her daughter's bravery. "I'll tell him you'll be down in a moment," she said.

After the door closed behind her mother, Jessie glanced at her reflection in the mirror. She was thinner in the face and had dark circles under her eyes from lack of sleep. Her waist was getting thicker, but so far she'd been able to hide it by hiking her skirts a little higher.

She felt the weight of dread pressing down on her. She didn't want to see Frederick. She didn't want to see anyone. She wanted to sit in this room until she became old and gray and everyone who ever knew her was dead and buried. "Oh hell," she spat. Crossing her room, she pulled open the door and started downstairs.

"Jessie, you look wonderful," gushed Frederick when he saw Jessie standing in the door of the parlor.

"Hello, Frederick," she said quietly. He looked the same as she remembered. Too thin, too citified. She couldn't stop herself from remembering James's tall, rugged, hard, masculine body, his shirt and trousers fitting snugly over his well muscled form, his gun and knife displayed prominently on his narrow hips. "Damn," she breathed as her heart fluttered at the memory.

"What's that, my dear?" Frederick asked as he crossed to take her hands in his.

"Nothing, Frederick," she responded. "It's nice to see you again."

"It's wonderful to see you again, Jessie. I'm so glad you came to your senses and returned home," he said.

Jessie felt her hackles rising at his choice of words. She hadn't come to her senses, as he put it. "Yes, well, I think you should know—" she began.

"Would you young people like some refreshments?" interrupted Rachel when she could see the path Jessie was taking.

"I'm fine, Mother," said Jessie, giving Rachel a dirty look for stopping her.

"I'd love something to drink," said Frederick.

"Lemonade?" she asked.

"That would be lovely, thank you."

Rachel looked at Jessie. "Won't you help me in the kitchen, Jessie?" she asked, afraid to leave her alone with Frederick.

"Certainly," Jessie replied sweetly, aware of her mother's tactics. As she left the room behind Rachel, she poked her in the ribs. "I wouldn't have bitten him," she said.

Rachel turned to face her daughter. "I wasn't worried about you biting him, although, I wouldn't put it past you. There's no reason to be rude to the young man. He just doesn't understand how you feel about Texas."

Jessie sighed. "All right. I'll be good."

"Good. Now you can go back and visit with Frederick while I get the lemonade."

Jessie turned around and headed back to the parlor.

The next hour was spent making small talk and Jessie was bored to tears.

"I think I'll leave you two alone for a few minutes," said Rachel.

Frederick smiled at Rachel as she left the room, then turned back to Jessie. "I've been waiting for a few minutes alone with you. Jessie, there's something very important I have to ask you."

James found Rachel and Sin's home at the end of an oak-lined lane. The structure was massive and beautiful, and he wondered why Jessie would ever want to leave it. Knocking on the door, he heard the sound echoing inside and waited, hoping Jessie was at home.

When the door swung open, James looked into the eyes of a stranger. "I'm sorry, I was looking for Jessie Braddock," he stated.

"This is Miss Braddock's residence," the butler answered.

"Oh, good, then I'd like to see her," he said, stepping inside the door.

"Please, sir, you cannot just enter and expect to see Miss Braddock. Do you have an appointment?"

"An appointment?"

"Is she expecting you?"

James frowned at the man. "No, she isn't expecting me, but I have something important to discuss with her," he said.

"Miss Braddock is entertaining a gentleman caller at the moment. I'll let her know you were here. Do you have a card?"

James stared hard at the butler. "No, I don't have a card, and I'm not leaving until I see her. So you can just run along and get her for me."

"James, is that you?" Sin asked, coming out of his study to see who was at the door.

James turned toward Sin, smiling. "Yes, Sin, it's me. It's good to see you again," he said, offering his hand.

Sin shook hands with James. "It's good to see you, too. But I have to admit I'm a little surprised. Jessie said you were about to be married. Did you bring your wife?"

"I didn't get married. Things didn't work out the way I expected," he responded. "I'd like to see Jessie for a few minutes, if I could."

Sin looked at the butler. "Where is Jessie?" he asked.

"She's with Mr. Chasen," the butler replied.

"Oh yes. Frederick has begun to court her," Sin informed James, a conspiratorial smile on his face.

James stiffened. "Is she engaged?" he asked.

"Not yet, but I doubt if it'll be too long. Frederick strikes me as being a persistent young man."

James felt a sudden urgency. "I need to see her, Sin," he said.

"James, what are you doing here?" Rachel asked as she approached from the parlor.

"I came to see Jessie," he said.

"I'm sorry, but I don't think Jessie will want to see you," she responded.

"Will you let Jessie decide that? Just let her know I'm here," he said.

"That's not possible. She's busy right now." Rachel glanced back toward the parlor door.

James noticed the direction of Rachel's attention and started for the door. "I'll only take a few minutes of her time," he said.

"No," said Rachel, following him. "I can't let you do this."

James grabbed the door handles before Rachel could stop him and swung the doors open. His eyes instantly found Jessie seated on a small sofa, Frederick at her feet, one of her hands in his. "I'm too late," he breathed.

"James!" Jessie said in horror at his finding her like this. "Frederick get up," she demanded.

Frederick stood up, confused and upset by the unexpected intrusion. He'd just proposed to Jessie and she hadn't given him her answer yet.

James's eyes narrowed angrily as his heart rebelled against the scene he'd interrupted. It couldn't be too late. He had to have a chance to speak to Jessie before she did something they both might regret for the rest of their lives. "You can't marry this man, Jessie," he said loudly.

Jessie raised her jaw defiantly. "How dare you burst in here like this," she said indignantly.

"Did you hear me, Jessie? You can't marry this man," James repeated.

"And why not?" Jessie demanded, outraged.

"Because you're not fit to wed," he answered loudly, his words meant to shock.

Jessie's mouth dropped open.

Rachel gasped, then covered her mouth with her hands.

Sin stepped forward. "Just what the hell do you mean by that?" he demanded.

"I mean, Jessie and I were lovers in Texas. I think that's why she came back here, to run away from me," James said clearly so everyone would hear.

"How dare you, sir!" said Frederick, advancing toward James.

Sin stepped closer. "You'd better be lying, boy, or there's going to be hell to pay," he said.

"Sin, wait," said Rachel, reaching forward to touch her husband's arm.

Sin looked at her in surprise. "You want me to wait? Didn't you hear what he just called our daughter?"

"Just wait," she said, fire flashing in her eyes.

"You son of a bitch," said Jessie, finally finding her voice.

"Jessie, please," said Frederick. "I'll handle this." He faced James head on. "I demand satisfaction," he announced haughtily.

James stared hard at the man for a moment, then threw back his head and laughed out loud. "You mean a duel? I'll give you a duel right here and now," he said, doubling up his fists.

Frederick's eyes widened in surprise. "I didn't mean fisticuffs," he said.

"Neither did I. In Texas we don't waste words or time planning how to knock someone on their ass. We just do it. If you've got a beef with me get ready to defend yourself."

"That's enough!" shouted Jessie, finally responding to what was happening. "James, get the hell out of my home and my life. Frederick, I won't marry you or anyone else, ever. I can't stand the sight of men!" She turned in a whirl and stomped from the room, running up the stairs as fast as she could.

"You heard her, James," said Sin. "Get out."

"But, Sin, I need to talk to her," James insisted.

"I'll see you out, James," said Rachel, taking him by the arm. "I have a few things to say to you, myself."

"But, Rachel," he tried again.

"Just be quiet and listen to me, James Bonner," Rachel said in a stern voice as she led him from the house.

Jessie lay awake in her bed and listened to the night sounds outside her window. It was nearing two o'clock in the morning, but she couldn't sleep. She was wondering why James hadn't married Carmen after all. She kept remembering how handsome he'd looked that afternoon when he'd burst in and ruined her reputation forever. "Damn you, James Bonner," she cursed. Grimacing, she had to admit there was a tiny part of her that was grateful to him for his behavior. She would no longer have to deal with Frederick or any other silly city man coming to call on her. Now all she had to worry about was telling her father that not only had she slept with James but she'd also conceived a child by him.

James looked up at the window above the trellis. He'd been surprised when Rachel had told him where Jessie's room was, and even more surprised when she'd encouraged him to see Jessie as soon as possible. "Here goes nothing," he breathed as he reached for the trellis.

Jessie heard a tapping on her window and felt a rush of fear along her spine. Turning her head, she peered beyond the glass. "James?" she whispered in surprise. Climbing from her bed, she went to the window and unlatched it, pushing it open. "What the hell do you think you're doing here?" she demanded in a whisper.

"Trying to kill myself," he responded. "Let me in." He swung one long leg over the windowsill, then pulled himself in.

"Do you know what my father will do to you if he catches you in here?" she said.

"I figure a bullet between the eyes would be his best bet. It's the only way he'll keep me from talking to you."

Jessie could hear the determination in his voice. "Fine," she said, going back to sit on the bed.

James followed and sat down beside her. Now that he was finally here he didn't know where to start.

"I'm waiting," Jessie said, impatiently.

James could see her in the moonlight that streamed through the window. Her black hair was loose and fell wildly around her shoulders. Her emerald eyes stared intently up at him. Her full lips were pursed slightly as she waited for him to speak. He lowered his gaze and could just make out the points of her nipples beneath the soft cotton fabric of her nightgown. His throat went dry and a surge of blood flowed downward, awakening the passion in his body.

"Well?" Jessie tried again.

James raised one hand and touched a stray curl that caressed her cheek. "I have something to tell you," he started, his voice hoarse with emotion.

Jessie sensed the change in him and felt her own body responding with a swift rise in her pulse and a heat flowing through her like molten wax.

"Jessie, after you left I found out you were right about Carmen. She'd never been pregnant, and she and Marco started the fire to get rid of you." He touched her cheek as he studied her beautiful face. "What if I'd lost you forever," he murmured.

"Would you have cared?" Jessie asked, her voice becoming breathy as she was mesmerized by James's gentle touch.

"I've been so stupid, Jessie. I don't know why it's taken me so long to realize how much you mean to me. I love you," he breathed, lowering his head to kiss her.

Jessie heard his words and felt his lips claim hers. She couldn't believe this was happening, it was too much, but she responded to his kiss by leaning into him, kissing him back with her very soul.

After a moment, James leaned away from her and looked down into her eyes again. "We have to discuss the Triple X," he said.

Jessie lowered her eyes. "It's yours James. I've accepted that."

"I want you to have it," he answered her.

"You want to sell it to me now?"

He laughed. "No, but I'll give it to you."

Jessie's eyes widened with surprise. "You want to give it to me?"

"As a wedding present."

Jessie took a quick breath. "A wedding present?"

"Yes, if you'll have me?"

"You want to marry me?"

"More than anything in the world," he said, lifting one of her hands to his lips. "Jessie, would you do me the honor of becoming my wife?" he asked.

Jessie hesitated only an instant. All her dreams were coming true. "Yes," she answered, her eyes filling with tears of joy.

James kissed her again, his lips covering hers tenderly, his tongue gently probing the sweet recesses of her mouth.

"James?" Jessie said, pulling away from him. "There's something else we have to discuss."

James gazed down at her with curiosity. "What?"

It was Jessie's turn to be nervous. "Well, I don't know how—"

"Just tell me, Jessie. You're going to be my wife, you can tell me anything."

"You're going to be a father," she said.

James sat very still as he digested her words.

"You're—"

"Yes. I'm pregnant."

James was stunned. "Is that why you left?" he asked.

Jessie nodded.

Letting his gaze drop to her abdomen, he reached out with one hand. "May I?" he asked in wonder.

Jessie took his hand and placed it over the small curve that was his child.

James felt as though his heart would burst with joy as he touched her. He was so full of love for Jessie, and now for the life they'd created, that he could barely contain himself. "How soon can we get married?" he asked.

"Is tomorrow too soon?" she asked.

"Not soon enough. I'm ready to wake a justice of the peace right now."

Jessie grinned. "I think we'd better tell my parents first."

"At least we'd better tell your father. I think you're mother all ready knew what was going to happen."

❊ Epilogue ❊

Rocking slowly, Jessie gazed out the window of her new bedroom in her new house on the Triple X. She could see James working in the yard from where she sat, and her heart was so full of love for him that it warmed her. She watched him in amazement, grateful for the love he gave her daily.

Squinting her eyes as another pain worked its way through her middle, she held on to the armrests of her rocker and breathed deeply. Looking down at her distended stomach, she smiled. "I suppose it's about time to tell daddy you're on your way," she said.

Standing up, she unlatched the window and opened it. "James," she called, her voice carrying across the yard. "Would you please come here?"

James felt the glow of love as he looked toward his very pregnant wife. "I'm just about through here. Can you wait for just another few minutes?"

"I can, but I don't think Rachel is going to be that patient," she answered, grinning.

James's eyes opened wide. Jessie had been calling the baby Rachel for weeks now. Did that mean—"Oh my God," he breathed. "Now?" he called.

Jessie nodded her head and pointed to her stomach.

"Oh my God," James repeated. "Tom, go for the doctor, please. It's time," he requested as he ran toward the house.

"Yes, sir," answered Tom, nervously dropping his hammer as he took off toward the barn to get a horse. Several other men who'd been working nearby also stopped what they were doing and began to run in different directions, each on his own mission to spread the news.

Jessie giggled at the nervous hustle that had started because she was going to have a baby.

"Jessie, are you sure?" James asked as he ran into the room and wrapped his arms around her.

She nodded. "I'm sure. I've been having contractions for hours already."

"Hours? Why didn't you call me sooner?"

"Because labor takes so long. Besides, I was watching you work. Do you know how incredibly handsome you are?" she asked.

James stared down at her. "I don't think that's important right now, Jessie. You're going to have a baby."

"It's because I think you're so handsome that I'm going to have this baby," she answered smartly. "Relax, James. This is only our first. I plan on having at least five or six more."

James took a deep breath. "Five or six more?"

Jessie nodded, feeling another contraction coming on. "Rachel is becoming impatient," she said, breathing slowly.

"What if it's a boy?" James said.

"It won't be," said Jessie with calm certainty.

Six hours later, Rachel Marie Bonner was born into the world. She had the same dark red hair as her namesake, and shared the startling green eye color of both her mother and grandmother.

Sometimes life comes full circle.

Let
Andrea
Kane
romance you tonight!

Dream Castle 73585-3/$5.50

My Heart's Desire 73584-5/$5.50

Masque of Betrayal 75532-3/$4.99

Echoes In the Mist 75533-1/$5.50

Samantha 86507-2/$5.50

The Last Duke 86508-0/$5.99

Emerald Garden 86509-9/$5.99

Wishes In the Wind 53483-1/$5.99

Available from Pocket Books

Simon & Schuster Mail Order
200 Old Tappan Rd., Old Tappan, N.J. 07675
Please send me the books I have checked above. I am enclosing $_____(please add
$0.75 to cover the postage and handling for each order. Please add appropriate sales
tax). Send check or money order--no cash or C.O.D.'s please. Allow up to six weeks
for delivery. For purchase over $10.00 you may use VISA: card number, expiration
date and customer signature must be included.

POCKET
B O O K S

Name _____

Address _____

City _____ State/Zip _____

VISA Card # _____ Exp.Date _____

Signature _____ 957-05

LINDA LAEL MILLER

- ☐ CORBIN'S FANCY .... 73767-8/$5.99
- ☐ ANGELFIRE .... 73765-1/$5.99
- ☐ MOONFIRE .... 73770-8/$5.99
- ☐ WANTON ANGEL .... 73772-4/$5.99
- ☐ FLETCHER'S WOMEN .... 73768-6/$5.99
- ☐ MY DARLING MELISSA .... 73771-6/$5.99
- ☐ WILLOW .... 73773-2/$5.99
- ☐ DESIRE AND DESTINY .... 70635-7/$5.99
- ☐ BANNER O'BRIEN .... 73766-x/$5.99
- ☐ MEMORY'S EMBRACE .... 73769-4/$5.99
- ☐ LAURALEE .... 70634-9/$5.99
- ☐ DANIEL'S BRIDE .... 73166-1/$5.99
- ☐ YANKEE WIFE .... 73755-4/$5.99
- ☐ TAMING CHARLOTTE .... 73754-6/$5.99
- ☐ THE LEGACY .... 79792-1/$6.99
- ☐ PRINCESS ANNIE. .... 79793-x/$5.99
- ☐ EMMA AND THE OUTLAW .... 67637-7/$5.99
- ☐ LILY AND THE MAJOR .... 67636-9/$5.50
- ☐ CAROLINE AND THE RAIDE............................. 67638-5/$5.99
- ☐ PIRATES.. 87316-4/$6.50
- ☐ KNIGHTS... 87317-2/$6.99

EVERLASTING LOVE: A collection of romances by Linda Lael Miller, Jayne Ann Krentz, Linda Howard, and Carla Neggers
.... 52150-0/$5.99

All available from Pocket Books

Simon & Schuster Mail Order
200 Old Tappan Rd., Old Tappan, N.J. 07675
Please send me the books I have checked above. I am enclosing $_____ (please add $0.75 to cover the postage and handling for each order. Please add appropriate sales tax). Send check or money order--no cash or C.O.D.'s please. Allow up to six weeks for delivery. For purchase over $10.00 you may use VISA: card number, expiration date and customer signature must be included.

POCKET
BOOKS

Name _____

Address _____

City _____ State/Zip _____

VISA Card # _____ Exp.Date _____

Signature _____

779-14